Book Four of the Roanfire Saga

C.K. Miller

Edited by Melissa Frey

Cover art, layout, and interior graphics by C.K. Miller

www.ckmillerbooks.com
ISBN-13: 978-1-7324544-4-6

To my characters who endure everything I put them through.

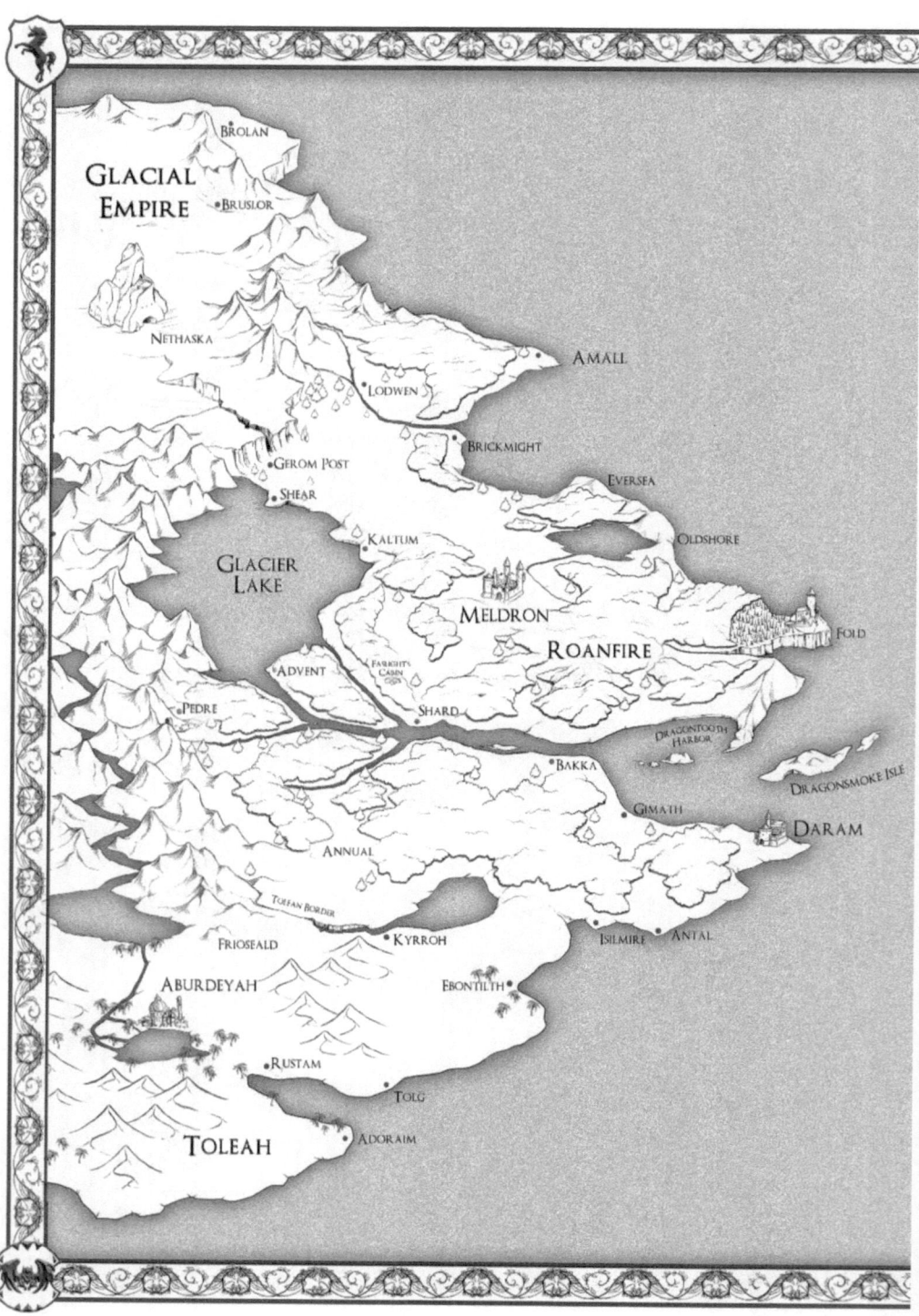

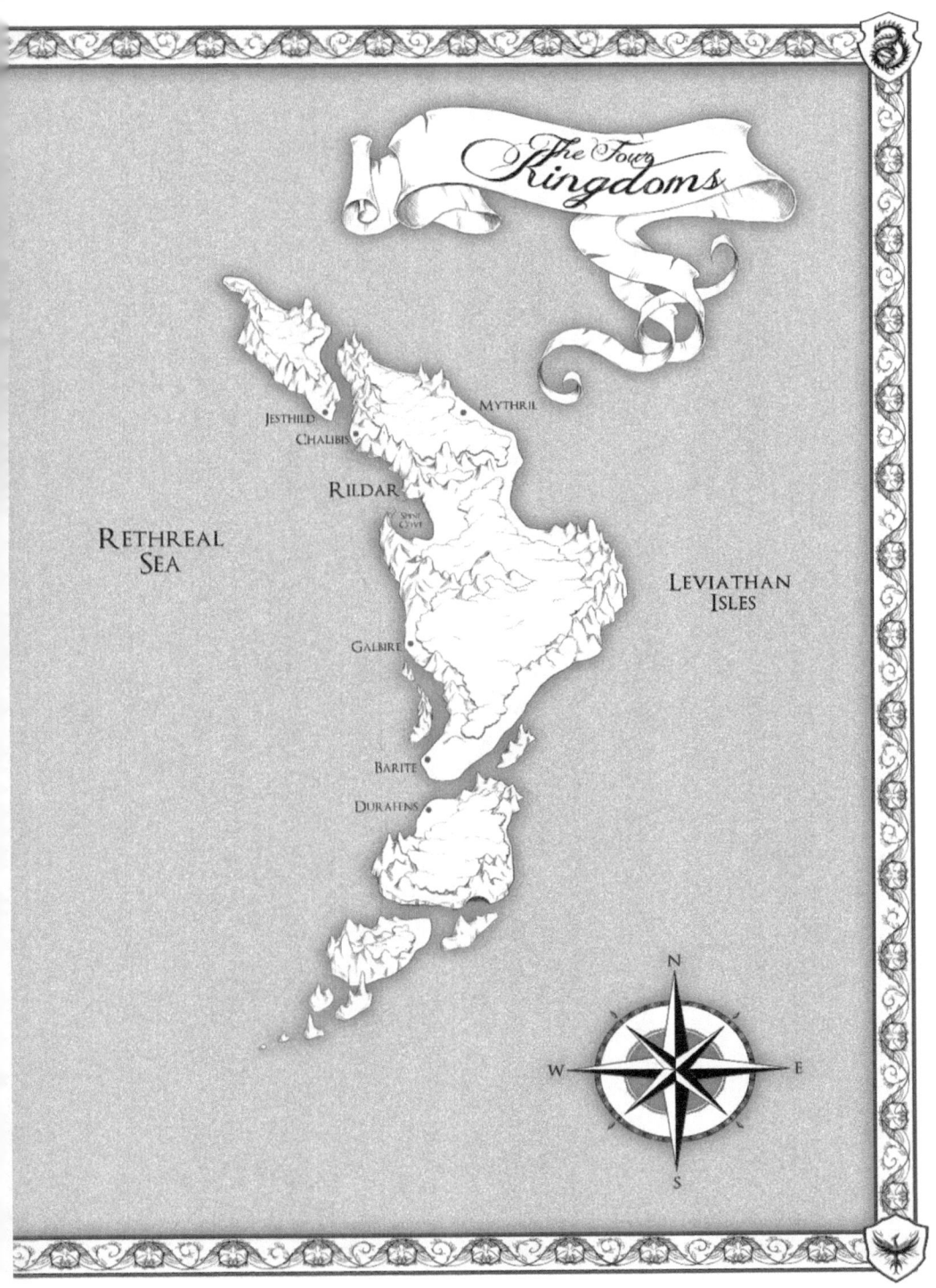

CK Miller

CHAPTER 1

POISON

Crimson painted the gray stone wall behind Prince Leander's back as he sagged against the spiraling staircase beside me. The same crimson traced sharp features of his angled face, leaking from a gash on his brow.

So much blood. So many wounds.

His exotic clothing hung in rags on his dark skin. The Deathbiters had shown no mercy, tearing into his face, neck, arms, back, chest, legs. One scratch from a Deathbiter talon was a death sentence, and Prince Leander had more lacerations than I could count. The only part of him spared was the lower half of his right leg.

"The White Wardent," he began with his Tolean accent full and strained, "has been my tutor since I could place one foot in front of the other."

Was he seriously trying to answer my question now? He needed healing. In truth, I couldn't comprehend anything more. Even if he told me exactly how to defeat Rion, my mind wouldn't have been able to understand. I still saw red: red stars, red fire, her red dress, her burning red threads reaching for souls and drawing them to her. I pressed the heel of my hand against my forehead.

"I did not know him as the White Wardent until I . . . until I had grown." Leander's teeth clenched as he placed a hand—the one with the emerald ring he always twisted—over a gash on his thigh. "He was only known to me as . . . Master Yona, a wise man with kind eyes that changed . . . changed color whenever elemental sprites were near . . . which there always were."

"Leander . . ."

"My father, Shah Milak, held him in high esteem until Master Yona began telling me stories of Roanfire." He continued as if he hadn't heard me. "Of curses and rubies . . . and princesses no longer born to the throne . . ."

"Leander, stop."

He sucked air through his teeth as his fingers dug into his thigh. "Yotherna and Alder are brothers . . . but Alder is not his real name. It is Karreth. He was in love with Rion, and he—"

"Hush, Leander," I pleaded.

Pinpricks of light flashed behind my eyes as I stared at him. There was something off about his face, something that should have alarmed me. But I couldn't place it. The more I thought, the more my head ached. The wonderful, handsome, noble fool had attempted to rescue Queen Lonacheska from Alder in the Deathbiter-infested night. He'd come back with the accursed ruby instead.

Slowly, my fingers uncurled, revealing a pale jewel sitting in the center of my sprite dust-riddled hand. No bigger than my smallest fingernail and set with a golden bail, it harbored the source of all my troubles. All my heartache and pain. All the losses I'd sustained. It should have been blood red and pulsing hot with fury, but right now, it was pale and harmless, almost white. A hairline fracture stretched across its surface.

That tiny crevice signified more damage than I'd ever dealt to this curse. I'd smashed it with hammers and rocks. I'd let it smelt in a forge until the golden bail burned away. I'd done everything I knew how to destroy this thing. So why did the crack on it not give me hope? The memory of what I'd done in order to create that fracture brought an ache to my core.

"Kea..." I didn't think Leander's voice could get any weaker. The muscles in his neck grew taut as he strained to lift his head from the wall. His honey-colored irises should have been radiating with the warmth of a sunburst, but they looked at me with the sickly shade of a spoiled gourd.

"I am sorry." His Tolean accent was thicker than I remembered, slurred. "It was... a mistake to not tell you sooner... what I knew..."

"Save your strength, Leander." I tucked the accursed pale ruby into my pocket then pulled his arm over my shoulders. My knees shook as I raised him up. A sour bite touched my tongue and stung my eyes as the pungent sulfuric stench filled the stairwell, coming from his wounds.

The poison already? I didn't remember it being so potent so soon. He had two weeks from now to have the poison withdrawn before he met the same fate as hundreds of Roanfiriens.

Together, we staggered back up the stairs.

"This is not... how my life should end," he muttered.

"Don't talk like that," I warned. But a terrible feeling crawled into my chest like an insect burrowing between slats of wood, hiding, gnawing against my heart with pain too deep to comprehend. I'd lost too much already.

Faces flashed behind my eyes. The stern face and gray-streaked beard of Eamon. King Sander's hollow eyes and his crown rolling beneath the armchair as he collapsed. Ropert lying on the floor of Queen Lonacheska's chamber with a new streak of white hair tainting his strawberry-blond locks. Lonacheska's dark eyes wide and tear-filled as Alder—that vile, deceitful viper—dragged her away.

"You... you need me." His eyes flickered like they wanted to burn bright but couldn't. "Not... much... time. She... she will break free."

Deadly heat radiated from his skin, and his eyes closed against the pain. Only then did I notice that dark lines crept down the flesh under his lashes, flowing to his cheeks like slender rivers on a map. I felt like they were screaming at me to see them, to realize their significance.

"Element . . ." Leander turned his face to the stone ceiling. "Four . . . souls . . . Four. I am . . . one."

He wasn't making any sense.

Then everything hit like a flaming arrow striking pitch. Panic exploded through my core. His dull eyes, the stench, the fever, the slurred speech, the lines streaking under his lashes. Those symptoms shouldn't have begun until the third day of infection.

I'd sustained just as many wounds if not more when the Deathbiters first appeared. I'd suffered for a week before symptoms like this emerged. This venom was different, more potent.

What had Alder done?

Kneeling on the cold stone floor beside Prince Leander, I watched helplessly as his faithful Ridarri warriors feverishly wiped at the wounds he'd sustained only hours ago. The washbasin's water grew more and more crimson with every wring of the towels.

The poison was taking hold. Leander needed magic. Now.

But I had nothing more to give. I'd just battled the Phoenix Witch, locked her inside her prison ruby with every crumb of strength I had left. I'd barely managed to pull Ropert back. I still didn't understand how I had found the strength to bring Leander here.

Feathers, I was tired.

I couldn't. I just couldn't. I had no more power to spare, no more mental capacity to deal with the suffocating draw of the poison flowing through his blood. It would drag me down with it. But if left untreated, at the rate he was deteriorating, Prince Leander would be dead by morning.

If only Broderick was here. He would know what to do. He could . . .

He would use sprite dust, I realized.

"Dust." The word slipped from my lips before I knew what I'd said.

Prince Leander's warriors paused and looked at me.

Healer Malcom's remedy was Prince Leander's only hope— the only thing I could think to stop, or at least slow, the spread of the poison until my strength returned.

The female warrior, the one I knew as Ciri, furrowed her dark brows at me. Her long silky hair, set in a high ponytail, fell over her shoulder. "What you say?" she asked in broken Roanfirien.

"The poison," I said. "We need to stop it from spreading. Do you have sprite dust? Water, wind, and earth?"

She turned to her male counterpart, Boma, a broad-shouldered man with muscles larger than Ropert's. She spoke to him in their native tongue, her tone filled with urgency. The large warrior rose and hurried to the wall of brightly colored reams of fabric hanging from the ceiling where it sectioned Prince Leander's chamber in half. His impossible garden was on the other side. The garden that had provided life-saving food to the inhabitants of Meldron castle for the past month.

I gazed down at Leander's clenched face as he lay among a bed of scattered pillows. This handsome, exotic prince had done more for Roanfire than anyone could comprehend. He'd stopped a war and forgiven King Sander for imprisoning him. Instead, he'd saved us from starvation and revealed the traitor in our midst. More importantly, he knew the White Wardent. He knew who I was, what blood flowed through my veins, and what I faced.

Boma returned with an intricately decorated wooden box. Kneeling beside me, he handed it to Ciri. As she cracked the lid, a flood of green, blue, and white light ignited the tattoos flowing across her skin in a beautiful radiance.

She displayed three thick cylindrical vials filled to the brim with beautiful glowing particles of dust. "Enough?" she asked.

"Feathers, yes."

Ciri and Boma provided me with everything else I asked for as I rolled up my sleeves. A clean bowl, water, towels, bandages, and most importantly, ashes from the fire. As I lifted the glowing sapphire vial of waterdust from the box, a soothing rush rippled through the glass and up my arm. I paused. Only one kind of sprite dust could be felt through the glass. The rarest and most potent of all: pure *gifted* sprite dust. This was dust given willingly, without the usual method of startling the sprites or holding them captive and forcing them to produce it. How in the blazes did they have so much of it?

Hurriedly, I popped the cork and tipped—

"*La tudlini!*" Leander jerked upright, striking at the air as if deflecting the assault of a thousand demon bats. His arm crashed against mine, and the vial of priceless dust flung from my grip. I flinched as it struck the stone floor with an audible clink. Dust exploded in a glittering blue burst as the vial rolled across the stone floor.

Boma gripped Leander's wrists. His muscles bulged as he wrestled his prince down, speaking powerfully to him in his own language.

The hallucinations already? That wasn't supposed to happen until the fifth day.

My reaction time was embarrassingly slow as I scrambled after the vial of pure waterdust. Ciri reached it first and helped me gather as much of the spilled powder into the bowl as possible. A stream of soothing energy tore through me as I touched the dust, like I'd slipped into a warm bath thick with steam, sinking to my chin in the water, my body weightless and floating. It was so calming and gentle, so desperately what my body needed right now. My head drooped to my chest, and my eyes began to drift—

No. Not now. I jerked my head up and shook the sleep away. Leander needed me. I could sleep later.

Crawling back to his side, I created Healer Malcom's ointment to the best of my memory, working the three glittering powders and black ash into a thick paste of midnight sky. It stuck to my fingers like mud, coating them with mesmerizing blue, white, and green stars.

"Hurry," Ciri urged me as the prince groaned through his teeth and arched his back. His hands clawed at the pillows beside him. Muscles and veins stood out in his neck and arms.

I spread a thick layer of glittering paste across his shoulder, letting it cover a gaping wound. Then the next wound and the next. I couldn't miss a single one. If anything was consistent about Deathbiter venom, it was that every superficial scratch had to be addressed with the same care. One bite or scrape was as deadly as one hundred.

Phoenix, please let this work.

As I labored, Leander's body slowly began to sink into the bed of pillows. A grayish pallor overshadowed his rich Tolean complexion, and the black veins trailed from his eyes like spiderwebs of tears. He looked so frail. Only a few hours ago, he'd been fighting alongside me, leaping with vigor and undeniable power from the Ridarri arts as he chased after Alder.

Boma leaned back, his stoic face growing taut as he watched his prince.

"Look for more wounds," I said. "We can't miss any."

Ciri and Boma began a painstaking quest to search Leander's body for marks. The lacerations on his shoulders and arms were most dominant, but they discovered two behind his right ear, where a strange mark was covered in blood. It looked like some sort of tattoo, but I couldn't make out the shape. A shield, perhaps? Whatever creature was painted on it had wings, but that was all my mind could register. Another wound hid under his armpit, and one lanced down the small of his back, which had punctured deep into his skin.

Finally, my fingers scraped against the bottom of the bowl, fighting for every speck of ointment to spread across the last wound on Leander's brow.

After making certain I followed the laceration into his hairline, I sat back. My eyelids burned. With the crackling fire blazing at my back and my hands caked with a drying coat of gray ash, I set the empty bowl at my feet and hugged my knees to my chest. It was all I could do.

Through the haze of drooping lashes, I watched Ciri and Boma wrap Leander's wounds with bandages. It was impossible to keep my eyes open any longer. I had to sleep. The sooner I could regain my strength, the sooner I could use my power to heal him.

How I hated this. Hated everything. Hated the loss, the exhaustion, the rage, the numbness crawling in. But most of all, I hated the feeling of helplessness and uncertainty. The feeling that everything was falling apart and there was nothing I could do to stop it.

CHAPTER 2

OBEY

*M*arrok pushed himself from the moonlit snow. The lingering pain in his skull was nothing compared to the taste that raged across his tongue. It was fresh and sharp, filled with the sweetness of revenge for what Master had made him do to Eamon Brendagger. He wiped the corner of his wolflike jaw with the back of his wrist as he eyed the thick, dark fluid dripping from the torn skin on Master's arm. He wanted more. He wanted to tear Master's pale, icy flesh from his bones, sever his limbs, and coat the snow with his blood.

Master. He didn't want to call him that anymore. This man was no master of his. This man was a malevolent, vile, and heartless creature, standing there with a strange black energy rolling from his cold skin. But this Shadow Viper's commands burrowed deep, like an anchor of a ship catching rock in the darkest parts of the sea. No matter how much Marrok wished to resist, his wolf-form obeyed the one who created it. It was as if his mind and body were as different as ocean and ship, one trying to swallow the other.

"Fetch her back." Master's deep voice burrowed into his chest, the command sinking deep and unrelenting. Master had always kept his face hidden beneath the cowl of a black hood, but now he revealed every angle of his terrible face. His one silver eye burned in the night, while the right one remained hollow and lifeless where a scar stretched over his skin. His silvery black hair hung over his shoulders like molten steel.

"Did you not hear me?" Master growled. "Fetch her back!"

Snarling, Marrok's body obeyed, sprinting after the shadowy footprints sinking deep in the snow. Deathbiters soared overhead as if pointing his way. The smell of the Shadow Viper's blood began to fade as a gentler scent touched the air, one tinged with rose, cedarwood, and fear.

She was just around the next cluster of trees. Even if his nose hadn't detected her scent and the Deathbiters hadn't been circling above her, the frantic beating of her heart would have betrayed her.

He slowed, his padded feet crunching softly in the snow as he stepped around the trunk of a dormant oak.

There she was, crouched in a snowdrift, back pressed against the shelter of sleeping trees, her dark eyes wide like a cornered doe. To her credit, she didn't scream. She didn't even try to run.

Not that she could with the child growing inside her womb. But perhaps she thought that by remaining perfectly still, he wouldn't see her.

He reached for her arm.

"Wait." Her breath puffed in frantic white clouds before her. "Don't . . . don't listen to Alder."

Alder? The name bobbed across his mind like an old crate scraping against the hull of a ship for the third time. He liked that new name for the Shadow Viper he'd once called Master. The girl had called him that. The one with the stormy-blue eyes and hair like the polished railing of a ship. The girl who held the name of Brendagger . . . just like Eamon.

The pregnant woman's swallow was as loud as a whip. "You attacked him for a reason," she pressed. "Why?"

How was this any concern of hers? She didn't know him. She didn't understand the strain dragging on his mind like a frayed rope on the rigging of a ship, threatening to break under the force of the opposing wind. Alder had ordered him to bring this woman back, and he couldn't refuse. The command burned through his blood and ached to the center of his bones. He would find no relief until it was finished.

"Come." He stepped aside.

Cradling the roundness of her belly, she stepped forward cautiously. Her heartbeat banged through his ears, the Deathbiters cried overhead, and the snow crunched beneath her feet. Underneath it all, he thought he could hear another fluttering beat, one coming from the woman's . . . stomach? The baby?

Her dark eyes met his. "Don't bring me back."

Like he had a choice. "Walk, or I shall drag you," he snarled.

She shut her eyes and hugged her shoulders, her entire body shivering as she turned into the coldness of night. He followed as she backtracked through the snow, her long white dress dragging behind her. He snorted. She wasn't dressed for this.

She paused and glanced over her shoulder. "You're not the monster I was expecting," she said.

The comment took him by surprise. What sort of monster was she expecting? "Keep walking," he snarled.

She did, but she stumbled on something uneven hiding beneath the snow, perhaps a rock or a protruding root.

A pop cracked through his ears as her ankle twisted. She caught herself on a tree, but once again, she didn't cry out. She didn't even yelp. All he heard was the sucking of air through her clenched teeth. This woman was stronger than he'd expected.

Approaching slowly, he lifted her into his arms, feeling the trembling stiffness in her body. What did Alder want with a pregnant woman from Meldron? This was madness. But what else could he do?

"I'm sorry," he whispered as he walked. He'd meant for it to come out in a regretful tone, but the words rumbled menacingly from his throat. He felt her stiffen.

"What . . . what do they call you?" she asked.

He glanced down at her. Why did she care? Why did she want to know? Everyone called him a beast, a monster. Only the girl in his mind called him by another name. What his true name was, he wasn't sure.

"Alder calls me Marrok," he said.

"Do you like that name?"

"I don't know."

"I am Lonacheska," she finally said, "Queen of Roanfire. But you may call me Lona."

Marrok paused. The Queen of Roanfire? By the moonlit scales of the Leviathan, what was Alder planning?

Hope flickered through my waking mind like a blade of spring grass punching through an endless winter. Ikane. My Ikane was waking up, questioning, realizing he was more than what Alder made him out to be.

A muffled voice cried from beyond the darkness of my lashes, and a harsh pounding against the door made me aware of my body—the pillows beneath me, the warmth of the fire radiating against my shoulder, the ache in my muscles. My eyes fluttered open to hazy light filtering through the arched windows of Prince Leander's chambers. Had I really spent the night here? Master Chanter would have my head if he knew.

I glanced at Prince Leander lying beside me, his body wrapped in bandages, his face pale and ashen.

Ciri hurried to the door, where the pounding took on a frantic edge. She cracked it open and peered out at two soldiers dressed in Meldron's colors of red and gold.

"Pardon the intrusion," a soldier said with a quick bow. "Something terrible has happened in the night, and the entire castle is on lockdown until we find answers. Please give Prince Leander our apologies for keeping him . . ."

The soldier's eyes flew wide as they fell on Leander's body.

"By the burning feathers of the Phoenix," the soldier breathed. "Please don't tell me he is dead, too."

Everything from the night before came crashing down on me like a crumbling stone tower struck by a catapult. King Sander. The soldiers. Ropert.

I staggered to my feet, trying to push through the door.

The soldiers barred my path. "I'm sorry, Lady Brendagger. We've been ordered to lock down this floor. No one comes in or—"

"I was there," I snapped, pushing against their arms. My stomach flipped into my throat as I caught sight of soldiers emerging from Queen Lonacheska's chambers carrying covered bodies from the room on stretchers. Two, then three, then four.

The soldiers tried to push me back, but I slipped under their arms as a fifth stretcher emerged. My feet stopped. The man's face wasn't covered.

Ropert.

Feathers, I'd hoped it wasn't true, that it had all been in my head or a nightmare produced by Rion. But the white streak of hair running from his temple into his thick mane of strawberry-blond locks was like a scar across perfect skin. I'd done that to him. I'd stolen too much of his life energy.

"Lady Brendagger." The soldiers tried to pull me back. "Please, come—"

"No." I twisted from their grips, rushing toward Ropert as he was carried down the hallway. I had to be with him. I had to make him understand that I hadn't meant for this to happen.

"Kea." A middle-aged man with white hair barred my path, catching my shoulders with surprising strength.

Why was everyone trying to stop me? "Let me go. I need to be with him. I need to—"

"Lady Brendagger!" the man snapped, shaking my shoulders until my head jerked.

Tears were already blurring my eyes as I glared at him. It was Master Chanter, Sander's right-hand man. The man who always looked out for the well-being of our king. The man who spied and killed and did whatever he had to in King Sander's shadow. He wore the guise of a servant remarkably well, but he was more than that. He was King Sander's closest friend and confidant. And now, his face was pale, his gray eyes churned with pain, and his hands trembled as he gripped my arms.

"Let me go to him. Please, I—"

"Ropert is unresponsive," he said. "There's nothing you can do for him."

A grinding lump solidified in my throat as I watched the soldiers turn the corner with his body.

"This . . ." I stammered. "This is all my fault." I had been blinded by Alder's impossibly perfect features and his flattering promises to teach me how to control the dark magic inside me. He had no intention of training me. He never had. He would have sooner watched, with a treacherous smile on his otherworldly face, as the magic tore me apart piece by piece.

"What do you mean, your fault?" Chanter demanded. He shook my shoulders again, his grip pinching. I deserved it.

I shut my eyes, letting the tears sting through my lashes.

"Kea. Tell me. Do you know who did this?"

I shook my head.

Master Chanter's grip on my elbow was fierce as he dragged me forward, into Queen Lonacheska's chambers. I didn't want to be here. Anywhere but here.

"Look!" Chanter snapped, spinning me to face the empty armchairs standing by the cold hearth. I knew what he wanted me to see, but I scrunched my eyes tight.

He jerked my arm. "Look at what happened to your king!"

I threw my hands over my face, trying to turn away. "I didn't know!" I cried. "I didn't . . . Alder. It was all a trap."

"What about Alder?"

"He . . . he is working with Rion. He had the ruby all along. The unsolved deaths. The servants . . . Lonacheska . . . I didn't know."

"What about Lonacheska?" He pinched my arms again, forcing my hands from my face. "Where is she?"

"He took her."

"Took her?" Master Chanter roared. His voice echoed through the cold fireplace. He nearly drove me to my knees in his rage. "He took her, and you did *nothing*?"

"I tried," I croaked. "I couldn't . . . Not after facing Rion . . . Prince Leander. He ran out to save her . . . but the Deathbiters . . ." I shook my head, fearing I wasn't making any sense.

"She speaks the truth," the soldier who'd come to Leander's chambers said. "The Tolean prince is suffering from numerous wounds. His chambers hold the stench of death."

I stumbled back as Master Chanter released me. He tore his hands through his white hair, pulling it from the pristine way he'd bound it at the nape of his neck. "Where did he take her?" he demanded.

"I don't know," I said. All I'd seen were trees and snow in my vision. They could have been anywhere within Roanfire. "But they couldn't have gone far on foot."

Chanter turned to the soldier. "Go. Tell Commander Tamian to organize a search party immediately. Hounds, trackers, archers, everything we have. They leave within the hour."

"Yes, sir." The soldier saluted and hurried out the door.

"As for you," Chanter growled at me. "I can't even look at you. Why didn't you wake me? Why didn't you alert the soldiers?"

"I thought . . . it all happened so fast. I—"

"That never stopped you before!" he bellowed.

My heart sank to the pit of my stomach. I should have fought harder. I should have done more. I should have at least ordered one soldier to find Master Chanter when I'd discovered Alder's treachery.

My eyes dropped, and the blurry shape of King Sander's crumpled form came into focus at my feet. The golden edge of his crown peeked from beneath the armchair beside him. My stomach flipped, and bile burned up my throat.

Dead. He really was dead. So was Eamon. Everything had really happened.

I had failed. The thought seeped into my mind like a cold breeze under the crack of a door. This was *my* doing. They were in my care, and I had been too overcome with my own uncertain grief to protect them. Instead, I'd placed their safety into Alder's hands. This was all on me.

Swallowing down the burning bile, I covered it with a forced numbness. I had to do something. "I'll go with them," I said. "I'll go with the search party and find her."

"I don't care what you do." Chanter spun away. I didn't miss the movement of his hand as he wiped his cheeks. "Go. Just go."

I stumbled out of the room, across the hallway, and braced my soot-covered hands on the stone of the arched window frame. My breath shook and fogged the glass. The courtyard stood below, the fountain sputtering icy water in the morning light like nothing had changed, like nothing was different.

But everything was different. Everything was wrong.

There's no coming back from this, I thought. *Roanfire is ruined.*

I wiped my cheeks fiercely. The ash streaked on my fingertips from the tears, revealing the glittering stars beneath. White and green . . . and blue? My hand froze. Was that blue sprite dust on my skin? When had I gotten waterdust on my hands?

Feathers. I shut my eyes. Prince Leander. When I'd scraped the spilled dust from the floor. I shook my head, almost laughing. Of course. Add this to my list of failures. If there was anything I believed about Alder, it was that the scarring to his face was caused by experimenting with sprite dusts. All four dusts together were a recipe for an eruption of raw energy. Even Broderick had tested them himself, creating what he called sprite dust explosives. All I needed now was firesprite dust to touch my hands, and I could lose them forever. At the rate things were going, it wouldn't be long.

"Lady Brendagger?"

I glanced over my shoulder to find Ciri standing behind me. Her dark, feline-shaped eyes gazed at my tear-stained face. Worry crossed her features, as if she wasn't certain she should ask anything of me in the state I was in. But her expression bothered me.

"Is Leander alright?" I asked.

She pressed her lips into a tight line and shook her head.

A fresh wave of adrenaline soared through my blood as I hurried to his room. "Did the dust help at all?" I demanded.

"Little." She held up her fingers, making a pinching motion. "But it no last."

Even that failed.

Pushing my sleeves to my elbows, we stepped into Prince Leander's chambers. The smell of Deathbiter struck me like the blow of an axe. The stench burned my nose and eyes. How I'd managed to sleep here during the night was beyond me.

Boma was kneeling beside Prince Leander, unwrapping his soiled bandages and washing away the ointment we'd placed on him in the night. The grayish undertone of Leander's skin made him look like he was covered in ash. His head rocked slowly back and forth.

The sprite dust, even as pure as it was, hadn't worked. It had simply delayed the spread of this heightened poison. Feathers, I wasn't sure I was ready. My mind continued to reel, to spin between hopelessness and numbness. Even Thrall couldn't find a perch suitable to stand on. But I couldn't wait anymore to find my bearings.

Prince Leander's muscles tensed, cords and veins protruding in his neck and arms as he arched back. He groaned through his teeth.

Gathering a shaky breath, I knelt beside Leander and smoothed his wild dreadlocks back. "I'm here, Leander. Hold on."

Once again, Ciri and Boma provided me with everything I asked for. But this time, all I needed was an ash pail and *a lot* of water.

I considered asking for firedust. Adding it to the water made washing the Deathbiter filth from my skin easier. I'd done it before, in the Glacial Empire, when I'd healed Erin. But it was the only sprite dust not embedded on my palms. Better not risk it. I'd scrub my hands raw if I had to.

I leaned over a festering wound reeking of death and decay on his arm. The blackened veins running through his skin were as prominent as the tattoos on his Ridarris' bodies. This was going to take everything I had.

Regardless, I plunged my hands into the ash pail and pushed the gray powder between the gaps in my fingers and up my wrists. My heart thundered. I barely had the strength to draw poison from the single wound on Erin's arm. And here, Prince Leander had numerous lacerations.

For the first time, I understood how intimidated Broderick must have been when he'd found me lying on my deathbed with wounds like this.

You can't do it, the thought forced into my mind. *The poison is too strong. Why even bother when you are only going to fail?*

I shut my eyes. I couldn't think that way.

Broderick's words echoed. *Focus, steady, release.*

I could do this. I had to.

Stretching my soot-covered hands over a wound on Leander's forearm, I closed my eyes against the black veins painting their way across his skin. Against the onlooking eyes of the Ridarri warriors. Against the vibrant curtains hanging in the center of his chamber, veiling the garden beyond. It was just me and the venom.

Breathe, I told myself.

Sparks of Etheria flashed through my mind, flooding the darkest corners with stars flickering awake in the night sky. I urged them forward, drawing them to the place in my heart that held the friendship Leander and I shared. It was still on shaky ground, still new and blossoming, but it was built on trust and honesty.

You're not as strong as Broderick.

The magic faltered.

Feathers, where were these thoughts coming from? It was like another voice in my head, a cynical mind trying to break me.

Of course.

I groaned inside. How foolish could I be?

Rion, I called to her in my thoughts. *I know it's you.*

Pity. She sighed. Her reply didn't come like the numerous voices in my head that I was accustomed to but as a thought, a weak reply. It seemed all she could do in her diminished state. *I had hoped to see you spiral into despair.*

Wasn't I already there?

I could feel her chuckle at my own despondent thought. *Are you really going to spend all this energy on a Tolean?*

He is my friend.

He owns slaves. Steals what life they have.

So do you, I snapped.

Ah. So you admit what I have done is equal to Toleah's crimes, and still you aid them?

That's not what I meant, and you know it. A black spark ignited through the numbness in my core.

Do I? she asked.

The black fire of Thrall infected my stars, threatening to smother them. It was true. The laws of slavery in Toleah ground against my core, against everything I believed. But the way Leander interacted with his Ridarri was different. I'd never seen a nobleman of Roanfire treat his servants with the same respect and equality as Leander did. And I'd never seen servants of

Roanfire care for their employers the way these Ridarri cared for their prince.

Etheria brightened, pushing the black flames of doubt away.

You are a traitor to Roanfire. Rion's thoughts grew sharper in my mind, biting. *First, you fall in love with a Leviathan prince—the enemy of our people. I overlooked that fault, thinking that he would make you see reason. Now that he's gone, you swoon over a man whose sole purpose is to oppress others.*

How dare she suggest I'd lost my love for Ikane. Never. Never in a thousand years would I stop loving him. *Hold your tongue, witch!* I snapped. This was hard enough without her infesting my brain.

Black encroached on my lights again, thicker this time, holding on like an axe biting into wood. Her words didn't anger me. It was her. The fact that she would not leave me in peace to heal a man whose heart was as good as Ikane's.

I dropped my hands, leaning back on my heels, letting the magic slip away. Prince Leander's head continued to rock back and forth, his dreadlocks a mess across the pillows. He arched his head back again, fists tightening, a horrible groan tearing through his throat.

His Ridarri watched me, hope and worry burning in their dark eyes. They loved their prince. They would do anything for him, and yet, here they sat, the most elite warriors Toleah had to offer, and they were helpless to save him.

If I was going to, I had to ignore her. Shut her out.

Inhaling the room's terrible mix of Deathbiter filth and exotic Tolean spices, I allowed Broderick's archery lessons to flex through my memories. The flare of sunlight reflecting on the icicles, cold biting my nose and fingers, my breath puffing white clouds, the feeling of the bow in one hand and the fletching brushing my cheek as I pulled. My breathing became steady. My muscles responded, my shoulders drawing back.

I could do this.

Lifting my hands again, I closed my eyes. In my mind, the white stars flickered awake. Rion's voices, more than one now, rose with them, taunting, a relentless barrage of lies twisted with hints of truth. But I focused on Leander. Nothing else mattered. He needed me.

And as everything around me faded, my stars remained pure. Like fragments of ore sitting in a heated clay crucible, they melted, sliding together, turning to liquid sunlight, ready to bend to any shape I desired.

Reaching to Leander, I hunted the black threads weaving through his blood. I didn't have to go far. His body was a snake pit of black, writhing with venomous strings twisting around his bones. I didn't remember the venom in Erin's body being this robust. It was like the difference between the fragile white roots of a budding flower versus the solid roots of an ancient oak.

I didn't need Rion's voices to put doubt in my mind. I'd never faced anything like this.

Regardless, I sent the golden-white energy forward, letting it bend and wrap around the blackness. The venom recoiled, jerking me like a wild stallion against its reins. I dug my heels in, muscles straining against the power threatening to drag me down.

You are not strong enough, Rion whispered.

I gritted my teeth as the black venom and my glowing white energy came to a standstill.

You can't take all this pain from him. It is a lost cause, child. Rion's red fire edged in. *But I can change his fate and make his life burn through eternity. Let me take him. Let me end his suffering.*

She was sincere. I almost felt her comforting hand on my shoulder, urging me to let go. Why did it tempt me? I knew her agenda. I knew what she would do with his life energy once she trapped it. But feathers, this was hard.

A groan pulled in my throat. My body trembled. Heat rushed to my temples, and my ears rang with blood pulsing through my heart.

Breathe. Broderick's voice reverberated through my memories. I could feel him beside me, his breath warm on my cheek as I held the drawn bow steady, aiming for the glistening icicle. *Remember to breathe.*

I sucked air through my nose. There was no releasing it in a steady, calm breath. All I could do was cry out as I dragged against the thick blackness. Inch by inch, the toxic thread's hold slipped forward. I was doing it. I was—

Like a grappling hook to a castle wall, the tail end caught, jerking my progress to a halt. I'd come this far. My energy shifted forward like a man changing grip on the rope of a fishing line, and I jerked.

Its hold broke.

My arms shot up, my body rocking as the resistance vanished. Eyes flying wide, I gulped air, feeling perspiration clinging to my skin and the burn in my muscles.

I'd done it. Flaming feathers, I'd done it.

My hands dropped to my lap, heavy with a thick black filth that clung to my skin like tar. The acrid stench filled the chamber with a renewed burn. It would get worse before it got better.

Ciri pushed the wooden bucket filled with water to me, her eyes flashing from me to Leander's healed skin. Her lips moved as if to speak, but she couldn't bring the words forward.

That was fine. I couldn't carry on a conversation now, anyway. The exertion it took . . . Feathers. I looked over Leander's body as I sagged against the bucket's edge, dropping my hands into the liquid. There were so many staring at me with a taunting blackness. Every wound would resist with the same vigor, and I felt as though I'd fought the battle for Meldron all over again after a single one.

"Thank you, Lady Brendagger." It was the first time I'd heard Boma speak in my language. His deep brown eyes glistened with gratitude and hope.

I wished he wouldn't look at me like that.

There was a good chance I would still fail.

CHAPTER 3

BLACK LEATHER

I couldn't stop. No matter how much my body protested. Whatever poison remained, even the most minuscule amount, would continue to kill Prince Leander if I did.

But I'd pushed past my limit five wounds ago.

My hands burned with rawness from scrubbing and stung where ash touched the broken skin. I couldn't even hold them over Leander's wounds anymore. I relied on Ciri and Boma to hold my hands steady. Boma even had his solid arm wrapped around my waist just to keep me from collapsing.

My stomach clenched, and bile rolled up my throat. Worst of all, my Etheric lights sputtered like a campfire caught in the rain, fighting to stay alight.

Leander lay on his side. He hadn't moved for hours. There were only three more wounds left. Three. That's all. The deep one on the small of his back and two on his side.

But I had nothing more to give.

I choked out a sob. He was going to die.

I warned you, Rion said. *This man was dead the moment he stepped into the night.*

Get . . . get out . . . of my head. I was even panting in my mind.

Darkness intruded, and my lights flickered out. My body sagged against Boma as my stomach twisted like a cloth being wrung out. Hot bile rolled up my throat. Throwing myself aside, I curled over as my stomach convulsed.

"Stop," Ciri whispered, her hand soft on my back. "Wait for strength."

I shook my head. "He doesn't have time."

"But you cannot continue," Boma said. His speech was nearly as perfect as Leander's though still touched with an accent.

I held my stomach, curled on my knees beside them. First Ikane, then Broderick. Eamon and King Sander. Ropert, and now Prince Leander? She was taking everything from me and breaking me more with every strike.

I glanced at Prince Leander, finding a strange shadow encroaching on my vision, making his grayish skin pulse and waver. There were only three more wounds left to heal. Three. It seemed so close and yet impossible. Could I really stop now and claim I'd done everything in my power to save him?

Ciri stroked Prince Leander's brow, her dark eyes shimmering. "He fades."

I reached for Boma's hand. "Help me."

His grip was firm as he drew me closer and allowed me to lean on his muscular frame. I envied that part of him now more than ever. I needed strength like his.

Then take it, Rion said with a venomous chuckle. *Imagine all you could do if you had the power of a hundred more like him.*

My eyes scrunched tight. I didn't have the strength or mental capacity to argue with her.

"Ciri," I urged. "Please."

A tear streaked down her cheek as she gently slipped her hands under my wrists and coated my palms with the dwindling soot from the fire's ash pail. Reluctantly, she held one of my hands over the wounds on Leander's side.

"Boma," I said.

He hesitated. "Perhaps . . . it is time."

"Boma," I snapped, though it came out much weaker than intended.

His jaw worked as he took my hand and held it beside the other.

I called for the power inside. A single star came forward, flickering like the dying ember it was. But as soon as I reached for it, it snuffed out. This really was it. This was all I had. There was nothing more I could do.

Boma must have sensed my deflation. He dropped my hand and pulled me to him, burying my head against his chest. "It is alright," he said.

But it wasn't. It wasn't. Only three more wounds . . .

A knock sounded on the door. Ciri wiped her cheeks and rose. I didn't dare look as the door creaked open.

"I was told Keatep Brendagger is here?"

That voice! My heart nearly jumped forward, pressing against my ribs like a prisoner pushing their face against the iron bars of a cell just to see a little further. Could it be? I pulled from Boma, arching my neck to look past his massive shoulder decorated with tattoos.

"Now not good time," Ciri said.

"I may be able to help," the voice answered.

"Let him . . ." I panted, "let him come."

The young man limped into the room, his black leathers creaking as he lowered himself beside Leander's body. Was this real? Was he really here? Perhaps I'd pushed too far and was seeing things.

The Broderick-like figure scanned my work. "I see you've kept up with your archery."

"Broderick." I breathed his name like a prayer and allowed my body to succumb to its weakness. Boma caught me. New tears rushed forward, blurring the image of Broderick's brown curls hanging over his eyes as he reached across Leander's body and took the ash pail.

"I hate archery," I sobbed, though it wasn't the complete truth. Archery had saved my life.

His smile, though marred by the scar on his lips, was a breath of hope. "I know." He plunged a hand into the gray powder. "I'll take it from here, Kea. Rest. You've done enough."

"Kea?"

My head rose slowly from my folded arms resting on my knees. I blinked up at the black-clad figure standing before me, his cloak draped over one arm. The light from the windows at his back silhouetted him in darkness.

The last time I'd seen him, he was lying on his death bed in Gerom Post, pale, unmoving, with shredded skin and bones crushed by Alder's pet, Marrok . . . my Ikane. There had been so much blood. Even now, as he sank to the wall beside me, a coppery undertone wafted from his perspiring skin.

Sighing, he leaned his head back against the wall. "That poison was . . . different."

I nodded. I wondered if he knew how close Leander had come to death.

This wasn't the reunion I'd hoped for. I'd imagined throwing my arms around his neck and crushing him in an embrace when he returned. But I barely had the energy to rest my head against his shoulder.

He laid his head on top of mine, an unspoken understanding and contentment radiating between us.

As we watched Boma and Ciri shift pillows and blankets around their resting prince, the painful question began burning through my chest, rising to my throat. I swallowed against it. Broderick wouldn't know anything. If he'd arrived in Meldron this morning, that meant he'd left Gerom Post before it happened.

Still, I had to know.

"Broderick?" I began.

He hummed.

"Is Eamon . . . ? Was he . . . was he alive when you . . . ?"

"Alive?" His head rose, his brow furrowing. "What sort of a question is that?"

I shut my eyes, wishing I hadn't brought up the subject.

"What happened, Kea?" he pressed. "Why are you asking me if Eamon is alive?"

I swallowed as the dream flooded my mind, and the tearing pain in Ikane's heart grew. Once again, I saw the glistening tears streaking down the rich brown fur on his cheeks when he'd realized what Alder made him do. "A dream," I whispered.

Fear soared through his blue eyes. "Your dreams have never been just dreams. What did you see?"

My eyes burned, but all the tears I could shed had been spent. I had nothing left. "Ikane," I said.

Horrified understanding filled his eyes. "No," he breathed. "How bad?"

I furiously wiped my cheeks but found no tears there. Still, I didn't want to say it.

"He's dead, isn't he? Marrok killed him."

Hearing him say it was like a new punch to my gut. "I'll admit it when the official news arrives from Gerom Post," I said. But who was I fooling? I already knew.

Broderick tore a hand through his brown curls. "We'll know for certain within the fortnight."

I hoped the news would never come.

Something flashed in his eyes as he gazed back at Leander, something I'd never seen in him before. It was dark and deep, churning with more than revenge. He reached across his body, dragging his cloak tight to his side. "Alder will pay."

The movement seemed off. I glanced down to where his arm should have been resting beside me.

"Broderick?" I asked slowly.

Broderick didn't look at me as he unclenched his fingers and allowed his cloak to fall free.

His arm. It was gone.

"Healer Malcom tried to save it," he whispered, "but the damage was too great and the infection too deep."

"Oh, Broderick."

He shook his head. "Spare me your pity. I don't need it."

I swallowed at his strength. If he could accept it, I would, too. He was adaptive. Perhaps he could manage to wield his axe and use his throwing daggers with one hand. But what about archery? He always seemed so at peace when he drew the bow and focused on his target. The only other time I'd seen him so serene was when . . .

My heart dropped into my stomach. "Your lute."

His eyes fell. There it was. The sadness. The pain. The ache in his heart that told him he would never be able to play the lute again. His fingers would never dance on the strings. His wrist would never drum a beat against the lute's hollow belly.

Reaching across his torso, he wrapped his fingers around the edge of his cloak that hid the missing limb. "It doesn't matter. I haven't replaced the one Ikane broke, anyway. Now I won't need to worry about the money."

Like that was truly a concern. He worked for the king's most trusted spy. He had all the money and means necessary. But perhaps this was his way of dealing with the ache of losing what he loved the most.

A new wave of guilt washed over me, and Thrall danced in it like a child splashing in summer rain puddles. I'd made so many mistakes. But the biggest one was trusting Alder. "I'm sorry, Broderick."

"It's not your fault," he said. "I don't blame Ikane, either."

"That's not what I meant," I said. "I'm sorry for not listening to you. You knew Alder wasn't who he said, and I ignored your warning."

"I didn't know what he was, Kea. I just didn't trust him."

"Prince Leander knew something was wrong, too," I insisted. "He recognized him, said he looked just like his tutor, Master Yona."

"Yona?" Broderick's brows rose. "As in Yotherna? The White Wardent?"

I nodded. "Alder is his brother."

"Brother?" Broderick frowned. "But that would make Alder over two thousand years old. He doesn't look older than twenty-five."

"I wondered that, too," I admitted. "I think they are both linked to the ruby somehow."

"And where is the ruby now?" Broderick's voice was darker than I'd ever heard it, and something black flickered around him.

I am here, my mouthwatering little assassin, Rion said. *I look forward to tasting your fighting spirit.*

I flinched as her thoughts infiltrated my mind and shifted my hip away from Broderick's side, worried that she could reach through me and take him.

Broderick's brows furrowed at my reaction. "Are you alright?"

"Not really," I muttered. With my ash-covered hand, I reached into my pocket and felt the cold surface of the whitewashed ruby on my fingertips. I withdrew her and opened my palm to him. There was so much I needed to explain.

"It's different," he said. "And is that a—" His eyes squinted as he leaned closer. "—a crack? Did you find a way to destroy her?"

I shook my head. The only reason I had the strength to break her was because I'd used Ropert—

"Flaming feathers! Ropert." I pushed against the wall and struggled to my feet.

"What about Ropert?"

"I'll tell you on the way."

"The way to where?" Broderick rose.

I wasn't sure. Had they taken him to the healer's billet? A private room? Or, Phoenix forbid, was he lying somewhere in a dark chamber alongside the other dead soldiers? Master Chanter would know, but asking him was out of the question.

"We need to find him," I said. "I . . . I did something that . . ." I steeled myself, swallowing the guilt. "I did something to him that I will never do again."

As we neared the healer's billet, I called out to the first nursemaid I could find. She was an elderly woman who shifted her linen-filled basket to her other hip as we approached, revealing the first signs of mourning in the castle—a black sash tied to her upper arm.

"Dear me, child. Are you alright?" she asked, her brows raising until her forehead was a wrinkled mass. "Are you in need of healing?"

Me? Why was she asking me? "We are looking for Sir Ropert Saded," I said. "Was he brought here?"

"I think you should be concerned for your own health, child." She extended one of her old hands. "Come. Let us get you cleaned up."

"I don't need a nursemaid," I snapped. "I need to know if Ropert is here."

She recoiled, holding her basket of white linens between us like a shield. "I . . . I only meant . . ."

Broderick placed his hand on my arm. "You do look like death, Kea."

I glanced at my hands. They were streaked with ash, raw and bleeding. My white cotton shirt was untucked, wrinkled, smudged with soot, and splotched with Prince Leander's blood. No surprise this woman thought I'd come for help.

"My apologies," I said to her. "I am simply in need of a new shirt."

"And a bath," Broderick added.

I ignored him. "Please, take me to Ropert."

The woman nodded. "This way."

A strange smell grew stronger through the hallways as we neared the healer's billet, sulfurous and peaty along with the sharp, sweet odor of herbs. It was almost as nauseating as the smells had been in Prince Leander's chambers.

We passed curtain after curtain separating beds occupied by injured soldiers or sickly individuals. Every now and then, someone would cough or groan from some part of the place. A new admiration grew for this old woman who had dedicated her life to healing the sick. How she could face this scene day after day was beyond my understanding.

The woman stopped at the far end of a row of cream-colored hangings and gently drew the curtain aside. "In here," she said.

I stepped into the room.

Ropert lay unmoving on the bed, white sheets tucked around his muscular body. They'd removed his shirt, probably to see if there was some external damage that had caused his unconsciousness. The only visible change I could see was the new white streak of hair at his temple. My stomach curled inward and folded at the sight. Still, I moved forward.

"Forgive me, Ropert," I whispered as I stroked his forehead. The pale strand of his hair flowed through my fingers. "I never meant . . ." I couldn't finish.

"We cannot determine his ailment," the nursemaid said, "but Healer Bandock is certain a poison was used. Some blend he isn't familiar with. There's no lingering smell on his breath or skin, no change to his eyes, no blisters on his fingers or rashes on his flesh. And no—"

"Thank you," Broderick interrupted. "Would you mind giving us some time alone with him?"

"Of course," she said, repositioning the basket on her hip. "I will return shortly." She paused at the curtain and watched me. "Shall I bring something for you when I return? A clean shirt, perhaps?"

"That would be appreciated," Broderick answered for me.

I took Ropert's hand in mine as the woman slipped away. It was warm—like it should be—calloused and scarred with strength just beneath the surface. The hand of my best friend, brother, and ally. I watched for the furrowing of his brow as I squeezed it or a hint of his infamous crooked grin or the flash of his unbelievably blue irises. But his face remained still, every crease and line soft and peaceful in sleep.

How much life energy had I taken? Was it more than his body could live without? Would he be in this state until he withered away? Or did he just need sleep? Deep, uninterrupted, sound sleep to recover?

Whatever happened, I would never use him or anyone like that ever again.

Do not make a vow you cannot keep, Rion said.

My jaw tightened. Did she really think I would do this to someone else?

"You blame yourself," Broderick said as he stepped closer. "I can feel it."

"I used his life," I said without taking my eyes off Ropert's serene face. "I stole it."

"From what you told me, he offered it."

My eyes rose to meet his. "That doesn't make it right."

"What if your roles were reversed, Kea? Would you have given him your life energy if he needed it?"

I glanced down at Ropert again. I'd give him my life this very moment if I could. Feathers, I hated it when Broderick was right.

"It's not weakness to accept help from others," Broderick said.

"But if it places them in danger? If I know they could die?"

Broderick reached across Ropert's body and took hold of my wrist, demanding my attention. "Kea. You are a soldier. You know better than anyone that fighting alone is not what we do. We form regiments and divisions. When we face an enemy on the battlefield, we gather in one unified group, knowing the dangers but also knowing that our chances of survival are better together."

"But Rion is mine to face."

Broderick retracted his hand as he looked down at Ropert. "I don't think that's true."

My brows furrowed. What did he mean by that?

Before I could reply, the curtain opened. I stiffened as Master Chanter stepped inside. He'd changed. His usual gray servant's robes had been replaced by a tailored midnight-black tunic and trousers—the color of mourning. Even the ribbon tying his white hair back was black. The shade made him appear younger somehow yet more dangerous, like his apprentice, Broderick. His gray eyes watched me, burning with something I didn't understand. I felt like he was measuring me.

He looked at Ropert. "How is he?"

"No change," I said.

Chanter nodded solemnly. "I . . . owe you an apology."

I opened my mouth to protest, but he raised a hand.

"No," he began. "I accused you of not sending guards to wake me or rousing soldiers to give chase as Alder stole our queen. Truth is, the four soldiers in Lonacheska's chambers were not the only casualties of the night. Alder's retreat was littered with death."

I swallowed.

"His magic is lethal," Chanter continued. "We lost eighteen soldiers last night."

Eighteen? I glanced at Broderick. Eighteen was a small platoon. Eighteen was a formidable group for anyone to contend with. But even together, they didn't stand a chance against Alder's dark power.

Chanter straightened as if trying to steel himself against his own emotions. A hint of concern flashed through his gray eyes as he met my face. "Are *you* alright?"

I wasn't. But what could he do about that? He couldn't bring Eamon or King Sander back from the dead. He couldn't restore Ikane. He couldn't give Broderick his arm back, and he couldn't wake Ropert from his strange death sleep.

I shook my head, looking away.

"When did you last eat?" he asked.

I couldn't remember.

"Slept?" he prodded.

"Who can sleep when a madman has kidnapped our queen?" I asked. "Has the search party already been dispatched?"

He nodded. "They left hours ago."

I shut my eyes. I'd wanted to be a part of it. I wanted to face Alder and bring Lonacheska back.

"Come, Kea." Chanter extended his hand to me. "I know your heart is breaking with the rest of Roanfire, but anything we do now will be ineffective and perhaps even detrimental if we do not care for ourselves first. You need to rest. Clear your mind and focus. It is the best chance we have to save our queen."

He was right. My mind had been spinning too fast for too long. Nothing made sense anymore. "I don't want to leave Ropert."

"I'll send for you the moment he rouses," Chanter promised.

I glanced at Broderick, who nodded. "Sleep, Kea. I'll stay with him."

CHAPTER 4

REGENT WANTED

*M*y eyes opened to morning light slicing through the gaps of the green drapes surrounding my bed. I didn't remember my room having a canopy-covered bed.

I'd grown accustomed to the small servant's quarters I'd been given above the kitchens where heat radiated through the stone from the mammoth ovens. But the swirling vines of gold and brown blossoms on the fabric reaching the carved wooden frame above was familiar. This wasn't where I should be.

Pushing the heavy blanket from my legs, I pulled the canopy aside. This was the room for Lady Brendagger—the room I'd been given when I'd first arrived in Meldron as Daram's representative. Nothing had changed from my time here. The painted walls, the writing desk by the window, the full-length mirror standing in the corner, the beautifully carved armoire, and the two chairs standing by the cold fireplace. The one on the right still sported the bite of my attacker's sword in its back from the time Archduke Goldest tried to have me assassinated.

I rubbed my temples. Chanter. I should have questioned or realized where he had brought me to bathe and rest last night. I would have insisted he bring me to my little servant's chamber above the kitchens. But I'd been too exhausted and too numb to comprehend.

A knock sounded on the door.

My head jerked up. Had Ropert awakened? "Enter," I called, eagerly climbing from the bed.

Two maidservants stepped inside, one carrying a tray with an arrangement of steaming dishes. They rattled as she set it on the table by the fire and replaced the items that had shifted during delivery.

"You look well, Lady Brendagger." The other maidservant said as she draped what I assumed to be my clothing for the day over the back of an armchair. "Astounding what a hot bath and good sleep can do."

I barely paid her any mind. My eyes were drawn to the clothing she'd brought. It was the color of midnight, trimmed with copper and wine-red flowers, evoking a sense of loss. Everything flooded back.

"Any news of Sir Ropert?" I asked.

She shook her head.

"What about the search party? Has Queen Lonacheska's trail been found?"

The maidservant glanced at the other, who had begun stoking the fire. "Forgive us, my lady, but we are not privy to such information," she said. "Though if you hurry, you could still make it to the royal counsel this morning. I'm certain they would be keen to share such news with my lady."

The counsel? The last time I was requested to be a part of the council, it had ended with me poisoned, Prince Leander locked away, and Toleah breathing war down our throats. Was this maidservant misinformed? Would they really be keen to share anything with me?

"Prime Minister Chanter would be pleased to see you there," she added, probably because of my confused expression.

"Prime Minister?"

"Ah, you haven't heard." A light grew in her eyes, like she finally felt she had some useful information to share. "A document was found in King Sander's possession that placed Master Chanter as Prime Minister in order to fill the needs of the kingdom should anything befall both him and the queen . . ." Her excitement faltered.

This was very unusual. A servant raised to the station of Prime Minister overnight? I knew Chanter had influence, but it was always behind closed doors and in shadow. Still, I had to commend King Sander for his choice. Chanter had no desire to rule. Chanter would do everything in his power to make sure the rightful heir sat on Roanfire's throne.

"Then let's hurry," I said to the maidservant.

Breakfast was rushed. My hair was braided back, and the maidservants helped me dress. I had expected Master— Minister Chanter to send me a corseted gown as he had in the past. But the black clothing provided was surprisingly . . . perfect.

Simple in cut, the tunic had been crafted with spectacular detail. The thick trim was laced with gold edging, containing vines of dark-green leaves and blood-red blossoms. It sang of sorrow, of the loss we had taken. Brass buckles clasped down my bust, coming to a snug cinch at the waist where the black coattails draped over my knees.

Black and blood. That seemed to be what my life had become.

You forget fire, Rion whispered through my mind. *What is life without the warmth of a fire?*

I should have known she would find my thoughts and scrape her blood-red nails down the fragile ache in my chest. I searched the room. Where was the stone? I scarcely remembered dragging it from my pocket before shedding my trousers last night.

A small flicker caught my eye on the top of the mantle. There she was. Pale and feigning innocence.

But something was different.

I stepped closer, scowling down at the cracked surface. Was she brighter than when Leander had handed her to me? A little more . . . pink? Her intent radiated hotter than the fire in the hearth. She was clawing her way out, slowly, diligently. The prison I'd locked her in was a sandbag in the doorway of an oncoming monsoon, and time wasn't on my side.

"Are you ready, my lady?" the maidservant asked.

I swallowed as I turned to her. Perhaps meeting with the counsel wasn't the correct course of action. My attention should be focused on Prince Leander and what he knew of the White Wardent.

"Will Prince Leander be there?" I asked.

"I . . . I do not know. They say he fell ill the night the queen was abducted. He has not been seen for several days."

"Days?" My eyes bulged. "How . . . how long have I been sleeping?"

"A little over five sunrises," she said, her hands raising. "It's alright, my lady. You needed the rest. Chanter has everything well in hand."

"Obviously not if we haven't found our queen!" I snatched the stone from the mantle, squeezing its deceitful warming surface in my fist. "Take me to the council chamber. Now."

As much as I wanted to keep the ruby as far from me as possible, I would not let her out of my sight again. Not after what Alder had done. And I would not risk anyone—such as these maidservants tidying my chambers—accidentally touching her surface, even in her weakened state. Another life could be all she needed to break free and destroy me before I discovered how to fight back.

Wise of you to be cautious, she hummed, *but unnecessary.*

Her words sent ice down my spine. She sounded so calm, so relaxed and placid, like everything had happened just as she had planned.

The heavy wooden doors of the council chamber groaned open. The long, polished table stretched into the room before me, surrounded by noblemen and women all dressed in their finest midnight clothing of sorrow. A dozen official documents bearing broken wax seals lay scattered on the table. One bore the black seal from the Glacial Empire. So they'd heard as well.

King Sander's empty chair at the head was like a punch to my stomach. A reminder of everything.

My feet stopped. I knew he wasn't here, but somehow I had expected to see him sitting in that chair. That's where he always was. I could almost see the ghost of his golden crown sitting on his rich auburn hair as his strong blue eyes looked out at me, pleading for counsel and love.

"Lady Brendagger." Chanter rose from his seat to the left of King Sander's empty chair. "My, but it is good to see you," he said. He smiled at me. There was sincerity in his eyes—and relief. "Please." He gestured to the seat across from him, Queen Lonacheska's chair. "Join us," he said. "We could use your counsel."

I blinked. Did he really just ask me to sit in the queen's seat? I wasn't even worthy of standing behind it as the rest of the bodyguards did for their noble charges. No, I would remain here, at the foot of the table where I belonged.

"What is being done about Queen Lonacheska?" I demanded. "Why haven't you found her yet?"

Chanter's smile faded. "Lady Brendagger. Please, sit." The sternness in his voice made me pause.

Very well. I would not make a scene. Perhaps they were already discussing the issue when I'd barged in. But I would not take Queen Lonacheska's place. Instead, I planted my feet where I was and clasped my hands at the small of my back in a soldier's stance. "I'm listening," I said.

Chanter sighed, shook his head, and returned his focus to the papers on the table. "As I was saying," he began, "news of King Sander's passing has spread to our neighboring kingdoms faster than anticipated. Condolences arrive by the hour." His eyes rose to scan those gathered at the table as he placed a hand over the letters. "However, along with their condolences comes a threat. We are vulnerable, and they know it. With Queen Lonacheska and her child missing, there is none left to claim the title of regent." His gray eyes stopped as they met mine . . . almost like he was asking me to take charge. Me. A simple soldier. A nobody. Yes, I had Noirfonika blood in my veins, but I was no ruler.

"I have done what I can," Chanter continued. "But the contingent from Toleah grows closer. I am told Ambassador Duqa Alaneek is with them."

Hushed murmurs broke out among the nobles. They knew the name and, from the sound of it, feared it.

"Who is this Ambassador Alaneek?" I asked.

"She is second in command to the king of Toleah," Chanter said. "She's known to Roanfire as The Hawk. Always vigilant, always ready to swoop down on vulnerable prey and destroy it."

"Then we must name a new regent before they arrive," a nobleman said. His face had paled. In fact, everyone in the room looked pale. Their eyes were wide with panic.

"I agree," a nobleman with angular-styled facial hair announced. "And since there is no blood-heir, it comes down to who holds the most power and land. According to that, I am—"

A woman held up her hand. "You have no right, Count Jergens. Just because you have the most land does not—"

"Have you forgotten who has been living among us for the last six moons? A great man who has saved us from starvation," I said. "Prince Leander won't let anyone harm us, especially not some woman known as The Hawk."

"Then why isn't he here?" the noblewoman asked.

"Prince Leander is still recovering from Deathbiter wounds," Chanter said. "Please, calm yourselves. King Sander was a man of wisdom and foresight. Before his passing, he made arrangements that would see Roanfire through a crisis such as this."

The room fell silent as the new Prime Minister waved to a servant standing against the far wall. The man approached with a scroll carefully balanced in his hands as if he were presenting Chanter with a priceless golden sword.

Chanter closed his eyes as he clutched the sealed scroll to his chest. "This is a dark time for Roanfire. Darker than we could have ever imagined."

He glanced up at me. The pleading in his eyes made me stiffen.

"I would not resort to this if we were not desperate," he said, "but we are. We are at the end of our rope, and what King Sander has decreed in this scroll is the only thing that can save us."

"May I?" the noblewoman asked, holding her hand out for the scroll.

Chanter did not remove his eyes from mine as he placed the scroll in her palm and allowed her to break the golden seal. The parchment unraveled. The room held its breath as she scanned the letters. Her brows grew narrower as she read on.

Count Jergens leaned forward. "Well? What does it say? What does King Sander want us to do?"

The woman glanced up.

Was she looking at *me*? I looked over my shoulder then back at her. She *was* looking at me, her eyes swimming with disbelief. I swallowed and shifted my feet. It took everything inside me not to lunge across the table and snatch the letter. What had Sander done?

"Give me that." Count Jergens reached across the table and snatched the parchment from the woman's hands. He hastily scanned the paper.

Perfect. Now he was looking at me, too.

"Who is regent, Jergens?" another nobleman asked. "What does it say?"

"It can't be." Jergens rounded on me, waving the paper. "Does Queen Lonacheska know?" His eyes were sharp and dangerous.

I didn't even know what the scroll said, but my heart thundered with suspicion. King Sander wouldn't be that desperate, would he? "Does she know what?" I demanded.

"It says here that you are his child. When were you legitimized?"

When was I *what*? I glowered at Chanter, and yet the floor seemed to buckle under my feet. My face grew cold. He couldn't have taken one moment to prepare me? To warn me? To just let me know this was King Sander's contingency plan?

"You mean King Sander appointed Lady Brendagger as acting regent?" a nobleman asked.

"Not regent," the noblewoman said slowly, her eyes still watching me. "She is the Princess of Roanfire."

All eyes turned to me.

I fell back a step, my jaw slack. I would not . . . I could not. King Sander had no right to legitimize me without my consent. I was no ruler. I knew nothing about governing a kingdom. I'd been trained in combat, not diplomacy. There had to be a mistake.

"Keatep Brendagger is from Daram, is she not?" a nobleman asked. "She's Master Eamon's daughter."

"Are you telling us that King Sander is her father?" the noblewoman asked Chanter. "How old is she?"

"She's nearly twenty years of age," Chanter said. "Well mature enough for this position."

"But that would mean King Sander had fathered her—"

"When he was a boy, yes." Chanter interrupted. "He was sent to the Glacial Empire far too young with a mind clouded by the idea that he should marry for love. He fell for another and fathered this child."

"Who is her mother?" Count Jergens demanded.

My eyes turned to Chanter. I'd wanted to know that, too, but I'd never had the courage to ask.

"She was a strong woman from the area near Gerom Post," Chanter said, his eyes warning the noblemen and women to drop the subject. "She died in childbirth. That is all you need to know. The child was given to Master Eamon to raise as his own. King Myron made certain he knew of her lineage."

I flinched as Chanter spoke of Eamon.

"The fact is that Keatep Brendagger Noirfonika is the first female heir borne to the throne since Queen Damita," Chanter declared. "And for the survival of Roanfire, we should honor it."

"She has been an asset," a nobleman mused. "She did defeat the Leviathan army."

"It's a desperate act," I snapped, finally finding my voice, "one you would be foolish to act on when our queen is still out there! It's treason! It's usurpation!" With heat rising to my face, I slammed my palm on the table. "Queen Lonacheska is alive and carries the future of Roanfire inside her. And you," I glowered at everyone seated around the table, especially Chanter. "You sit here in your fine black clothing discussing her replacement rather than making every effort to restore her!"

"The trail has run cold," Chanter said. "We have exhausted—"

"Then gather fresh horses and hounds! Send word to every town and hamlet. Call on the neighboring provinces—"

"We've done all that," Chanter said. His calmness irritated me.

"It's only been four days!"

"It only takes one to ruin a kingdom!" Chanter snapped, redness rising to his cheeks. "And every day that passes, others scheme to take the throne. Threats lie within just as they do without. Neighboring kingdoms like Toleah and the Leviathan pirates will come to conquer!"

Dragging my hand from the table, I curled it into a fist at my side. "Tomorrow, I will go."

"Tomorrow is King Sander's funeral," Chanter reminded me darkly.

"Fine. Then I will go the following day. But I will hunt down Alder and bring our queen back before this so-called 'Hawk' arrives." Turning away, I made for the doors.

"What makes you think you can do what our armies couldn't?" Count Jergens called after me.

I stopped. "Because I have more at stake than any of you," I said then marched from the room. I had mourned King Sander's death. Now I wanted to kill him all over again.

"Lady Brendagger?"

I glanced up at the maidservant who'd accompanied me here now standing in the hallway.

"I beg your pardon," she said with a bow, "but I just received word that Sir Ropert seems to be waking."

My heart jumped. Oh, how I needed his counsel, his humor, or just his friendship.

But then my feet slowed. Would he give me any of that after what I'd done to him?

CHAPTER 5

WHITE LOCK

*M*y knees ached as they knelt on the stone floor beside Ropert's bed. His hand lay in mine, lax and unmoving. His eyes remained shut, his face soft, his breathing deep. They said he'd stirred, but since I'd arrived, I'd seen no sign of him rousing.

I ran my fingers through the bone-white streak in his hair as worry gnawed on my insides. Even if he did wake, he would hate me. He would fear me. He would know what I was capable of and keep as far from me as possible.

Or he will revere you, Rion slipped into my thoughts. *Now that he has tasted your power, he will worship you and understand what he could become. He could be eternal. So could you.*

Shutting my eyes, I pressed Ropert's knuckles against my forehead. "What must I do to be rid of you?" I whispered.

Her voices laughed. *My dear Phoenix Daughter. You and I are the same. We hold the same power and the same strength. The only difference is that I have embraced the souls that come to me, whereas you push them away. What do you—*

Souls do not come to you, I snapped in my mind. *You take them. You steal lives that do not belong to you.*

I save them. Why can you not see? They feel no more pain. She genuinely sounded perplexed that I could not understand. *With me, they can be with their loved ones for eternity.*

Until you use them like you did King Sander.

For every good thing, there is a price to pay.

And when you rise? I demanded. *What then? Every soul you have bound within your prison will be consumed.*

Not consumed. Transformed. Turned into my eternal flame.

I shook my head, pressing Ropert's hand more tightly against my forehead. There was no reasoning with her. In her twisted mind, she believed she was saving souls. Souls that hadn't lived a full life. Souls that would never learn or change or grow. Souls that could never find peace in her.

You, too, could be free of this sorrow, she said. *Become my new vessel. Let me be reborn in you. The people already look to you for salvation, yet you fear to rule Roanfire. You needn't do it. I can take this burden from you. Let it go. Let it slip away. Let your worries, sorrows, and pains be swallowed up in my immortal fire.*

You snake! My Etheric lights sparked to life, slapping her away, pushing her back. *You only want power! You care nothing for life.*

I am life itself! she cried. *With or without you, I will be reborn.*

"Dagger?"

My eyes snapped open. "Ropert."

Ropert's eyes were tired, narrow slits as he watched me, those beautiful crystalline blue irises shining through his lashes. He gave me a weak, pain-filled smile. "You can stop crushing my hand now."

"Oh." I pried my fingers from his hand then leapt from the ground and embraced him. I inhaled his scent of steel, leather, and strange herbs the healer had placed on his skin. He was alive. He was alright.

"Forgive me," I whispered into his shoulder. "Please, forgive me."

His hands were warm on my back but strangely weak as he held me close. "For visiting me without bringing pastries? You should be sorry."

I laughed through my tears, holding him closer. The ease with which he turned the darkest situation into something bearable was magical. The entire kingdom was in mourning, yet here I was smiling through the tears because of Ropert.

"I . . . I had a terrible dream." His tone turned more serious as he whispered into my hair. "At least, I hope it was just a dream. Alder had the ruby. And Rion took King Sander . . . the soldiers . . . me. Did I really see a burning woman surrounded by red stars?"

The joy he'd brought evaporated as my grip around his neck loosened. I couldn't even look at him as I sat upright.

"King Sander is dead, isn't he?" he asked.

I wiped my cheeks furiously, angry at the new tears. "You were dead, too." I tried to ignore the churning in my stomach. "I tried. I trapped her, but it's not going to last. She's going to break free."

"Hey, Dagger." Ropert propped himself up on his elbow. "It's alright."

What was wrong with him? Why were his eyes burning with pride instead of anger and fear? He should hate me.

"I gave my energy willingly, and I would do it again. You brought me back," he reminded me. "You were incredi—ugh." With a wince, he pressed the heel of his hand against his temple. "My head." He dropped back onto his pillow.

I'd never seen him so weak. I brushed his hair back, swallowing my tears. I had to be strong for him. "Rest, Ropert."

He shut his eyes against my touch. "What happened, Dagger? I can't remember anything after . . . after you pulled me out of that strange place full of stars."

Where was I to begin? "Alder kidnapped Queen Lonacheska," I said.

"What?" he demanded. "Has she been recovered? Please tell me Alder is behind bars."

"No prison can hold a man like that," I said. "Even so, we'd have to find him first. Master Chanter, now Prime Minister Chanter, has sent out search parties but to no avail."

Ropert blinked at me.

"I'm leaving the day after tomorrow to search myself."

"Whoa." Ropert held up a hand. "Prime Minister Chanter? How . . . how long have I been sleeping?"

"Nearly six days."

He shut his eyes with the same dismayed expression I had probably given the maidservants who attended me. "Anything else?" he asked.

"The Deathbiters' venom has changed. It's more potent. Instead of a fortnight, it kills within days. If Broderick hadn't returned when he did, Prince Leander would be dead right now."

Ropert's eyes opened. "Thundercrack is back? How is he?"

"Sound," I said. "But he . . . he lost his arm."

Ropert winced.

"And there's one more thing," I began slowly. I wasn't sure I wanted to tell him, but I needed his guidance. "Apparently, King Sander had me legitimized as his heir without my knowledge. Because we cannot find Queen Lonacheska, the counsel is desperate to name me their princess before an embassy from Toleah arrives. You should have seen their faces when Chanter told them that someone known as The Hawk was arriving with them. Cowards. All of them."

Ropert's bright blue eyes stared at me, through me, unblinking. Perhaps I'd thrown too much at him at once. He'd just woken up from being . . . dead, after all.

"Did I . . . did I hear you right?" His eyes focused on me again. "I thought I heard you say they want to name you princess? As in heir to the throne?"

"I won't accept, though," I said. "Ropert, Queen Lonacheska is still out there. She's alive, and she needs us. Naming me heir is . . . is . . ."

"Treason?" he asked.

I smiled. At least someone understood. "It's stealing the throne from her child. King Sander's true heir."

"Logically, you do have claim to the throne," he said. "But you?" His mischievous smile tugged on the corners of his lips. "You'd make a terrible queen."

I chuckled and pushed my fist into his shoulder. Normally, I would've slugged him good at a comment like that. But I was still worried about his condition. He looked so pale.

He rubbed his shoulder playfully, acting as though nothing had changed between us. Then his smile faded. "We need to find Alder. We need to bring Lona home." Reaching across his body, he dragged the blankets from his torso and tried to sit.

"Ropert, no." I placed a hand on his shoulder. "You need to rest."

"Apparently, I've been sleeping for six days. How much more rest do I need?"

But even as he spoke, I could see the dizziness sweeping over his eyes. My arm shot out to steady him.

"Please, Ropert."

He held onto the edge of the bed and closed his eyes. "I just need—"

"Why didn't anyone tell me?" The curtain flew to the side as an elderly man with a long white beard stormed into the chamber. His dark eyes found Ropert then flung spinning daggers my direction. "What are you doing here?"

I returned the daggers with my own eyes. Healer Bandock. I'd rather face a hoard of Leviathan pirates than this ancient, egotistical healer.

"You," he growled at me as he marched to Ropert's side. "This man is ill, and you try to pry him from his bed before I have examined him? Once again, you attempt to undermine my expertise as a healer. The king's own physician!" He urged Ropert to lie back. "I should have you removed at once."

"She was just informing me of the events of the past few days," Ropert said. To my surprise, he allowed Healer Bandock to guide him back to his pillow. Never before had Ropert given in so easily. "She meant no harm."

"No harm? Bah! All this girl does is bring bad luck. Pirates, traitors, poison, and now this." Bandock turned his focus to Ropert's eyes, tugging the bottom lid down until pink was exposed. "The last thing you need right now is to be weighed down by the troubles plaguing this castle. It isn't good for your recovery."

"You don't even know what's wrong with him," I muttered.

Bandock whirled to me. "What was that?"

Ropert shot me a look that said I wasn't helping. "I would rather be informed than be kept in the dark," he said.

Bandock turned back to Ropert. "Open your mouth, and stick out your tongue."

Ropert did, and Bandock scrutinized the pinkness of his throat. "Well," Bandock grumbled as he leaned back. "I don't see anything wrong with you. You're slightly dehydrated, and your eyes are slow to dilate. Other than that . . . what happened in the queen's chambers? Were you poisoned?"

Ropert rubbed his forehead, scrunching his eyes. "I don't remember. All I remember is fire."

"Fire?" Bandock asked.

"It's nothing," Ropert said quickly. "But you are right about one thing. I am dreadfully thirsty. Is there a horse trough nearby?"

Bandock scowled at him. "I'll send for water. But you"—he pointed at Ropert—"you stay in bed. And you." Now, he jabbed a bony finger at me. "Leave him be. He needs rest."

I moved for the curtain, but Ropert grabbed my wrist.

"Just a moment longer," Ropert said to Bandock. "I need her company more than I need silence right now."

Bandock scowled. "Very well. But only a few minutes. And stay in bed." With that, he stormed from the room.

Ropert tugged me back to his side. "I'm sorry, Dagger."

"What for?"

"I . . . I feel useless. My head . . . everything is spinning."

I clutched his hand in both of mine. "It's alright, Ropert. You were . . . dead."

He gave me a pathetic chuckle. "Now I can add that to my life history. 'Sir Ropert rises from the dead after a battle with a burning witch,'" he announced in a performing tone. "All jesting aside, Dagger, what do you know about Alder? Were you able to interrogate the bounty hunters who tried to abduct you?"

I'd completely forgotten about that incident. The bounty hunters must have some insight into what Alder was planning, even if they didn't know it.

"Ropert." I placed my hands on his cheeks. "You are brilliant!" After planting a kiss on his brow, I hurried for the curtain. "I'll be back."

"Does that mean you'll bring me some apple fritters?" he called after me.

I chuckled. I'd bring him a basketful if the cook would allow it.

CHAPTER 6

SAVE A LIFE

I held the torch high, its orange glow flickering across the glossy surface of the damp stone walls as I descended the slick stairs. The sharp, fermented scent of rotting fruit and sulfur of human excrement grew so strong, I could taste it.

A shiver ran down my spine. I'd been behind one of those doors before, lying on flea-ridden straw, awaiting my sentence. The hazy memory of King Sander leaning over me, tenderly brushing my hair back, pleading with me to remember anything about King Myron's murder pulled a lump into my throat. What more could I have done to save him?

Someone coughed in the distance, and a steady dripping noise echoed through the corridor lined with cell doors. Even in the meager light, I could see my breath.

"Can I help you?" The gray-haired guard on duty rose from his stool in the corner.

"I'm here to speak with the captured bounty hunters."

He led me to a cell at the far end of the corridor and unlocked the door. "I'll be right outside," he said.

Nodding, I stepped inside, the torchlight falling across the forms of two men sitting against the wall. Iron shackles rattled as the older bounty hunter squinted up at me with a dirt-smudged face. But the younger hunter, the one with the shaved head, kept his face bowed to his knees.

"What do you want?" the older man demanded, shielding his eyes from my light. "We've already told you. We did not poison King Sander or his soldiers."

"Is that what they think you did?" I asked.

His eyes narrowed at me. "Who are you?"

"I'm asking the questions."

"We're bounty hunters," he snapped. "Not assassins."

"We're fools," the younger hunter mumbled into his knees.

The older man hardened his face. "The only thing we did was try to collect a bounty. As hunters, we have certain exemptions."

I'd heard the same defense before. "Not when it comes to collecting a bounty set by Leviathan pirates," I said. "That is treason."

"We didn't—"

"Don't lie anymore, Pa." The young man raised his shaved head but still didn't lift his eyes to meet mine. "We knew."

"Caleb," the old man warned, "don't."

"Why?" Caleb demanded. "We knew the bounty was set by pirates, but we didn't care. The money was too good. It would have allowed my Pa to retire, and I . . ." Chains rattling, he pulled his hands to his clean scalp and ran them back to his neck. "I would have been set for life. I could have finally married Adeline and given her the life she deserved."

Keeping the torch high, I crouched before them, firelight falling across their dirt-smudged faces. Caleb, at least, seemed willing to talk.

"I don't care about the bounty," I said. "If you help me, I will see the charges of treason and manslaughter are dropped. I know you are innocent of that."

Caleb's hands lowered. Then he glanced at his father with pleading hope. "You mean . . ." He finally met my eyes. "You can free us?"

If only they knew the power the council was prepared to give me.

"I want to know about Alder," I said. As his name left my lips, a brief sting pricked my temples. It felt like a needle. I flinched but refrained from rubbing the side of my head. I couldn't show weakness. Not to these men.

"What do you want to know?" Caleb asked.

"Hold on," the old hunter broke in. "Don't say another word, Caleb. This is our bargaining chip."

"I already gave you a deal," I said. "What more do you want?"

He turned to me. "We'll tell you what we know, and in return, you'll release us and give us five hundred gold to compensate for our unlawful imprisonment."

"You have committed treason by trying to fill a Leviathan bounty," I said, "but I can spare you the executioner's sword."

The old man's eyes narrowed further. "But we'll be branded. That alone is a death sentence."

It had been over a year since the glowing iron had marked my flesh. The scar on my shoulder now held the perfect shape of a Phoenix and Leviathan serpent locked in battle. Yes. They would bear the same mark. That, I could not spare them. "I can see that it isn't made public," I said.

He shook his head. "That's not good enough."

"Why fight it, Pa?" Caleb demanded.

"Hush, son."

"No." Caleb dropped his hands and looked up with bloodshot eyes. "I will accept my mistakes, and I will pay penance for it." He turned to me. "Alder approached us in Kaltum with the opportunity to make a fortune in filling the bounty for Lady Brendagger. The sum was too great to refuse, even if it was set by pirates. And Alder, already bound for Meldron, had a way for us to enter the castle and get to her. He didn't even want his cut. All he wanted was for us to get the girl out of his way."

I tilted my head at the young man. He didn't recognize me as their quarry. Then again, the brightness of my torch might have made me appear as a silhouette to them. "And you didn't question why?" I prodded.

"We asked," Caleb's father answered, "but Alder said it was better we not know."

Of course he did. The more he kept from them, the more I wouldn't be able to—

Another prick of hot pain flared through my skull. This time, my hand flew to my forehead, but by the time I touched my brow, the pain was gone.

"Help me understand," I said. "Lady Brendagger was the soldier who they say defeated the entire Leviathan army. She was the one who put fear into their hearts. Her name alone kept Roanfire safe. And you were willing to turn her in to the very pirates threatening our shores?"

Caleb was shaking his head before I even finished my question. "It's a lie," he said.

"Excuse me?"

"Alder made us see reason. Lady Brendagger did nothing against the pirates. It was all conceived to put fear into the hearts of men and raise her station. We heard the stories. But really? Who can believe that one woman destroyed an entire army or survived the Deathbiters' lair or frightened off a beast that tore twenty seasoned warriors apart? It's too much to even consider."

I sat back. Well. He wasn't completely wrong. I *didn't* destroy the Leviathan army. That was Rion. But the rest? Yes, if I were in his shoes, I'd find it all too farfetched to believe.

"Besides," Caleb's father continued. "Alder said the pirates wanted the girl alive. What harm could it do?"

That piqued my interest. "And where were you to take her?"

"We were to leave a message in the hollow of a tree at the edge of the Dead Forest," Caleb said, "where the Fold River meets. We would arrange the exchange from—"

His words were drowned out by another flash of hot energy slamming into my temples. What was going on? The last time I had pain like this . . .

Rion!

I reeled inward, folding into the mental energy of the ruby inside my pocket. Sure enough, there was a crack in the polished sphere I'd trapped her in—a jagged line like a lightning bolt on the surface. Hot red fire smoldered beneath.

I was wondering when you'd notice, she said. *Did I not give you enough signs?* There was a dangerous smile to her voices. A slender thread of fire wormed from the fissure and snapped against my mind with a crack. Sparks danced behind my eyes, blinding me both physically and mentally. Hand flying to my forehead, I rocked forward onto my knees, almost dropping the torch.

A strangled cry rang through my ears, but it wasn't mine. It echoed across the cell walls. Tearing my eyes open, I found Caleb curled over, fingers digging into his scalp.

"Caleb?" the old hunter leaned over him.

He reveals too much, Rion said. She was reaching through me, a burning thread trailing from her prison into Caleb's mind like a parasite, tugging on the star that was his soul. His very life.

"What is happening?" the old hunter cried, his eyes wide and pleading as he looked at me. Then his expression changed. His mouth dropped open, his eyes going rounder. "You're her," he breathed. "You're Lady Brendagger."

He glanced at his son again, at his body curled in pain, at Caleb's nails dragging down his skin, leaving shredded red lines on his shaved scalp.

"Please," the old hunter cried. "Please, stop. We are sorry. We didn't mean—"

He thought I was doing this.

Slamming my eyes shut, I called to the white sparks of Etheria, driving them forward until they wrapped Caleb's life energy in a fierce embrace of light, and pulled. She would not have him. She would not have a single soul more to add to her sea of terrified spirits.

Oh? Rion chuckled. *Was the taste of Ropert's soul that addicting? Very well. I shall let you have this one.*

Wait—what?

She let go.

Caleb's life force jerked back, whipping into my mind like a broken chain. He crashed against my memories. Like a caged bird, his white star darted from one part of my mind to the next, bruising every thought and moment as he tried to escape.

The torch slid from my hand and thumped against the soiled hay.

"Caleb!" the old hunter's cry shredded my heart. It was the cry of pure horror and loss, the cry I'd heard in my own heart over and over again.

I chased after Caleb's star. *Caleb. Caleb, stop. Let me help you. Don't fight me, please!* I had to return him, send him back. But he darted through my fingers like a fish in water. Didn't he realize I was trying to help him?

Congratulations, my child, Rion chortled. *You have just saved your first life.*

My stomach rose and fell as if I stood on the bow of a ship. I whirled away, bracing against stone. I hadn't saved a life; I'd taken it. Ripped it from Caleb's body like it was nothing.

A dreadful warmth radiated against the back of my neck, almost like Rion was leaning over me, whispering into my ear with hot, violating breath. *And this will be the only life I let you take.*

Let me? I cried in my mind. She'd tricked me. She'd let him go, knowing that I would pull too hard. After what I'd done to Ropert, I'd vowed to never touch a fraction of another's life energy, not even breathe it. And here I held one captive in my mind, his power radiating like a tempting burst of adrenaline. Power that would enhance mine and give me strength to seal Rion away again.

Do it, she urged. *Use him. Taste the power.*

"No," I whispered, balling my fists. She was toying with me, stabbing me where she knew it would hurt the most. I called on my own lights—the fragile fragments of Etheria. They sprang to life in my mind like the stars winking awake in the night sky. *I'm not like you,* I thought to her and sent the stars flying in her direction like a hundred arrows.

She recoiled into the fissure, sucking all her fire and force inside. The Etheric lights slammed against her prison. Thudding noises reverberated through my mind as the lights burrowed into their target at the same time, creating a fragmented seal over the gap she'd escaped from.

It would hold, for now. But feathers, I was tired. If she hadn't been cut off from her endless source of power, she would have easily overtaken me. Phoenix, if she had taken Caleb, I don't think I could have subdued her.

But Caleb . . .

The guard burst into the cell. His brows furrowed as he took in Caleb lying on the ground with his father sobbing against the young man's chest. Hurrying over, he placed his fingers against the young bounty hunter's neck.

"What happened?" he demanded.

"It was her!" Caleb's father cried. He faced me with tears streaming down his wrinkled cheeks. "She did this."

The guard looked at me.

I shook my head, swallowing the bile in my throat. I had to send Caleb back before it was too late. His energy continued to lash through my mind like a panicked bird.

He was so unlike Ropert. My friend had been calm and accepting of his fate, making it so easy to carry him back. But Caleb? I couldn't get him to hold still long enough to touch him. He struck another memory, and a blinding flare burst through my temples.

Caleb. The panic in my voice faded to a desperate plea. What could I say that would get his attention? *You're dying, Caleb. Let me help you. Let me guide you back. Think of your father. Think of the girl you want to marry. You are leaving them behind. They need you. They love you.*

He smashed into a corner of my thoughts, bumping against memories so they drifted out of place like untethered boats in water. But there he paused, his yellow-tinged star flickering.

I'm going to send you back, Caleb. I never meant for this to happen. My weakened Etheric lights came forward, sputtering softly as they knit together, slowly crafting a slender bridge. It grew thinner as it stretched to his mind. Gritting my teeth, I pushed more energy to the end. He had to make it back.

Go, I urged.

Caleb timidly moved forward. He was going too slow. I couldn't hold our minds together forever.

Hurry.

He latched onto the bridge and slid away.

Wasteful, Rion's voices came strong and sharp. As I strained to hold the bridge, I missed the thin ribbon of burning light streaking after him. It harpooned into his back, his light lurching to a halt in the space between minds.

Rion, no! I cried.

It is rude to return a gift, Rion snapped.

Caleb cried out as he was dragged back.

I lunged after him, my frail lights whipping around. But Rion was too quick. Like a viper, she pulled him through a splinter-like gap in her imprisonment. I slammed into her cage like someone crashing against a closed door and peered through the crack.

Oh, what a terrible vision she was. So beautiful and so dangerous. Orange, red, and blue flames rippled up the strange fabric of her blood-red gown as if it were made of burning water. The white hollowness of her eyes seared into my core like a piece of overheated iron in the blacksmith's forge. Light blossomed to her face from Caleb's trembling star in her coppery hands. She held him firm—just as she had King Sander—her red-painted nails clutching him like the bars of an iron grate.

She smiled at me. *Come and get him.*

I couldn't. If I made the gap wide enough for me to enter, she would break free. And I had nothing more to give. My stars flickered and waned around me, dropping away like spent fireflies. Why was I so weak? I couldn't save Prince Leander on my own, and I couldn't save Caleb, either.

Her white, hollow eyes narrowed at me. *You see? You do not have what it takes. You are not willing to make the sacrifices necessary to become more.* Her hand tightened around Caleb's star. He flared with panic.

Don't . . . My voice was weak and frail, even in my mind. It was happening all over again. *Don't do it.*

Her ruby-red lips spread into a dangerous smile. Then, like crushing an insect, her hands slammed together, and the star flickered out. Brilliant orange light surged from her hands, up her arms, and into her center. Eyes closing, her head tipped to the sky as the star's life energy flowed across her skin, brightening every strand of her bone-white hair.

Again. She'd done it again. Stolen and absorbed a life right before me, and I was powerless to stop her.

Her smile was lethal and bright as she turned to me. *I will rise,* she promised. With a thrust of her hand, a bolt of fire surged from her palm in my direction.

I reeled away. My frail lights snapped together to form a shield. The crack of thunder rattled my mind, ringing through my ears as the firebolt struck. Sparks shot through the weakened gaps in her prison, spitting through like sparks from an uncontrolled fire, pelting me with stinging fragments of hot embers.

So much power from one life.

Panic flooded my core as I lowered my stars and whirled back to the repaired confinement. Had my hasty patchwork withstood her blow?

There were no new cracks I could see, and the new line of cobbled fragments mending the lightning bolt fissure seemed to hold together, though some looked molten and warped like melted pools of wax.

So much destruction with one life. Caleb's life.

He was gone.

The guard lifted the burning torch from the ground and swiped at the smoldering hay with a gloved hand. He then stood. The torchlight cast deep shadows across the old hunter's trembling shoulders as he wept over his son.

"Did you do this?" the guard demanded of me.

How I wanted to say no with a clear conscience. But it *was* my fault. I'd let Rion play me. Yet, how could I explain it to a man like this? A man who could only see what was before his eyes?

"No," I said weakly.

"Liar." The old hunter's head came up, his bloodshot eyes burning with hatred as they found me. "I believed Alder when he said the stories were false. But now I see they were true. Every single one of them. You are no soldier," he said. "You are a witch."

I swallowed. It was not the first time I'd been called that.

"You deserve the bounty on your head," he continued. "Whatever the pirates want with you, I hope it involves pain. Lots of excruciating pain." His voice broke. Squeezing tears through his eyes, he lowered his head to his son's chest and wept.

"Lady Brendagger," the soldier's voice rang through my ears like a distant call. "Come away."

Why couldn't I move? My knees ached. I wanted nothing more than to leave this rancid dungeon, but I couldn't tear my eyes from the father weeping over his son. I'd done this. Rion had tricked me, but I should have known better. I should have been more careful, more controlled. I . . . I had stolen Caleb's life, and Rion had used him like something expendable and worthless.

"My lady?" The soldier stepped closer, the torchlight blurring shapes together. "My lady, come away."

I couldn't look at him. I couldn't look at anything else but the mourning father. My fault. All my fault.

"Kea." Something about this voice seemed different. It wasn't the guard. Warm hands gripped my shoulders and urged me to my feet. The same hands steered me away from the scene and through the cell door. I didn't hear the lock click or the jangle of keys. All I heard was the old man's weeping as the strong arms guided me down the corridor, away from the noise and up the stairs. Still, the weeping followed me. Light stung my eyes as we emerged into a hallway lined by windows, but I didn't close them. I couldn't. They felt like they were held open by invisible fingers.

"What happened? What's wrong with her?" someone asked. Somewhere, in the back of my mind, I thought it sounded like Broderick, but I couldn't be certain. I wasn't certain of anything anymore.

"She is in shock." This accented voice came from the strong hands holding my shoulders. "Something terrible happened in that cell."

CHAPTER 7

HUNTING

*T*he enclosed stone walls around him felt like a trap. He hated this place. Even with wooden beams stretching high to the vaulted ceiling of the corridor, mimicking the feel of the forest, he felt exposed. Every wooden door had either disintegrated in this desolate place or had been stripped away for firewood. There was no place to hide his monstrous form, no shadows to sink into, no breeze running through his fur.

Only one door was constructed of new timber with a heavy iron lock on the outside. Right now, the lock was open. Alder was inside, speaking with the woman who called herself the Queen of Roanfire. Alder had ordered Marrok to wait for him here, and like a faithful hound, he did.

Wary eyes watched him from every corner. Faces of men and women who called themselves Leviathan pirates, dressed in rough leathers and furs, peered from corridor openings and judged him from tapestry-covered doorways. Several had hands resting on hilts of weapons. They didn't quite fear him, but they were cautious around "Alder's pet"—at least that's what they called him.

Marrok's gaze kept wandering to a doorway with a tattered gray sheet hanging over the entrance. He'd seen that hole and frayed corner in the fabric before. Even that coppery rust-colored stain in the center seemed familiar. But how? He'd never set foot in this crumbling fortress before, had he?

As if stirred by a ghost, the curtain moved aside, and a young woman ducked into the same corridor in which he now stood. His heart fluttered at her image. It was her. The girl who held the same name as Eamon Brendagger. What was she doing here? How?

She seemed younger and more innocent somehow, like this was a memory of who she had been. Scales, she was beautiful. He always felt she was, though the hatred Alder had instilled in him clouded his feelings. He wouldn't push them aside any longer. Like a river, he would follow any path his mind took him. He had to, or he would drown.

The young woman scanned the corridor, looking past him as if she didn't even see him standing there, focusing on the spiraling stairway at the far end. Dropping the curtain, she limped forward, holding her side. Was she injured? He . . .

Aye. He remembered. She had been shot by an arrow. He'd cleaned the wound at her back, redressing it daily, watching it slowly heal and scar.

Her feet stopped as she came closer, then she turned and looked directly into his eyes. At him. Not through him. Not like the eyes of a memory. How could those incredible storms see him so clearly? She wasn't real, was she?

He extended a clawed hand, wondering if he could touch her.

"Ikane," she whispered.

He stopped.

"I've done something terrible." The innocent worry in her eyes changed, morphing into eyes that had seen too much, eyes that were rimmed red with pain. Her hair altered from its long and braided state to short and blunt, as if cut by a knife at her shoulders. Three stripes of coral-pink scars appeared on her *supple skin. Even her oversized shirt constricted and changed to a tunic of black.*

He blinked. This wasn't a memory any longer. He could feel it. This was real. The girl was in his mind. She was here.

He should be angry. He should feel violated and flouted that she had come without his consent. But he couldn't keep from wondering why she was weeping. She had always seemed so strong and sure of herself before—so sure of him. Now, it was like the main mast in her had snapped. Although he denied it, her unsolicited reassurance had fueled his sails.

"What happened?" he asked, his voice low.

"I was tricked." Her eyes dropped as she hugged her shoulders. "Like you, I was deceived into taking an innocent life."

She knew. Marrok's heart clenched. The sharp coppery taste of Eamon's blood exploded in his mouth. He'd tried to bury the pain—it was the only way he could function. Now, it came crashing down on him like a rogue wave over a ship, slamming him into the deck, hurtling his body against the railing with such force he couldn't breathe.

He staggered, his back hitting the wall as if she'd punched him.

"Oh, Ikane." Her eyes shimmered as she met his again. "I need you back. I . . . I'm breaking."

Him? What was she talking about? He didn't know her, did he? Memories flashed then vanished as if they were a part of someone else's mind. Was it her mind? Was she planting these thoughts into his head the same way Alder did?

He couldn't take this anymore. Slamming his eyes shut, he pressed his clawed hands over his face. "Leave me alone."

"Ikane, please."

Oh, how her voice tore at him. There was so much pain. He didn't want to hear any more.

"I've tried to do this without you," she continued. "I've tried to accept it. But I can't. I know you want to believe me. Please. Even if you don't believe in me, believe in Eamon. Believe that he loved you. He died to save—"

"Do not say his name!" Marrok swiped a clawed hand at the image. The young woman's form disintegrated, turning to wisps of curling smoke.

"I miss him, too, Ikane." Her voice whispered from somewhere beyond his mind as she faded.

He crouched on the stone, burying his wolf face in his hands. She knew what he'd done. She knew.

My mind stung from the blow, but the weight of something heavy prevented my hand from rising to my temple to comfort myself. A blanket?

I had a faint memory of someone leading me from the dungeons and into this room. Broderick and Prince Leander had been here, but I didn't remember falling asleep. Yet here I was, sitting in an armchair before the crackling fireplace with a blanket draped over my shoulders and a crick in my neck.

Still, I felt cold. Numb. Perhaps it was better this way. Perhaps Ikane had the right idea. Bury the pain. Drown it. Pretend it wasn't there.

Untangling my arms, I finally massaged my temples until the stinging pain subsided and brushed my hair from my face.

Alder had taken our queen to Fold. I recognized the tattered gray curtain hanging over the door as much as Ikane did.

But the fortress was crawling with pirates. Were they working with Alder? What had he promised them? What about the crippled people who lived there? Torquin and Malese? Had the pirates killed them?

My hands curled into fists. I'd always said that if I had the power, I would change the living conditions for those people. But now, I was probably too late.

The door cracked open. I glanced up as warm light spilled into the room behind a head of brown curls. Broderick peeked inside. His timing couldn't have been any more perfect. I needed advice, and he was by far the best person to give it.

"You're awake." He stepped inside and closed the door behind him. "How are you feeling?"

If I considered any part of how I was feeling, I would melt into tears again. No. I had to focus. "I know where Alder took Lona," I said.

Broderick's brows shot up as he limped to the armchair beside mine and lowered himself into it. "Where?"

"Fold. He has her locked in the Fold Garrison."

"Did you see this in another dream?"

"The problem is," I began, ignoring his question, "the place is swarming with Leviathans. Have there been any reports of pirate ships?"

"Some," he said, "but they have been sighted near the coast of Oldshore, not Fold."

"Well, they're in Fold, like termites." I rubbed my neck. "How do we keep overlooking them? Twice now, they've built an army in the Dead Forest."

"It's hard to keep track of open spaces like that with the Deathbiters roaming the night," Broderick reminded me. "Termites? How many do you think there are?"

"At least twenty that I could see."

Broderick leaned back in his seat. "Their ships typically carry fifty men, so we must assume there are at least that many."

"We need to send out scouts and spies," I said. "We need to gather information and gauge their defenses and numbers. Despite Fold being an old and crumbling fortress, its location on the cliffs makes it difficult to attack. The only path to advance is exposed by the dead stumps of trees. The soldiers would be picked off by archers before we reached the ruined walls."

Broderick just stared at me.

"Do you have nothing further to add?" I asked. "Am I overlooking something?"

"Kea, I . . . what happened in the dungeon last night?"

Letting the blanket slip from my lap, I rose and moved to the fire. I didn't want to talk about it. "Don't change the subject. We are speaking of Queen Lonacheska's rescue. How many scouts do you think we'll need? Fifteen? Perhaps fewer to avoid detection?"

"Kea."

"I should lead the party," I continued as I placed a log on the smoldering embers. Sparks leapt up, falling on the back of my hand like Rion's ashes. How I was beginning to hate fire.

I shook my head. No. No more of that.

"I know the Dead Forest better than anyone," I said. "I've learned to listen for the subtle crack of the rotting trees before they—"

"Kea," Broderick snapped, leaning forward in his seat. "What happened?"

Wiping my hands on my hips, I stood. I looked at his boots first, then the swirling designs in the rug, then the shadows dancing under the armchairs. Anything but him. I feared if I met his eyes, I would break. I was finally feeling productive and in control.

"I need your advice, Broderick," I said. "I need to know what to do about Alder."

Broderick stood and limped over to me, the firelight flickering on his black trousers. "Your thinking is sound," he said. "Gathering intel would be the first step. And yes, I think you should go. But Kea, I think you also need to share whatever distressed you last night."

I swallowed the rising lump in my throat and turned away as a shudder flowed down my spine. "I'll deal with it later."

Broderick's fingers were gentle as he tucked my hair behind my ear. "I'm here for you, Kea. Leander is, too. He's worried. We both are."

I looked up at him. Feathers, I shouldn't have done that. His eyes were so full of concern and friendship that my heart began to tremble.

"He knew to come looking for you last night," Broderick said. "He said he felt something was wrong. Kea . . . the bounty hunter . . . he's dead."

I spun away, hugging my shoulders. "Leave me."

"Kea, please."

"I said, leave me!"

Silence followed as Broderick processed my outburst. I hadn't meant to hurt him. I just didn't want to talk about it.

"Will I see you at the funeral this afternoon?" he asked.

"I will be there."

He limped for the door then paused and looked over his shoulder. "Talk to someone, Kea. Anyone. I don't care if you decide to share it with a rat gnawing on your boots under the bed. Get it out." With that, he slipped out the door.

Share what I'd done? Why? What good would it do anyone? It wouldn't help stop her. Oh, how I wanted to speak with Eamon. I needed his wisdom and guidance. Although he may not have had the solution, he always had a morsel of insight that left me feeling chastened or emboldened, or both, like he did back in Gerom Post when Broderick had been on his death bed.

You're holding a knife to your own throat, he'd said. *You won't be able to move forward holding on to guilt.*

But this was different, wasn't it?

I didn't remember entering the corridor. I didn't remember walking to a familiar chamber at the end of the hallway. I brushed the sturdy door with my fingertips and traced the black ironwork of the frame. My forehead fell against the wood as my hand hung heavy on the lever.

"Eamon," I whispered. Gathering a shaky breath, I pushed the door open. Dust danced in the patch of harsh golden sunlight streaming through the frosted window, falling across the gray blanket that stretched across the empty bed. The corners were tucked so tight it held the air of a tombstone. And lying on the bed was an obsidian sword. Ikane's sword.

The empty room screamed for me to believe, to accept, to live with the hollow void of loss left in my chest. But the room still smelled of Eamon. Of leather and iron, of his earthy musk and a hint of his past demon, wine. Today, I didn't hate it. I relished it.

I stepped inside, wanting more, wanting to feel him close, wanting some sign that the dream hadn't been real.

But I'd felt Ikane's heart break. I tasted the coppery flavor of blood on his tongue. I'd felt the sticky redness crusting under his destructive claws.

I paused by a tall shelf that stood against the wall. A handful of books sat there: *The Saga of Sir Ebardus*, *The Art of Longsword Fighting*, *The Book of Bricot Wymerus*, and *Poems of the Heart* by Lady Elain Runelace. I'd seen this book on Eamon's shelf back in Daram. It always struck me as unusual for such a hardened warrior to have such a romantic book in his possession.

Carefully, I pulled it from the shelf, feeling the grooves of the gold embellishments on the green leather gliding under my fingertips. It fell open to the first page as if he'd unfolded it to this section over and over. A handwritten message sat under the swirling title.

My dearest Eamon,

I used to dream of someone like you. Someone who would hold me tight, love my eyes, and adore my smile. Someone who would see me through the darkest days, dry my tears, and crush my fears.

And now that you are mine, I see so much more. Every time you walk through the door, my heart melts like the wax of a burning candle. Every time you smile, I see stars light the heavens. And in your arms, I fall into a universe that is our own.

Eamon, my love. Burn bright for me. Remain as strong as your sword and as gentle as the moonbeams that reflect upon your blade.

My heart will always be yours.

Your bride forever,

Veronika

The letters blurred. This was his wife's handwriting. The wife he'd lost to the Leviathan pirates—the woman who'd given me my name. No wonder the book remembered this page so well. I could see Eamon reading this passage repeatedly as he pulled the mouth of a wine bottle to his lips.

Closing the book, my eyes fell to the sunlight reflecting on Ikane's obsidian blade lying on the bed. Ikane had been for me what Eamon was for Veronika.

A gentle knock sounded on the open door. I turned to see Prime Minister Chanter step into the room. The sadness he carried in his gray eyes deepened as he glanced at Eamon's empty bed.

"You already know," he stated soberly.

This was it. The news of Eamon's death had finally reached Meldron. I swallowed and gave him a single nod.

"How long?" he asked. "How long have you known?"

"Since the night before King Sander's murder," I whispered.

"Why didn't you say anything?"

When would Chanter stop asking me that question? I hadn't been able to say anything. I had been too distraught, too shocked, too filled with Marrok's pain. Alder had it all planned. He'd meant to render me useless in defending Lona's child against his dark power. Seeing Eamon killed had certainly accomplished this.

"Forgive me." Chanter lowered his eyes. "That was inconsiderate. Take heart in knowing that Master Eamon Brendagger will be honored alongside King Sander in the funeral ceremonies today." He took the book from my hands and slid it back onto the shelf. "I truly mourn for you, Kea. I cannot imagine the heartache you must be feeling. Both men were fathers to you."

I swallowed.

"Broderick tells me that you know where Alder has taken our queen."

Good. He was changing the subject to something I could tolerate. "Yes."

"Then you must go," he said. "Oh, don't look so stunned. Broderick pled your case. Your knowledge of the Dead Forest will be crucial. But he also said Leviathan pirates have infiltrated Fold. This is news to me. I've had no such reports."

"That is what I saw," I said. "But I don't know how many we will be facing."

He nodded. "I will handpick fifteen soldiers to accompany you."

"I'd like to have a say."

"Of course," he agreed, which startled me a little. "I've taken the liberty of hiring a new bodyguard for you." Chanter gestured to the doorway as a man stepped into view. My breath caught, threatening to tear my emotions free of the numbness I'd caged them in. Caleb? His head was shaved, yes, but he was broader and more muscular with hard, arrogant eyes. This wasn't the man I'd killed. A thin, dark beard covered his squared jawline. He wore an iron pauldron and vambraces, but his gauntlets and the rest of his armor were constructed of leather, like he was slowly piecing a suit together as he could afford it.

With a hand resting on the hilt of his sword, he tipped his head to me. "It is an honor, Lady Brendagger."

My face snapped toward Chanter. "You're replacing Ropert?"

"Ropert can barely stand on his own," Chanter reminded me. "If you intend to go after our queen tomorrow, you will need someone like Sir Ian watching your back."

I shook my head. "It does not matter how strong or skilled Sir Ian is. I need someone I can trust."

Sir Ian stepped forward. "You can trust me, my lady."

I shot him a warning glare. "Trust is earned," I said, "not declared."

"If you would give me the opportunity, I will prove myself to you. I can be as loyal to you as Sir Ropert was."

My jaw tightened as I closed my eyes. This was not the place to have this argument. This was Eamon's room. A shrine. "Out," I snapped. "Out of this room. Both of you."

Sir Ian's hard, arrogant eyes glanced at Master Chanter.

Chanter nodded. "Go. I will reason with her."

The muscles in Ian's jaw worked as he turned away.

"Kea, I know you are—"

"I don't want to talk about it."

"You need a bodyguard."

"Then assign me Broderick. Besides Ropert, I trust him more than anyone."

Chanter frowned. "Broderick cannot protect you the way he used to."

Was he really looking down on Broderick because of his missing arm? It was the Dead City all over again, people being shunned, despised, and undervalued due to infirmities, whether they were inflicted by accident, injury, or suffered from birth.

"Give Sir Ian a chance, Kea." Chanter's hand rested heavy on my shoulder. "His reputation is exceptional. I would not have chosen anyone less for the future Princess of Roanfire."

How dare he remind me. I hadn't accepted, and I wouldn't.

"Don't look at me that way." Chanter dropped his hand. "It was King Sander's wish. Through this, he guaranteed Roanfire would be safe. You want to speak of trust? He trusted you, Kea." Then Chanter's eyes softened. "I trust you, too."

I raised an eyebrow at him. That was news to me. We always seemed to be bickering.

"We can discuss this later," Chanter said. "Right now, it is time to honor the men who gave their lives to keep Roanfire safe."

And the numbness settled back in.

CHAPTER 8

THE BIGGER MAN

*O*range flames licked up the wood, sparking and crackling, growing hotter against my cheeks. Plumes of thick gray smoke rose to the equally gray sky, filling the air with the acrid stench of burning flesh. The silhouette of King Sander's body warbled under the rising heatwaves.

It was like losing him all over again.

I'd watched him die the first time as life drained from his eyes and his body crumpled to the floor. And then a second time, as I faced Rion in the confines of the ruby and watched as she trapped his soul in her hands and suffocated his glow. Now, a third time as he lay upon the pyre, dressed in golds and reds as flames curled around his body, eating away at the last of his memory.

I was so sick of fire.

"Dagger." A hand touched my elbow.

I glanced up. "Ropert!" He was here, on his feet! Granted, a nursemaid stood under his arm to help him walk, but he looked good. He smiled weakly as the nursemaid released him to me. Chanter hadn't been exaggerating. He was still so weak. But I would gladly carry his entire weight on my shoulders. This scene was easier to bear with him at my side.

He rested his head on mine as we watched the black smoke rise to the sky.

"He was proud of you, Kea," Ropert whispered.

"I miss him," I said. Though I wasn't sure if I missed Sander or Eamon more.

Ropert's weight on my shoulders seemed to grow heavier. "I should have acted faster," he said. "I should have struck Alder down when I had the chance. He even said it was strange how I was immune to his power."

I glanced at his red-rimmed eyes staring stoically at the flames, his stubbled jaw held strong. "No, Ropert. Rion would have only taken you sooner."

"Then perhaps she would have used my soul instead of his," Ropert whispered. "He would still be alive, and Roanfire would be safe."

"Ropert."

"You know it's true." He looked down at me with his bright blue eyes. "We are soldiers. We have sworn to protect and defend with our very lives, and I failed."

"You did not fail," I said. "You gave your life to protect. Feathers, you were dead, Ropert."

"I can't help but feel like I did something wrong."

I watched the flames a moment longer. "You're holding a knife to your own throat," I said.

"What?" He looked down at me.

"It was something Eamon said to me. You cannot move forward if you hold on to guilt."

He smiled. "Wise words. When are you going to listen to them?"

"We're talking about you, not me."

"I think those words were meant for both of us."

We watched the flames a moment longer, feeling the heat radiate against our faces.

Finally, I shut my eyes. "I've seen enough."

Ropert gave me a gentle squeeze. "Alright."

We turned around, pushing our way through the crowd. But my feet slowed when I found Prince Leander standing at the edge of the crowd, honoring King Sander in his own way. Though he wore a long, black sleeveless coat in symbolism of mourning, he was the only one wearing color in a sea of gloom and black—his signature blue turban. He looked well, even with the solemn expression on his face. His golden eyes locked on mine through the crowd.

"Leander," I whispered to Ropert. "I should speak with him."

But Ropert resisted my urge to steer him toward the Tolean prince. "Later," he said. "There will be time to deal with princes, monsters, witches, and rubies. Right now, we celebrate the memory of King Sander and Master Eamon Brendagger."

"I don't feel much like celebrating," I muttered.

"Then we eat pastries until you do." He winked.

I wasn't sure my stomach could even handle water, but the idea of sitting at a table with him was a comfort I needed. I gave Leander an apologetic smile and turned away.

The gloom of the castle covered us as we stepped inside.

"Who's the shadow?" Ropert asked, jerking his head slightly toward Sir Ian who trailed silently behind us with a hand on the hilt of his sword.

"My new bodyguard," I grumbled. "Minister Chanter appointed him."

Ropert stopped. He forced himself to stand taller, taking weight from my shoulders. "New bodyguard, eh?" Turning around, he scrutinized the arrogant-eyed man from head to foot.

Sir Ian raised his chin, almost like he was challenging Ropert to find fault with him. Ropert glanced at the sword at his hip.

"Are you any good with that?" Ropert asked.

"Any intelligent person would see that I am," Ian declared.

I bristled. Did he just insult Ropert?

But Ropert didn't seem to take offense. "Where did you learn to fight?"

"Are you trying to intimidate me?" Ian demanded, his eyes darkening. "I know you, Sir Ropert. I know you are an expert in the broadsword. I know you were schooled by Master Eamon Brendagger before the man became a drunkard. Commander Holdan replaced him, though my mentor, Master Hugo of Brickmight, was far more accomplished in swordsmanship."

Another insult? I glanced over at Ropert. Was he just going to take this? And what gall to tarnish Eamon's memory on the very day we honor his sacrifice, releasing his soul to rest.

"I've worked as Count Sternrod of Oldshore's security officer," Ian continued. "I have acted as bodyguard to Lady Grandiberg, Duchess Phillipa, and the young Baroness Heather of Annual. Believe me, Lady Brendagger has not been in better hands."

A third insult? Ropert had to be fuming. I certainly was.

But he remained as calm as placid water on the surface, even smiling a little. "Impressive," he said. Then he extended his hand. "I am glad to see Lady Brendagger in exceptional hands."

Sir Ian's face softened with a pacified smile at the compliment and gripped wrists with Ropert. Ian's face didn't just look arrogant anymore. He *was* arrogant. The more he spoke, the less I liked him.

"Join us for a treat," Ropert urged. "I hear they have apple fritters in the kitchen."

What in the blazes was Ropert doing? My hands were balled at my sides, ready to smash the smugness from Ian's squared jaw. If he thought he was superior to Ropert, he was sorely mistaken. Even in Ropert's weakened condition, my friend held more muscle, stood a hand taller, and wasn't as soft as Ian around the midsection. Besides, I wanted to spend time alone with Ropert, the way we used to in Daram.

But Ian nodded.

"After you." Ropert offered and stepped aside.

Ian's chest inflated like a proud rooster as he strode past.

Ropert leaned against me again, his weight somewhat heavier than before, like speaking with Sir Ian had drained him. We shuffled down the corridor after Ian.

"You don't need to befriend him," I whispered.

"Who says I'm trying to make a new friend?" Ropert whispered back.

"Then why invite him? He insulted you three times."

"Did he?" Ropert gave me his notorious sly grin. "Fuel a man's ego, and he won't notice suspicion," Ropert said. "I'm not done with him yet. The fact that he hasn't offered to relieve you of my burden tells me much about him. He's slothful, facile, and conceited. Notice anything else about him?"

I watched Sir Ian walk, his shaved head held high, his hand still resting on the hilt of his sword as he strutted forward. He made no effort to step out of the way as servants weighed down by heavy trays of roasts and other confections were forced to step aside.

"He's inconsiderate."

"And?" Ropert pressed.

What did he want me to see? We'd already concluded Sir Ian was not a likable character.

"He's walking ahead," Ropert said. "A good bodyguard always watches their charge's back. He may have a remarkable list of former employers, but they're just that. Former. I think there is a reason he no longer serves them. I bet you ten silver he'll feign injury or turn tail and run at the first sign of trouble."

Even in his weakened state, Ropert was more of a bodyguard than Sir Ian. I held him tighter. "I wish you were coming with me tomorrow," I said.

"As do I," Ropert admitted, allowing true sorrow to slip into his tone. I couldn't imagine how vulnerable and fragile he felt. Even when his arm had been burning from the inside out, he was still strong and capable.

CHAPTER 9

FRITTERS

The rich smell of herbs, onion, and garlic permeated the stone walls as we neared the kitchens. Only the cook, a dozen servants, and twenty scullery aids bustled by the three mammoth ovens. But the mess hall, adjacent to the kitchens, stood empty. Everyone was in the Great Hall, partaking in King Sander's funeral feast.

Sir Ian approached one of the eight long tables in the room, removed his sword belt, and dropped it on the edge with a thunk. Sitting on the bench, he slapped the table with the flat of his hand. "You there," he called to a serving boy. "Fetch me a mug of ale. Bring two more for my friends."

Again, Ian was proving to be an unreliable bodyguard. Soldiers on duty were forbidden to drink on account of being compromised if there was an unexpected attack. How much more did a bodyguard need to remain sober?

"No ale," Ropert insisted as he slid his arm from my shoulders and lowered himself to the opposite bench. "But I'll take a mug of cider and twenty apple fritters."

The serving boy paused, his face perplexed, wondering if he'd heard Ropert right. "Twenty, sir?"

"Be glad he didn't ask for fifty," I said as I sat beside Ropert. "Just bring whatever you can. I'll have cider as well."

The boy nodded and hurried away.

I turned to Ropert. "Did you really think you could ask for twenty fritters? They've all been prepared for the feast in the Great Hall. We'll be lucky to share one between the three of us."

"No one appreciates them like I do," Ropert insisted. "Besides, I would eat one hundred fritters in King Sander's honor."

"I would be honored if you would allow me to assist." Prince Leander's accented voice carried through the empty kitchen as he approached with Boma and Ciri on his tail. "Though I have not yet sampled these apple fritters."

He held up a hand as the benches and table scraped against the stone floor when we moved to stand.

"Oh no. No need to rise." His golden eyes found mine, his smile like a summer morning. "I am here as a friend."

He looked well. Incredible, actually.

"Sir Ian." Leander turned to my newly appointed bodyguard. "Congratulations on your recent promotion. I am certain you will serve Lady Brendagger well."

"I intend to, Your Majesty," Ian said. His eyes strayed to Ropert, something fierce burning in them. "With me by her side, you'll have nothing to fear."

"That's it!" I snapped, slapping my hand on the table. "Insult Sir Ropert again, and I'll have you locked in the pillory. Every insult, one day. You're already up to four. Ropert may no longer be my bodyguard—not that it was my choice—but he is still my closest and dearest friend."

Ian raised his hands. "I only said those things in jest." Although Sir Ian leaned back, his posture was still defensive. "Sir Ropert understands. Don't you, Sir Ropert? We bodyguards simply have a competitive nature."

"It's alright, Dagger." Ropert placed his hand over mine.

"No, it's not." My head was beginning to throb. "I'm not going to stand by and listen—"

"Do not take it personally, Sir Ian," Broderick interrupted as he stepped from behind one of the wooden beams. How long had he been there? He slid onto the bench beside me, his eyes hidden beneath his mop of brown curls.

"It's been a stressful day for Lady Brendagger," Broderick continued. "Having her old bodyguard replaced so abruptly cannot be easy for her. Sir Ropert has been by her side since childhood. I'm sure you understand."

My fists clenched. "Do not take his—"

Broderick held up his hand, and I bit my tongue. Hard.

"Let her have this last evening with him before your journey tomorrow," he suggested. "Go. Attend the feast in the main hall. Relish your last day as a free man before your every breath becomes her will."

Sir Ian raised his chin. "Where Lady Brendagger goes, I go."

Broderick leaned over the table, his black leathers creaking. His eyes went dark. "I am Prime Minister Chanter's pupil. Do you think she is not safe with me?"

"You're a cripple," Ian said as he glanced down at Broderick's missing arm.

Black flashed behind my eyes. "Five days!" I snapped.

"Why?" Ian demanded. "That wasn't an insult. It was truth."

"Leave!" I stood. My hand flew to my hip, catching the hilt of my sword in a fist. "Go, before I run you through myself!"

"But I am not to leave your side."

"Then I am ordering you to take the night off!"

Prince Leander stepped forward and placed a hand on Ian's shoulder. "No need to fear. We will see her safely to her chambers tonight."

Ian scowled at each one of us. Finally, he stood, dragging his sword from the edge of the table. "I shall see you in the morning, my lady." He bowed then turned away.

My breath came hard through my nose as I watched him leave. How could Chanter think this man was a good replacement? No one could replace Ropert. Not even in his frail condition.

Prince Leander pushed his cobalt-blue turban from his head as he slipped onto the newly vacant bench. Boma and Ciri sat on either side of him. "Take a breath, Kea," he said.

I inhaled sharply.

"One more," Broderick urged.

Prying my hand from my sword, I rubbed my aching temples and sank down between Ropert and Broderick. "Did Chanter know he was such a—"

"—pretentious over-plucked peafowl?" Ropert finished. "You know, if you were to paint a line down the back of his head, it would look like the backside of a pig. Minus the tail."

I gaped at him. So did Broderick, Leander, and the others.

Then, despite myself and the steady ache in my skull, I laughed. Broderick joined, then Leander. Ciri smiled with a questioning look on her brow, like she hadn't fully understood but enjoyed seeing the smiles on our faces. Boma remained as stone-faced as ever.

I wiped the corners of my eyes as the serving boy appeared with three mugs in one hand and a plate in the other. He seemed confused at the change in our company. Hesitantly, he set the mugs down. The plate clanked softly against the table, holding three small broken rings of fritters with burnt edges.

"Wait," the boy said. "You're . . . you're the Tolean prince." His eyes went as wide as coins as he gaped at Leander. "F-forgive me." Bowing, he snatched the plate away from Ropert's reaching hand then scampered off.

"My fritters," Ropert whined.

"Are fritters good?" Ciri asked.

"Only the best," Ropert said, his eyes brightening. I hadn't seen them light up like that since he stopped courting . . . why couldn't I remember her name? She was a sweet merchant daughter in Daram. She'd desired marriage but wanted Ropert to leave Daram's militia and practice a safer trade, like candle-making or cobblery. She said a soldier for a husband was too uncertain. But it was Ropert's dream.

"They're apple rings fried in a honey-sweetened batter," Ropert continued. "The finest ones have a dash of cinnamon." He closed his eyes as if he could taste them already.

Ciri smiled. "You like eat sweet things?"

"I just like eating," Ropert said with a smile of his own. Flaming feathers, he was blushing. His cheeks were actually growing pink.

The boy returned, but this time, he was accompanied by two more serving aids. They carried three trays towering with warm apple fritters, soft gingerbread sweets coated with some sort of white glaze, and fresh mugs of spiced cider.

Ropert ran his tongue across his lips as he reached for a batter-fried apple ring and popped the entire thing into his mouth. White sugar stuck to the corner of his lips.

Ciri gestured at him to clean it.

"Would you like anything else, Your Highness?" the boy asked Leander.

Leander lifted one of the plates of apple fritters and held it out to the group of young servants. "Take," he urged.

The servants looked at each other.

"We all honor King Sander tonight," Leander said.

The boy timidly reached out and took one small apple fritter from the corner, clearly not wanting to offend the Tolean prince, but he didn't eat. Hesitantly, the others followed suit.

"Sit." Leander waved to the end of the table where the benches sat vacant.

The poor servants looked horrified.

"Leander," I began, "it isn't custom for our servants to eat and sit with those they serve."

He tilted his head at me, his gold-embellished dreadlocks falling over his shoulder. "Do they not labor just as hard?" He set the plate back down and turned to the servants. "I did not mean to offend. Go and enjoy your treats in honor of your king."

The servants smiled and turned away, comparing fritter sizes as they went.

"Sometimes I wonder who oppresses more," Leander mused. "The Toleans with their slavery laws or Roanfire with the abuse of their servants."

"There is abuse in every culture," Broderick reminded him, quietly eating his own treats.

"Truth," Leander agreed.

"Come on." Ropert set his mug down on the table, wiping cider from his chin with the back of his wrist. "Let's not spoil this with talk of politics. This is a celebration, remember?"

I raised my mug. "To King Sander."

"To King Sander," the others chimed in.

I lowered my mug and looked deep into the amber liquid. *And to Eamon Brendagger*, I thought. Then took a drink.

CHAPTER 10

TOO MUCH

As Deathbiters began rattling the windows, Broderick assisted Ropert back to his room while Prince Leander and his Ridarri warriors escorted me to mine. There were more guests in the castle tonight—people who'd remained too long after nightfall to make their way home. I held onto Leander's strong arm as we stepped over many who had curled up on the hallway floors to sleep. Their presence made me nervous. Rion still scratched against her prison wall, lancing fiery pangs every now and then as she bit deep. She was hungry for lives like these.

The image of Caleb collapsing onto the filthy hay shot through my memories, turning into his frantic star rebounding across my mind. If she could, she would do to these people the same thing that she'd done to the young bounty hunter.

"Your mind is distant," Leander commented. "Share your thoughts?"

I inhaled through my nose, trying to push the image of Caleb aside. I didn't want to speak of it, even if Broderick said I should.

Leander watched me with his honey-colored eyes. They were so warm and open, so eager to understand and help. And he could. Finally, he was well enough to share what he knew about the White Wardent, and my mind was finally sound enough to comprehend—at least, I hoped it was.

"Yotherna," I said.

Leander looked ahead, his eyes growing distant, and nodded. "Ropert's hair," he said. "Drained of color . . . of life."

I cocked my head at him.

"The White Wardent received his name the day he forged the Phoenix Stone. The creation of it drained his life," he said.

My jaw dropped.

"He should have died over two thousand years ago," Leander continued. "But like Karreth, or Alder, his life is linked to the ruby. Until she is destroyed, the brothers cannot die."

That meant I couldn't defeat Alder without destroying Rion. A terrible thought raced through my mind. "Is . . . is Ropert now linked to the ruby?"

Leander shook his head. "He is linked to you."

I rubbed my throbbing forehead, scrunching my eyes tight. "How am I supposed to defeat her, Leander? I'm no closer than the day I found her in the tower."

We stopped as we reached my door, and he faced me, his golden eyes drawing my full attention. "You are closer than you realize, Kea. Your training in Etheria and Thrall is vital to this. I have felt your power. Your control and mastery are increasing."

"It isn't enough." I shook my head, wishing the piercing redness would stop. "I don't have the strength on my own. I've tried."

Leander placed a hand on my shoulder. "That is why the White Wardent created the four keys to—" He flinched, his hand flying to his temple. His face scrunched in pain.

Boma and Ciri stepped forward, but Leander held up a hand. With golden eyes squinting through the pain, he looked at me. "It's her."

I sank into my mind. *Rion!*

He's mine, she hissed from behind her prison. Her burning thread reached through a crack, hooking Leander's soul.

My mind froze. It was just like Caleb. I wanted to wrap Prince Leander's green energy in my white lights, shield him, draw him to me in a protective embrace. But what if it happened again? What if I stole his life force the way I had done to the young bounty hunter?

"Kea," Leander's strained voice pulled on my ears, dragging me back to the hallway where we stood. His face was filled with so much pain. He staggered forward, pushing me back against the wall. With one hand braced beside my head, he clutched my wrist in the other like a vice. "Mend her prison," he urged. "Let me help."

His green energy was . . . stretching for me. Like a man reaching for a saving hand to keep from dropping off a cliff. Didn't he know what would happen? I was not a place of safety. I was his demise.

He cried out as Rion pulled with renewed vigor.

Kea, please! This time his voice was in my mind. He was already too far. His green energy blurred into her red thread, turning it an ugly shade of brown as she inhaled him. Feathers, she wasn't just taking his energy. She was already absorbing it!

Instinct made me reach out. I could not let him suffer like this. My white lights touched his, and like spring unfolding before my eyes, his energy flowed around me, through me, with me. Every white light flared with a verdant radiance. They expanded like the roots of a mighty tree burrowing into the earth to restore its strength.

With him here, I could breathe. I could stand to be in Rion's presence without her fire piercing my soul. It was . . . it was too much.

Rion cried out as her thread burst into fading embers, unable to hold on. *You are taking him,* she warned. *Just like you took the bounty hunter.*

She was right. I had to stop. I let go of his energy, hoping he would recoil and slide back into his body, but he clung to me like moss on a tree.

Seal her prison, he said.

Leander. Go back. Stop.

Seal her! His voice was sharper and more demanding than I'd ever heard. *We need more time.*

I'm killing you!

You will not. He drove his energy deeper.

The sensation of a cold tear streaked down my cheek as I embraced his power. I vowed I would never do this, but he dove into me without restraint, giving me everything.

Our merged lights surged forward in a storm, surrounding Rion's cracked and patched prison. They turned into vines spreading across the surface, twisting, knotting into taut chains around every smooth edge until her red light disappeared and the pounding in my head dropped away.

It was enough. He could stop now. I pushed, both mind and body, with everything I had left.

I gasped as my muscles gave out.

Leander's strong arms caught me before I crumbled to the stone floor. Good. He was strong. He was alive. He was . . . stroking my cheek, his golden eyes wide, staring at me.

"Kea, you *abiun*," he said. From his tone, I assumed it was a word akin to fool. "You gave me too much."

Me? He was the one who'd given me his life.

He gave a command to Boma in his native language as he slipped his arm behind my knees and lifted me from the floor. Why was I so drained? Leander's energy made me feel invincible while I'd contended with Rion. But now I felt as though I'd faced her alone.

Boma opened my door. Leander carried me to my bed, and Ciri moved the pillow under my head as he laid me on the blankets. Sitting on the edge, he brushed my hair back.

"You should not have done that," he said softly.

Why was he blaming me? He was the one who reached. I said no. I warned him. "I'm sorry," I breathed. "I didn't mean to use you."

"Not that," Leander said. "Do you not feel it? I am strong while you are weak."

I blinked at him.

His smile was sad and sympathetic as he allowed his warm fingers to trace the side of my face. "You are too resistant. I gave, and you returned more."

"More what?"

"More life."

Was that what I'd done?

"You must be careful," he said. "Push too hard, and you could give me all."

I shut my eyes. "Would that really be so bad?"

"Do not say such things." I felt his hand rest over my heart. "And do not resist me now." With those words, I felt his verdant energy again, leaking into me. What was he doing? Strength seeped into my body, enough so I could raise my arm and grip his wrist.

"Stop," I croaked.

"Just a little more," he said.

My grip grew tighter as my strength returned. Finally, I could shunt his hand away and break our connection.

He straightened. "You are too good for this world, Kea. You value others more than yourself, which will make your task of destroying the Phoenix Stone much more difficult." His golden eyes scanned my face, like he was seeing me in a new light. "Rest now, Kea."

He stood and motioned for Ciri and Boma to follow.

"Leander," I called.

He paused, glancing over his shoulder.

"Forgive me."

"There is nothing to forgive," he said. "I gave."

My lashes fluttered with exhaustion as he moved to the door. Before my eyes closed, however, I thought I saw Boma catch Leander as Ciri pulled the door shut.

CHAPTER 11

IKANE DIED

*M*arrok crouched at the top of the crumbling stairs, peering around the broken stone banister as Alder greeted the new arrival of pirates below. In the past, this large hall would have been a place to host great gatherings. Now, it was cold and dull, littered with bedrolls and gear from the Leviathan pirates who seemed to flock daily from the sea. Another ship had dropped anchor last night.

Alder extended his hand in greeting to a pirate who looked strangely familiar. The man was tall and lean with broad shoulders that gave him a powerful edge. A sword hung at his hip, and two large hunting knives were tucked into his belt at his back.

A smile twitched on Marrok's lips when the pirate refused to clasp hands with Alder. At least Marrok wasn't the only one who disliked the darkness surrounding Alder. Instead, he looked behind him and waved two pirates forward.

Chains rattled as they dragged a prisoner between them whose face was concealed by a cloth sack. His legs stumbled awkwardly, more than simply having his senses cut off. The man's clothing hung like sheets on limbs too thin and frail.

Alder dropped his hand. "Who is this?" he demanded, glowering at the prisoner. He didn't even try to hide his scarred face anymore. No hood, no patch. His silver-black hair hung down his back like molten black steel. "You were to bring me an army. Not prisoners."

"You needn't concern yourself with him," the pirate answered. He waved to the men holding the chained captive. "Find the dungeons, and take him there. Then spread word."

"Word of what?" Alder asked as the prisoner was dragged away.

The new pirate folded his arms across his chest as he scrutinized Alder's tall frame. "So you're the traitor to Roanfire."

"My loyalties lie with whomever can provide me an army," Alder said.

"And what do you give us in return?"

"Half of Roanfire," Alder replied, almost too quickly, "when we've conquered it, of course."

The pirate threw his head back and laughed. The sound echoed through the Great Hall, drawing the attention of several pirates resting in corners. "And you aim to do that before we have captured the Brendagger witch?"

Marrok's smile faded. The girl?

"Roanfire's bounty hunters are spineless eels with warts for brains. My men would have her bound and gagged in a day if you—"

"I have done my part!" Alder's deep voice rose above the laughter. A darkness rippled around his countenance, causing the pirate to take an unwilling step back. Even Marrok's ears flattened. He knew what Alder could do with that darkness.

"The king is dead," Alder said, "and I have the queen locked in this keep. That is more than the pirates have ever accomplished. Keatep Brendagger is nothing. When I am done, she will not be in our way."

The pirate's arms unfolded. "I want her. I want to see her bleed for what she did to my brothers."

"Oh, she'll do more than bleed." Alder's eyes rose to the top of the stairs. A crippling chill ran down Marrok's spine as Alder's silver eye saw into the shadow where he hid.

"Then you will bring her to me?" the pirate demanded.

Alder turned his attention back to the man. "I will."

The pirate's handsome face turned dark. "You will have your army, and I will have the girl. She will pay for what she did to our army. For what she did to Dran." His fists curled, and Marrok could hear the creak of his leather gloves up the stairs. "And for what she did to Ikane."

Marrok stiffened. That name. It was the name the Brendagger girl called him.

"Ikane is dead," Alder said. "She killed him in Meldron."

The pirate's dark eyes snapped to Alder. "That is not what I've heard."

Alder waved a hand dismissively. "I am not interested in your brotherly quarrels. Do what you must. Provide me with an army, and you will have—"

Marrok's mind wandered. Ikane? That name sounded so strange, and yet he was beginning to feel that it was true. The pirate was looking for Ikane. Why? Scales, this was irritating. Perhaps the Brendagger girl would be able to tell him. But first, he had to help her, warn her. But how? She slipped into his mind without warning, always gentle and timid, like she didn't want to violate him. But right now, he wanted her here.

The murky chamber suddenly shifted, growing brighter with vibrant ribbons, evergreen boughs, and gold-plated chandeliers. Candlelight fell across a red carpet that flowed down the stairs, leading to the center of the chamber where . . .

The girl. She was here, standing in the center of the room, dressed in a flowing blue gown the color of crystal-blue water. She was beautiful.

He glanced at Alder and the new pirate, but they didn't seem to notice the changes.

She looked down, smoothing the watery fabric of her gown like she didn't understand why she was wearing it. Was this another memory? This had to be a royal reception of some sort.

No, a coronation! He remembered! She wore that gown at a coronation that he was commanded to attend. She had been the most breathtaking thing in the room.

But something dark tainted the memory. He was supposed to do something terrible at this event, but he couldn't remember what it was. All he could remember was the feeling of dread and heartache and how beautiful she was.

Her blue eyes rose to his. The sadness in them was deeper than the darkest parts of the ocean and more troubled than waters torn by a hurricane. He leaned out from his hiding place, one clawed hand reaching for the stairs.

"Brendagger," his mind called out to her. "You're in danger. That man is looking for you."

She tilted her head at him. "You . . . you're warning me?"

Annoyance flared inside him. "He's a pirate, and from the way he's addressing Alder, I assume he is a leader."

She squinted toward Alder and the pirate then looked back at him. "I . . . I don't see a face. Is he a prince?"

"Perhaps."

"Your brother." She sounded like she was making a conclusion.

"I have a brother?"

"Six. Though one was killed in Meldron."

"Was it Ikane who died?" he asked.

"No, it was Dran. You are Ikane."

"But . . . Alder said Ikane died. That you killed him."

She shook her head sadly. "Ikane. You killed Dran to defend me."

"What?" Scales, things were sounding more and more ludicrous the more she spoke. He looked back at Alder and the new pirate who were now walking side by side toward a doorway at the back of the Great Hall, locked in conversation.

"Then why does that pirate want to find Ikane?" he asked. "And why does he want to take revenge on you for . . ." He rubbed his temple and let out a low growl. This was too confusing.

"For destroying the pirate army?" she finished. "For Dran's death and your desertion?"

"But why did Alder tell that man that you killed Ikane . . . me?"

She held out her hands with a shrug. "I don't understand the mind of a liar, Ikane. All I can say is that he wants to control you and control the situation. The only way he knows how to accomplish this is to lie and manipulate."

Marrok took several crawling steps down the stairs toward her. "Who am I?"

"Marrok!" Alder's voice cracked through his mind like a whip, shooting a black lightning bolt through his skull. Marrok stumbled into the stone railing, catching himself against it. Squinting through the black pain, he found Alder watching him below, his silver eye burning with warning.

He had no choice.

He glanced back at the center of the room where the girl had stood, but she was gone. The red carpet was gone. The candles and decorations were gone. Everything had returned to its dull and dusty state.

"What are you playing at?" Alder's voice rippled through his mind. "I ordered you to stay hidden."

Marrok gathered himself together and slinked back up the stairs into shadow.

"What are you looking at?" the new pirate asked, following Alder's gaze up the stairs.

Marrok leaned back.

"Something I will need to deal with shortly." Alder's voice was dark as he turned away. "Come, Your Highness. I believe Queen Lonacheska would be offended if you were not introduced."

Marrok sank to the floor at the top of the stairs, resting his arms on his wolf knees as he rested his head against the stone banister. He'd hoped speaking to the girl would have given him *answers, but now he seemed to have questions arising from the depths of his mind like debris from a sunken ship after a storm. Only he felt like the storm was just beginning.*

CHAPTER 12

POCKETS

"Leave those," I said.

The maidservant's hand stopped as she reached for the thick metal faulds lying on my bed. Normally, they would attach under the breast and backplate that was currently being buckled together under my arms. But I could not wear the full suit of armor for this quest.

Protection from the Deathbiters at night was imperative, but this was a stealth mission. The loose faulds would clang and rattle against my hips. I needed to be selective in my armor choice. I would have to rely on my double layered gambeson and chainmail instead.

"Bring the armguards," I said to her.

It had been months since I'd worn this majestic suit of armor. Despite it being in the hands of an expert blacksmith for repairs, there were new dents and scrapes that marked the horrendous battle it had endured with the Leviathan pirates. It was fit for a queen, originally crafted for Queen Damita. A warrior queen like . . . like me, I realized.

"Lady Brendagger?" Sir Ian called from the door. "Sir Broderick Ironshade is here."

"Then let him enter." Ian knew I permitted Broderick's company without needing an introduction, especially today, when I'd given him an assignment.

Broderick entered, purposefully avoiding eye contact with Ian.

"Did you bring them?" I asked.

He pulled the pair of beautiful, sea-serpent adorned, black steel weapons from under his cloak. Morning light lanced through the window, striking the surface with a blinding glint.

The maidservant finished with my armguards in time for me to reach out and take one of the weapons from him. It was the most balanced sword I'd ever held. To create one sword like this was a feat, but to create two identical ones with the same perfect balance? The blacksmith who forged these was a master at his craft. One of these days, I would commission a sword from them, even if they were a Leviathan pirate.

"What changed, Kea?" Broderick asked. "Why are you bringing these?"

"I had another dream of Ikane," I said. "He's doubting Alder more and more."

"And you think he will come to you?"

I tilted the sword until my reflection warped on its polished surface. I looked so different from the woman who'd stood at the bottom of the staircase last night. I had been so young and innocent then. "I can hope," I said. "I know this may be in vain, but perhaps seeing these weapons again will help Ikane's memories return."

"I hope you're right." Broderick placed the other sword on the armchair by the hearth. "Chanter says he's ready for you in the courtyard. He's assembled the soldiers to accompany you on—"

The door burst open with a crack. Sir Ian barely caught it as it rebounded off the wall.

Chanter stormed inside. "Did you approve?" I could almost see steam rising from his crimson ears. What did I do now?

"Approve what?" I asked.

"Prince Leander's company. He's preparing to come with you."

I stiffened. "What?"

"He's a prince. The heir to the throne of Toleah," Chanter raged. "Do you realize what this could do? The diplomatic party from Toleah will arrive within the week. If anything happens to Leander while under our care, we will be ruined. We cannot risk any—"

"You don't need to remind me," I said as the maidservant proceeded to buckle my sword belt around my waist. "I will speak with him."

"Perhaps you should stay," Chanter suggested. "Let someone else head the reconnaissance mission. Like it or not, you are now Roanfire's future. You have responsibilities. Taxes must be collected to feed and house the army we will need to raise to fend off the Leviathans. There are three outstanding land disputes near Annual. And the recent shipment of Toleah's rations must be distributed to the villages most in need. With the change in Deathbiter venom, we need to take a closer look at curfew. We've lost so many cattle and livestock to them that even Toleah's rations aren't enough. We need to find a way to eradicate them."

I gave him a sideways glance. "Do you think I'm trying to find Alder for entertainment?"

"That's beside the point."

"No, it's not. It *is* the point. I will find a way to bring back Lonacheska. And I will return before The Hawk arrives."

"Every kingdom knows we are vulnerable," Chanter warned. "Not just Toleah. Roanfire needs someone they respect and fear to make a stand."

"And you think of me?"

"Don't you see?" Chanter asked. "You already have a relationship with Prince Leander. The Leviathan pirates fear you enough to place a bounty on your head. You've even made an impact on the Glacial Empress, who has expressed a desire to visit. Think of all the good you could do. Royal blood flows through you, Kea." He set a scarred hand on my shoulder, his gray eyes burrowing deep. "You are the best and only choice Roanfire has right now."

I raised my brows. "What do you think the Glacial Empress will do when she comes to visit and finds her daughter in the hands of Leviathan pirates?"

Chanter dragged a hand down his groomed beard.

"I will have Queen Lonacheska back on the throne in a fortnight," I vowed.

"A fortnight," he repeated with a tone that seemed to count down the days to the end of the world.

I snatched my old, patched, fur-lined cloak from a chair and swung it over my shoulders.

"We have nicer cloaks, Highness," Chanter said.

I gave him a look. I would not be called by that title. "Do they have pockets?" I asked.

"I . . . er, no. I don't think so. I could have the seamstress—"

"This one is fine," I said. I worked the three wooden toggles down my neck. Even if they did, this cloak was from Ropert. I wouldn't have replaced it if half of it was burnt away.

Chanter turned to the servant. "Don't just stand there. Take Lady Brendagger's things to the stables."

"Thank you for all your help today," I called after her.

"You needn't thank a serv—oh, never mind." Chanter sighed.

Tucking Ikane's swords into my belt, I turned to the final object for this journey: the small wooden box that could fit in the palm of my hand, sitting on the mantle. A copper lock kept it closed tight. The ruby sat inside, nestled in the ragged scrap of cloth I'd taken from one of her mummified corpses a lifetime ago. I could feel her heat radiating through the wood.

A fortnight might be too long.

"I should speak with Leander," I said.

"May I suggest you scrutinize the soldiers I've chosen for the mission first?" Chanter advised. "It will give them time to prepare."

I nodded. That was sound advice.

Thirteen hand-picked men and women stood before me with hands clasped at the smalls of their backs. Morning light illuminated their stoic faces. I recognized none of them. Although they looked fit and capable, I knew nothing about their backgrounds for stealth or tracking. Why was Broderick not among them? He was the only one who could keep my heart and emotions in check. But he trailed Chanter like his shadow as we walked down the line.

This must have been how Commander Holdan had felt all those years ago as he scrutinized us back in Daram. I missed the simplicity of those days.

We reached the first soldier, a short woman with a crooked nose. It had obviously been broken years ago. Scarring touched her cheek, common to archers where fletching tore into the skin.

"Sergeant Lillian Shaw has the reflexes of a cat," Chanter informed me. "She can release six dangerously accurate arrows in the time it takes to draw a single breath."

Feathers, that was remarkable. She would do.

Chanter motioned to the next soldier in line who stood a little taller as we approached. "Master Sergeant Johnathan's navigational skills are extraordinary."

That was good. We needed someone like that.

We moved on. They were all good choices: fast, quiet, tenacious, observant, reflexive with exceptional stamina, and proficient in multiple weapons. But none of them were Broderick.

"One change," I said, turning to Chanter. "I want Broderick."

Chanter's brows narrowed. "Kea. He's no longer—"

"I trust him," I said. "These men and women may be skilled and formidable, but I need at least one person I can trust with my life."

I felt Sir Ian bristle beside me at the statement, but I didn't care. Broderick's smile from behind Chanter's shoulder made the insult worth it.

Chanter sighed. "Are you sure?"

"Yes," I affirmed.

Chanter glanced over his shoulder. "You heard her. Pack your things."

Broderick bowed, gave me a grateful nod, then hurried away.

Chanter dismissed a man in the middle of the row then turned to the others. "Gather your things. You leave within the hour."

The men and women dispersed. I felt good about the troop we'd assembled. If all went well, we would be back with a full report in a few days.

"What precautions will you be taking at night in defense against the Deathbiters?" Chanter asked as we walked across the courtyard to the castle.

"Armor," I said, rapping my knuckles against my breastplate. "We will make fireless camps in the densest parts of the woods. It will hinder their flight a little and keep us concealed. I want every soldier supplied with firedust. If we do find ourselves under attack, it will be vital to our defense."

Chanter was nodding his approval. "And when they are bitten?"

I didn't raise a brow at the question. He was right. It wasn't a matter of "if" they were bitten. Every one of us would be infected at some point during this quest. "Healer Malcom's sprite dust remedy is effective for smaller wounds," I said. "We will need more dust for that. Broderick and I will draw out the poison from deeper infections." This was another reason I needed Broderick with me. I could not do it alone.

"It seems you have given this a great deal of thought," Chanter mused as he opened the door for me. "It is good to see you like this."

"Like what?"

"Like a leader. You are taking initiative, organizing, delegating, doing the things a ruler of a kingdom would do."

"I'm just comfortable with military movements, that's all," I replied. "Eamon was . . ." My voice broke. Why was it so hard to speak his name?

Chanter placed a hand on my shoulder. "He taught you well. And King Sander's stratagem flows in your blood. Between both of them, I believe Roanfire has a chance."

Torchlight flickered on the stone walls as we walked the corridor. I paused at an intersection. One direction would lead to the healer's billet and Ropert. Pungent herbal scents emanated from that direction, especially peppermint and eucalyptus.

The other would lead to Prince Leander.

I would have to keep my visit with Prince Leander brief if I was to say farewell to Ropert, too.

"I hope you can convince the prince that his decision to accompany you is a dangerous one," Chanter said. "We almost lost him to the Deathbiters before. I will see to the gathering of sprite dust immediately."

"Chanter," I called, looking over Sir Ian's patchwork of armor. "Will you please take Sir Ian to the armory? His leather body armor is not suited for this. I can see myself to Prince Leander's chambers."

"As you wish, Your Ma—" Chanter stopped himself. "My lady."

I still wished he wouldn't call me that. Going from corporal to lady was bad enough. But Your Majesty? That was a title I hoped I would never have.

I glanced over my shoulder as Chanter and Sir Ian walked down another corridor. There was a lightness about Chanter that I hadn't seen for some time. It was a familiarity of his employment, a purpose in serving.

The sacrifice he must have made to accept the position of Prime Minister must have been as much of a burden to him as accepting the title of princess was for me.

CHAPTER 13

RIDARRI ARTS

I stood outside Prince Leander's chamber, eyeing the wood grains and ironwork of his door, listening to the movement beyond. From the sound of it, he was packing like a madman. How could he be moving so quickly after what had happened last night? I'd seen him collapse, hadn't I?

I shook my head. I didn't know what to believe anymore. I wasn't even sure what I would say to him. He'd given me his life force to strengthen Rion's prison, and he did so with a passion and vigor that terrified me. He hadn't questioned or hesitated. It was like he'd waited his whole life for a moment like it.

What if he did it again? I couldn't have him with me for that reason alone.

Gathering a shaky breath, my hand finally rose, and I knocked.

"Enter!" Prince Leander's clipped voice called.

I pushed the door open then paused and blinked at the sight before me. He . . . he wasn't packing.

The morning light slanted through the open windows, falling across his glistening bare chest as he parried punches dealt by Boma. They moved about the room like feral cats.

He was fast, almost as if I hadn't taken anything from him the night before.

"I'll be . . ." he began as he whipped his leg into Boma's ankle. The large man teetered off-balance. Spinning again, Leander knocked Boma back with a kick. ". . . right with you."

Instead of crashing onto his back, Boma controlled his fall, his feet flying over his head in a roll, and was back in fighting position in a blink. He lunged at Leander.

This was incredible. What I wouldn't give to move like that. So smooth, so precise and fierce. Ropert would have adored this. This was the true Ridarri arts in action, something he'd kill to see.

Prince Leander's muscles rippled across his bare torso as he ducked under Boma's arm, his physique rivaling Ikane's. No trace of Deathbiter remained on his flawless dark skin save three faint scars on his shoulder and neck—the final wounds Broderick had healed.

"Lady Brendagger," Ciri waved to me from her position along the wall, urging me to come. I skipped past the fight, barely evading Boma's backward retreat. My armor ground against the wall as I pressed my back to it.

"Training fight," Ciri explained.

"You mean a spar?" I could not take my eyes off the scene. Leander's strikes were like lightning. He must have hit Boma somewhere on his leg, because the Ridarri buckled and staggered back.

My enthusiasm faltered when my eyes fell on the three packed bags sitting by the door. Chanter was right. He intended to come, but like any dedicated warrior, he wasn't sitting idle while waiting for the rest of the party to finish preparations.

Ciri shunted my shoulder in time to spare me a collision with Leander as Boma drove him into the wall between us.

Leander flashed me a brief, breathless smile, like this was simple child's play. "One moment," he said then slipped to the side as Boma's fist flew at his face.

Somehow, Leander trapped Boma's arm and struck his temple at the same time. Dizziness swept through Boma's eyes. With the larger warrior stunned, Leander whipped Boma around. Now, Boma was against the wall. He threw his arms up to shield his face as Leander struck him with both knee and elbow then spun and landed a final kick to Boma's abdomen, causing Boma's body to rebound off the wall.

"*Muntahi*," Boma groaned as he hunched over and held up a hand. "*Muntahi*."

Leander dropped his hands. He said something to Boma in Tolean, bowed to him in a gesture of gratitude and respect, then clapped the warrior on the back. Boma coughed and held his side.

Ciri stepped forward and took Leander's jaw in her hand, turning his head to study a red mark on his cheek and lip. Apparently, Boma had landed some good blows of his own.

"I have had worse," Leander said as he gently pulled her hand away. He turned to me. "I was not expecting to see you here this morning."

"No?" I found it strange how easily my initial frustration returned even after the thrill of such an impressive display of martial skill. "Would you have preferred to surprise me by joining the mission without my consent?"

"So you have heard." Breathing hard, Leander grabbed a towel from the back of a chair and dabbed the glistening perspiration from his neck. "I did not intend to offend you, Lady Brendagger. I simply wish to see you safe."

The little black spark inside me flickered awake. "Me? You were the one who almost died last night."

"And if you had not been there, she would have succeeded."

"If I had not been there, it wouldn't have happened," I shot back.

His smile faded as he dropped the towel onto the seat of the chair.

"I don't know what your secret is," I began. "You fought like a lion just now without a hint of what happened last night. But I saw you collapse outside my door." I watched his face for any sign of vulnerability. "Ropert can barely walk almost a week later."

Leander grabbed his sleeveless coat from the back of the chair and slipped his arms through it. It did little to hide his glistening bare chest full of muscle. "Accompany me to my garden," he said, gesturing to the reams of fabric dividing his room. "There are new blossoms that need pollinating before we go."

I folded my arms across my chest. "You are not coming, Leander."

I wasn't sure he'd heard me. He simply walked to the curtains and pulled one aside, urging me to enter.

"Please?" he begged. Feathers, his eyes. Somehow, they pulled me forward, and before I knew where my feet had carried me, I stepped inside his impossible garden. The smell of moist soil filled my body with a rich and grounding sensation, filling my lungs with an energy I could only glean from the earth. Healthy leaves exploded from pottery and raised beds with vines meandering across the floor and up the walls. White and yellow blossoms stood open, ready for the painstaking task of hand pollination.

"Those are unique swords," he stated as he handed me a little wand with a piece of cotton on the end. "Those belong to your Leviathan pirate, do they not? The one who has been transformed?"

I glanced down at my waist where Ikane's swords sat snugly against my hip. "Don't change the subject."

Turning away, he gently tucked his wand into the mouth of a blossom, hands working so gently I was sure he could stroke a butterfly's wing without causing harm. And yet, watching him fight was like watching a hawk dive from the sky for prey.

He was as lethal as he was gentle. "Do you expect to meet him on this quest?" he asked.

"I . . . I don't know."

"Broderick is accompanying you." He said it as more of a statement than a question.

I frowned, uncertain if he was judging my choice due to Broderick's missing arm and twisted leg. "He's strong, Leander."

"I know," Leander said as he finished a set of blossoms and moved to the next. "And you wish for Ropert to come?"

I wished that more than anything.

His golden eyes lifted slowly, catching mine like a snare. "You would rather have two men who are weakened by their own bodies at your side than me?"

"They are not royalty," I snapped. "An entire nation won't come crashing down if something happens to them."

He tilted his head at me. "Unlike my Ridarri, my skin is plain to hide my expertise, and yet I allowed you to witness my abilities, hoping you would see that I am not a hinderance but an asset. To you, to your kingdom, and to fighting Rion."

I set the wand down on the garden bed. "I can't ask you to do more for Roanfire than you already have."

"I am not doing this for Roanfire." His eyes locked on mine, so golden and vibrant against his dark skin it was like looking at a sunrise. My heart fluttered strangely, and a terrifying sensation ran down my spine to my limbs. I hadn't felt anything like this since . . . since I'd first met Ikane. Worse yet, I feared that I was beginning to reciprocate—

I shook my head. No. Ikane was coming back. His mind was waking. I would not allow my head to be turned. Leander was a man unlike any I'd ever met. Kind, selfless, wise, strong, and—flaming feathers—he was exotically handsome. But one thing just wasn't right. He wasn't my Ikane.

"I need to go." I backed away.

"Kea." Leander followed as I pushed through the curtains and hurried to the door. "It is not what you think," he said.

I didn't know what to think anymore, but one thing was certain: He would not be coming with me. I pulled the door shut behind me then turned to the guard standing outside. "Lock it," I commanded.

His eyes flew wide. "What?"

"Lock it."

"But that's . . . that's . . ."

"Unlawful detainment of royalty," I finished. "I know. Do it."

He swallowed hard as he produced the key, but he moved too slowly. Snatching the key from his hand, I stuffed it into the lock and heard the click as it latched.

I stepped back. What had I done? This was exactly what Master Chanter and King Sander had done to me time and time again. Now I understood. They had done it for my own safety, even though I did not agree with them.

"Kea?" Leander called through the door. "Do not do this." Once again, he showed so much strength in his calm demeanor. There was no pounding against the wood or rattling of the lever.

I swallowed. "Unlock it when the sun reaches noon hour," I ordered the guard.

That would put enough distance between us to make it difficult for Leander to catch up before nightfall. Hopefully, he would see reason and remain in Meldron until I returned.

Turning away, I hurried down the corridor, too flustered and eager to flee to consider visiting with Ropert. I would be back in a few days, anyway. He would understand.

"Soldiers!" My voice rose above the commotion of snorting horses and side conversations. Sir Ian and Broderick sat astride their horses beside me as the twelve soldiers silenced. They were all outfitted with snug-fitting armor that moved silently with their bodies. Sir Ian sat as proud as—how did Ropert put it?—an over-plucked peafowl in his new shiny metal plating. Even Broderick had replaced his usual leather armor with dark steel as a shield against the Deathbiters. The fewer injuries we had to heal, the better.

"You have been chosen for this reconnaissance mission in an effort to rescue our queen who is being held captive by Leviathan pirates in the ruins of Fold," I began. "You don't need me to remind you of the danger. Although this mission is intended to be brief and quick, our nights will be long, and we *will* face Deathbiters. We have a remedy of sprite dust prepared as well as other means to draw out the poison." There was no need for me to go into detail about what Broderick and I would be doing.

I looked them over. "If any of you desire to be excused from this expedition, you will not be disgraced or condemned for it."

Silence stretched through the courtyard, save the snorting of horses and the sputtering of the fountain. No one moved. Not even a flicker of exchanged glances as they considered the danger.

My heart swelled with pride. With men and women like this fighting for Roanfire, we could conquer.

CHAPTER 14

SPRITE DUST

The violet-orange sky through the budding foliage marked the end of our first league. I held up a fist.

"We make camp here. No fires. Shelter the horses in those pines." I gestured to a tight cluster of evergreens to our right. Their thick, needlelike branches meshed together like a wall. It was a risk to separate ourselves from our mounts, but if they became spooked or cried out in the night, this would at least safeguard the soldiers' concealment.

"We will camp in the smaller cluster over there," I continued. "As long as we stay quiet, we may come away unscathed by Deathbiters tonight."

And only tonight. Tomorrow, we would arrive at the edge of the Dead Forest where trees and foliage were sparse or nonexistent.

The soldiers dismounted and stretched without groaning or complaint and began stripping gear. Save Sir Ian. He let out a loud groan as he dismounted and arched his back.

"I'm not accustomed to so much heavy armor," he defended when Broderick shot him a look.

I swung from my saddle and moved my hips in an effort to release the tightness there. Then I tugged at the neck of my armor. I wasn't accustomed to so much armor, either. Although it was fashioned to be light, riding in it for hours had felt like I was carrying an entire castle wall on my shoulders.

Broderick stepped beside me. "You're doing well, Kea. See how the soldiers move without complaint? I've never seen a troop so agreeable and emboldened."

I reached up and began stripping my gear from my horse, including Ikane's swords that had been strapped to its saddle. "Chanter chose well," I said.

"You made the final call," Broderick reminded me.

I smiled. I had to admit, this *was* empowering. For the first time in months, I felt in control, like I knew what I was doing and where I was headed. I had a clear goal and a clear mission.

If only things with Rion could be so simple.

"Enough idle chat." Sir Ian shoved his horse's reins at Broderick. "Take the horses over. You can manage that with one arm, can't you? I'll stay with Lady Brendagger."

My hand shot out, latching onto Sir Ian's gauntleted wrist as the black spark ignited in my mind. "Don't you dare speak to him like that."

"Kea." Broderick's voice was calm and level beside me as his eyes fixed on Sir Ian. "I'm sure he's just too exhausted to do it himself. I mean, I would be, too, if I had to wear so much armor."

Sir Ian jerked his arm from me, his ears flaring bright red. A vein protruded on his brow, which would have been hidden if he'd had any hair. "You dare insult me? I am Lady Brendagger's bodyguard, who is soon to be Princess of Roanfire."

I opened my mouth, but Broderick was quicker.

"And I'm the apprentice of the man who hired you." He leaned closer, eyes narrowing dangerously. "I had a say in his decision, and I am beginning to regret it."

Sir Ian stiffened, then he not only snatched my horse's reins but Broderick's also and marched all three of our mounts to the appointed evergreen corral.

I shouldered my saddlebag and clutched Ikane's swords in my hand as I watched him leave, still biting my tongue at his remark. "I want Ropert back," I muttered.

"As do I." Broderick hefted his own gear. "Take a breath, Kea. I can feel your Thrall bubbling over."

I hadn't even noticed how large the black flame in my mind had become. It was leaning toward a memory, ready to find whatever anger and pain was hidden inside. Heeding Broderick's advice, I inhaled and closed my eyes. The black flame ebbed away.

"Come on," he said. "We should claim our spot of ground before all the ones without lumps are taken, not that any of us will sleep much tonight."

I followed him into the trees, pushing the thick, needled branches from my face. The soldiers' bedrolls lay scattered under the tight evergreen boughs. It was a good spot, well-concealed, and dense. Even if the Deathbiters found us tonight, flying through these trees would be problematic for them.

Dropping my bags, I crouched under a pine tree and tested the ground for lumps. A long root rippled under my glove beneath the bed of pine straw. It probably wouldn't be that noticeable through my armor, anyway.

I desperately wanted to shed the breast and backplate, though. I was not looking forward to sleeping in my armor.

"Lady Brendagger?" someone called through the trees. It wasn't full dark yet, but still, they were supposed to keep their voices down. "Where is Lady Brendagger?"

I ducked out of my shelter and dusted my gloves off on my cuisses. "Hush," I snapped at the soldier. "I'm here."

She pushed a pine branch away as she hurried to my side. "Four riders," she said, "coming fast."

Broderick stepped beside me. "Friend or foe?"

"Tolean," she said.

It couldn't be. I exchanged a look with Broderick then turned back to the soldier. "Did you see a blue headdress?"

"Yes," she said.

I shut my eyes. "Charred rachis. It's Prince Leander." Dragging my hand down my face, I shook my head. I had no choice now. I couldn't leave him to be exposed to the Deathbiters, and sunlight was fading fast. "Let them camp with us," I muttered.

She saluted and turned on her heel.

"They must have ridden hard to catch up to us," Broderick said.

A part of me wasn't surprised. Leander *was* resourceful. But I told him no. I warned him. My fists clenched as I turned back to my pine shelter.

"You're not going to greet him?" Broderick asked.

"He wasn't supposed to come in the first place."

"I assume Ciri and Boma are two of the riders accompanying him," he said. "Aren't you curious to see who the fourth rider is?"

I paused. Part of me *was* interested, but the disappointment was stronger. "No," I said. "See they are made safe for the night, but tomorrow, they go back to Meldron."

"As you wish," Broderick said.

I unraveled my bedroll and sat with my back propped against the rough pine trunk. Chewing on a piece of bland venison jerky for supper, orange flickered awake around the edges of my vision as Mina's sprite gift ignited in my eyes.

The sunlight was gone. A quietness settled through the trees, the dense branches muffling all sound. Still, my ears strained for the dreaded screech of the Deathbiters.

The branches of my shelter moved as someone ducked inside, the edges of his strong frame burning with Mina's light. Crouching, he smiled at me. A crooked, mischievous grin that I knew too well.

I almost forgot my own order for silence. "Ropert!"

He crawled to my side and sat down, our shoulder armor clanking together. He reeked of peppermint. I didn't understand. How was he moving so well? The last time I'd seen him, he was leaning on everything and anything just to stay upright.

He scanned the thick canopy. "This is nice."

"How?" I whispered. "How are you here?"

"What? Are you not happy to see me?"

I wanted to slug his shoulder, but that would make too much noise. "Of course, I am. But you were so . . . so weak."

"Scoot," Ropert said as he shifted his hip into mine, forcing me to relinquish my perch against the tree trunk. Putting his arm around my shoulders, he pulled me against him and leaned back, our armor grinding. I rested my head against his breastplate, wishing I could feel his heartbeat underneath.

"It was Prince Leander," he whispered. "This strength is not my own."

My head lifted as I gazed at him. Feathers, no. Had Leander given Ropert some of his life energy? Was that even possible? "What?" I asked.

"Sprite dust," Ropert explained. "Apparently, if all four are administered correctly, it can restore vitality." He let out a soft laugh. "There is so much we still don't know about the power of elemental dusts."

I blinked at him. Sprite dust? Was that how Leander had restored his own energy so quickly after Rion's attack?

I laid my head back onto Ropert's shoulder as he gently took my gloved hand in his. He stroked my forefinger with his thumb like he was pondering what lay beneath. "Do you still have the sprite dust embedded in your skin?"

"Yes," I whispered. "Three."

His thumb stopped moving. "Three?"

"Earth, wind, and water," I said.

He let our hands rest against his breastplate. "I'd watch out for firedust."

He didn't need to tell me. I knew. "You smell," I whispered.

"Yeah, peppermint," he admitted. "The oil helps with the headache."

"Headache?"

"Don't worry about it."

A screech penetrated the thick canopy overhead, but neither one of us moved. It was wonderful to have him here.

Ropert's thumb stroked the back of my hand as we sat there. I probably should've thanked Prince Leander for this, though I was still livid with him for challenging my request.

For now, there was nothing I could do, save listen, watch, and wait until morning.

CHAPTER 15

THE WOLF

*M*arrok stood in the tower, inhaling the scent of the sea blowing through surrounding rows of arched windows. He didn't feel so confined here. A rhythmic, near undetectable rumble rippled under his feet as the sea pelted the cliffs below the garrison. To his left, pale foam broke along the beach.

Further inland stood the dilapidated buildings of the decimated city of Fold. But that was not what drew his attention. It was the ocean, stretched before him like a blanket of blue, the horizon bleeding into the night sky speckled with stars.

It was impossible to focus on just one. They burned together, an endless sea of light scattered across the sky like beacons. Or maps. Aye, somehow he could see maps in the stars, guiding him to a marina sheltered by rugged cliffs somewhere far across the sea.

He shook his head. Why did these images keep flooding his thoughts? It was like things sparked through his mind from long ago. Or had it really been that long? He looked down at his hands, at the claws and deep leatherlike skin on his palms, at the rich fur covering the back of his fingers. His hands hadn't been like this then. They'd been smooth and humanlike, like . . . like Eamon's.

"Marrok."

The deep voice sent a tremor through his spine. No matter how much he despised this man, he held too much power over him. His bones still ached from the torture, and random bolts of pain seared through his muscles. All because he had taken a few steps down the stairs without permission.

He crouched, lowering his ears, as Alder entered the circular chamber. His long steely hair blew behind his shoulders as he stopped at the window, gazing out at the same sea that had brought Marrok peace moments ago. Then Alder's silver eye turned to him, burning. The other gazed at him with an eerie white haze.

"The goddess has spoken to me," Alder said. "She needs our help."

Marrok flinched as Alder rested a hand atop his head. Even through his fur, he could feel the cold sting of his touch.

"The Phoenix Daughter has betrayed her," Alder continued.

Marrok hated the way he trembled under this man's touch. A man. A mere man of flesh and blood. A man he wanted to tear into.

Alder finally removed his hand and turned back to the sea. "The Phoenix Daughter has found one who can give her strength enough to bind our goddess. A prince from the kingdom of the desert lands to the south. You will know him by the blue cloth he wears to cover his head."

Marrok hardened his eyes. He knew the next words to come from Alder before he spoke them.

"Kill him," Alder said, his silver and white eyes flashing.

The order burrowed into Marrok's blood, coating his bones, filling his muscles with the desire to break and destroy. Scales, it ached. Yet, he knew it was another terrible decree like the one given to kill Eamon. It was wrong.

His claws dug into the stone at their feet, leaving long lines of silver in their wake.

"As for our goddess," Alder continued, "it is time to retrieve her. Bring her back to me."

Marrok dared to look up at Alder's terrible face with the moonlight falling across his pale skin. The girl. The Brendagger girl. She had the Phoenix Stone where the goddess resided.

His body trembled with the desire to kill, yet his mind cried at the horror of doing it. He had to leave now, before Alder gave him further instructions that he could not ignore.

"Marrok!" Alder called after him.

Marrok stopped.

"I want you to sink your teeth into her flesh. Make her bleed."

Marrok shut his eyes. The command was now embedded into his flesh.

"Now go."

Blood pumped through his muscles, driving his body forward on all fours as he tore down the circular stairway. Stone flashed by. Doorways blurred past. And before the horror could settle, he was weaving through the decaying stumps of the Dead Forest, heading for Meldron.

I jerked awake. Ikane's energy boiled through my blood, flooding to every limb like wildfire. Ropert's arm tightened around me, holding me firm and silent at his side. He was still outlined in Mina's glowing orange light as he lifted a finger to his lips. A Deathbiter cried out overhead, but its screech was distant and non-threatening.

Charred rachis, Ikane was headed this way! He was after Prince Leander. What was I to do? We were trapped. We could not move without drawing attention from the Deathbiters, yet every moment we lingered, Ikane was drawing closer. This was not going to happen again. First Broderick and then Eamon. I was not going to lose another friend, and I was not going to let another death weigh on Ikane's shoulders.

Pushing off Ropert's chest, I flipped the edge of my bedroll to reveal Ikane's swords nestled beside my pack.

Ropert grabbed my wrist. "What are you doing?" His breath was warm against my cheek as he whispered.

"Ikane is coming," I whispered back.

He released me, his eyes churning with thought even in the darkness. Because he realized the same thing I did. There was nothing we could do until dawn—until the Deathbiters were gone.

"When?" he breathed.

At the speed Ikane was going, he would be here by daybreak. But could he keep up that pace through the night? Would he? He knew Alder's orders were wrong—I felt his resistance. Yet the command burned through him unlike anything I'd ever experienced. No matter how much Ikane's mind refused, his body would be compelled to obey.

"Morning," I said.

"Target?"

"Leander and . . ." Flaming feathers. Me. I was his other quarry. He was coming for me and the ruby, which was sitting in my belt pouch.

Ropert reached across me and lifted one of Ikane's swords from the ground. Pine needles fell across my lap as he sat back, twisting the weapon in his hands. I wasn't sure how well he could see, not with Mina's gift brightening my vision. But he must have had some light or he could not have stared at the obsidian blade so intently. Then he looked at me. There was something in his eyes that promised a solution, something I had refused to consider.

I shook my head. Ikane's memories were returning. All he needed was a little more time.

Ropert pursed his lips, his eyes still fixed on mine, begging me to weigh the consequences.

The idea was like a knife against my heart, held there by some unknown shadow. I couldn't . . . I just couldn't . . .

"Leander won't be the last," Ropert whispered.

I shut my eyes. It was the truth. If Ikane couldn't find his memories soon, he would kill again and again, all at Alder's behest. And each killing would add to Ikane's guilt until he broke.

My hand trembled as I took Ikane's sword from Ropert and laid it across my lap. I caressed the weapon. I had until morning to decide. Dawn would determine the fate for many people. For me, for Leander, and for Ikane.

I thought relief would wash over me like a bucket of fresh water under summer heat when the violet-orange light breathed across the sky, my firedust gift ebbed, and the Deathbiters dispersed. Instead, dread clutched my chest.

Climbing from the pine canopy, I scanned the trees for a blur of darkness, any indication of a predatory beast ready to tear into me. But the dense trees that had been our safety through the night suddenly became our nemesis. I couldn't see. Even the soldiers as they gathered their bedrolls and gear were barely visible.

With Ikane's keen sense of smell and hearing, we were all prey.

"Kea." Broderick said as he approached, smiling blissfully. "We survived our first night without a scratch. Even the horses were safe. You could not have chosen a . . ." His voice faltered. "What's wrong?"

"We need to move," I said. "Get the soldiers to the main road. Now."

Broderick's brow furrowed. "What's going on, Kea?"

"Ikane."

Broderick's eyes darted around the trees, his face growing deathly pale. His throat moved with a deep swallow as he absently tugged his cloak tighter over his missing arm.

I'd been subtle, but there was no time to break the news gently. I quickly placed my hand over his. "He's not here for you." Was that really any more comforting?

"Lady Brendagger?"

Prince Leander's accented voice tore my gaze from Broderick. He approached with Ropert right beside him. He wore a simple suit of bronze armor, probably borrowed from Meldron's armory, which blended well with our surroundings. However, his cobalt-blue turban was wrapped around his shoulders, a bright beacon of color in a sea of gray, brown, and green.

"Take that off," I snapped. "He's looking for that."

Leander tugged the blue cloth from his neck. "Who is?" he asked.

I scanned the trees again. Ikane could be watching us at this very moment, smelling my fear, listening to every frantic beat of my heart.

"Everyone to the road," I ordered, pushing through the trees. At least there, our visibility would improve. "Everyone on Prince Leander. He is the target."

"I appreciate your concern, Lady Brendagger. But my Ridarri and I can—"

"Not this time," I said. This was a creature I was not willing to take risks on.

Branches swung back as we punched through and staggered onto the muddy path then scanned up and down the tree-formed corridor. Good. All the soldiers were here, holding weapons, expressions alarmed and uncertain.

"Circle," I ordered, "Prince Leander in the center."

Boma drove Prince Leander to the center of our small platoon and stood at his back. Ciri joined them. The rest of us stood together, shoulder to shoulder, encircling the Toleans.

"Lady Brendagger. What is going on?" a soldier demanded.

"Listen up!" I called over my shoulder, eyes still peeled on the trees and shadows. Sunlight lanced through the branches, casting a hazy glow on everything that would make him a little more difficult to see. "You've all heard of the beast. Half man, half wolf. He's faster, stronger, and bigger than any of us." My words sank deep into my own mind, hitting a nerve. "He has been ordered to kill Prince Leander."

"By whom?" another soldier asked as her eyes scanned the brightening woods. Her bow lay ready in her grip with an arrow nocked to the relaxed string and three more in her hand for successive firing. Good. She would need the speed.

"The man who kidnapped our queen," I said.

"Dagger," Ropert's voice was soft beside me. "Have you decided? It's either him or us."

My stomach churned, and I swallowed hard. "Him," I whispered. My eyes blurred as the word escaped my lips. Ropert was right. We'd seen firsthand what Ikane was capable of. Even with such elite soldiers around us, we would be hard-pressed to land a single blow on Ikane. Still, my sword remained steady, raised to strike.

"I'm sorry, Dagger," Ropert whispered to me, then he turned his next words to the soldiers. "We aim to kill! No mercy! If you have the slaying blow, take it!"

"Kea," Broderick said as he moved through the inside of the circle. "Take this."

I glanced over my shoulder as he pressed a small leather pouch into my hand.

"Careful," he warned. "It's a dust bomb. There is a glass vial inside filled with firedust. Once it breaks, you have three seconds before it combines with the others and bursts."

He had at least a dozen more strapped to his belt, and he moved through the circle, handing one to each of us.

I flinched as an archer raised her bow, aiming it into the shadows of the trees. Movement caught my eye. My heart thundered, and I almost crushed the small pouch Broderick had handed me. But it was small and gray, with large ears flattened to its back as it darted from one bush to another. A rabbit.

She lowered her bow.

I tucked the loop of the pouch into my belt, not wanting to accidentally trigger an explosion.

"Don't let your guard down!" Ropert called.

"I thought Lady Brendagger was in charge," Sir Ian muttered from the other side of Ropert.

"She is," Ropert said.

"Then let her make the calls."

The black fire ignited in my mind. This man was facing a life-or-death situation, and he was worried about rank?

Lowering my sword, I broke from the circle, wheeled to face him, and grabbed the neck of his breastplate. My face was inches from his arrogant eyes.

"You are dismissed as my bodyguard."

"But Prime Minister—"

"—has no authority here!" I shunted him back. "I am in command!" I could feel my blood boiling and the black fire inside surging with the energy. "*I* choose what is best for me and all parties involved. You have shown nothing but contempt for those who have been most faithful to me."

Sir Ian's chest puffed out as he straightened. "I have had more years of combat experience than you've been alive. I've mastered the sword and mace, and I've skill in battle axe and spear. My aim with the throwing knife is unmatched. After all this, you mean to tell me I am less qualified than that whelp?" His eyes burned as he scanned Ropert from head to foot.

"Dagger," Ropert said. "Let it go. We don't have time for this."

"Kea." Broderick took three cautious steps toward me. "Breathe."

I didn't want to breathe. I was tired of trying to subdue the anger inside. I wanted to unleash it on Sir Ian, make him see just how insignificant he was.

"Movement!" a soldier shouted. "East!"

We turned as an archer raised her bow and fired three shots at a shadow blurring through the trees. All three of them missed.

She cursed and reloaded her weapon as another archer took her place.

He was circling us.

"Watch your back!" I cried.

The large shape dove into some underbrush. Three chipmunks and a squirrel darted across the forest floor. Then everything was silent. My eyes ached to see movement, squinting, searching.

I lost him.

"Anyone see him?" Ropert demanded.

We stood silent, hunting, our breaths coming hard.

Where in the blazes was—

"Kea!" Leander shouted.

The massive dark blur shot from the trees and rammed into my side, tearing my feet from under me. The impact against my breastplate jerked my head forward. Pain flared through my chin as it struck the metal edge of the gorget around my throat.

"Dagger!" Ropert roared. "Fire! After them! Go, go, go!"

CHAPTER 16

DENTED ARMOR

*M*y vision blurred with pain, but I could still make out his thick tail lashing behind him as he carried me over his shoulder. I pulled my core muscles tight to alleviate the constant impact of my abdomen against his shoulder.

Branches whipped by as he punched through the trees. Behind us, the branches fell closed, concealing the panicked troop giving chase. A chorus of three concussive bursts rippled after us. I flinched at the blinding light sparking through the trees.

Broderick's dust bombs! Mine was still tucked into my belt. *Phoenix, please, don't be broken.* I fixed my hold on my sword still in my hand, turning it to Ikane's ribs. One slice, and I could stop him. But why couldn't I do it? He was going to kill me. He was going to take the ruby tucked away in my pocket.

But his first order had been to eliminate Leander. Why hadn't he? Was it because I'd had him hide the blue cloth and made his target harder to find? Or had he been too difficult to get to with us surrounding him?

No. With a body like this, Ikane could have plowed through us and snatched Leander the same way he'd snatched me.

What if . . . what if Ikane was resisting Alder's command? What if he didn't want to kill me, but he simply wanted to speak with me alone? I could show him his swords and . . .

Charred rachis. In my panic to get Leander to safety, I'd left them under the tree.

Ikane's feet dug into the earth as he skidded to a stop. The shift in momentum pulled my body from his shoulder. I hit the earth, rolling along the forest floor. A crack resonated through my ears as my back collided into the trunk of a giant tree. The old arrow wound flared with dizzying pain. My leg seized.

Feathers, not now. Involuntary tears blurred the image of the massive figure lumbering over me.

My sword. Where was my sword?

Instinct told me to search my waist. My hand found the small pouch from Broderick instead. It was hot, even through my glove. Tearing it from my belt, I pitched it to the side.

A flash of blinding light erupted before it even struck the ground. I threw my arm up, shielding my face as shards of glass, metal fragments, and dirt shot toward me, hitting my armor. Apparently, more had been inside that pouch than sprite dust.

The noise had been too much for Ikane. He hunched on the ground with his hands thrown over his ears. This was not a good start to negotiating.

"I'm sorry, Ikane. I didn't mean to."

His black eyes shot to me, churning with pain and rage. "What magic is this?" he roared.

Where was my sword?

I dragged myself backward, trying to shield myself with the trunk of the tree, my left leg still locked in seizing pain. "It was an accident. Please, Ikane. I just want to talk."

He lunged forward, swinging one of his clawed hands at my face. I dropped to my side. A deafening crack rippled through my ears as the tree groaned. Splinters hit my armor.

"Ikane!" I held up my hand. "Ikane, stop. It's me. Kea."

His claws flew for me again.

I rolled away from the tree, avoiding the worst of his blow as it bit the base of the trunk. But I felt the terrifying tug of his claws ripping the chainmail sleeve on my shoulder. My sword! Metal glinted against the blade as it lay among strewn pine needles.

But charred rachis, my leg. It was still locked in a taut spasm. I couldn't bring it up under me to run. Still, I clawed my way toward it.

Pressure clamped down on my leg. I whirled as he dragged me to him—under him. He set one massive hand on my breastplate, his claws grinding against the metal as he leaned over me, pressing me into the earth. My armor groaned then buckled with a crack, caving in on my chest. I gasped, clutching his massive wrist in both hands.

"Ikane!"

He leaned in, jaw opening, rows of white, sharp teeth aimed at my throat.

I would not let him kill me like this! I forced my eyes to meet his—those black pools of nothingness trembling with a desire to remember. "Eamon." My voice was strangely calm and resigned, though the pressure on my chest may have had something to do with that. "Eamon Brendagger."

He stopped, his jaw closing as he watched me. "Eamon," he breathed, as though he were reminding himself of the man. His black eyes seemed to flicker with recognition. "Brendagger."

The pressure on my armor eased as he moved away. I gasped for air, desperate to expand my lungs, but the concave form of the breastplate continued to push against my chest. I had to loosen it.

Ikane tensed as I raised my arm.

I froze, worried I would trigger his instincts. "I can't breathe," I said. "I just need to . . ." I slowly reached across my body and unlatched the buckle under my arm. The cracked breastplate popped up. I lay back, inhaling deeply, feeling a few new bruises stretch across my ribcage. The taut grip of muscles in my back finally relaxed and my leg stopped cramping, yet something was still pressing against my lower back where I'd struck the tree.

"You're . . . you're not in my head," he said.

My heart fluttered at the sound of his beautiful Leviathan accent through my ears, though his voice was rough and deep.

"I am not," I whispered. Slowly, carefully, I propped myself onto a shoulder then pushed to a sitting position. A terrible ache in my back, right in the area of my belt, almost made me stop. The small wooden box containing the ruby had been in the leather belt pouch strapped to my back. The box must have shattered against my spine.

Ikane's ears swiveled behind him. He looked over his shoulder, his eyes darkening. I swallowed as his claws dug deep grooves into the earth at his feet. "The man from the desert," he said. His nostrils flared as if he could smell Leander's Tolean spices.

"He's a friend," I said. "You may not know him yet, but he wants to help."

Ikane's gaze snapped back to me. "Help with what?"

"Help you be free of Alder."

Something dangerous flashed in his eyes, then it ebbed like a receding wave on the beach before crashing against the shore again with threat. Ikane could not simply destroy Alder, or he would have done so already. He was bound to Alder in a way I could never understand. Loyalty was there, even if it was compelled. I began to wonder if my choice of words had been the right ones.

I glanced at the trees as I heard shouts somewhere in the distance.

Ikane snorted and shook his head. "They come," he growled.

I held my breath as he crawled toward me. "You don't need to run," I said. "They will listen to me . . ." Feathers, he was huge. A hulking mass of teeth, claws, fur, and muscle. The buckles and edges of my metal brace bit into my skin as his hand crushed my wrist.

He jerked me to my feet. My teeth slammed together as something in my shoulder popped twice, as if it had been pulled from its socket then slipped back into place. I felt so feeble and frail around him. Even a simple tug like that could dislocate limbs.

He snarled. "It's hard enough not killing you."

Then, dragging me behind him, we continued through the woods.

Amid the pain, I glanced at my sword lying half-buried in pine straw as we stepped over it. All I had now to defend myself was a boot knife and, hopefully, our memories.

CHAPTER 17

ONE BITE

He slinked through the underbrush, sliding through low-hanging branches like a cat—a very fast cat. He left no trace of his steps, even in the soft earth. No wonder we couldn't track him. He knew how to move, knew where to place his feet.

I, however, stumbled after him, snapping branches, tripping over roots and rocks, mud caking to my boots from melting snow. Sweat dripped down my neck, despite the darkening clouds rolling over the sky. My back bit with every step. I needed to rest, to catch my breath, to assess my injuries. But he didn't stop.

I had no idea where he was taking me. We weren't headed toward Fold, but we weren't headed for Meldron, either. I felt like Ikane was simply wandering about.

"Ikane?" I finally dared to speak.

His grip clamped down on my wrist so hard, I felt the metal give way. I didn't think his grip could be any stronger. I inhaled sharply through my nose as the vambrace crushed into my bone, threatening to break it. He jerked me to face him. His eyes were burning black again, fueled with a need to break and tear.

I swallowed. Asking him to rest was not an option. I had to bring his mind back. "Is Lonacheska alright?"

"How . . . how do you know her?" he asked.

"She is my friend and my queen."

His dark eyes flashed with humanity, burning with . . . hope? Yes, that was the only way I could describe it.

"Did she . . . did she know Eamon Brendagger?" he asked.

"Yes," I answered more quietly, feeling the rawness of pain in my chest.

His grip on my arm relaxed. "I shouldn't have killed him." He looked at his hands, at those lethal claws that I knew he doubted were real. "I remember. I was a boy, a human boy. He taught me to wield dual swords." His hands snapped into fists, the rage returning.

I couldn't imagine the torture in his mind right now. The way his body ached to tear into me like a starving man tearing into a raw piece of meat. He was doing far better than I'd expected.

"I have your swords," I said. "I brought them—"

He roared, slashing into a tree beside my head. I flinched.

"It hurts!" He spun away, smashing his fists against his head again and again.

"I know."

"You *don't* know!" He spun back to me, the hunger returning to his eyes. "I see the way blood pulses in your throat. I hear the frantic beating of your heart. I can smell . . ." His nostrils flared as he stepped closer. His eyes grew darker, more wild and primal. I was losing him.

"I can smell the fear on your skin. I need to bite . . ."

My back hit a tree as I retreated, my heartbeat rising to another level of panic, my breathing coming fast through my nose. What had Alder said? *I want you to sink your teeth into her flesh. Make her bleed.* He didn't need to kill me. He just needed to taste my blood.

My hand trembled as I bit the fingertips of my glove and tore it off. Frantically, I unbuckled the dented vambrace.

Dropping it, I pushed my sleeve up to my elbow, exposing bite-mark scars that he had given me what seemed like a lifetime ago.

The hunger in his eyes was insatiable.

I swallowed. If this was what he needed to be free of this torment, then I'd endure a moment of pain. I held my arm out to him. "All you need is to bite. Make me bleed," I said. "That was all Alder commanded you to do."

Pain flashed across his features as he tried to resist Alder's command.

"Can you do that?" I asked. "Just one—"

He sprang forward. His hands snatched my shoulders, claws scraping against my armor as he drew me to him and bit down on my arm. Pain flared through my skin as individual teeth punctured. My eyes slammed shut, mouth opening to let out a cry—but I did not release a sound. I ground my teeth together as my bones shifted under the pressure, threatening to break.

The tension in his body was incredible, a fraction of his true power. He was holding back. Somehow, he resisted the instinct to jerk his head and tear flesh from bone.

All at once, his muscles eased. Releasing me, he pulled away, stumbling back like a drunk man, licking my blood from his lips.

It was done. One of Alder's terrible orders had been accomplished.

He wiped his wolf jaw with the back of his wrist as a mixture of gratitude, guilt, and relief flooded his eyes. "Why . . . why would you do that for me?"

I pulled my sleeve over the bleeding injury, holding it to my chest. "You would do the same."

He cocked his head at me. "I . . . I don't think I would."

Perhaps not this Ikane. But my Ikane would.

A cold drop of water struck my cheek. I glanced up, finding that the clouds had built into a thick gray blanket across the sky. Another droplet struck my forehead as a third hit my breastplate with a *tink*. The morning had come with the promise of sun and the warmth of spring, but now . . . I squinted as something black darted across the treetops with long leathery wings. Was that a Deathbiter? It couldn't be. Not during the day.

My blood ran cold. The clouds. The rain clouds were hiding the sun. I remembered that terrible day in Glacier Pass when a strange mist arose and clouds covered the sky, bringing the Deathbiters with it. It was when Ikane had been taken from me and changed into the creature standing before me now.

I turned back to Ikane, feeling the hot, sticky blood seeping through my sleeve as I held the injury. The Deathbiters didn't bother him. Perhaps they wouldn't bother me, either, as long as I was with him. But what about Ropert, Broderick, Prince Leander, and the others?

A cry tore through the sky above. My eyes shot upward. There they were, spinning through the treetops in search of prey.

"You fear them more than me?" Ikane ventured.

I found myself taking steps toward him. "Yes," I said, not daring to raise my voice above a whisper.

He blinked at me then looked up and snorted, his own disdain for the creatures evident. Even if I'd only felt it in a dream, I knew the way their screeches pierced his ears.

"This way," he said, turning to the woods.

I followed him through the underbrush, pushing pine branches away with my shoulders as I tried to stem the bleeding of my arm. I was not looking forward to when my adrenaline waned. The pain of this bite would be enough to make a seasoned soldier cry.

Rain began pattering against my armor in a steady thrum of soft *tinks* as we slid through a wall of branches and emerged at the base of an ancient tree. It was breathtakingly magnificent. I'd never seen another tree like it. Roots arched upward like a miniature citadel, covered in splotches of whitish lichen, thick green moss, and shelf-like mushrooms that could pass as organic terraces for the elemental sprites.

"Inside," Ikane ordered.

I ducked through the arching branches as the mossy-scented air filled my nose. Licking the rain from my lips, I sank to the earth between the tangled roots. Water dripped from the gaps like a leaking roof and pattered on the soft earth by my boots. My body trembled, though I did not feel cold.

Ikane curled up between twisting vines on the opposite side of the shelter, his face turned to the downpour pelting the forest beyond. His deep-brown fur glistened with raindrops. It would have been a serene sight, like the time I remembered watching him stand on the bow of a ship, relishing the ocean air against his skin. But his tail twitched, his hands curled, and his black eyes strayed to me. He was still fighting. Still resisting Alder's other commands.

I had to keep him distracted.

"You didn't answer me before," I said. "Is Queen Lonacheska alright? The baby?"

His jaw worked. "I do not know," he finally said. "Alder will not let me see her."

A shiver ran down my spine.

My body stiffened involuntarily as Ikane turned to me and approached on all fours. My heart was running like a herd of panicked deer, and I knew he could hear it. His body was so imposing, like a giant steed whose muscles rippled beneath its coat, boasting power, strength, and speed. Yet there was a softness around him as his fur glistened with moisture, and sadness touched his eyes.

He stopped before me, his breath hot and filled with a slight sweetness. How I missed his scent of steel and mint. Not the overpowering mint that had accompanied Ropert last night, but the subtle hint of something cooling and warming at the same time.

"Why do I know you, and yet I can't remember?" he asked. His large dark eyes searched mine, scanning my face, lingering on the scars marring my skin. I swallowed as he reached up. Holding firm, his cold claw brushed a strand of wet hair from my cheek. "Your eyes are like the sea," he said. "Like . . . home."

Did he realize what he was saying? Somewhere inside, he knew his place was on the Rethreal Sea, sailing the waters, feeling the wind through his hair and the salt on his skin, using the stars to guide him.

"I want to help you remember," I whispered.

His hand dropped, and his head tilted as if to ask *how?*

"I don't know what Alder has done with your memories," I said. "All I can do is share what I know and what memories I have of you and me. The rest will be up to you."

He raised his head, the decision to trust me churning behind his eyes like black water.

"Do you remember when we first met?"

His head shook slowly, eyes not straying from mine.

"It was in Daram. You had come to warn Eamon of an impending Leviathan pirate attack." I smiled softly at the memory of him standing there, gazing up at Daram's tallest tower. "We sparred. It was the first time I'd ever faced a dual-sword wielder. You were magnificent." The memory of his green eye flashing as his obsidian blades struck mine tainted my smile with sorrow. How I missed his mismatched eyes.

He sat back on his heels, listening.

"We traveled to Meldron together for King Sander's coronation." I bit back the truth of why he had come. Would reminding him of his coerced mission to assassinate the king trigger something in him? My poor Ikane seemed to always have his own will squelched by someone. First his brothers, then Rion, and now Alder.

"The coronation," he said slowly. "You wore a gown the color of the sea."

My heart leapt forward. "Yes. Yes, I did."

"We danced."

"Yes." My vision blurred with moisture. Something changed in his eyes, the left one. Was that green shimmering around his black iris? Frantic, I blinked the tears away, needing to see. Whatever green I'd seen was gone.

"You were . . . angry with me," he said darkly.

Perhaps I hadn't seen it at all. My smile faded. I didn't want him to remember that part, but it was the truth and our past.

He shook his head as if trying to wake himself.

I was losing him. "No, Ikane. Don't try to understand."

He turned away, clutching his head in his hands.

"I was wrong then, Ikane," I said. "I just found out that you were a Leviathan pirate, my sworn enemy. But I'd already fallen in love with you. You held my hand when I had nightmares. You saved me when I was dying. You brought me to the Fold Garrison and nursed me back to health."

That seemed to trigger something in him. His back muscles rippled as he dropped his hands. "Fold." His voice was so low, I barely heard it. "Alder. The Phoenix Stone."

I'd lost him. The command to bring the ruby back to Alder had taken hold. I couldn't let him have it. Once he had the Stone, he would go after Leander.

He spun to me, black eyes burning with feral rage. "Where is the Phoenix Stone?"

I held my hands up, my blood coating them. "Ikane, please. You are stronger than this. You resisted this long. Try—"

I slid down the roots, letting his hand whip over my head. A loud crack, like an axe splitting wood, filled my ears as he hit the roots of the tree beside me. Debris rained down on my armor. I may have avoided the first blow, but I was now trapped between moss-covered roots, unable to roll or move away.

"Ikane," I cried, throwing my arms over my head, frantically trying to find words that would bring him back. "Don't let Alder win! You are not his pet! You are not his pawn!"

"Then what am I?" he roared.

I blinked between the gap in my arms, finding his dangerous form standing over me, chest heaving, his hand trembling in the air, ready to strike. He wanted to. I could see it in his eyes, but he was fighting it again.

"You are someone I will always love," I said. If it was the last thing he heard me say, at least he would know that I loved him until the end. Just like Eamon.

This wasn't his fault.

He dropped on all fours over me, his hot breath stinging my skin. "Where is the ruby? I feel it. Give it to me! Give it to me now before I . . ." His eyes shut tight, face contorted in pain and frustration. "Before I kill you like I did Eamon."

My lips pressed tight at the agony in his voice. He didn't deserve any of this. But I could not give him the Stone.

"Give it to me!" Spittle hit my cheek.

Shutting my eyes, I shook my head, preparing for the tearing of my skin.

He roared. The tree groaned as he tore into the protruding root beside my head with his teeth, jerking the bark away like Ropert did to bread. Splinters and pieces of wood hit my face. His claws finished the job, ripping the root from the earth as easily as pulling a sword from the abdomen of a foe. I tasted dirt and felt it in my teeth.

"She'll only destroy you!" I cried. "She will destroy all of us."

He gripped the neck of my armor and jerked me closer. "She is my goddess," he snarled.

I'm here. Her voice hummed like a whisper in my mind. Ikane froze as well. He'd heard her, too.

Her belt, she instructed. *She has me in a pouch on her belt. Take it.*

He acted, slamming me down like nothing more than a rag. Something cracked in my chest, and it wasn't the dented breastplate giving way under the blow.

I couldn't breathe. My heart suddenly felt heavy and constricted. I waited for it to beat as Ikane tore my belt from my waist. I waited for it to beat as he turned to the rain pelting the earth outside. And I still waited for it to beat as his blurry shape slipped through the underbrush, tree branches swaying in his wake.

Thick, consuming blackness swarmed my vision.

I thought I could bring him back. I thought I was strong enough to inspire him, but all my efforts only reminded me of how weak I really was. And it hurt. Feathers, it hurt.

More than my lungs screaming for air. More than the non-beating of my heart.

CHAPTER 18

ORDERS

arrok slammed into the crumbling trunk of a tree, feeling the ground shake at the impact and the branches shudder. Heavy raindrops shook free of the branches, drenching his fur as he leaned against it. He had the Phoenix Stone now. All he needed to do was return it to Alder, and the pain in his limbs would lessen—just like it did when he'd bitten the Brendagger girl's arm.

He still didn't understand why she'd done that for him. It was like she knew the pain in his body, understood the pull and unquenchable desire to complete Alder's demands. She had stared at him with those stormy-blue eyes like the embrace of the sea keeping ships afloat. And the constellation of freckles across her skin was like a map, a direction, pointing his way home.

He glanced over his shoulder. She knew him. He believed that with all his heart—if he still had one.

And he knew her. But his memories of her lay fragmented across his mind like a shipwreck.

A horrible screech tore through the trees, followed by another and another, a chorus of angry cries grating on his ears. Squinting against the rain pelting his face, he looked up. Black shapes shot across the sky, all heading the same direction, all converging on . . .

Spines, they were after the girl. They could smell her blood. Even he could taste it on the air.

A strange sensation flowed through his muscles, building in the center of his chest. He had to save her. Adrenaline pushed to his limbs. With the stolen belt clutched in one hand, his legs pushed his massive body through the forest, weaving between the blurring trunks of trees, crashing through rain-soaked branches.

He burst through the wall of underbrush, arriving at the ancient tree just as the bats plummeted.

The girl lay crumpled on her side where he'd left her, wet hair clinging to her face. The raindrops pinging against her armor almost masked the weak and erratic beat of her heart.

She was no stranger to battle wounds. The three faint scars stretching across her face were evidence of that. But this was something greater. Had he done this? He tried not to hurt her after she'd offered her arm to him. But she was suffering.

The first filthy creature dropped from the sky, arcing toward the tree's base. Ikane tore across the clearing, skidded into the shelter, and spun as the Deathbiter scratched its way in. His claws sliced into the animal, knocking it from the wood with a shower of splintered roots.

Another took its place.

He tore it from its perch, pinning it to the ground with his claws. The wings flapped wildly against his arm. With a quick bite and twist of his head, the creature stilled. He glanced back at the sleeping girl.

Why did it seem like he'd done something like this before? An image flashed through his mind, of his hands wielding two obsidian swords, cutting down blue-painted faces as this girl— yes, this same girl—lay unmoving on a battlefield. She was even wearing the same armor.

Two more bats entered.

At least a dozen swarmed outside, perhaps more.

Settling in, Marrok found a rhythm, a form of peace and acceptance as he stood over the unconscious, armored girl. This was his element. This was what he was meant to do. To kill and destroy . . .

And to protect.

Warm light radiated against my eyelids. Sweet birdsong and chirping squirrels hummed through my ears. The sweet scent of cleansed earth filled my breath, mixed with . . .

I choked. A sour, acrid burn stung my nostrils. My eyes cracked open to the rays of sunlight shining through the gaps in the tree's roots. Broken stems hung overhead, held together by fragile clusters of moss, while others bore deep, white, linear scars. Dismembered, twisted bodies of Deathbiters lay scattered across the opening of the tree's shelter.

The aftermath of the dream. Ikane . . . where was he?

My chest screamed in pain as I pushed myself from the damp earth, and my heart flew into a pummeling frenzy against my ribs, every beat like the bolt of an arrow hitting my torso. Phoenix, something was very wrong. I'd never felt anything like this before. The pain went deeper than muscle or bone.

Gritting my teeth, I slipped the damaged armor over my head and allowed it to crash to the earth beside me. The rounded curve of my breastplate bore a deep crater the size of a horse's hoof sitting over the chest, and a crack ran through the metal surface like a scar. It was damaged beyond repair.

I stretched for the buckles of my right greave, which was also dented and cutting into my shin, but leaning forward sent a new wave of pain through my core. Lying back again, I closed my eyes and inhaled slowly, shallowly, trying to calm the dangerous beating of my heart.

A shadow fell over me. My eyes opened. Ikane's majestic wolf face looked down on me. He actually looked concerned.

The ache in my chest took on a new edge. I wanted him back. Feathers, I wanted him back.

"Ikane."

His ears twitched. "Your heart."

I winced as I placed a hand over my chest, feeling the tenderness inside.

"Your heart is . . . bruised," he said.

I looked up at him, at his rich brown fur glistening under the shafts of light breaking through gaps in the tree, at his dark eyes, at his majestic wolf face. Somehow, with the way he was looking at me, my heart was beginning to mend. My hand raised, and without intending to, my fingers brushed the fur on his chest.

He jerked back.

"I'm sorry," I said quickly. "I . . . I didn't mean to."

His eyes fell on my dented armor lying beside me, a memory churning inside. I could see it.

"You've seen that armor before, haven't you?" I asked.

He nodded slowly and reached out, touching the dented breastplate. His claws made a gentle *clink* as they tapped against the metal. "I . . . I remember a man with an axe—a battle axe. He had blue paint across his eyes."

"Your brother, Dran."

"I . . . I killed him." His voice held so much sorrow. "Alder lied to that man."

"What man?" I asked.

"A pirate who came to Fold. He was asking about . . . me. About Ikane. Alder told him he was dead." He looked at me. "That you killed Ikane and Dran."

This was not a conversation to have on my back. I pushed myself from the ground, my heart banging harder as I tried to sit.

Growling, he pressed me back down by my shoulder, trying to be gentle, but it still felt like a boulder slamming into my core. Yet, through the pain, my heart fluttered, soaring with untamed hope as he leaned over me. I didn't think a creature like this could show so much concern.

"I didn't mean to hurt you," he said.

As I rested my head against the ground, I gripped his wrist, feeling the hardened muscles beneath the soft warmth of his fur. "I know."

He watched me with those black eyes, studying my features, taking me in like he was trying to remember every part of us. Of who we used to be.

Wait. Was that . . . ?

I wanted to sit up, look closer, see his eyes more clearly.

His eyelids blinked again. Yes! There it was! A faint edge, a rim of blue and green around the edges of those obsidian stone irises. He was waking up! He was remembering.

I reached up, brushing the tips of my fingers against the fur around his jawline. And he let me. He even relished it, closing his dark eyelids as he leaned into my touch, like he'd done so many times before.

Then his eyes tore wide. The rim of blue and green burnt out, and his eyes grew dark and distant like something else was calling to him, ensnaring him.

I dropped my hand. "Ikane?"

His eyes hardened at something I could not see. He growled. "Aye."

"Ikane, what's wrong?"

He flinched, ears lying flat against his head as if something invisible had struck him. "Aye . . . Master."

My heart flew behind my spine. He said the name through clenched teeth, like Alder had forced him to say it. Ikane's midnight-black eyes dropped to me.

"Bring the Phoenix Stone." His voice was low and monotone, like the words were not his own. His hand, still resting on my shoulder, clenched. His claws dug into my thick padded gambeson and chainmail, puncturing through like arrows. I inhaled sharply through my nose.

"No, Ikane." I clutched his arm tighter. He had been free. Or at least a part of him had been, and Alder had stamped him out, crushed him under his boot.

Shutting my eyes, I fled toward his mind, seeing the darkness shrouding it like a gray mist. I hesitated. He hated it when I pushed into his thoughts, and I did not want to trigger anything that would push him farther from me. But Alder was inside, scattering the mending memories like a madman tearing through someone's private chambers.

The pain in my chest increased tenfold.

Alder's darkness turned on me. *You think you can undo what I've created?* His deep, resonant voice boomed through my mind like boulders tumbling from a mountain. *He is mine.*

I would not invade Ikane's mind, but that didn't mean I couldn't strike back. I gathered fragmented stars of my white energy, inhaling as Broderick had instructed until an arrow formed.

Alder's apprehension rose as my Etheric lights grew taut like the string of a bow. I'd struck him before, and he knew I could do it again.

Get out of his head! I released. The power flew forward, careening toward him like a true arrow.

His gray shadow curled inward and vanished like a puff of smoke drifting away in a breeze.

My arrow struck Ikane.

A thousand sparks exploded outward, shooting across his mind, penetrating his scattered memories.

My eyes flew wide as he roared and reeled away, clutching his head.

"Ikane! Ikane! I'm so sorry. I didn't mean to!" I cried. I didn't care how much it hurt my heart. I sat upright and reached for him.

But he staggered away like a drunk man, shoulder hitting the fractured roots near the entrance. His body spun as he collapsed onto his side in the clearing.

I clawed my way after him, moving too slow. "I didn't mean to, Ikane. I was trying to help. I only wanted to get Alder out of—"

But he kept moving like he hadn't even heard me. Snatching up my belt, he sprinted into the trees and disappeared behind swaying branches.

I sagged against the tangled roots as tears stung and blurred my eyes. Why? Why did I keep doing this? First Caleb and now . . .

Rion and Alder knew how to use my strengths against me, forcing me to make irreparable errors that didn't just make my soul bleed but left festering wounds on the inside. It was the horror and ache of watching fire and smoke consume the bones of a home.

"I'm sorry, Ikane," I whimpered into my hands. "I'm sorry."

I'd lost him again. It was my fault. And this time, I felt it was eternal.

"I'm sorry."

CHAPTER 19

BRUISED HEART

*T*here!" someone shouted through the trees. "I see her. Over there!"

I sagged against the trunk of a massive oak as a flurry of bodies wove through the forest toward me. Stumbling through the woods had been like walking under the numbing waves of the sea, shapes blurring together, noises muffled, body pressing on until the pain had been driven to the depths.

Now, as my senses were forced to stir, I squinted at the bright beams of sunlight lancing through the treetops. My heart throbbed against my ribs with an inconsolable restless gait, rattling my bones with every arrhythmic pump.

"Dagger!" Ropert burst through the underbrush, catching me under my arms before I slid to the ground. I cried out at his crushing embrace folding over my chest. He brushed my hair from my face. "Hold on, Dagger." Slipping his arm under my legs, he lifted me from the ground. "Broderick!" he shouted. "Over here! We found her! She's alive!"

Broderick's head of brown curls appeared. His keen eyes and expert hand flew over my injuries. Pausing at the bite mark on my arm, his brows furrowed. "I expected worse."

"My chest," I croaked, tugging at the neck of my gambeson. I felt like the weight of the heavy padding was forcing my heart to beat faster.

He tugged the lacing open. Cool air hit my exposed skin.

"Flaming feathers," he breathed. "Bring her back to camp. Hurry."

Trees whirred overhead, the cloudy sky flashing between the budding branches of spring as Ropert's strong body carried me forward. He lowered me to a bedroll someone had hastily spread out, gently resting my head on some sort of makeshift pillow Ciri placed there. Ropert stroked my forehead once more.

"Help me get her armor off," Broderick demanded as he dropped to his knees beside me.

"Leander?" I croaked as Ropert and Ciri began stripping my armor. I didn't see Leander. Had Ikane gotten to him?

"I am here," Leander's accented voice came from somewhere beyond my line of vision. Ropert moved away and allowed the handsome, foolish Tolean prince to kneel beside me. He took my hand, caring not for the blood saturating my sleeve and staining my fingers.

"Go back to Meldron," I said. "Go now. While you have the—"

I cut off with a gasp as Broderick's hand slid under my tunic and touched the deep puncture wounds on my shoulder. Pulling his hand away, he rubbed the crimson stickiness between his fingers. "You're going to need sutures," he muttered.

I gripped Leander's hand more tightly, feeling the cold of his emerald ring dig into my skin. "Go, Leander."

His hand gripped mine like a vice. "I will not leave you in this state."

"Rachis, Leander. Ikane will come for you next. As soon as he delivers the stone to Alder, he will kill you."

His golden eyes shattered like the sun had fallen to the ground and rolled away. "He took the Phoenix Stone?"

"There is no time to explain." I craned my neck to look at Boma and Ciri. They were my only hope. "Please, take him back to Meldron. He's not safe here. Ikane . . ." My voice faltered. Ikane was dead. After striking him the way I did, I had ensured that he was permanently lost to me. It was the final spark to his funeral pyre. "Marrok will destroy him."

Leander leaned forward, his dreadlocks falling across his shoulders as he stroked my forehead. "I am more secure with you than anywhere."

I shook his hand from my brow. "You don't understand." I turned to Broderick. "Tell him, Broderick. Make him see."

Broderick's eyes remained focused as he studied the bite mark on my forearm. "He didn't kill you." His voice was distant and thoughtful, like he believed we had misjudged the creature Alder had created. "Perhaps there is some good left in him."

I pulled my arm away from both Leander and Broderick, the black spark of anger and frustration rising inside, clawing to be released. "He's gone!" I snapped, trying to stay my tears, still seeing the explosion of my power ricocheting inside Ikane's mind. "It's undeniable this time. Alder made certain of that."

The throbbing in my chest tore a path to my throat. My breath came shallow and strained, air suddenly becoming trapped in my throat as if the wind had died and all fluttering banners stilled.

"What is wrong?" Leander asked.

Broderick leaned down and pressed his ear against my bruised ribs. His body shot upright. "Winddust!" he called. "Does anyone have winddust?"

"You're the dust boy," Ropert said.

"I used it all for the bombs."

"Here," Ciri said, handing Broderick a vial of something so bright it blinded my blurry vision.

"Hold her head back," Broderick ordered, tearing the cork off with his teeth then spitting it away. Leander's warm hand slipped under my neck. The vial clanked against my teeth as he tapped the dust into my mouth.

Cherry blossoms danced on my tongue. Autumn leaves swept down my throat. A gust of warm crispness expanded in my chest like wind filling the sails of a ship, and the despondent beating in my chest folded inward.

Leander lowered my head as the wind stroked my skin, rippled through my blood, and touched every strand of hair. I felt as though I could sail with the clouds, whisper through the trees, experience everything at once. It was amazing.

"No." Broderick pushed me down when I tried to rise. "You have more than cracked ribs. Your heart is bruised."

"Feathers, Dagger," Ropert said. "Why aren't you wearing your armor? You should have been—"

"My armor caved." My voice sounded strange, breathy and light, like everything about me had turned to air. Marrok had fought so hard against his instincts to kill. It didn't seem right. "It just caved."

Broderick looked at Leander then Ropert. "She can't go on. If she strains herself, her heart could stop."

"I will take her," Leander offered.

"I feel fine now," I said.

Broderick's eyes fell to me. "You need to go back to Meldron. I am not gambling with this one, Kea."

"And I will go if you are with me," Leander said with a sly grin. He was learning from Ropert.

For the first time, I knew my limits. They were right. I was finished. This was as far as I could go.

"How long before she heals?" Ropert asked as he knelt beside Broderick, assisting him as the healer began pulling cleaning alcohol, bandages, and needle and thread from his healing kit.

"I can't say for certain," he admitted. "The damage is deep. It could be weeks. Perhaps months."

Months? I shut my eyes. This was not what I wanted to hear. But I could feel it. The damage to my heart was not something I could ignore or push through like I did with so many other injuries. This was dangerous.

"Lona doesn't have that much—"

"I know the Dead Forest, Dagger," Ropert interrupted. "I'll lead the mission."

"But you've only been there once," I reminded him. "And you were half-conscious with fever."

Ropert held up the needle and squinted as he threaded it. "Better semiconscious than torpid," he said. "It'll be alright, Dagger. This way, we all get what we want. Leander goes back to Meldron with you, Sir Ian is reinstated as your bodyguard, and I get to spy on some pirates."

"Where is Sir Ian?"

Ropert shrugged. "Last I saw, he was tending to the horses. He'll be puffed up like a proud peafowl once he hears the news."

I allowed my head to sink back against the makeshift pillow. "Alright."

Ropert brushed his calloused hand over my hair. "It's the right choice, Dagger." When had he grown so much? His crystalline-blue eyes still held their mischievousness, but a flourishing wisdom was building behind them, a wisdom I respected.

"Let's get her patched up," Broderick said.

Shutting my eyes, I dove into my mind. My empty, uninhabited mind. Rion was gone. I couldn't feel her or mend any cracks in her prison walls or sense her next moves. Sinking deeper, I dared to stretch my mind, letting it flow through the trees, weave around stone and fallen logs, and slip across the threshold of the Dead Forest where young life fought to reclaim the land. I could feel him, a spark of something blue shimmering at the edge of my attention.

His mind was as solid oak, chained with no key to fit the lock and no hammer strong enough to break it. Even if I could breach his wall, he loathed it when I tried. The same way I hated it when Rion entered mine.

I could only hope that he felt my remorse flood from my own mind, like a cottage door with warm light spilling out into a rainy evening. But the doubt encircled my welcome like ravenous wolves, quelling any hope of him ever reaching back.

I'd destroyed him.

CHAPTER 20

ASK ALDER

"Attack!"

The cry flared at the edge of my consciousness, pulling me back to every ache in my body.

"We're under attack!"

Deathbiters? I stirred, every muscle protesting movement. My eyes struggled to open. Light still touched the scattered gray clouds overhead in shades of orange. It wasn't Deathbiters.

Shouts and the clashing noise of metal against metal rang through the trees.

Broderick appeared, his eyes wild as he tore the blanket from me and slipped his hand under my back. "Up, Kea. We need to go."

"What's going on?"

"I don't know. But we need to get you out of here."

I placed a bandaged arm over my chest, relying solely on his strength to help me stand upright. Squinting through the white flashes of pain behind my eyes, I watched my soldiers spiral and engage an enemy slipping through the trees as lithe as serpents, striking with teeth of sword, axe, and knife. Three of my handpicked elite warriors fell.

If these were the Fold raiders Ikane and I had trained, I could reason with them. Torquin would recognize me. I could make this stop. But none of these shadows looked deformed. None held withered arms or legs. None of them fought with hunched backs or twisted bodies. They were solid warriors, swift and dexterous, wielding finely crafted weapons and wearing exquisitely designed leather armor edged in fur.

My heart flew into a painful fit of erratic beats as the stripe of blue paint across their eyes became clear. Leviathan Pirates. They'd found us first.

Prince Leander appeared at my side, his hands raised, his golden eyes alert.

"Thundercrack!" Ropert bellowed over his shoulder as he rushed toward the enemy. "Get Dagger and Leander out of here! Protect them at all cost! Go!"

Ropert barreled into the chest of a pirate and threw him over his shoulder. The man landed on his back and met Ropert's blade with his chest before he could think to roll away. Ciri rushed forward like a cat, sailing around him—*with* him— like a dangerous wind circling a mountain.

When had they grown so harmonious? It was like they'd been fighting together for years, knowing each other's moves, balancing each other's strengths and weaknesses. It was beautiful.

And it ignited a strange prick in my chest. That was supposed to be me. Ropert and I were a team. We'd always had each other's backs.

My ribs screamed as Broderick pulled my arm over his neck. "Come on." Urgency filled his voice as he turned toward the horses who were tossing heads, stamping hooves, and pulling on their reins. Boma worked to untether four of them, keeping his movements soft and fluid.

I glanced over my shoulder one more time, watching Ropert and Ciri make quick work of their attackers. Their movements were so crisp and perfect. Ropert slipped into a strike, letting the pirate's weapon fly past his head. Without using his sword, he smashed his fists against the pirate's arm. Then, in a flurry of movements, he struck the man's throat and solar plexus.

I'd never seen him move his feet so smoothly, gliding perfectly around his attacker and landing a solid blow to the back of the pirate's neck with the pommel of his sword. The Leviathan sprawled facedown at his feet.

The Ridarri arts. He must have been learning from Ciri.

Something caught the corner of my eye. My heart couldn't seem to decide whether to stop or fly into a wild gallop.

The man looked like Ikane.

He burst from the trees like a lion. Tall and dark, with broad shoulders and lean hips, moving like a broken dam as he ripped through the soldiers with a broadsword. His deep-brown hair flew around the blue-painted streak across his eyes. He crushed a soldier underneath his blows—not the smooth lethal lighting strikes Ikane used, but the barbaric violence the pirates were known for.

His difference became clearer the more I watched. His jawline was stronger and covered with dark stubble, unlike Ikane's usual clean-shaven face, and his hair was shorter. This could only be one of Ikane's brothers.

Broderick tugged me forward. "Kea."

Gritting my teeth, I tore my eyes away from the man and set my boot in the stirrup. I pushed off Broderick's knee, swinging up. But my body stopped with a jerk as a pair of solid arms crushed my waist, lifting me backward.

Feathers, my heart! I cried out in agony as my fingers ripped from the saddle.

Another pirate bore down on Broderick, a crack sounding as his fist struck the assassin's jaw. Broderick's head of brown curls rocked to the side.

"Broderick!" I cried, fighting against the pirate dragging me back.

Red dripped from the split in Broderick's lip as he struggled to regain composure. He ducked away as the pirate lunged for him with a set of daggers so long, they looked more like short swords. A red slash appeared on my horse's thigh as the Leviathan's first swipe missed. The stallion flinched, crying out, dancing away.

Leander appeared like a falcon swooping down on prey. I heard the crack of his strike against my attacker's windpipe. The crushing arms holding me released. My heart jolted as my boots hit the ground, and I stumbled into Leander's arms. He spun me behind him, shielding me with his body as four other pirates converged.

"Go," he ordered me, barely looking over his shoulder.

I swallowed. It wasn't in me to run. But I staggered back as a Leviathan sword raced for Leander's head. He ducked under the blade, plunging his elbow into the man's sternum. Another crack sounded as he struck the inside of the pirate's knee. The man cried out, his leg buckling.

The tip of another pirate's sword flashed silver as it raced for Leander's back like a spear.

"Behind you!" I cried.

Leander's body shifted easily, like water moving around a stone. His hands moved too quickly for me to determine what strikes he delivered, but the pirate's arm went rigid and his sword clattered to the earth within a breath. Leander's arm wrapped around the pirate's neck, whipping the man around to use as a shield when another sword came arcing at him.

Tossing the limp body aside, Leander's leg came up like a club, striking another pirate in the side of the head. The man's eyes turned white as they rolled back, and his body collapsed like one of the decaying trees in the Dead Forest.

He was incredible. But the pirates, too, had noticed. More were converging on him, seeing him as the main threat.

I held my side as adrenaline soared through my blood. I wanted to fight. I wanted to help, but I was weaponless and without the skill of a Ridarri. Where in the blazes was Boma?

Or Sir Ian? I hadn't seen a trace of my supposed bodyguard since . . . since Ikane had taken me, I realized. He'd been missing this entire time.

A flash of blinding white light burst across the camp, followed by a deafening lightning crack that shook the trees and rattled my ribcage. My ears rang as I spun to Broderick. His attacker staggered away, screaming into his hands that were covering his face. Blood leaked through his fingers. The smell of lightning and burnt flesh filled the air.

"Kea, now!" Broderick roared, frantically waving me toward the horses.

I glanced back at Leander, who was already engaged in another fight with three more pirates. But once again, he was the dominant warrior. I was glad he was on my side.

"Kea!" Broderick snapped.

A hand jerked my arm. My body whipped around so forcefully I thought I heard my ribs crack again. My heart felt like it was beating through tar, everything moving in slow motion as I came face-to-face with my attacker.

Ikane? I shook my head. No. But it was like looking at his twin. "Teilo?" I asked.

His dark brows furrowed as he considered me, but only for a quick moment. Then his deep-blue eyes hardened like the ocean freezing over, and his sword came up like a lightning strike, freezing against my throat. "How do you know Teilo?" he demanded.

I swallowed, feeling the cold blade sting my skin.

The man's grip tightened as he pulled me closer to him, closer to his sword. I arched back, sucking air through my nose. If I couldn't calm my heartbeat soon . . .

"Answer me!" the pirate prince demanded in the same beautiful Leviathan accent Ikane had.

"I . . . Ikane," I choked.

He shoved me back. "Bind her," he commanded as I staggered into the hands of pirates. "I want her alive."

No amount of adrenaline could numb the pain flaring through my shoulder and chest as they wrenched my arms behind my back.

Broderick lunged forward, raising his battle axe. But the Leviathan prince parried with ease before advancing, driving Broderick back with the sheer power behind his blows. Broderick sank between the trees as his axe was battered from his hold. The pirate prince pursued like a wolf.

Ropes coiled around my wrists, and hands pinched my arms as the Leviathan pirates grew thicker around me, preventing me from seeing anything beyond their painted faces. I searched for Leander, finding his dreadlocks spinning behind a crowd of pirates choking him back. There were too many, overpowering our small troop five to one. Still, I dug my heels into the earth as they dragged me farther into the trees.

"Ropert!" I cried.

Flaming feathers, where was Sir Ian?

"Ropert!" My scream shredded my throat. This was exactly what Minister Chanter had feared—that I would be taken captive or killed when Roanfire needed me the most.

My boots stumbled and tripped over broken shrubbery and dead leaves as the cries of battle grew more and more distant.

How had things gone so horribly wrong?

Splinters of tree bark slid down the neck of my tunic as the pirates pulled my arms back, looping a rope behind the trunk to both of my wrists. An unwitting cry of pain ground through my teeth as they pulled it tight.

Without a word, they left me there to watch as handfuls of Leviathan pirates trickled back into their camp, which they'd set up just inside the boundaries of the Dead Forest. How long had it been since I'd seen this place? New blades of grass and shrubbery peeked little green fingers from the soil, ready for spring, ready to flourish here once again.

The pirates were exposed here, but so were any incoming threats. It was a tactical position. One I would have approved of if not for the Deathbiters. How did they shield themselves at night? I saw no torches, brasiers, or shelters. Just a smattering of canvas tents and scattered firepits throughout the dead stumps of trees.

I twisted my wrists against the ropes, gauging the tightness and quality of the knots. Then I laughed at myself. These were pirates. They spent days, weeks, years perfecting their knot work. It was life or death on a ship. The fact that I had even suspected sloppy knot work showed just how disheveled my mind was.

Commotion ensued as a pair of Leviathans staggered into the camp: Ikane's brother and the pirate whose face had been blasted by Broderick's dust bomb. With the wounded pirate's arm around his shoulder, the prince carried the man across the barren landscape into a tent across the way. When the flap closed, cries of pain ensued.

Licking the dryness of my lips away, my mind turned to the flecks of sprite dust glittering in my palms. The same dust that had created Broderick's weapon. The shimmering particles embedded in my hands were one element away from becoming one of them.

Alder had warned me about their unstable condition when combined. But seeing it firsthand was . . . was something I hadn't expected. Like I hadn't realized just how dangerous my situation was.

I folded my legs under me, watching the Leviathans putter about the camp, sorting through spoils, tending to wounds, and building up fires for the evening. It was just another day for them. Another day of raiding, plundering, and destroying. Seeing this reminded me of why my prejudice against Ikane had been so strong when I'd first discovered who he was.

I counted twoscore Leviathans, three times the number of my small reconnaissance troop. My stomach churned at the thought of Ropert, Ciri, Broderick, and Boma surviving those odds. If there were this many out here patrolling the edge of the Dead Forest, I dreaded to discover the number infesting Fold.

My eyes snapped back to the tent as the flap ripped open and Ikane's brother emerged, his dark eyes locking on me. He placed a hand on the hilt of his sword as he approached. If he meant to intimidate me and succeeded, I would not show it.

Planting his soft leather boots before me, his deep-blue eyes stared at my face, measuring, questioning, curious. Silence stretched on as I stared back, studying his features. This wasn't Teilo. Teilo, as I understood, was the sixth of the seven princes, Ikane being the youngest. This man was too mature, with soft creases at the corners of his almond eyes—but no less stunning.

"Where is Ikane?" he finally asked, his voice deceptively soft. "How do you know about Teilo?"

I narrowed my eyes at him. "Are you working for Alder?"

The corners of his lips pulled into a smile as he crouched before me. "Bold little soldier, aren't you? Avoiding my questions without so much as a twitch of the eyes. Tell me, are you afraid?"

"Answer me," I snapped. "Are you working for Alder Grayhorn?"

He rested his arms on his knees. "I work for no one."

So he wanted to play word games. "Fine. Are you working *with* him?"

"Why? Do you not approve?"

My heart hurt, beating so hard it throbbed into my temples. So it was true. Alder had somehow convinced the Leviathan pirates to side with him. "What did he promise you?" I demanded.

The prince settled back with a smile. "I think you don't realize who has the advantage here, little soldier. I ask the questions. I want to know what happened to my brother, Ikane."

I hardened my eyes. "Ask Alder."

His smile faded. "That is a brave accusation."

"It's the truth."

His eyes scanned my bandaged limbs, missing armor, and patched gambeson. "Your wounds. What are they from?"

"Ask Alder," I repeated slowly.

"So stubborn," he said. I stiffened as he brushed my hair from my cheek, his touch deceptively gentle. I knew what he was capable of. "Your soldiers fought like lightning eels to protect you. As would I for such a rustic beauty."

"You will maintain your distance, pirate."

He retracted his hand. "Authority," he mused. "You are accustomed to giving orders. I can hear it. Perhaps you are not the lowly soldier I assumed. Your scars suggest years of battle. Are you a commander or a general, perhaps? What is your name?"

"You first," I said.

He smiled. I hated how much he reminded me of Ikane.

"Your bravery is admirable," he said. "Very well. I am Benroar Ormand, third Prince of the Leviathans. Now." He paused. "It is your turn."

It seemed he didn't recognize that I was the very Lady Brendagger he'd set a bounty on, and I intended to keep it that way as long as I could.

"They call me Dagger," I said.

He tilted his head, waiting.

"Is that all you are going to give me?" he asked. "No family name? Title? Rank?"

"Why should that matter?"

He sighed, shaking his head as he looked down. "You're going to be a difficult one to break." Standing, he dusted his hands on his trousers. "Perhaps you'll be a bit more accommodating once you're begging for water or meat." He turned away.

"Benroar!" I called after him. "I mean it. Ask Alder about your brother. He knows exactly what happened to him."

Benroar glanced at me over his shoulder, his face devoid of emotion. "He says Ikane is dead."

"He isn't. He's very much alive."

Benroar seemed to take in my words a moment, then he moved back to the tent he'd come from and ducked inside.

My body shuddered as I exhaled the tension in my muscles. Prince Benroar, deceivingly gentle and soft-spoken, intimidated me like a battle-ready cavalry standing on a hillside. Perhaps it was his resemblance to Ikane or the way his eyes remained so cold even when he smiled.

Leaning my head against the tree, I watched the long afternoon shadows grow darker as the sunlight faded somewhere behind the dead stumps reaching to building rainclouds in the sky.

No one made a move to take cover. As the light sank away, black-winged creatures soared among the midnight rainclouds, utterly disregarding the camp where scattered campfires sizzled and sparked. Alder was protecting the Leviathans. He had to be.

I glanced at the thick branches of the living woods to my left, a good five rods away. Even if Ropert, Leander, and the others had survived the attack, any attempt to spring from those woods and rescue me would be met with death. Phoenix, please, let them to have survived the attack. Let them find shelter from the Deathbiters.

CHAPTER 21

PRINCE BENROAR

*S*lushy white pellets showered my body and melted against my skin with an icy sting that sank into my bones. It was like the seasons couldn't decide if they should hang on to winter snow or warm to spring showers.

Stuck in their battle, I shivered, my lips trembled, my fingertips burned with cold. There was nothing I could do save let my head hang, watch the slush pelt the padded gambeson on my lap and melt under the moonlight, and pray my heartbeat didn't get any more erratic.

The noise of boots sinking into mud drew closer. I lifted my head, finding Prince Benroar standing before me, holding up a flickering lantern. A blanket draped over his arm, mocking the cold in my bones. At this point, it would take more than a blanket to warm me. But he made no motion to relieve my trembling. Instead, he turned his face to the sky, his damp hair shimmering in the lantern light.

"Not the most comfortable night to be sleeping under the stars, is it?" he mocked.

I couldn't still the shaking of my body or the quivering of my lips as I stared at the woolen blanket.

Benroar crouched, holding the lantern high. The light chased the edges of Mina's gift from my eyes.

"Your lips are blue," he said.

I looked away.

"Don't be an idiot," he said. "Tell me what I want to know, and I'll give you warmth and rest in my tent. How do you know Ikane? How do you know that Teilo is here?"

I forced myself not to look up. Teilo was here? My eyes scanned the moonlit streams of water running under my folded legs as this information dug into my mind. Teilo was the brother Ikane would do anything for, the like-minded one, the one his brothers threatened to kill if Ikane didn't do as they demanded. Even before he had been turned into this beast, Ikane had still been controlled.

But if Ikane knew Teilo was here, would he find himself again? Would he . . . ? I shook the hope from my mind, pushing it down. Ikane would tear me apart before I had the chance to utter Teilo's name. And this time, it wouldn't be because Alder had ordered him to. Ikane would kill me of his own volition.

Still, I couldn't let Benroar know that I had been taken by surprise or that he was feeding me more information than I was giving.

"Come now," Benroar urged, impatience growing in his voice. "There is a bowl of hot venison stew sitting on my table for you."

I licked the cold rain from my lips. I wanted it more than he knew, to stop the shaking and the terrible ache it caused in my chest.

"Ikane was my f-friend," I said.

He smiled. "Now we're getting somewhere. You say he *was* your friend. Why past tense?"

Now I looked up at him, watching the melting pellets glisten on his dark hair. "Because of what Alder did to him."

Benroar's face darkened. "And we're back to Alder," he muttered. "What has Alder supposedly done to my brother?"

"Ask him."

"I'm asking you."

"You w-won't believe me."

"You underestimate what I can comprehend, little Dagger."

That name tore my heart in half. Ikane called me his Little Brendagger and Ropert called me Dagger as long as I could remember. Hearing Benroar say it was like a violation of both.

My body shivered. I shut my eyes. I couldn't talk like this. I was too cold. In too much pain.

Benroar set the lamp on the ground and cupped my jaw in his warm hand, lifting my gaze to meet his. I inhaled sharply as he leaned close. His breath was balmy on my frozen skin, smelling of rich herbs from the venison stew he'd suggested could be mine. The warmth radiating off him sent a shiver down my spine. Then his deep-blue eyes scanned my face, lingering on my lips.

If I hadn't been so cold, I would have spit at his Ikane-like features.

"You got a bad dose of it, didn't you?" he finally said.

"Don't pretend you c-care," I said through chattering teeth.

"Not all Leviathans are heartless, Little Dagger." He released my jaw. Reaching around me, he tugged on the knot binding one of my wrists. Blood rushed through my shoulders, chest, and arms, burning like hot coals inside my skin as I dragged my hands forward—one sporting the other end of the rope like a bracelet.

Taking my elbow, Benroar pulled me to my feet and wound the rope around my wrists in front. "You'll tell me what I want to know, or I'll bring you right back. Understand?"

I wasn't sure if he could tell I was nodding through the shivering of my body.

After draping the blanket around my shoulders, he lifted the lantern from the wet earth, took my bound hands, and guided me across the open landscape into his tent.

I swallowed as we drew near. The way he'd looked at my face—at my lips—I knew I was not safe with him. Yet, I needed the warmth he could offer, or I would not survive the night—not with my heart throbbing so painfully as it was.

Benroar pulled the flap of his tent aside. "After you."

Cautiously, I ducked in. The temperature difference was immediate, stinging my cheeks and fingertips with warmth. I small firepit sat in the center, glowing with hot embers. A cot, table, and chair stood against the walls. From the scattering of papers, dirty dishes, candle wax drippings, and rumpled blankets and furs, I surmised that this tent had been here for some time. Even the firepit was rimmed carefully in stone. This was a military outpost, probably stationed here to prevent the very thing my troop had tried to do. They had simply spotted us first.

Benroar entered and set the lantern on the table. He removed the candle from inside and began lighting the candles clustered at the edge of his table. There sat the bowl of venison stew, rich with meat, steam curling into the cold night. I swallowed hard.

"You should get out of your wet things," Benroar said as he tousled his wet hair then shook his head like Ikane used to. His dark hair stood wild.

In my mind, I stiffened, everything inside me tingling with unease. But I forced my face to remain expressionless. My body, however, betrayed me by trembling violently. The warmth of his tent seemed to make it worse.

He shrugged as if my comfort made no difference to him then gestured to the folding stool by the table with worn leather stretched across the seat. "Eat. Stop your shivering so we can have a proper conversation."

I wasn't sure that was all he wanted to do. Still, I moved forward, scanning the tent for anything I could use to defend myself. I'd seen him fight. I would need to strike first, fast, and hard. I could use the candles, pitch the hot wax into his face. That would buy me enough time to steal the sword in his scabbard. But first, I wanted the soup.

"Do you intend to make me eat with my hands bound?"

"You can manage." He smirked then moved to his cot, removed his cloak, and sat on the edge. "I know a fighter when I see one. I see it in your eyes. You're as dangerous as they come."

Well, I'd tried. I slowly lowered myself to the stool.

He smiled, nodding to the hot stew. "Eat."

With my hands still bound, I cupped the wooden bowl. Oh, it was warm, stinging my fingers. I lifted it to my lips.

Benroar leaned forward on his knees. "Your wounds," he began, nodding to my bandaged wrist and torn gambeson. "Deathbiters?"

I swallowed the warm stew, feeling it sink into my stomach with heat, and lowered the dish. But the taste was lost as my body clung to survival. "No." I glanced at the chunks of meat and other vegetables floating in the thick broth, but only briefly. I had to keep my eyes on this pirate prince.

"Then where did you get them?"

I'd wanted him to hear the news from Alder, but he was ready and willing to listen to me now. "Ikane," I said.

His brow furrowed. "What?"

"These injuries were from your brother, Ikane."

"Ah," he said, leaning back with a knowing smile. "Then you know what he is. You must be special to him, indeed. Not all survive his attack as a lycanthrope."

He didn't understand . . . or he didn't know. I lowered the bowl to my lap, allowing the radiating warmth to seep into my damp trousers. "How long have you been in Roanfire?" I asked.

"Not long enough," he said.

"Have you heard rumors of a giant beast, half-man half-wolf, who can destroy entire squadrons? Tear a man apart with his bare hands? Rip out his throat?" A lump grew in my own throat as I spoke, but I shook it off.

Now Benroar tilted his head. This had sparked his interest.

"Alder," I began, "transformed Ikane into a half-breed pet whom he calls Marrok."

The pirate prince straightened, something churning in his eyes. He'd seen Ikane in his twisted form. I knew he had. He just didn't know that the creature slinking into shadows at the top of the stairs or creeping through the hallways of the Fold Garrison was his brother.

"Alder locked Ikane's memories away," I continued. "He does not remember who he is. He does not remember you or Teilo . . . or me."

Benroar's dark eyes watched me. Silence stretched on with only the pattering of the slush against the canvas tent filling the void. I took another sip of the stew, allowing a thick, tender piece of venison to slide into my mouth.

"You were right," Benroar finally said. "It is hard for me to believe you."

I felt my heart drop and all hope with it.

"But that doesn't mean I don't," he added, looking up at me. He stood.

I leapt to my feet. I would not be caught in a vulnerable position. I'd toss this soup at him if I had to.

He took a step closer. "You fear me."

I wanted to say I didn't, but in my current condition, I was no match for him. If it weren't for the terrible, unwieldy throbbing in my chest, I was sure I could hold my own.

But now that he was standing over me like a lion over prey, adrenaline soared. My heart thrummed like a hummingbird's wings inside my ribs. Everything inside the tent warped in my vision. My head felt as if it would float away. The bowl tipped, hitting the edge of the table, spilling at my feet. I braced myself against the edge. I could not fall unconscious here.

"You don't look well," Benroar said. "Is it your fever?"

I shut my eyes, trying to stop the spinning. But the noise of the pattering rain on the canvas grew more and more distant. *Feathers, not here.*

I clutched my heart as I tipped. Benroar's arms caught me, so solid, strong, and human, like Ikane's used to be. But they were also rough. My teeth slammed together as my resoluteness faded. Staying strong was no longer my priority. Surviving was.

Benroar's hand fell over mine. He pulled at them, clearly wanting to see what damage I was protecting. My heart raced faster. Was that really all he was after?

But he was stronger and pushed my bound hands away, drawing the neck of my tunic aside. His face hardened as he took in the deep-purple-and-red bruising there. "Ikane did this to you?" he asked.

"It was Marrok."

He scoffed as he released my hands. "Marrok. Ikane. What's the difference? He's always been a monster."

Something inside me broke as he said that, something that I hadn't even known was whole and holding onto hope. I thought he'd come to save his brother. But his tone indicated that he had come for Ikane with a completely different motive.

"Sit." Benroar spun me over to the cot. The back of my knees hit the edge, giving me little choice.

"You need rest, but I'll not have you soiling my bed with your soggy clothes," he announced. Reaching into a bag sitting at the foot of the cot, he shook out a large cotton shirt and tossed it at my lap. "Change."

I glanced at my bound wrists still protecting my chest. "You'll have to unbind me."

My heart throbbed harder as he drew a knife from his belt. Kneeling before me, he slid it between my arms, touching the edge of the rope. "Try anything, and this blade will sink into that purple bruise on your chest. Understand?" His breath was hot and smelled of an herb—not minty like Ikane's, but more earthy and sage-like.

"The same goes for you," I warned.

A smile spread on his lips with a chuckle. "I like you." He jerked the knife against my bonds, and the ropes fell away. I hadn't realized how much my wrists were aching until they were freed.

He stood and sat down on the stool, stabbing his knife into the tabletop.

I clutched his dry shirt in my hands. "You're not going to give me privacy?"

"This is my tent," he said.

He wasn't going to make this easy. I'd changed countless times in the barracks filled with soldiers, men and women alike. I'd learned some tricks to maintain my modesty, but with my ribs so sore and movement limited . . .

"At least turn your back," I reasoned.

"So you can stab it?" he asked. "Not a chance."

"I don't have a weapon."

He smiled. "I know."

He made my blood boil. And worse, seeing a face so close to Ikane's treating me the way Ikane never would, made my heart ache all over again.

I glowered at him as I kicked my boots off then began unbuckling the greaves on my thighs and remaining armor on my leg. The bracer on my wrist I removed last, tucking it under my thigh. It wasn't much of a weapon, but there was a sharp edge to it that—if I used it right—could cause some damage.

I wished I knew the Ridarri arts like Prince Leander. I wouldn't need a weapon. My entire body could become one.

Benroar watched me struggle to pull the heavy chainmail over my head.

"It would be much easier if you allowed me to help," he said.

The chainmail crashed at my feet, my body feeling weightless for the first time in days. I pushed my damp hair back and faced him. "You know, Ikane changed the way I thought about Leviathan pirates. But you? You're reminding me why I took up the sword in the first place."

He laughed and leaned forward, bracing his elbows on his knees, lacing his fingers together. "And just how did he change your mind about us pirates? Woo you? Run his hands through your hair? Pull you close, and show you passion?"

"No," I snapped. "He showed me kindness, compassion, and respect."

His smile faded. "Well." He leaned back. "I'm not Ikane."

He could say that again.

With my eyes staying on his, I jerked the buckles open on my gambeson and shrugged it from my shoulders. Another shiver tore through my body as cold air hit the final layer of my wet shirt.

Benroar's eyes grew deeper, greedier.

"You're a pig," I muttered as I grabbed his dry cotton top. Ropert would have come up with a much more inspired insult, but it was the best I could do.

I wanted to turn my back on him. But turning my back to an enemy would be a fatal mistake. Slowly, I pulled one arm from my shirt, slipping it though the neck, while keeping my chest covered.

His eyes scanned my skin—the numerous rose-gold stripes crisscrossing up to my shoulder, cutting down my back, sliding up to where the mottled rose scar blossomed on my throat.

The hunger in his eyes washed away. "What happened to you?"

"Were you expecting the flawless, supple skin of a lady?" I asked. Holding the neck of my shirt over the bruises on my sternum, I wriggled my other arm through, setting my teeth as the fabric snagged on the new sutures in my shoulder.

He stood abruptly. My hand clutched the bracer tucked under my thigh as he snatched my bandaged forearm.

"This mark," he said, leaning over the old traitor's brand on my shoulder. His fingers traced the raised image of the phoenix and the leviathan serpent locked in battle on my skin. "A traitor's brand?" he asked. "You're a friend to us?"

"I'm a friend to Ikane." I jerked my arm from his grip and grabbed his borrowed shirt from the bed.

He looked at me—not at my lips or womanly curves, but at me. The look alone stopped my heart from trying to escape the confines of my chest.

"You're as mystifying as a siren song," he said.

"I'm as simple as the rain pelting the tent if only you'd listen."

He sighed then moved to the fire . . . keeping his back to me. I raised an eyebrow at the rippling muscles in his shoulders as he added new logs to the flame. "Anyone who has survived what you have deserves more than to be heard. Forgive me, Dagger. I have mistreated you."

He said my name simply, respectfully. Was it really as effortless as showing him the brand to prove that I was no enemy?

Quickly, I pulled his shirt over my head, hiding my body inside as if it were a tent. It smelled of mildew, salt, and sea— like him.

"You don't even know what happened," I said as I wriggled my rain-soaked shirt down my legs.

"I can speculate. I've seen Ikane hurt people before."

"Phoenix, no," I snapped, appalled that he would think that Ikane was capable of something like this. "These scars are Alder's doing."

Benroar's head lifted, but he didn't look back at me. "Again, you blame Alder. What has that man done to you?"

"He's no friend to anyone," I said, struggling to remove my sticky, wet woolen stockings and trousers.

"He's kept his word to us."

I dragged a fur over my bare legs and tucked them under, keeping the bracer close. "He's manipulating you."

Now Benroar's head tilted my direction. "How?"

"Using you to take over Roanfire."

Benroar stood and dusted his hands off on his trousers. "You seem to have a twisted view of who is using whom. I needed his help to infiltrate Meldron. Roanfire will be ours by the planting season. All that stands in our way now is a soldier by the name of Keatep Brendagger. Do you know her?"

Thankfully, my shivering helped keep my face from showing any emotion. "All of Roanfire knows of her," I said. "They say she is a hero."

His eyes darkened as he sat down and grabbed the hilt of his knife still embedded in the table. "Not in our eyes. She has power too strong for any one person to wield. Power that my people have feared would arise since we were driven from Roanfire's shores."

I narrowed my eyes at him. "Power?"

"Legend tells of a jewel, a lost heirloom." His knuckles turned white as his grip tightened on the knife. "We believe it has been found by Keatep Brendagger." He said my name through his teeth. The anger burning in his eyes was like an inferno, waiting to unleash the moment he found his target. It was so strong that even my little ember of Thrall could smell it like fresh-baked bread wafting down the street.

He tore the knife from the table. "She must be stopped."

Pushing the dark magic down, I hugged the gray-and-white fur tighter, hiding my frozen hands inside. I wanted to tell him that Alder was in possession of this ruby at this very moment. That he was siding with the danger he wanted to beat down. But Benroar wasn't a fool. He would wonder how I knew, and he would realize that I was the soldier he was looking for.

"No one should have that much power." I whispered.

He cocked his head. "Are you on our side?"

I shook my head. "I am loyal to Roanfire. But I do hope for peace between our people."

"That brand on your shoulder says otherwise. We could use someone like you."

"I won't spy for you, if that's what you're suggesting."

"Roanfire rightfully belongs to us. Simian Ormand was tricked by Rion Noirfonika to hand over his land centuries ago. She was corrupt and devious. Alder promised to help us reclaim it."

Alder was good. I could see his plan now. He spoke the truth. He would help them conquer Roanfire, but in the end, it would become Rion's kingdom. The Leviathans were nothing but tools to him. "He's lying," I muttered.

"Alder has cleared the way for us to march straight into Meldron and take it." He leaned forward again, resting his elbow on his knee while holding his knife casually. "Your king is dead, and we have your queen locked in our stronghold, guarded by an army of over eight thousand men."

It took everything inside me to keep my brows from shooting up, but inside, I choked. Eight thousand? That was twice the number Rion had devoured the first time. How in the blazes did this go unnoticed? How had we not seen the ships coming and going? And how was a desolate place like this sustaining so many?

"Ah, look at me. Revealing vital information when you have yet to share anything with me."

"I already told you where to go to get the information you want."

"Alder." He chuckled, but there was an uneasiness to it, like he was uncertain he wanted to speak with Alder again. I didn't blame him.

"Tell me one thing," he said. "Where did you meet my brother, Ikane?"

"In Daram," I said. "He was looking for help from a warrior there."

"Help?"

I met his eyes. "You know what Ikane was doing. He was trying to warn us about you. My home was Daram, and you destroyed it."

"That we did," he said, but his tone wasn't that of pleasure or triumph. It was tainted with remorse. That piqued my interest about this man. Was he not as ruthless as I thought?

"You didn't agree?"

"It's complicated," he said and pinched out a candle. "I think we've talked enough tonight. Rest. It would be a shame for you to die of fever when you've already survived so much."

I pulled my knees up, hugging the blankets and furs around me.

"You know, it's easier to sleep when you're lying down," Benroar suggested as he extinguished all the candles with a pinch. Only the glow of the crackling fire radiated against our faces.

"Where will you sleep?" I asked.

"Are you offering?"

"No, I . . ."

"You'd be warmer."

"I'm warm enough."

Chuckling, he reached over. My hand dropped to the cold bracer still sitting beside my thigh, fingers curling around the curved metal. But he simply grabbed one of the many furs scattered across his bed and dragged it to him. "Can you blame me for trying? A beautiful warrior in my bed with nothing but my shirt to cover her. Ikane was a lucky man."

He shrugged the fur onto his shoulders and folded his arms on the tabletop. "Sleep," he ordered.

Slowly, I sank onto my side, curling my legs tight and holding the metal bracer even tighter.

He rested his head atop his arms and closed his eyes.

I had to find a way out of here before he discovered who I was. Traitor's brand or no, he wouldn't protect me once he knew I was Keatep Brendagger.

CHAPTER 22

PRISONERS

$\mathcal{M}$y body ached like it had been thrown from a horse, trampled, and thrown again. The drizzling sound of rain no longer pattered overhead, and a warm light radiated through the canvas with the promise of sun. My hand still held the bracer like a weapon.

And then I remembered where I had fallen asleep. My eyes shot wide, and, despite the ache in my muscles, I sat up. The table and stool where I'd last seen the Leviathan prince stood empty. My clothing hung by the fire, which had been built up again, draped over barrels and other crates.

"I said no prisoners." An angry voice from outside spread through the tent. It sounded like Prince Benroar. "Now you bring me two?"

Climbing from the bed, I snatched my trousers and shoved my legs inside.

"This one is from Toleah," another voice said. "It took four men to hold him down."

I stiffened. Toleah? Stumbling to the tent door, I peered through the cracked flap with one eye. Benroar stood with his back to the tent, hands on his hips, speaking to a group of pirates holding prisoners. Flaming feathers, they had Prince

Leander! He knelt between two pirates, ropes looping around his torso in layers, with his hands bound behind his back. Another rope cut into his mouth, and more cords stretched from his ankles into the hands of two more pirates, no doubt to keep him from kicking his way free—which I knew he could.

I tried to see the other prisoner, but the body was hidden by the tent flap and a group of pirates. All I could make out were the dirty white cotton sleeves of a shirt and dark leather boots.

Leander's golden eyes glowered at Benroar as he approached. "Toleah?" Benroar mused. "What would a Tolean be doing with a Roanfirien scouting party? And one who fights like a Ridarri without the symbolic tattoos."

Leander's golden eyes burned as Benroar approached and grabbed a fistful of dreadlocks. He jerked Leander's head to the side, checking something behind his ear—the tattoo I'd seen while tending to his Deathbiter injuries. Leander's eyes slammed shut as his nostrils flared.

"Ah!" I could hear the smile and realization in Benroar's voice as he found the mark. He released Leander's hair then gave him a mock bow. "Your Highness. What an honor to have the prince of Toleah in my camp." He turned to his warriors with a smile, raising a fist. "We came to conquer one kingdom, but now we have the leverage to conquer two."

The pirates around him chuckled and cheered.

Leander jerked against his bonds, but they held him firm.

"And who is this other one?" Benroar turned to the last prisoner. I craned my neck as he reached for them in a motion that indicated he'd grabbed the prisoner's hair or neck. Feathers, I couldn't see.

"This man," a pirate announced, "is the personal bodyguard of Lady Keatep Brendagger."

Was it Sir Ian . . . or Ropert?

The pirate's voice went dark. "She was there, Prince Benroar. She was within our grasp, and we failed."

Benroar frowned as he dropped the prisoner and stepped back. Slowly, his eyes lifted to the tent. "Probably not . . ."

My face grew cold. Even at this distance, I could feel his hatred churn, feel the storm rising, rippling across the way. Thrall flickered awake again, wanting to partake.

Staggering back, I snatched my bracer from the cot, searching for a way out, another weapon, anything. I hurried behind the smoldering fire. At least it would buy me some time. Still, I wished I had time to replace my stockings and boots.

Daylight flared into the tent as the flap was pushed aside. Benroar's tall frame filled the opening, and with him, an air of danger.

"Do you have something you need to tell me, Dagger?" Benroar spat. "Or should I say Brendagger?"

I swallowed hard, moving with him as he circled the fire, keeping it between us.

"You thought you could hide your identity behind beauty, scars, treacherous brands, and lies?" he demanded. "Take advantage of my sympathy?"

"I did not mean to deceive you."

Lightning flashed in his raging sea-blue eyes, and his hand fell to the hilt of his sword at his hip. If it left that scabbard, I wouldn't stand a chance. Still, I shifted my stance, holding the bracer like a minuscule, useless shield, watching his weapon.

"I'm not your enemy, Benroar."

"An entire army of Leviathan pirates are dead because of you!"

"That wasn't me! Don't you think if I had magic I would have used it to flee this camp by now? It was the ruby. The one you spoke of. Yes, I found it. But I have been trying to destroy it."

Silver glinted as his sword peeked from its sheath.

"Alder has the Phoenix Stone," I said quickly.

His hand froze. "What?"

"He sent Marrok to take it from me. That's where these injuries came from." I placed a hand on my chest. "Please believe me. I am doing everything in my power to destroy her."

"Her?"

Was now the time to explain? It sure wasn't the time to lie. "Rion Noirfonika's soul is inside that stone," I began. "It was designed to hold her until she gathered enough power for rebirth. She's a curse to us all, Benroar."

He circled again, and I moved in kind.

"You lie," he said. "If you meant to destroy it, you would have done so."

"It cannot be crushed by a hammer," I said. "I've tried. I let it smolder in a forge until the setting melted away, but the stone remained whole. It can only be destroyed by magic."

"But you don't have magic." His head tilted suspiciously.

I bit my lip.

"You do, don't you?" His eyes narrowed.

"I did not use it against the pirates in Meldron."

"But you have used it."

I wanted to say no with a clear conscience, but I couldn't. I had used my powers by accident several times, hurting my friends and frightening soldiers. There were witnesses. I couldn't lie, but telling the truth could be just as dangerous.

I lowered my hands. "Please, just ask Alder about it."

He straightened, and his own hand dropped from his sword. "I intend to." He held out his palm, indicating the bracer.

Reluctantly, I handed it over.

He turned it in his hand. "If you truly do have magic, why would you choose to use this as a weapon?"

I swallowed, waiting, watching his eyes as they processed his own question.

Finally, he pitched the bracer across the tent. Striking the canvas with a dull thud, it dropped to the earth. Then he stepped around the fire, and his hand shot out and pinched my elbow in a vicelike grip.

"Alder will know what to do with you," he said. With that, he dragged me outside. Sunlight struck my eyes, forcing me to squint against the brightness. Cold mud slid between my toes as I stumbled after him and into the crowd of Leviathan warriors.

Jerking me to his side, he raised his voice. "The hunt is over! Keatep Brendagger is ours!"

Noise erupted from the gathering crowd. Some were cheers, others were snarls, and three pirates—that I could see—spat my direction. Panic filled Prince Leander's golden eyes. He fought against the hands of his captors, managing to get a foot under himself, but the moment he did, a pirate tugged on the rope attached to his ankle, sending Leander to the ground.

"Kill her!" someone shouted. "Kill her now!"

"Her blood will be ours," Benroar assured them. "But there are questions that need answering." His dark eyes looked down at me, flaring with a warning that if he discovered that what I'd said was false, he would run me through.

"Bind the prisoners over there," he ordered, gesturing to a cluster of dead stumps reaching to the sky. A prisoner already sat in the mud there with his hands stretched behind his back, his head hanging low. I didn't recognize him.

My heart began an aching throb as Benroar shunted me into the arms of pirates. Their grips were pinching and harsh, almost as if they were trying to break my bones. Pain flared through my head as someone struck my temple. I flinched as something cold hit the back of my neck, trickling down my spine. I could only suppose it was spittle.

My captors shouldered me through the mass of angry faces, deflecting the harshest blows. Still, I would have new bruises.

Spinning me around, they lashed my arms around the trunk of a tree beside the stranger. Leander was also brought forward and strapped to another trunk in an inhumane standing position. They bound his feet and arms to the tree, wrapping the ropes twice around his torso and thighs. They did not underestimate his skill.

Once again, I could not see the fourth prisoner through the mass of pirates. I ached to know if they had captured Ropert or Sir Ian, but the commotion across the way indicated he was also being restrained.

I gritted my teeth as my arms were pulled taut. The cords around my wrists bit deep, and my fingers cried for blood. A pirate stepped around the tree, his face hard. He was young, not much older than myself.

"This is for my father," he snarled as his fist slammed into my gut. All air pushed from my lungs in a painful burst. I gasped, hanging on my ropes, wishing I could curl over.

Pirates laughed. Some jeered. Leander fought against his bonds, golden eyes burning with fight, nostrils flaring. Muffled noises came from behind the gag over his mouth.

A strange redness flashed behind my eyes, biting my temples with burning pain. My heart tore into panicked beats. This wasn't from the punch. This was . . .

There you are. Rion's voices spoke like thunder, rumbling together. Heat bled from my temples into the rest of my body and soul like a tumbling rockslide of glowing coals.

It had happened. Alder had freed her. Ikane had given him the Stone. She burned with access to all her power—everything I had tried to sever from her.

In a desperate panic, I called my white stars of Etheria to me, throwing up a wall, protecting my mind. The familiar pounding against my temples resumed as Rion knocked and scraped. But she wasn't anxious or incensed. No, she pounded and scraped with intimidating deliberation, like a monster in the night whose sole purpose was to cause fear.

Your time has come, Phoenix Daughter. There was a smile in her voices.

I gasped and choked for breath as the air grew thick and heavy. Tender patches of spring grass grew brittle under my feet. The moss clinging to dead trees turned brown and shriveled. Saplings wilted, and the muddy ground cracked into mosaic patterns as all moisture sucked away. It crusted against my bare feet, turning to dust.

The jeers from the pirates faded as they backed away, looking around with wide eyes. Only Benroar stood forward, his eyes dark as he watched me.

"I . . . I'm not doing this," I gasped.

"Kill her," a pirate said. "Before she kills us all."

This was not good.

Benroar's sword hissed from its sheath, and sunlight glinted against the polished edge. He took a step forward.

Leander's muffled protests grew louder.

"This isn't me!" I cried. "I lifted the curse from the Dead Forest when I found the Phoenix Stone in the ruins of the Fold Garrison. This death around us? It means the Stone has been returned. Alder has it! Please, Benroar. If you believe anything I said, believe this. We are all in danger here."

I flinched and slammed my teeth together as Rion struck hard. Bowing my head, I felt the familiar trickle of blood run down my nose and touch my lip. "Please . . . believe me."

A silky whiteness wrapped around my mind. The fire faded as it pulled my mind away, dragging me deeper . . . deeper . . .

CHAPTER 23

HIS TRUE FORM

*T*he smell of lilies flooded my senses, pungent and sweet. It was his smell. Yotherna. The smell that always accompanied my visions of him. But this was the first dream where I felt the ground beneath my feet. Not the sensation of boots on a hard surface, but the touch of a cool stone floor under my bare soles.

"Keatep." His voice was so close and so real, as if I actually stood before him. Not the hazy echo of a dream. The sound through my ears was vastly different from the creamy voice in my visions. He sounded tired and weak, his voice shaking with effort.

Why couldn't I see him? Why couldn't I see anything? I could feel the warmth of sunlight dancing on my face and a hot breeze brushing my skin, but my vision remained black.

I groped the air, stumbling forward. "Yotherna? Where . . . where am I? Why can't I see?" My fingers brushed against something soft and flowing. Fabric? A curtain. The sheer white curtains I'd seen flowing in the breeze every time we met in this strange dreamland, I realized. But this was beginning to feel less and less like a dream. I tightened my hand around the fabric to be sure, to see if it would fade when my fist clutched tight. It didn't. The fabric remained, the texture soft against my skin, real.

"Be still, child." He gathered a rattling breath. "You are in a place . . . between minds. A place . . . between reality and a dream." He inhaled, the sound rough and frightening against my ears.

"What is wrong with you?" I asked. "Why does your voice sound so different?"

For a moment, only the sound of his labored breathing filled my ears, like he was struggling for the right words. Then, like a black fog evaporating in the morning light, the darkness over my eyes began to fade.

White, green, red, and blue sparks danced around the form of a man who gradually came into focus, sitting in a cradle of vibrant blue, green, and yellow embroidered pillows. His white hair draped over a large cushion supporting his back. He was beautiful. An angelic version of Alder—young, lean, with perfect features, dressed in white robes of Tolean design.

The lights floating around him were sprites! Dozens of elemental sprites whirred by. His eyes morphed between pale green, blue, and pink blush, like ink swirling in water as coordinating sprites drew closer.

"This is not . . . how I had hoped to meet," he said with a forced smile.

He looked so vulnerable, so frail. This was not the man from my visions.

"I have wanted to come to you," he said. "Guide you. Be by your side as I should have with the first princess of Roanfire. But . . ." His hand jerked on the pillow beside him, like he was trying to lift it. He couldn't. He couldn't move at all. The pillows around him were his support, holding his body upright, cradling his limbs.

Feathers, what had happened to him?

His image blurred and shifted, like he was splitting in two. Like a ghost leaving a body, a transparent form of himself rose from the weak body lying on the pillows. Standing tall and strong, he glanced back at his disabled body, which now lay on the pillows with eyes closed.

"The day I trapped Karreth was the day I became this," the ghostly version said. His voice was strong again, creamy and rich—but also filled with a dreamlike essence. He looked back at me. "Forgive me, Keatep. It is easier for me to speak to you in this form."

I swallowed, comparing both versions of this man. "What happened to you?"

"It happened the day I trapped Karreth in the rocks of Glacier Pass."

"You trapped him there?"

He nodded, sadness spreading through his flickering eyes. "You were never meant to face him. He was to remain sealed away until one from the Noirfonika line would put an end to both the Phoenix Stone and our link to her. End us all."

"What?"

His eyes shimmered pale blue then morphed to violet and silver. "Centuries ago, before Roanfire was born, my brother, Karreth, fell in love with the young rising queen, Rion Noirfonika. They were wed, and soon after their third child was born, Rion fell ill with an incurable disease. Fear overwhelmed their sanity. They searched desperately for a way to save her and tampered with dark magic."

"Thrall," I whispered.

He gave me the slightest nod and swallowed hard. "They began forging the Phoenix Stone, but Karreth failed. He came to me for help. I loved my brother and could not bear to see him in so much pain."

"So you helped," I said. "You finished what they had started."

"Yes, and by so doing, we have become ensnared by her. Our lives are bound to the ruby as much as hers is."

"You mean . . . Alder cannot be killed unless the ruby is destroyed?" I asked.

"Yes."

I blinked. "And you?"

He smiled. "Sweet Kea, do not mourn for me. My time has long been overdue. I have yearned for the end, to rest both soul and body since the day Rion devoured the life of her firstborn daughter. I felt the corruption, the change, the growing hunger, and I did nothing to stop it. When Karreth gifted the ruby to a princess who passed away before her first year, I finally found the courage to confront him. Our battle was sore and long." He looked back at his crippled form. "Merchants from Toleah found me under the rocks and brought me here, where I have watched, mourned, and strived to aid the princesses tormented by Rion's curse."

This was why he had not come to me. He couldn't. Instead, he'd stretched his mind across Roanfire to guide me as best he could, like he was doing now.

"How?" I asked. "How do I do it? Please, tell me." I clutched onto the curtain, afraid the dream would vanish before the answer came—as it always did. "Tell me plainly. No riddles. No mysteries."

He watched me a moment longer. "Your heart?"

"It'll mend," I said.

"In its fragile state, it may not be able to handle the truth." He reached a pale hand toward me, his slender fingers lifting to my heart. "I can mend what is broken there now, but you will need to mend what will break after."

His words were like the apprehensive shaking of the earth as an army approached fortress walls. Did I really want to hear the truth? Did I really want to know what terrible thing I had to do to defeat Rion?

What choice did I have?

Yotherna's cold fingers touched my chest. His face grew tight with concentration as white light flared across my skin, sinking deep with warmth. The bruised pounding of my heartbeats no longer ached. Even my ribs stopped throbbing with every expansion of my lungs.

I hadn't realized how shallowly I had been breathing until this moment. I inhaled the warm air around us, smelling the heat *of the Tolean desert and the hint of lilies wafting from Yotherna's skin.*

He stepped away. "What I am about to tell you can break you, Keatep. Are you truly prepared?"

"I am." This was what I had been waiting for, searching for, begging for.

He inhaled slowly through his nose, closing his eyes. "Rion has stolen endless lives," he began. "She feeds on frightened and uncertain energy. Though it may seem endless, it is weak. However, a single life given willingly holds more power than a hundred thousand frightened souls."

That word resonated through my mind with terrifying truth. Willingly. Ropert had said as much when I'd nearly destroyed him.

"You have felt the strength within you as the keys offered their energy."

I had. I remembered the strength and power that flowed with my Etheric lights whenever they were near. Ikane's blue energy had helped me first. Ropert . . . my dear Ropert. I'd almost killed him by using too much. And Leander's power was firm and grounding. I had yet to experience Broderick's support, but I'd felt him before, when I had been recovering from my initial Deathbiter attack. I hadn't known it at the time, but now—

Why did Yotherna look so somber? Wasn't this a good thing? Wasn't this hope?

His eyes flashed green as an earthsprite fluttered by. "You cannot face her alone. You know this. The four keys are your strength. You have the sword, who is also the energy of fire. You have felt him and used him."

"Ropert," I whispered.

"You have the compassion of a prince," he continued, "raised and tutored for this purpose—the energy of the earth."

"Prince Leander."

Yotherna continued. "You have uncovered the shadow in light and wisdom, who is also the power of the wind. The young assassin named Broderick."

He didn't need to say it. The last was water. Ikane. The friend and foe. I knew it.

"So," I began, "if they help me and work together, we can end her?"

He nodded once, but his countenance didn't lift.

"What's wrong? What aren't you telling me?"

Yotherna's eyes shimmered blue. "There is no delicate way to say this, Keatep. You will, in the end, kill them."

"What?" My face went cold.

"You will need all the strength they can offer."

I began to shake, and my heart throbbed hard and fast. My hand dropped from the curtain, my lungs suddenly finding the air hard to breathe. "No. You don't mean that. They are strong together. Like an army. We support and protect each other. We watch each other's backs. We . . ."

Yotherna was shaking his head.

"You . . . you want me to take their . . ." I couldn't say it. I couldn't finish. Tears burned my eyes as I choked on the air. My heart ached more than I thought possible, more than losing Eamon and King Sander, more than when it had been bruised and broken.

I understood now why he had healed me. I staggered back, hoping to fall out of this nightmare, wanting to get as far away from the paralyzed marble man as possible. How could he do this? How could he design something so cruel?

"I wish there was another way." The ghostly form of Yotherna gathered a shaky breath. Something glittered down his perfectly chiseled cheek. A tear. How dare he weep. He did this! He created the curse, and I was the one who had to sacrifice my dearest friends to destroy her. Hadn't I lost enough already?

"No." Why was my voice so silent, so strangled? I wanted to scream it. Feel the word tear through my throat, scar it, permanently ring through all ends of Roanfire.

There had to be another way. Something Yotherna hadn't tried. Something he'd overlooked. "They'll be fine if they are together," I said, my voice holding a pleading edge. "I won't need to use all of their strength."

His ghostly image moved closer. "I'm afraid not."

I jerked away as he raised a hand to my shoulder. "Get away from me!"

He froze, pain filling his beautiful, perfect face. He was weeping. "I am sorry."

"You . . . you're a monster." Now, my voice found its strength, booming through the dream. "You're just like her. You're just like Alder!"

Thrall flickered awake and tasted the rage rising inside, growing larger, wrapping its black mist around me. And I let it. I let the darkness of Thrall seep into my mind and wrap around my memories like a black fog rolling over the sea. It covered anything light, anything that would have anchored my mind and helped me withstand the blows of the angry waves. Why should I try to resist when I was going to lose everything, anyway?

"No, Keatep." Yotherna's voice was like a single beam of sunlight forcing its way through the clouds, trying to offer hope. "Don't give up. Please, don't give up. You are all Roanfire has left."

"Then Roanfire is lost!"

He flinched as black smoke rippled out with my cry, striking him. His ghostly white skin hissed as mottled blackness spread. Even his physical self—the paralyzed form of a man lying on the pillows—groaned as blackness spread up his neck. Tears leaked from his closed lashes.

"Rion cannot be right!" I screamed. "I am not like her!"

"You are nothing like her, Keatep," Yotherna said, his face contorted in pain. "Take comfort in knowing that I, too, will perish the day you shatter the Phoenix Stone. The magic will end. You will never need to wield it again."

"But they are my friends!"

"Would taking the lives of strangers make a difference?"

I shook my head, tearing my hands through my hair as Thrall continued to swirl around me like the smoke from a recently extinguished candle. "I can't do it ... I won't. I ..." I was breaking. This was what I had searched for. An answer, a solution. But I never imagined that I would lose the very things that motivated me to fight.

"Their sacrifice would be saving everyone from the burning tyranny Rion will inflict," Yotherna said. "Heroes. Legends who would never die."

He sounded just like Rion. "Shut up," I growled, shutting my eyes. "Shut up." I hated him. Hated him more than Alder and Rion combined.

He was right. My heart could not take this.

Turning around, I fled to the edge of this dreamlike reality. Darkness closed in, and the ground beneath my feet disappeared. I was falling. And I hoped I would fall into a forever nothingness.

CHAPTER 24

NUMB

My eyes cracked open. Brown earth looked back, parched and fractured, holding imprints of a dozen boot prints from the pirates who had bound me here. It was dead, just as I felt inside.

Long shadows stretched from a patch of withered grass at my bare feet. Dry. Everything was dry, parched, brittle, like raindrops had never touched the earth. The spring blades of grass hung limp and brown, moss crumbled, and the infant trees dropped their petals. Rion had claimed her place in Fold once again, sucking it dry of life.

No birds sang. No wind rushed by. Even if it had, I couldn't have felt it. I barely felt my body at all, even though I knew it was aching.

I lifted my head, barely seeing the two figures bound to the trees across the way through the strands of hair falling over my eyes. One was the prisoner I'd seen before. He sat silently in the roots of the tree, head of dark hair bowed, clothing torn and old, limbs as thin as a starving child. A thin beard covered his youthful jaw. A boy. No older than eighteen. Only two years ago, I had been his same age—when the nightmares first began. Now, I felt like I had aged into an old, battered woman.

My heart plummeted further at the sight of the man—the bodyguard—tethered to the tree beside him. Blood streaked down the side of his face, staining the cotton shirt at his shoulder as it dripped. The white stripe in his hair stood out like a warning, reminding me of everything Yotherna had said. I was Ropert's undoing. I was going to kill him—if the pirates hadn't already.

"Ropert?" I croaked his name.

He didn't move.

I shut my eyes.

Kea? The voice was soft and gentle, flowing with grounding green energy, politely entering my mind like a friend looking in on someone ill. *Are you alright?*

What are you doing here, Leander? Lifting my head, I glanced beside me. Leander was watching me through his bonds, a rope still cutting into his mouth.

His golden eyes shimmered with concern. *You are burning with Thrall,* he sent to me.

So what if I am? I looked away, glowering at the pirate campfires being lit for the night. Prince Benroar stood there, his hand on his sword, speaking with a handful of Leviathans. Why hadn't they fled the Dead Forest? More importantly, why hadn't Rion taken them already? Why hadn't she taken any of us? She was free, wasn't she? I still felt her constant hammering in my skull.

What happened, Kea? Leander pressed.

I glowered back at him. *You knew. You knew I would be forced to steal . . . take . . . use your soul in order to defeat her. Why didn't you warn me? Why didn't you run?*

Because this is my destiny.

No. It isn't. Your destiny isn't to die by my hand. It's wrong and twisted, and Yotherna should have never designed anything so . . . so heartless.

If I can save your life, then I will gladly do it.

I turned away again. I didn't want to be saved.

The boy stirred. His face scrunched in pain as he lifted his head and squinted at us. He looked just like a younger version of Ikane, with dimpled cheeks and a dirt-smudged jaw clinging to hints of childhood. I squinted at a pendant hanging around his neck. It looked like two swords crossing . . . two swords just like the ones Ikane used.

"Teilo?" I asked.

He blinked at me. "Do I . . . know you?" His voice was hoarse, broken.

It *was* Teilo. The dark vapors of Thrall dissipated as my heart reached out to the brother Ikane had tried to protect all these years. But . . .

"I thought you'd be older," I said. "I thought Ikane was the seventh prince. The youngest."

"Ikane?" His green eyes lit up. "You know him? Is he . . . is he alright?"

My gaze dropped. "No, he's not. He hasn't been for a while."

The light in Teilo's green eyes faded.

"Why did Benroar bring you here?" I asked.

Teilo scoffed. "Because he knows Ikane will do anything to protect me. Even come back to us," he said. "I keep telling him I'm not worth it, but he won't listen. He's determined to make my brothers see Roanfire for what it is—or was. He thinks we can make peace."

"Do you think we can?" I asked.

He let his lower lip slide between his teeth. "I want to. With the right people, I think it is possible." Then he shook his head. "But that's beside the point. If you know where Ikane is, can you get a warning to him? This is a trap, and I am the bait, as usual. Benroar has orders to kill him for betraying us."

"Orders from whom?"

"High Prince Accalon, our eldest brother."

That was a name I hadn't heard yet. "Is he here? Accalon?"

Teilo shook his head then sucked air through his teeth as the motion caused him pain. "He hasn't left the isles."

"How many of you are there? I was always led to believe that there are seven princes."

Teilo gave me a crooked, weak smile, showing an adorable dimple on the side of his cheek. "We are nine in total. Not all brothers, though. And I am the youngest." He said that last part darkly, like there was more to his story than he was willing to tell, something that bordered on years of abuse and heartache—just like Ikane had endured by the hands of his brothers.

"So there are sisters in your family, then?"

"Aye. But only one living. Kindra. Pray you don't ever meet her."

Why hadn't Ikane ever told me this? This boy was revealing more than Ikane ever had. A part of me awakened. If Ikane couldn't protect Teilo anymore, then I would.

A commotion erupted at the edge of the camp. Pirates rose to their feet as a pair of horses approached bearing two cloaked riders. One, I knew. I'd recognize his tall, lean form and black attire anywhere. His steely hair flowed down his back as beautifully as Yotherna's white strands. Alder.

The other rider seemed familiar. A woman. It was hard to determine any more than that at this distance, as a hood shrouded her face.

Benroar approached them in greeting, taking the reins of Alder's horse. Alder's silver eyes glanced in my direction as he dismounted. He said something to Benroar, who also looked over his shoulder at me.

Hate clawed its way forward, feeding into the dark magic already swirling inside me. I wanted to release it on him, on all of them.

Alder raised his arms and helped the woman from the back of her horse. She linked arms with him, and I stiffened as the motion revealed a crimson-red gown beneath her dark cloak. Then he led her forward, following Prince Benroar as they approached us.

Somehow, I couldn't take my eyes off the woman. She walked with a familiar grace, yet it was tinted with an arrogance I didn't remember. Golden rings adorned her fingers, glinting in the fading daylight. Her blood-red painted lips held a strange smile.

Alder stopped a few paces away, his silver eye watching me intently. His other eye—though milky-white and dead—still seemed to see through me. He smiled, looking terrible and beautiful all at once.

"Leave us," he barked at Benroar.

The pirate prince hesitated, and I hoped my expression would convince him to remain. He glanced at Teilo then turned and walked back to the tents.

"Keatep Brendagger, darling," Alder said in his deep voice that always made my chest rumble. "I didn't believe it when they said you were here. A great warrior like yourself, a woman capable of unimaginable power and magic, bound to a tree, prisoner to Leviathan pirates. I see you've made some progress with your use of Thrall. Isn't it invigorating?"

I hardened my eyes at him, and my blood-starved fingers curled into fists behind me. "Where is Queen Lonacheska?"

"What? Do you not recognize this beauty standing beside me?" He brought the woman forward.

My heart pounded harder as I noted the roundness of her stomach beneath the cloak. She reached up and pulled the hood from her head, revealing locks of long golden hair and the face of my queen. But her eyes . . .

I gasped. They burned white like overheated coals in a forge, illuminating her skin.

"Rion . . ."

"Hello, Phoenix Daughter," she said.

My stomach clenched. It was the voice of my queen but the words of my enemy. Red shimmered at her throat as she stepped forward. The ruby. She was wearing it.

"You look surprised to see me," she said.

Feathers, scales, honey puffs, and whatever curses Leander used in his native tongue. She was here.

I stiffened, holding my breath when she stopped before me. Heat radiated from her hand as she lifted it and set it against my cheek. There was no time to think, no time to reach for the white lights of Etheria. Just fire. Bubbling hot oil slipping down my throat, smoldering coals filling my chest, smoke burning my nose and eyes.

"You can end this," she whispered.

I cried out wherever I could, however I could. Body, mind, soul . . . it didn't matter. The scream was all I had left, all I could manage through the pain.

"I will give you one last chance to become the honored host of my reborn self," Rion continued. "To rise with me, through me, become me."

Everything inside me turned black, cracking, breaking apart as her fire tore through everything I was. I could smell her— burnt flesh, melted ore, snuffed out candles, lightning, ash. Or was that me?

"What do you choose?"

I'm here, Kea! Leander's rich energy expanded like a spring meadow in the mountains. He surrounded me as if I'd stepped into the warm embrace of a forest, the shelter of a mighty oak standing against an onslaught of wind. Green light began wrapping around my white stars like warm earth around a seed. He enveloped me in vines and flowers and curled through my center with life.

Rion flinched, her hand retracting quickly. Her white eyes burned as she turned to Prince Leander. "So that was you." She moved toward him. "Back in Meldron, that was you as well. My, but you are succulent."

I gasped and panted for breath. Blood dripped from my nose, turning into red pearls in the dry earth at my feet. "Leave him alone," I panted.

One touch. That's all it would take, and she would have him.

She didn't stop.

I shut my eyes and reached for Leander's energy. I had to protect him, build a wall around him before she stole his soul and added it to her millions.

He reached back, wrapping my Etheric lights in his verdant power. He gave me everything he had, like leaves bursting magically from an ancient tree. It terrified me. But without it, I could not help him.

I created a shield around him, snapping it tight just before her hand touched his jaw.

Her brows furrowed when she could not take him. She pulled the rope from his mouth, letting her finger trace his bottom lip as she tilted her head at him. "She's protecting you, isn't she?"

Leander jerked his face from her touch.

"Very well, then." She turned her attention to Ropert.

Feathers, no. "Ropert!" I called. "Ropert, wake up!"

He didn't move.

Rion's sable cloak dragged in the dust as she approached him.

Ropert, please! Again, I shut my eyes and raced to him. His mind was shut, asleep, lost to me.

Leander's green energy brushed up against mine. *I am still here, Kea. Together, we can help him.*

He was offering more, but I'd already used too much.

Hurry, Kea, he cautioned, *or she will take him.*

What else could I do? I accepted Leander's strength and built another shield, wrapping Ropert's sleeping mind inside. Again, Rion was too late. As she placed her hand atop the white strand of hair on his head, she frowned.

I glanced at Leander. Panic flooded my bloodstream when I saw him hanging by the ropes in weakness, his dreadlocks falling over his face. He was alive, yes, but severely drained. And I had done it to him.

Rion spun to me again, rage burning in her eyes. It was too painful to see the fire in the face of the beautiful, loving Queen Lonacheska.

"What is the matter, my love?" Alder asked her. "Why have you not taken them?"

"She is shielding them from me," Rion answered.

Alder's silver eyes flashed to me. "What do you want to do with her?"

Rion approached him, caressing her swollen stomach like Lona used to. "Do you think she can be broken?"

Alder's smile sent ice down my spine. "She is already breaking. I can sense it."

"Then do what you must. I have waited centuries to be reborn, and my patience is gone. We will keep this child as a precaution," she said as she caressed her belly again, never taking her white eyes off me, "but I want her. She is strong, already feared and respected by the people, and already claimed as Roanfire's rightful heir."

"As you wish, my love." Alder stalked toward me, standing tall and dominating, swirling with the black vapors of Thrall.

"What?" I called after Rion. "Too cowardly to do it yourself?"

"No, Phoenix Daughter," she said as she walked away. "Wise enough to know that I do not have the restraint to keep you alive long enough to break you."

CHAPTER 25

TWISTING MEMORIES

Alder's arctic hand circled my throat and closed around my windpipe like an ice-crusted rope as he smiled. That smile alone nearly cracked my resolve. Thrall seeped from him, leaking into my mind like smoke under the gap of a door. It reeked. It forced my jaw tight and locked my muscles. It spurred my heart and raced with heat through blood and bone.

I strained against the ropes, needing to run, move, strike at something, anything. It was the same anger burning inside Ikane. The same unrelenting urge to kill and destroy.

Then he bent it inward. Rage sank into a memory and split it like glass. It was the day I met Ikane—the day I'd bumped into his tall, handsome frame back in Daram, with the sun shining on our shoulders and the breeze from the sea caressing our faces. But instead of a gorgeous stranger apologizing, his face darkened, and his green eye turned black. Even the sky dimmed.

His hands pinched my shoulders, drawing me so close I could feel his warm, minty breath on my skin. His eyes scanned my features, trailing the three scars across my face, lingering on my lips. Then his mouth slammed against mine, hard and angry, biting.

My heart flipped and banged, fighting against its cage as I pushed against his solid chest. This was wrong. All wrong. This wasn't Ikane. This was . . .

He pulled away.

My mind spiraled back into my aching body with my arms twisted around the rough trunk of the tree. I gasped as Alder released my neck.

"That was what you wanted that day, wasn't it?" he asked. "For him to kiss you? Take you in his arms and show you passion?"

I shook my head, trying to shake the image of Ikane's dark face from my mind. That wasn't what I'd wanted. I hadn't known anything about him then, but I'd wanted to. I'd been desperately attracted to him and wanted to know everything.

Alder pinched my jaw in his hand, lifting my face to his. "What about this memory?"

Thrall drove me back like a whip, carrying me to the empty training arena of the Daram fortress. I barely had time to react as Ikane's obsidian sword bit into my shoulder. Holding the wound, I staggered away.

This wasn't real. This wasn't happening.

But the image of Ikane advanced. His twin swords lashed around him, his green eye smoldering into black. The sky behind him didn't glow orange with the rising sun as it had that day but curled with a blood moon at his back, glinting against the polished edges of his swords.

"Ikane, stop!"

Instinct made me raise my weapon, but whatever vision Alder was twisting through my mind made it as effective as smoke. Ikane's sword cut through it like it wasn't even there. His blade stung my side like a whip, slicing into skin and rippling against the bones in my ribcage. I cried out, clutching at the wound. Warm blood leaked through my fingers.

How could this pain feel so real?

His second blade hit the inside of my thigh with a sickly noise. My leg buckled. White sparks flashed across my vision as I fell to my knees. "Ikane . . ."

Ikane stood over me, chest heaving, swords at his sides. It looked just like him, felt like him, smelled like him. But it wasn't him.

"This isn't real . . ." I gasped. "This is all in my head. Alder is doing this."

Ikane slipped both swords into one hand and reached down, cupping my jaw, forcing me to look up at him. "Is it?" he asked.

I froze as doubt twisted inside. Was this . . . was this really who Ikane was?

He dropped my chin . . .

And I crashed back to the tree as Alder's hand fell away. I gulped, blinking through the tears blurring the darkening sky, waiting for the pain in my side to abate.

"Let me know when you've had enough," Alder said. "Thrall is endless. Memories are endless. And I find so much pleasure in the infinite ways a thought can be turned."

"What are you doing to her?" Teilo's voice rang out behind him. "Leave her alone."

I inhaled sharply as Alder's icy hand slipped to my cheek. He didn't give me time to breathe.

Stars opened up, endless and thick, blanketing the sky and reflecting on the night-blackened water carrying our ship. Feathers, no. Not this memory.

I tried to move, rise from the crates and leave Ikane's side as we lay on the deck of the *Otaridae*, but my limbs remained frozen. This was the first of many nights where Ikane had comforted me after my nightmares. The first night we spent under the stars.

"They never change," Ikane said as he lay beside me. "Every night they burn, constant and strong . . . just like Rion one day will." He propped himself on his elbow and placed a hand on my cheek, forcing me to look into his damaged eyes. "Will you help her?" he asked.

I had to stop this. Alder was ruining every memory Ikane and I had ever shared. What would be left if this continued?

I grasped Ikane's wrist, trying to pull him away. "This isn't you."

He pinned my arms to my sides and leaned closer, his dark hair falling over his eyes. "Help her, and this will stop," he whispered into my ear, his breath warm and wrong. His lips touched my neck. What was Alder doing?

I struggled against his arms. "Ikane, no."

He bit my skin.

"Stop! Ikane, no!" The truth slammed into my chest. My teeth slammed together. "Alder, stop this!"

I snapped back to reality as Alder's cold hand dropped away.

Hanging by the ropes binding me to the tree, I blinked through tears. I hated this. Hated him. Hated how he was twisting Ikane. I couldn't take another . . .

He reached a hand for me again.

"No," I panted. "Please, no . . . no more."

He paused, cocking his head to one side. "Indeed? I thought it would take more than this to break you, darling."

I let the tears slide, let the sobs escape. This was too much. Rion could take my life. She could take my friends. She could destroy everything, but ruining the precious memories I had left? That was more than I could bear. I wished Yotherna hadn't healed my heart. It would have given out long before this moment.

"Don't touch her again, you hear?" Teilo barked.

My heart flickered as this young man tried to help. But there was nothing he could do. No more. No more fighting. This had to end.

Alder sighed with disappointment. "I had one more treat I was looking forward to sharing with you." Then he smiled.

"Why not? It'll only be a moment." He stretched his hand out again, reaching for my waist.

"No. Please, no!" I fought against the restraints.

"She said no!" Teilo's voice rang.

Yet Alder's cold touch slid around me and drew me forward . . .

I found myself in Ikane's strong arms. We stood in the center of Meldron's grand ballroom. Golden chandeliers glowed overhead. Colorful fabrics and decorations spun around us. The air was filled with perfume and wine. King Sander's coronation.

"That dress does something for your eyes," Ikane said, not hiding his Leviathan accent again. "Like the sea after a storm."

I shut my eyes. His scent washed over me. Mint and sage with a hint of steel. "Stop . . ."

But he guided my body into a spin, the dress swirling around my legs as we danced. I had loved this moment. Loved and hated it as I had just discovered who he truly was: a Leviathan pirate prince sent to assassinate King Sander. But I had already fallen in love with him.

He spun me back into him, arms wrapping around my belly. They were not firm and guiding as they had been that day but angry and crushing.

"Might I steal your lovely partner for a moment?"

My eyes shot wide as King Sander's voice infiltrated the warped memory. Sander held his hand out for me to take.

"Certainly, Your Majesty," Ikane said with a bow, sliding a hand behind his back.

My heart thundered in my chest. Something was about to happen. I could feel it. Something twisted and wrong—

Like a wolf, Ikane sprang forward. The silver edge of a knife slid into King Sander's abdomen.

Why couldn't I move? Why couldn't I do anything but watch as King Sander's eyes flew wide? As his jaw opened in a strangled cry?

Ikane twisted the knife then tore it free. King Sander clutched his stomach, catching the blood leaking from the wound, turning his crimson tunic a shade darker. He staggered back and collapsed to the floor.

Alder released me.

I swallowed air, fighting the tears and rage and hate.

"That one was my favorite," he said. "I never tire of seeing King Sander crumble to the earth."

"You . . . you monster."

"Don't pretend you are not," he said. His hand reached for me again. I flinched as his cold fingers tucked my hair behind my ear. "There is a monster in all of us. Even you. I think you wouldn't be so terrified if you embraced your own."

This time, I felt his Thrall search and sink inside, finding the memory that I associated with my own inner beast.

Crack. Thunder tore from my chest. It surged through the icy walls of Glacier Pass, a whirlwind of raw emotion sweeping away everything in its path, grinding at ice, shredding Deathbiters, disrupting the horrid black vapor leading the demons to me, to us.

My knees hit the ice. This was the day the Deathbiters had taken Ikane. The last time I saw him or felt his true self. It felt like a lifetime ago, and somehow I was glad he hadn't been there to witness what I'd become.

"Enough." The word broke through my cries. I could endure any physical pain he inflicted. I could endure Rion's fire. But not this.

Alder drew me back to the thick, stifling air of the Dead Forest.

I shook my head, slamming my eyes tight against the tears streaking down my cheeks like banners of defeat.

"Rion will be pleased."

I was ashamed of how I flinched when he let a finger slide down the side of my face. He turned away. Mina's gift of light flared around him as he walked to Prince Benroar's tent.

Night. I didn't even know how late it was. Fires smoldered in the distance as if they'd been burning for hours. Pirates no longer huddled by them.

"Scales, I've never seen someone so . . . so dark. Shadows sink into him," Teilo said. "Are you alright? Did he hurt you?" His face was illuminated by the firedust in my eyes, his dark brows knotted with worry.

I couldn't look at him. Alder had hurt me where I couldn't heal, broken me where I couldn't rebuild. Everything I'd fought for was destroyed, and everything I still loved would soon be nothing because of me. Rion could end it. And I wanted her to.

A groan came from Ropert. His head lifted, revealing a swollen eye and blood coating the side of his face. "Dagger?"

I pressed my eyes tight, pushing the tears through my lashes. Why did he have to wake up now?

He glanced at his surroundings then groaned. Leander still hung unmoving on his tree, but Teilo tipped his head in greeting at Ropert.

"I'm Teilo."

"Ropert," he replied uneasily, one eyebrow raising at Teilo's casual manner. "You . . . look a lot like Ikane."

"You know my brother, too?" Teilo asked.

"We were friends . . . well, sort of. Things were a little rocky for a while."

"What happened to him?"

Ropert looked at me, and I purposefully averted my eyes, disengaging from the conversation.

"He was . . . how would I explain? Captured by Alder's demon bats and turned into a hybrid wolf monster?"

"Uh . . ." Teilo said.

"Kea could explain it better," Ropert said. I felt his eyes on me, even in the darkness. "Are you alright, Dagger?"

"The man, Alder, did something to her," Teilo explained.

Concern radiated from Ropert. "Dagger?"

I didn't answer.

"Dagger, please."

Everything was wrong. If I fought against Rion, I'd lose him. If I didn't, I'd lose him, anyway. I could spare myself the guilt of killing him if I just gave myself to her. I didn't want to do this anymore. I was tired. Tired and defeated.

"She seemed the most startled when she saw a woman with him," Teilo began. "She called her Rion, I think."

I wished Teilo would stop.

"Rion?" Ropert repeated, his voice filled with alarm. "Flaming feathers, Dagger. What's going on? What happened?"

"Leave it alone, Ropert. It's done," I said. "Everything will be over shortly."

"What will be over shortly? You sound like you've given up. This isn't like you."

"I've made up my mind," I whispered.

"About what?"

"She knows," Leander's voice whispered from his tree. "She knows, and she has not accepted. She would rather give herself to Rion than use the power we offer."

"What? Dagger, no. Rion will destroy everything."

"Everything has no meaning if you're not in it," I said. "Ikane is already lost. I've already failed."

Warm light flared from the tent as Alder emerged holding a lantern aloft.

I heard tree bark crack and rope groan as Ropert pulled against his restraints. "We need to get out of here," he grunted. "Come on, Dagger. Use your magic. Do something."

"I'm done fighting, Ropert."

"You don't mean that."

"I do."

The air felt heavy between us, like a haze of smoke blowing in from a raging brushfire. I hated the feeling. Ropert and I were inseparable. We'd been brought to Daram at the same time, trained together, become brother and sister in a way blood could never replace. We'd fought and disagreed before, but this was the first time I actually felt his disappointment inside me.

Alder drew near, the light of the lantern falling across our faces, warping the sprite dust vision in my eyes. He paused a moment, watching me like someone scrutinizing a piece of art.

"You will make a beautiful goddess," he said. "Rion is pleased that you have finally accepted your role. The ceremony will take place at dawn, once you've been bathed and clothed in something more fitting." He withdrew a small dagger from his belt.

"Stay away from her," Ropert growled.

Alder cut the rope binding my arms around the tree. I fell forward on my knees. My shoulders cried out, and my hands pulsed as I caught myself against the dusty earth. Alder's grip was firm as he grabbed my elbow and lifted me up.

"Please, Keatep," Leander pleaded. "Do not lose hope."

They didn't know what they were saying. Alder had shattered my hope. Nothing mattered anymore. My bare feet kicked up dust as I staggered beside him, letting him lead me away.

"Do not worry about your friends," Alder said. "They will be the first to find eternity in the Phoenix Goddess. There is no greater honor."

My feet planted. This . . . this wasn't right. Rion intended to kill them. She would steal and take and torture. Yet, they offered themselves to me—begging me to let them serve and lay down their lives in a way they wanted. Shouldn't I at least give them that?

Alder's hand tightened as he jerked me forward. "Come on."

I twisted. His grip came loose. My legs found strength as they propelled me forward. He cursed. A clatter of metal and glass sounded behind me, and the lantern light vanished. Mina's gift flared in my eyes, opening a path through the trees. If I stayed this course, I could reach the dense forest of the living woods and—

My head jerked back, my hair stinging my scalp as he pulled me against his chest. His arm slid around my throat. My cry was cut short as he clenched tight, cutting off my air.

"Don't make me hurt you," he warned. "Rion would not be pleased."

He spun me around, squeezing my jaw in his hand until my teeth cut into my cheeks.

"No more fighting." His perfect face was inches from mine. He reeked of Thrall, thick and pungent, dangerous and ashen. "Understood?"

No one told me what to do. My knee came up. But he was faster, deflecting my blow with his leg. His silver eye flashed as he twisted my arm back, smashing my chest into the trunk of a crumbling tree. Bark scraped my cheek.

"You insolent whelp!" he growled. Grabbing my hair again, he slammed my head into the tree.

Sparks flashed across my vision as a bolt of pain shot through my temple. Darkness swarmed through him, leaking into my soul, searching for another memory to twist and tear apart.

"Go on. Keep resisting. I enjoy this," Alder breathed into my ear.

I cried out, trying to seal my mind away, but he sank deeper, finding the memory of Ikane tending to my injuries while hiding in the ruins of the Fold Garrison. Not again.

Something knocked into Alder. His hold on me tore away as his body spun and staggered for balance.

I whirled, watching as the creature skidded to a halt on all fours, claws digging into the earth, kicking up dust. Was Mina's light playing tricks with my eyes?

His fur shimmered with orange light, his teeth and claws gleamed, and the spiraling hilts of two swords were strapped to his back. His pointed ears fell flat against his head as his snout pulled back into a wrinkled snarl. But the most impossible sight was green. It pulsed in his left iris like a lonely firefly.

"I am no longer under your control."

CHAPTER 26

I KNOW YOUR THOUGHTS

*I*kane." I barely dared to say his name. Tears blurred the glowing edges of his frame. Dare I hope? After everything Alder had put me through, was there a chance this was real? Was I really looking into solid blue-green eyes? Or was my mind playing tricks on me? Oh, Phoenix! I never thought I'd see those colors again.

Alder regained his balance, his steel-black hair falling in lethal strands across his face as his eyes burned into Ikane. "You . . . I should have suspected when you failed to kill the Tolean prince." Thrall writhed through his fingers and crackled with blue-gray energy. "Shame. You were the jewel of my creations."

Alder was going to destroy him.

Every muscle in my body ignited with fire. I lunged, burying my shoulder into Alder's ribcage. I felt the impact ripple through him as we collided into a tree. His fingers dug into my arms, and Thrall ripped into my skin. With unnatural strength, Alder pitched me aside. I hit the earth, dust exploding across my tongue as I tumbled.

Tossing my hair off my face, I pushed myself from the ground, searching for Ikane. He wasn't where I'd seen him.

Even Alder scanned the trees, his hands curled, Thrall rolling between his fingers and up his wrists like smoke. "Show yourself!" he roared.

A black blur rushed at Alder. He cried out as Ikane's claws slashed across his back. Spinning, he released a bolt of black energy. The darkness missed and clapped against a brittle tree trunk as Ikane disappeared. Bark exploded. I raised my arm, shielding my face from the spray of splintered wood.

Lowering my arm, I searched the trees again. He was too fast, even for Mina's firedust to illuminate him. "You can't kill him, Ikane," I called to the darkness. "He is linked to the ruby."

"Shut up," Alder snapped, spinning in circles.

Ikane rushed him again. This time, Alder struck. Mina's firedust flared around a tuft of fur flying from Ikane's shoulder as he blurred past. He blended into the trees again, silent.

I staggered to my feet, glancing at my companions bound to the trees not ten yards away. Pirates were rousing at the noise caused by Alder's use of magic. I'd have to act quickly if I was to free any of them.

Sprinting to the nearest tree, I landed on my knees and began untying the knot on Teilo's wrist.

Alder cried out again. In the corner of my vision, I saw him go down on one knee. He flung a bolt of Thrall wild, the black vapor launching through the dead stumps.

"What's happening?" Ropert demanded, craning his neck to see me.

"It's Ikane," I said as I worked. "He's back."

"What?"

A hound-like whimper shattered the night just as Teilo's arm came free. I spun in time to see Ikane's powerful form stagger into a tree, holding his side. Alder rose. Thrall surrounded him, filling his cloak and raising his hair as he took heavy steps toward his prey.

"Ikane!" I called. "Run, Ikane!"

He pushed off the tree and rushed toward me on all fours. Alder's blast of Thrall followed him, hitting the ground at his heels. The spray sent broken clumps of dirt into my face as Ikane's arms wrapped around my torso.

"No!" Alder roared after us. "She's escaping! After them!"

I clung to Ikane's neck as he darted through trees, burying my face into his fur. Was this real? Was he really back?

I flinched as he crashed into the living woods. Branches whipped against my arms and stung my skin. Yet even knowing pirates were pursuing us, knowing Alder was there, knowing Rion infested my queen, knowing my friends were captive and fated to die, I could finally breathe. I was with Ikane. My Ikane.

Sweet, earthy scents arose as Ikane slowed. His arms loosened and gently lowered me to the ground. Pine needles and dead leaves crunched under my bare feet as I looked up at him.

His eyes scrunched tight as he staggered back, clutching his side where Alder had struck him. Mina's gift highlighted a black mottle of burnt fur and flesh. Blood leaked through his fingers.

"Ikane?" I sank with him to the earth.

The brows of his wolf face furrowed as he watched me, his beautiful eyes shimmering with tears, standing out like jewels in the starless night.

His palm slid to my cheek, warm and rough. "Little Brendagger."

I let out a strange sound, not knowing whether to laugh or weep. "You came back."

His eyes closed as his hand dropped from my face. "I'm so sorry, Kea. So sorry. For everything. For . . . for Eamon."

"No, Ikane. It wasn't your fault," I said. "You weren't in control."

"It doesn't matter." His teeth snapped tight. "I still did it."

"Alder did it. Not you."

His head shook. "You don't understand."

"I do. Oh, I do," I said. "I've been in your head, Ikane. I know your thoughts. You didn't remember him. All you could feel was Alder's order burning through your body, tearing you apart from the inside."

His body shook. Tears slid down his cheeks, glittering against the rising sun. "It hurts . . ." He curled over until his head rested on my shoulder, fur brushing my cheek. "Kea, it hurts." A long, heart-wrenching whimper pushed through him, like the sound of a hound crying alone in the night.

My own heart reached back, toward his pain. I slid my fingers through his fur, holding his shaking form as he allowed grief to swell and break. It washed over me, etching a fresh path through my heart.

But the pain was changing. Eamon was gone, yes. But his martyrdom had awakened the first spark of doubt in Ikane. The doubt that brought Ikane back. Eamon, in his own way, had saved Ikane—again. It was just how I imagined the great Eamon Brendagger's life coming to an end. Sacrifice. Sacrifice to save another.

But for Ikane . . . would he ever heal? Would he ever be able to forgive what he'd done? It was a pain I could not take away from him, no matter how many times I assured him that his actions were involuntary. And if I had been in his place . . . I probably couldn't forgive myself, either.

I held him tighter. "You are still my Ikane," I whispered.

He sobbed harder, his arms wrapping around me. I kissed his neck, smelling the steel of his swords and the earthy wildness of his fur, and let him weep.

Slowly, the shaking of his body stopped. He drew back then flinched and sucked air through his teeth. His hand flew to his side as he glanced down at the wound, wolf brows furrowing.

He wasn't healing. In fact, the wound looked worse, oozing blood and blackness.

"Let me," I said. The edges of his fur had melted away, leaving a festering patch of burnt skin and muscle. Could Etheria cure this? Was there poison inside? Knowing Alder, it wouldn't have surprised me. But my wounds didn't sting the way Deathbiter venom did.

Regardless, I let my hands hover over his side and closed my eyes.

Ikane's massive hand wrapped around both of mine. He pulled them to his chest. I could feel his heart beating.

"Don't squander your magic on me," he said. "I deserve this."

"Don't say that."

His eyes closed. "How can I not?"

"I am no better, Ikane. I've hurt my friends with magic. Pushed them away, placed them in unspeakable danger. I even . . ." I choked. "I even killed a young man with magic because of Rion. We are both monsters, Ikane."

His hand pressed mine more firmly against his chest. "You are no monster."

I was. Feathers, I was more of a monster than he knew. He had just come back, just found his freedom, and Yotherna wanted me to take his life.

"How did you do it?"

"Do what?"

"Free your mind," I said. "I tried to get through to you so many times. Alder had sealed everything away."

Ikane clenched his teeth as he reached up and drew one of his obsidian swords from the makeshift scabbard at his back. Mina's orange light touched every edge. The spiraling hilt of the serpent body, the three horns protruding from the arched head, the detail in every scale and tooth.

The swords? Were they what brought him back?

"It was Teilo," Ikane said.

I tilted my head at him.

"And these weapons," he added. "Teilo gifted them to me the day I left to find Eamon. It had taken him an entire month to forge one. And two more to make the second a perfect match." He let his thumb glide along the edge and tilted the blade, catching the first raindrops against its polished surface. "Even a master could not have forged more exact weapons."

"They are exceptional," I said.

"It has been over two years since I've seen my brother, but the moment I saw the pendant around Teilo's neck, everything opened. I remembered."

Was it really that simple? Just seeing his brother and the pendant necklace? No. It had to have been an accumulation of things. Eamon's death had been the first crack. The doubt inside Ikane had been growing ever since. Teilo had just been the final key.

"We must get you back to Meldron," Ikane said.

"But Ropert, Leander . . . Teilo."

Ikane's beautiful, mismatched eyes burned into mine. "Aye, they need help. But what can you and I do alone? You must go, Kea. Heal. Regroup. Gather an army. March on Fold, and drive the Leviathans back to their isles for good."

"You'll come with me?"

"I will go with you as far as the city wall."

I didn't like that answer. "Stay."

"Look at me, Kea. I can't."

Cloudy moonlight filtered through the trees across his deep-brown fur, contouring every sculpted muscle in his body. "You are magnificent, Ikane." I brushed beading raindrops from the fur on his shoulder, where another wound from Alder's magic festered and bled. "The people will see you as—"

A terrible screech tore the moment apart. His eyes snapped to the sky. Five or six black silhouettes—outlined by the orange-red fire in my eyes—darted over the treetops, circling and arching back.

"They're hunting us." The fur across Ikane's spine bristled.

I licked my lips, barely daring to breathe.

Ikane slowly drew his feet under him. "Go. Get under that pine."

We moved silently under the thick fans of pine branches. Shoulder to shoulder, with my back pressed against the rough trunk, I struggled to see the sky. Five or six black blurs had turned to ten. No, fifteen. Twenty? I couldn't keep track. They were moving too fast, swarming overhead. Which could only mean one thing.

They knew we were here.

My heart slammed against my chest, pumping adrenaline to every limb.

"Take this," Ikane said, pressing the cold hilt of his sword into my hand.

He, in turn, extended his lethal claws. They flashed with an orange-red outline like throwing knives. His ears pivoted wildly.

"Ready yourself," he said with a low, warning growl. "They come."

And they did, screaming through the growing rain.

CHAPTER 27

DEATHBITERS

*T*he branches overhead came alive with movement and noise as Deathbiters crashed into them. Raindrops and pine needles were knocked loose, pelting my face as I focused on their advance. Leathery wings folded as the screeching creatures clawed their way toward us.

At least the trees acted as a barricade. They would give me time to fight off the ones that broke through. The air, despite the rain, grew thick with their sour, acidic stench.

I wished I had my armor. In the very least, a leather tunic. Anything but a thin cotton shirt and trousers. No doubt, I would face the burning sting that would come with their strikes. But for how long? How soon would day break and save us?

Foul air wafted against the back of my head as a Deathbiter soared past. I dropped as Ikane's hand whipped out, snatching the creature's wing midair. He continued the creature's momentum, guiding it into the earth. There, he tore it apart like something feral.

Another bat dropped from the branches before me. It screamed, opening its horrid mouth to reveal fangs dripping with venom. Launching itself from the ground, it kicked up pine needles and dead leaves. I swung. Ikane's sword didn't even shudder as it impacted sinew and bone. It was a clean cut. Effortless. The Deathbiter split in two and dropped.

"Behind you!" Ikane roared.

I spun as another creature climbed down the trunk of the tree, opening its maw. My elbow flew back, impacting its head. A resonating crack sounded as it dropped to my feet. Its wings twitched.

Ikane grabbed my wrist. "This way."

Something in my shoulder popped as he launched forward, dragging me under the sheltering branches of another pine. He stopped, rounding on the Deathbiters behind us. I held my aching shoulder as I glanced back, watching the swarming Deathbiters fight their way out of the branches to give chase. Clever. Ikane was using the forest to our advantage. If he didn't have to worry about me, he could've outrun them.

"Keep moving," I urged him.

His eyes scanned me, the question of *Can you keep up?* burning in his eyes. He noted the way I held my shoulder and shook his head. "We fight," he said. "It won't be long before daylight. We can hold out."

A Deathbiter dropped between the trees. Its wings opened just before it impacted the earth, and it soared directly for us, sliding under the branches with ease. Ikane caught its face in his hand, smashing it down into the earth just as three more followed.

"Get down, Kea!" he cried.

I dropped into a crouch as he sliced his claws into the first. The second crashed into his shoulder. A yelp escaped him as the creature bit down. I raised his sword as the third came soaring for me, cutting it in two.

Ikane ripped the Deathbiter from his shoulder, silencing its cries. An eruption of screeches followed, shadowed by a strange rushing noise coming from above.

Ikane's ears twitched. "Scales," he breathed. He spun to me. "Down!" he cried.

I sank to my knees as he launched himself forward, curling his large hybrid body around me. The impact of a Deathbiter rippled through his torso. Then another and another, pummeling into his back like the explosion of stone from a shattered castle wall. He roared in pain but did not release me. He curled tighter, shielding my face from the onslaught of dozens more.

"Ikane," I cried. They were killing him, tearing him apart. Strangled yelps, snarls, and whimpers tore through his throat. Deathbiters shrieked. Leathery wings beat through the rain around us, suffocating, burying. Ikane's body jolted at every impact.

I slammed my eyes shut. I had to do something.

Turning inward, I touched the flickering white stars of Etheria, the armor, the fortress. This was power meant to protect and shield, but it felt incomplete without the life energy of my friends. Regardless, it would do nothing against the Deathbiters.

What I needed now was the magic I vowed never to use again. I needed Thrall.

I turned to the sable little flame simmering in the corner of my mind. It had destroyed the Deathbiters before. Vanquished them to nothing but ash. But if I was to use it, I needed to feed it. I needed to let it taste some form of rage in my heart.

I didn't want to. It terrified me. It tore my mind apart every time, altering memories to suit its insatiable need for anger.

Ikane yelped, his protecting grip growing tighter as he trembled against the Deathbiters' onslaught. Warmth dripped from his shoulder, hitting my neck, and a coppery scent I knew well filled my nose. They were tearing him apart.

I had to stop thinking. I had to act. I had to find the anger and rage in me, but right now, all I wanted was to protect Ikane. But that was the emotion that fueled Etheria. How could I stop—

Alder. I let his name simmer in my mind, his deceptively perfect features filling the forefront of my thoughts. His silver-black hair, his pale skin, his steel-colored eye and the scar stretching over the other. The man who had changed Ikane into this monster. The man who deceived me. The man who created the Deathbiters. The man who had kidnapped our queen. The man who was working with Rion.

Thrall expanded as I held these thoughts out like a morsel of food to a starving dog. It snapped the pain from me, the raven fire expanding with power. It stretched to another memory.

No. My white lights of Etheria barred its path. It would heed my commands. It would only get what I offered. And it would do as I bid.

A strange sensation filled my core, easing the painful beat of my heart. It was like . . . like archery. Like I was standing in the Glacial Empire again, cold air burning my nostrils, sun on my shoulders, fingers aching, back straining as I drew the bowstring back. The arrow's tip resting on my finger, the fletching balanced against my cheek.

Balance. This was it. Etheria and Thrall together. A shield and sword.

Release.

The power expanded from my body, taking all my strength with it. It flowed through Ikane, blasting against the hoard of attacking Deathbiters like the blow of a great hammer from within. Cracking noises pelted the trees as Deathbiters were knocked back. Shrieks silenced.

We remained still, breathing hard, waiting, listening to the rain patter against the treetops. Were they gone? Ikane's trembling arms squeezed me to his chest, threatening to crack my ribs all over again as he let out an agonizing whimper. The smell of blood was thick. How badly was he hurt?

"Ikane?" I breathed, barely finding the strength to set my hand against his chest. I paused. It was soft, smooth, like the texture of . . . skin.

I lifted my head, forcing Ikane to release.

My breath stopped. Everything around me fell away as I stared at the face looking back at me. Smooth skin, angled features, human. Under an untamed beard covering his jaw, the familiar X-shaped scars sat pink against his cheek. His deep-brown hair lay long and wild over his shoulders but still perfect. So perfect.

Was this real? I lifted my hand to his cheek. He was warm.

"Why are you looking at me like that?" He blinked, his eyes flickering with confusion at the sound of his own voice, no longer tinged with an animal growl. "What . . . ?" His voice faltered, and he lifted his hand from my back. His eyes widened as he turned his palm toward him, studying every finger. "I . . . I'm human?" His question hung in the air like he didn't believe it. He looked at me, his beautiful green-and-blue eyes filled with so many questions. "How?"

I didn't know. And truthfully, I didn't care. What mattered was that he was back and whole and with me. I wanted to throw my arms around him, pin him to me, smother him with kisses, but my use of power had drained me too much. All I could manage was a smile as I lay in his arms.

His beautiful eyes shimmered. "I'm human." The relief in his voice was tangible as he pulled me to him, rocking.
At that moment, I hated the weakness of my body more than Alder. I wanted to stay with him, hold him, speak with him, reunite with him, but my eyes closed. I felt my muscles go limp, then my mind slipped away.

CHAPTER 28

BLACK FIRE, WHITE STAR

he subtle sound of water dripping onto the ground filled his ears. Not the soft, ever-present pattering of rain, but the aftermath of one giant drop falling from a sagging branch at a time. Birdsong rang through the trees, and the bright chatter of squirrels filled the morning air. The noise of a rabbit nibbling on firm dandelion greens sounded nearby. But the most gratifying noise was Kea's heartbeat pounding strong in his arms.

His eyes cracked open to morning light reflecting on endless diamond drops of rain glistening on pine needle branches above. The sky was clear, promising sun and warmth.

Glancing down, he found his Little Brendagger curled against his bare chest. He stroked her damp hair from her face—with a human hand. Human. He still couldn't believe it. Somehow, her explosion of power had not only destroyed the Deathbiters and healed every wound on his body but had also changed him back.

She hadn't stirred since. His brows furrowed at the sight of a tear in her sleeve as the stench of Deathbiter filth wafted from her. He hadn't seen the wound last night under the cloak of his blood soaking into her shirt or the overwhelming acidic stench around them. The morning light revealed a red gash on her skin . . . with black spidery veins running around the edges. She'd been hit. For all his shielding, she'd still been infected with their venom.

Carefully slipping his arm from under Kea's head, he sat upright, stroking her hair once more. It was time to end Alder. That shrouded wraith had turned him into a monster, locked his memories away, enslaved him, made him hunt and kill his own friends and family. His jaw ached as his teeth ground together. As long as Alder and Rion lived, Kea would never be safe. No one—

He turned his head as a heartbeat encroached on Kea's slumbering pulse somewhere in the trees behind him. Nothing but pine trees and thick underbrush watched him in return, but he could hear it drawing closer, each beat growing louder and increasing in speed.

Fear. He knew the sound. Whoever it belonged to had seen him. And whoever this heartbeat belonged to, they possessed ghostly stealth. Even straining his senses, he heard no sound of earth shifting beneath boots, no breaking branches, not even the subtle swoosh of a branch sweeping across clothing.

He sniffed the air, approval and admiration running through his chest for his stalker. Nothing but damp earth, rotting leaves, and a subtle sting from the surrounding corpses of Deathbiters. This prowler was clever enough to stay downwind.

Muscles coiling in preparation and ears strained, Ikane waited as the heartbeat slinked closer. The pounding of fear shifted to something strong and dangerous: determination. His hunter was preparing to confront him.

Ikane reached for one of his swords, tilting his head as movement caught the corner of his eye. A hooded man stopped at the edge of the trees. His black leathers and cloak glistened with moisture, indicating that he, too, had spent the night in the rain. Ikane raised himself up, holding his sword as he faced the man. The weapon felt right in his grip, like a long-lost friend.

"State your business," he demanded, doing his best to hide his Leviathan accent.

The man stepped closer, holding a leather pouch high. Ikane's eyes narrowed. That was the same pouch Kea had tossed from her belt the day he'd first abducted her. It had burst with a crack of thunder and light, paralyzing his acute hearing for several painful moments. His eyes tracked the glinting throwing knives attached to the man's bandoleer.

"Thundercrack?"

The man lowered his arm. "Ikane?" He removed the hood from his head, revealing a mass of brown curls and eyes filled with hopeful suspicion. "How?"

Broderick was alive! The last time Ikane had seen him, he . . . The taste of Broderick's blood exploded across his tongue all over again. The sensation of his bone crunching in his teeth rippled through his jaw. A shudder moved down Ikane's spine and settled in his throat like rocks—too heavy to vomit and too large to swallow—as he noted the empty space where Broderick's arm should have been.

He'd done that.

No. His hand tightened around the hilt of his sword. Alder had made him do it.

"I . . . I'm sorry, Broderick," Ikane said. "I never meant to hurt you."

"I don't blame you, Ikane. I never did." Broderick tucked the dangerous thunder pouch into his satchel, never moving his eyes from Ikane's. "I can't believe you're here . . . human. How did . . . ?" He gestured to Ikane's bare torso. "How did this happen? How did you break Alder's hold on your mind?"

"It was Kea," Ikane said, stepping aside.

Worry flashed across Broderick's face when he noted Kea lying on the ground. Rushing forward, he dropped to his knees beside her and pulled the strap of his satchel over his head. His fingers hovered over the blood staining her shirt.

Ikane could only imagine what it looked like. "That isn't her blood," he said. "At least, not all of it. Deathbiters attacked us last night. She has one wound I can see, but I don't think that is what has made her so weak."

Broderick found the gash in her arm then began searching her body for more. "Only one?" he asked. "Are you sure?"

Ikane crouched. "It's all I can smell."

Broderick blinked up at him. "How are you unscathed?"

"She used some sort of magic . . . I've never felt anything like it."

"Did she use Thrall?"

Ikane shook his head slowly. "Yes . . . and no. I can't describe it. It was like . . ." His eyes fell on his twin swords. "It was like the balance of my swords—lethal but controlled."

Broderick tilted his head. "Etheria?"

Ikane shook his head again. "I know what pure Etheria feels like. It was there, too . . . but this was more of a melding of both?"

"Both?" Broderick gazed down at Kea as if she'd transformed into another creature. "Is it . . . possible?" He shook his head as if trying to convince himself it wasn't true. "No. No one has ever managed that before. Not even the White Wardent."

"Managed what?" Ikane asked.

"To use Thrall and Etheria together. Though I suppose it is possible if one's mind is strong enough."

Ikane looked down at Kea's serene face. Scars from her first encounter with the Deathbiters shone on her skin like stripes of rosy sea coral touched by sunlight through water. Another scar, in the shape of a rose, peeked from under the collar of her shirt. She'd survived a Deathbiter attack just like the one they'd endured last night—without magic. She'd fought burning nightmares until her nose, ears, and eyes bled. She'd been hunted and betrayed by her own people, and still she defended them. Even after the Phoenix Witch infected him and forced him to crush her throat, she followed, refusing to let him carry the burden alone. She never gave up.

"She's one of the strongest people I know," he said and stroked her damp hair back. He could never get enough of the feeling of her smooth skin and soft hair under his human hand. More than anything, he wanted to feel her lips against his again.

"We need ash," Broderick said, "and fast. Alder has changed the Deathbiter poison somehow. Symptoms develop five times faster. She'll be dead by tonight if we wait."

Ikane nodded. Finding dry wood in this damp forest would be a challenge, but Ikane accepted it.

"Hold a moment," Broderick said. He unclasped his cloak and held it out. "You look cold."

Ikane hadn't realized how cool the air was or the prickling across his bare skin. Strange what months of living under a layer of fur could do. "Thank you." He swung Broderick's warm cloak over his shoulders then began searching the ground under the densest trees nearby for dry timber.

Soon a fire sparked, popped, and cracked with moisture, filling the air with the stench of smoke. Ikane didn't like it. It was like a beacon to the enemy. As soon as they could create enough ash to heal Kea, they would move. Already, veins of black spread down her cheeks.

He prodded at the burning wood with a stick, hoping to speed the process along. "Broderick?" he asked.

"Hmm?"

"What is that . . . that thunder pouch you were holding?"

"Thunder pouch?" Broderick seemed perplexed, then his eyes lit up. "Oh. You mean the sprite dust explosives. Clever, isn't it?" He reached inside his satchel and removed the pouch he'd been holding earlier. "It holds all four sprite dusts. One dust—I chose firedust—is contained in a glass vial in the center. Shatter that, and you have a few seconds before they become unstable and burst." He handed Ikane the pouch. "I like your name for it. 'Thunder pouch.'"

"Thunder explosive is more like it," Ikane said, weighing the pouch in his hand. He could smell the dusts inside, a mixture of hot and cold movement. That was why Kea had tossed it away. The glass vial inside must have shattered. She could have hurled it at him. She could have gotten away, but she didn't. He gazed at her peaceful face, at her dark lashes lying against her cheeks.

She'd stayed with him. Despite the fact he could have killed her—and almost did—she stayed.

Broderick chuckled. "Careful. Ropert wouldn't like you getting too clever with naming things. That's his specialty."

Ikane's smile faded. Benroar had Ropert. He had Prince Leander and Teilo, too. Scales, Teilo. His little brother. How much had he endured on Ikane's behalf? "We need to get them back," he said.

"How?" Broderick asked. "Negotiate?"

Ikane shook his head, handing the thunder pouch back to Broderick. "I can count on one hand where negotiations haven't come to blows amongst my brothers. No. Trying to talk would be like trying to sail backward in the wind."

"Keep it." Broderick pushed the pouch back. "So you're saying that there is no choice but war."

Ikane turned his eyes to the glowing orange embers in the fire. "Aye. War . . . again." It hadn't even been a full year since the last one.

"Do you think we stand a chance?" Broderick asked. "I mean, with Alder and Rion on—"

A noise in the woods jerked Ikane's attention away. Snapping twigs, boots crunching in the dead leaves, heavy breathing, and a pounding heart. He stood and spun toward the source. "Were you followed?" he demanded of Broderick.

Broderick rose slowly. "I don't think so . . . Feathers, the smoke from the fire."

Ikane's fists curled. It was too late to do anything about that now, and they needed the ash to heal Kea. He shut his eyes, letting all his senses flow to his hearing and smell. One heartbeat. That's all it was. They could contend with that.

"Stay here," Ikane said as he removed Broderick's cloak and draped it over Kea. It would only hinder his movements. He snatched up his swords. "I'll head them off."

"Who?"

He wasn't sure. All he knew was that they were coming fast and reckless. Keeping low, he slid into the trees, keeping his senses open and trained on the singular heartbeat. It was approaching from the left. A branch snapped like the crack of a whip against his sensitive ears, and the steady pounding of hurrying feet stumbled. A grunt sounded. Whoever this was, they were not hunting them. They seemed more like they were running from something.

Movement flashed between the trees—dark hair, a filthy white shirt, brown vest, and black trousers. The body was masculine but half-starved and stumbling forward. The smell of blood and Deathbiter filth filled Ikane's nose.

He sank behind the tangled branches of budding underbrush, sliding both swords into one hand. He would not be needing them.

The man stumbled between the nearby trees, glancing over his shoulder—the shoulder he clutched as blood oozed onto his sleeve. The sight blasted against Ikane's chest like a hurricane force gale. Before he knew what his body had done, he rose to his feet.

"Teilo?"

Teilo stopped, his green eyes wide with spidery veins of Deathbiter venom weeping down his cheeks. "Ikane."

Ikane's swords slid from his hand and crashed to the earth as he sprang forward, wrapping his brother in his arms. Teilo returned the embrace. He was thin, trembling, and burning with fever. But thank the Leviathan, he was alive. Alive.

He crushed his brother to him. "I thought you were dead."

"Scales, Ikane. If you don't let me breathe, I will be."

Ikane released him and blinked the tears from his eyes.

"How is it you've gotten stronger?" Teilo asked, rubbing his chest. "You've always been stronger than any of us, but this?" He gestured to the rippling muscles of Ikane's abdomen.

"Never mind that," Ikane said. "What are you doing here?"

"What else? I'm the leash, as always."

Ikane frowned. "What did they want from me now?"

"Accalon and Benroar wanted you to come to my rescue so they could kill you for betraying Dran." A smile spread across

Teilo's lips, and his dimples became more prominent. "But I thought I'd give escaping a go."

Ikane let out a sober chuckle. "Well, you're free now. They can't hold you against me anymore."

Teilo shivered and stumbled back as pain crossed his face. Ikane caught him.

"When will it end, Ikane? When will all this war and bloodshed stop?"

Ikane didn't have an answer. He wanted peace as much as Teilo did. But even if Kea destroyed the Phoenix Stone, the history of plunder and war between the Leviathans and Roanfire ran too deep. "Come. I'd like you to meet some friends." Ikane said as he gathered his swords.

"You still have those?" Teilo asked, indicating the twin weapons.

"I wish I could say they've never left my side," Ikane said as he slipped Teilo's arm over his shoulder. "But aye, they have saved me in more ways than one."

CHAPTER 29

I'M HERE, KEA

I can get her back to Meldron in three days," Ikane was saying.

My neck ached as I turned my head toward the sound of his voice and the rhythmic grind of a whetstone against metal. I knew that sound well. I'd come to love it and understand that it was a part of who Ikane was. When we had hidden ourselves in Fold, he would oil and polish his swords every night, whether he'd used them that day or not.

"What about the Deathbiters?" Broderick asked. "Alder has them actively hunting you now. I don't think hiding under the shelter of pines will spare you anymore."

My eyes cracked open to afternoon sun breaking through rainclouds, lighting three figures sitting around the remains of a dead campfire. So it had been real. I'd been in Ikane's head, witnessing everything.

Ikane was sitting beside me, one of his swords propped upright between his legs. The muscles in his back and arms rippled with every stroke of the stone against the weapon. The tattoo of the Leviathan crest, a pair of twisting sea serpents, stood out against his shoulder. How had I ever hated that? It was beautiful—a part of him.

Teilo stiffened as he noted my fluttering lashes and slapped Broderick's shoulder twice. "Oi. She's waking up."

Ikane immediately turned to me. "Thank the winds of the sea," he breathed, setting his sword aside. He'd shaved his handsome jawline clean and had bound his wild, tangled locks at the base of his neck in a rough knot. He was perfect. My heart fluttered as he slipped a hand under my back and helped me sit upright.

His brows furrowed. "Are you alright? Your heart—"

"It's fine," I said, feeling heat rise to my cheeks. I clutched Broderick's cloak to my chest.

Teilo grinned. "Scales, Ikane. She's got it bad for you."

Ikane cuffed his brother's ear but smiled nonetheless as Teilo flinched away with a chuckle. "Kea," Ikane began. "I'd like you to meet my brother, Teilo."

I blinked. Ikane's eyeteeth were longer than I remembered. Wolflike.

"We've met," Teilo said with a dimpled smile. "In truth, she was the one who helped me slip the ropes. Thank you for that."

I nodded to him.

"How are you feeling?" Broderick asked me. It was so good to see him here and unscathed from the attack, but there was something burning in his eyes. Suspicion? Uncertainty? Wonder?

"I'm fine," I said slowly. "Thank you for healing me." I touched the torn part of my sleeve.

"Your heart?" he pressed. "Your cracked ribs?"

I understood now. I'd only been missing for a few days, and already those devastating and debilitating injuries had healed. "I had help," I said, hoping my tone conveyed that I did not want to speak of it further. Bitterness curled inside me. Yes, Yotherna had healed me, but he'd only done it so that I could endure the news of what I was to do next.

"Any news of Ropert and Prince Leander?" I asked, needing to change the subject.

Ikane looked at Teilo.

"They were alive when I left," the boy said. "Benroar said something about using them, but I don't know what for."

"Ransom, I bet," Broderick suggested.

"No," Ikane said, his voice dark. "Not with Alder there." He looked at me, his green eye burning. "Alder will make them suffer to get to you."

My heart clenched. And Rion would be battering against their hastily crafted shields to get to them. They were out of time already.

"Is there a weakness in the walls somewhere?" I asked Ikane. "A place we can infiltrate? Something we didn't notice when we were there?"

Ikane shook his head. "There is no weakness. Even in its ruined state, the front walls are solid, and the back is protected by the cliffs."

My mind reeled, thinking back on the time I spent there under Ikane's care. There was no way in, except . . .

The caves.

The map! The map I'd found in the Glacial Empire of the cave system running beneath the old garrison. I'd brought it back with me. We could use that. It had to work. It was the only way in.

I rose to my feet, dragging Broderick's cloak with me. "We go back to Meldron," I said. "We give our report and raise an army. They will march on Fold and draw the pirates' attention." I handed Broderick's cloak to Ikane as he stood. "As for us, I know of another way in."

"What way?" Ikane asked. "There is no other way."

"The caves," I reminded him.

He straightened. I could see the doubt in his eyes but also confidence in me.

"There is still the issue of getting to Meldron with the Deathbiters pursuing us," Broderick said. He squinted at the sky. "And I suggest we come up with a plan quickly."

"I think . . ." I began. "I think I can help with that."

Broderick tilted his head at me. "You can shield us from the Deathbiters the way Alder does?"

I shook my head. "I don't know how Alder does it," I admitted. "But I think I found another way." There was something about the magic I'd used the night before, the blend of Etheria and Thrall. I'd released the power so forcefully it had obliterated the demon bats. But if I managed to keep a steady hold on it, I was sure I could repel them.

But for how long? One explosion had left me drained and unconscious for hours. Could I repel the Deathbiters all night long?

I glanced at Broderick and then Ikane—and my gut churned as I momentarily saw them as fuel, objects of power, something to keep me strong. This was the way Rion saw everyone.

Clenching my fists, I turned away. "Let's move," I said, turning west, bare feet and all. "We need to cover as much ground as possible before nightfall."

Ikane, Broderick, and Teilo scrambled to gather what little supplies we had and hurried after me.

"Scales, Ikane," Teilo muttered in a whisper, though I could tell he'd meant me to hear him. "You didn't tell me she's both pretty and fierce. She's like a forge."

"No," Ikane said. "She's like a star."

I smiled. I knew what stars meant to him. They were hope and home, a map leading him to safety. They were his life. And then the image of Rion's numberless cloud of frightened stars burned into my mind. My smile faded. I was a star he should not follow.

Broderick, ever the prepared man that he was, gave me his extra pair of stockings to cover my feet. It alleviated the worst the forest floor had to offer, though I still yelped when a rock or a pine needle splinter made me stumble. Yet I pushed on hard, watching every change in the sky as it slowly morphed from bright spring blue to small tufts of clouds edged in yellow-orange and violet. Finally, sunrays lanced like a warning through the trees: Her light and protection were waning.

We were four days from Meldron on foot. Two on horseback. And if Ikane were to run alone, he would make it in half that. My heart thrummed in my chest, my mouth was dry, and despite the cool air, my palms were damp and clammy. I rubbed them down my thighs. How could I do this? How could I shield us all from the Deathbiters throughout the night?

I needed strength—something more than what my own body held. Was taking life energy from my friends really the only way? It didn't seem right. How did Alder manage? Was he really that much stronger than I was? Or was it his link to Rion that gave him more power than was humanly possible?

I started as a warm hand slipped into my palm. Ikane squeezed it, his eyes smiling gently, confidently, approvingly. "You're exhausting yourself with worry. I feel it in your heart and smell it in your blood."

I squirmed a little. Was this how he felt when I was in his mind? "I'm worried I'm not strong enough," I said then shook my head. "No, I *know* I'm not strong enough."

"I'm here, Kea."

"You don't understand."

"I do," he said firmly, his hand squeezing mine tighter. "I understand completely, and if it is life energy you need to get us through the night, Broderick and I are prepared."

My footsteps faltered. "How . . . how do you know about that?"

"I've known since the first time I shared my life with you. It frightened me at the time. I was so weak after . . . and I'm ashamed to say I pulled away after that."

So that was what he was hiding from me when we were heading to the Glacial Empire. He knew. He knew I could kill him, and it terrified me.

"I'm so sorry, Ikane."

"Don't be," he said. "I've accepted it now. I'm sorry it took me so long to admit it."

My head shook wildly. "Do you know what you are saying? I am not Rion. I will not use your life like that." Sliding my hand from his, I turned on my heel and hurried forward.

"Kea." Ikane's hand caught my wrist. "I am not asking you to be like Rion. I am asking you to accept my help. I don't like this any more than you do. If we could, Broderick, Teilo, and I would wield our weapons against the Deathbiters tonight. But we know how effective that is against a swarm." He took my shoulders in his hands, turning me to face him. "This is how we can help. Do you intend to make us stand by and watch as you raise the sails alone? You said it yourself, you do not have the strength. But with all of us together, we stand a chance."

Why did he have to make so much sense? I hated it. "I don't want to become like Rion," I whispered.

He placed a finger under my chin and gently raised my head. "You are nothing like her."

But the seed of doubt had been planted, spreading roots. More and more, I found myself thinking like her, wanting more power. Was it really wrong if I intended to use it for her destruction? I feared it was something more—that I actually pursued the power because it made me feel . . . invincible.

"Is everything alright?" Broderick asked as he and Teilo caught up to us. He glanced at the pine needles, dead leaves, and dirt clinging to the knitted fabric of the stockings. "Is it your feet?"

"I'm fine," I said.

"It's the Deathbiters," Ikane said. "She needs our help."

Broderick nodded thoughtfully. "Then let's make camp while the sunlight is still on our side."

"Do we have time to hunt?" Teilo asked, his green eyes pleading for a positive answer.

I hadn't even thought about this young man's need for food. He was half-starved before he'd come to us. A small slice of jerky as his only meal of the day wasn't going to bring back his strength.

I looked at Ikane. "You haven't lost your touch for rabbit hunting, have you?"

He smiled crookedly, flashing one of his sharp canines at us. "I'll be back."

With that, he slipped into the forest.

Broderick slid his satchel over his head and set it on the ground. "Let's hurry with the fire. I trust your ability to shield us, Kea. But I'd rather not attract the Deathbiters if we can avoid it."

I couldn't agree more.

With the fire put out, our bellies satisfied, and backs pressed together, we waited under the sheltering fans of pine for the deep-violet light to sink into black. Ikane wrapped an arm around my shoulders, drawing me to him under the warmth of Broderick's cloak.

Broderick busied himself by unpacking his satchel and taking inventory: five "thunder pouches," as Ikane called them, a healing kit, dried herbs and mushrooms that were most likely poisonous, rope, flint, a whetstone—the one I'd seen Ikane using earlier—a bar of soap, a comb, three daggers, an old leather-bound booklet, a charcoal pencil, and two extra vials of glowing fire and winddust.

The sprite dust vials made my heart race. That and the dust glowing in my palms. I wanted my gloves. The last thing we needed was light drawing the Deathbiters to us. I tucked my hands under my armpits as Broderick slipped his vials back into his bag.

Teilo, on the other hand, curled onto his side and tucked his arm under his head. Within moments, his breathing deepened.

Ikane shrugged at my expression. "He's a pirate. He's slept in ships rocking more than a desperate mother trying to soothe a wailing child. He's slumbered while bound to masts and wedged between crates with cold seawater as his blanket. This is a peaceful moment for him."

"He's also young," Broderick interjected. "His growing body needs more rest."

Rest. I hadn't rested since my nightmares began two years ago, and I felt like I had been running ever since.

"Are you ready for this?" Ikane asked.

I glanced at the sky, or what I could see of it through the pine branches. Mina's light had grown brighter, edging everything in her orange glow, which could only mean one thing: It was dark. The Deathbiters were out there somewhere, hunting us.

I gathered a deep breath. "I don't like this," I whispered.

Ikane's arm tightened around me. "It's alright."

"Please, if I am taking too much, I beg you to make me stop," I said. "Both of you."

They nodded.

What in the blazes were we getting into? This was unexplored magic. Even if I managed to repel the Deathbiters through the night, would Ikane and Broderick have the strength to walk in the morning? Would I? Or would we be trapped here in an endless cycle of survival?

The first screech sounded overhead. To think these creatures had once been unassuming little flying mice, only coming out to feast on insects at night, caring for their offspring, and avoiding all human contact. Alder's magic had twisted them into something grotesque and . . . unhappy. Like Ikane had been. Perhaps that was why they were so desperate to attack. They were in pain. And the only way to release their pain was to bite and claw, let the poison flow.

Ikane's fingers laced through mine like a grounding link, and he nodded.

With another nod from Broderick, I shut my eyes and sank into my mind. Etheria flickered with white stars at my empathy for the creatures whose simple, unassuming lives had been turned upside down by Alder.

And then the black fire of Thrall ignited, flashing like sparks leaping from flint strikes as I remembered the sting of the Deathbiters carrying Ikane away. The black fire roared as it caught the memory. While it swelled, it reached for more, overwhelming the shimmering white stars of Etheria. No. I had to balance them, feel equal parts of empathy and rage.

Focus, steady.

Broderick's words flowed through my mind, and with it, his silvery breath of wind. Etheria leapt forward, blocking Thrall's path like a wolf blocking the escape of sheep.

What was missing from Broderick's encouraging words was *release.* There would be no release this night. I would need to find stable ground, equal parts aggression and protection, a steady push and pull.

Ikane's blue energy seeped through every crack, filling the gaps as white and black sparks knit together.

Black solidified to the pointed tip of an arrow while white formed the featherlight fletching at the back. They met in the center of the shaft, spiraling together like dancing suns of black and white, blue and silver. This was it. Balance. A deadly place between two opposite points.

But the arrow was nocked to the bowstring of my mind, pulled taut, stretched back until the fletching brushed my cheek. This was the part I feared most, the strength I needed to hold it here. Even I knew it was foolish for archers to pull their bows before the advance of an enemy. It was exhausting.

We are with you, Kea. Ikane's soothing voice assured me, and with it flowed another wave of blue energy. The strength was overwhelming, soothing even, making my efforts frighteningly easy.

Not too much, Ikane.

I'm alright, he assured me. *It's working, Kea. The Deathbiters are arching away.*

That was good. Now all we had to do was hold it.

All. Night. Long.

Wind told me I was alive. Water surrounded me like the arms of my love, never afraid to touch what was most broken inside me. And between the two, I was safe. A cooling wealth of life and movement spun around me, rhythmic, peaceful, hypnotic. It was the balance of knowing everything was wrong but facing it with friends, grace, and hope. The darkness was just a moment to endure.

Kea? Ikane's voice rushed through my mind, breaking the hypnotic rhythm I'd found. "Kea?" My ears opened to the sound of his voice.

I blinked against the subtle rays of light peeking over the treetops. Morning already? And I didn't feel exhausted? Tired, yes, but not so drained that I couldn't walk. Did that mean—?

I jolted upright, out of Ikane's arms.

His eyes snapped open. "Kea?"

I was shaking. "Are you alright? Please—"

"Hush." He pushed himself to a sitting position and touched my cheek, eyes shining with . . . pride? "It's alright. You did it. *We* did it. We're alright."

I glanced at Broderick, who was sleeping tranquilly on his side, and Teilo, who'd rolled onto his back. I blinked at the treetops, half expecting to see Deathbiters clinging to branches. Nothing. It was peace and birdsong around us as if nothing unusual had ever happened.

I had actually done it and hadn't harmed Ikane and Broderick in the process—in fact, they seemed . . . rested. If that was even possible.

Ikane shook Broderick's shoulder and tossed a pinecone at

Teilo, hitting his head. "Rise up, slumber-noggins. Time to meet the road. We've got a long way to travel yet."

CHAPTER 30

PIRATE PRINCES

*T*here it was. Meldron castle, towering above the clay-tiled rooftops and smoking chimneys like a protector and beacon. But even as sunlight glinted against windows, highlighted the tracery, and enhanced the beauty of every decorative stone, I felt an emptiness dominating towers and spires. King Sander was no longer here.

"Let me go ahead," Broderick said as he slipped off his satchel and handed it to Teilo. "Minister Chanter will want to know."

I nodded, leaning heavily on Ikane's shoulder. Three nights of shielding us from the Deathbiters was beginning to show for all of us. Dark circles had crept under Broderick's and Ikane's eyes, and our pace had slowed to the point where Teilo could overtake us. At least we would be in the shelter of sturdy walls tonight.

Broderick hurried ahead as the rest of us limped down the hillside after him.

"Enough of this," Ikane said. He spun to me, slid his arm behind my legs, and lifted me into his arms.

"Ikane, no."

"Your feet are bleeding. I can smell it."

"I've come this far. I can manage a few more furlongs."

"Let him be," Teilo said, flashing his dimples with a wink. "Ikane's been dying to hold you, anyway."

For the first time, I noticed a rosiness flush Ikane's tanned cheeks. "Remind me again why we saved you?"

"You didn't," Teilo said. "I got away."

I bit my lip as a smile crept across my face. They were as bad as Ropert and I were. Then my smile faded. Ropert, Leander, Queen Lonacheska . . . the baby. Why did everything good have to be overshadowed by darkness?

It wasn't long before Broderick returned with a handful of soldiers and three extra horses, who carried us the rest of the way into the city. Minister Chanter was waiting for us in the castle courtyard. His brow furrowed as he watched Ikane then wrinkled further at the sight of a younger version of the pirate prince riding beside me. Ikane held Broderick's cloak tight around his bare torso, hiding the tattoo on his shoulder.

Stepping forward, Chanter took hold of my horse's bridle. "Bless the Phoenix, you're safe," he said. "What news of Lonacheska?"

"It isn't good," I whispered.

Chanter's face turned a shade whiter. "And Prince Leander? Where is he? His Ridarri returned empty."

Hope swelled. "Boma and Ciri?"

"Only the woman," Chanter said, shaking his head. "We have no word of the other."

Feathers.

"And why . . ." He lowered his voice. ". . . why are they here?" He shot a warning look at Ikane and Teilo. "Pirates? And isn't he the one who tried to kill you?"

I didn't like his reaction, but it was to be expected. "They are our allies," I said. "I expect you to treat them with the same respect you hold for me."

"Of course." Chanter waved to a pair of maidservants standing nearby.

My feet ached as I dismounted. If I could've avoided walking for a week, that would have been bliss. "I will give you a full report tonight when the counsel convenes."

"Yes, Your Majes—" He cut himself off as I shot him a warning look.

I had not been officially crowned princess, and I would avoid it if I could . . . though things were not flowing in my favor.

"Also, send for our best captains. And have the head librarian bring the map I brought back from the Glacial Empire. Send for Ciri as well. I want her there."

Chanter straightened, and a certain satisfaction radiated from his gray eyes. He liked my commanding tone. He liked my initiative. Even though I hadn't accepted my role as the Princess of Roanfire, he already saw me as such.

"It will be done," he said. "See her to her room," Chanter instructed the maidservants. "Send for Healer Bandock immediately, and see that she is bathed and fed."

I glanced at Ikane and Teilo. "Give them rooms near mine."

Chanter's pride faded. "As you wish."

With my arms around their shoulders, the maidservants led me into the castle. All I could think about was a hot bath, ointment for my feet, clean clothes, and a full night of blissful sleep.

I felt strange standing at the head of the table. This was King Sander's position, not mine. But all eyes were trained on me, expectant, hopeful, wondering what direction I would take to return Roanfire to stability.

Teilo and Ikane, who were now shaved and clean, sat beside me, with Broderick and Minister Chanter across from them. Ciri sat at the table as well, her face stoic and cool, but I could see the fear and panic burning in her catlike eyes. She was worried about Leander, as was I.

Captain Tamian had been summoned, along with four more captains I had only heard about, but their reputations were formidable. I was confident they would be able to complete the tasks I set out for them. The head librarian sat at the far end with a scroll on the polished wood before her. She bounced her knee under the table, waiting.

My feet ached. My heart throbbed. But I could do this. This wasn't a meeting of diplomacy or negotiations. This was a battle plan. War strategy. This was what I was good at.

Gathering a deep breath, I addressed everyone present.

"Thank you for coming," I said. "As you know, I recently headed a reconnaissance mission to the Dead Forest after receiving word that our queen was being held captive there by Alder Grayhorn and the Leviathan pirates. As you can see, it did not go as planned."

"How many pirates are there?" Captain Tamian interrupted.

I opened my mouth to answer, but Minister Chanter raised a hand. "Let her finish her report. Save your questions for after."

I swallowed. Right. I had so much to learn about holding an effective meeting, especially with so many moving parts.

"Out of our party of twenty souls, only Broderick and I have returned. My bodyguard, Sir Ropert, and Prince Leander of Toleah are currently in the hands of the pirates."

"Flaming feathers," Chanter groaned, putting his head in his hands. His head rocked back and forth. "This is a disaster."

Ciri's lower lip quivered, but she remained firm and composed.

"I, too, was taken captive for some time. While there, I learned that the Leviathan pirates have taken the Fold Garrison. Their numbers are eight thousand strong."

"And growing," Teilo interjected. As all eyes turned to him, he sank back into his seat. "Sorry. I should not have spoken out of turn."

"No," I said. "Please. If you have anything more to add to this news, I will hear it."

"And who are you?" Captain Alexandra demanded, her face hard.

"This is Teilo Ormand, seventh of the Leviathan princes and our ally," I said.

The captains looked at one another. "A Leviathan?"

"A prince," I snapped. I hated the prejudice radiating from them. Still, I understood. I had once been just like them. But they needed to see that they were allies, not enemies. "In fact, you are honored to be in the presence of two Leviathan princes seeking peace." I gestured to Ikane as well. "They have come to help us drive the pirates back and rescue our queen."

"Let him speak," Captain Tamian said.

Teilo glanced at Ikane who nodded to him.

"While I was held prisoner by my own brothers, I overheard a conversation between the man you know as Alder Grayhorn and Prince Benroar that another five ships are expected within the month. Each one carrying at least one hundred more pirates."

Quiet murmurs broke out among the captains. I felt their panic. These reinforcements would make their army eighty-five hundred strong. I exhaled sharply, steeling myself. It would all work out. We just had to attack before the additional ships arrived, drive them back, and return Leander and Queen Lonacheska before the Ambassador from Toleah arrived. Easy.

"This is nothing we haven't faced before," I said.

"This is twice what we faced before," Captain Alexandra snapped. "Not just the pirates, but if Toleah discovers what happened to their prince . . . Can you do it again? Use your . . . magic or whatever it was?"

I flinched. Feathers, this was getting complicated quickly. "I cannot," I said simply, hoping she would accept, "but the strategy I have developed will hopefully spare both armies from annihilation."

Chanter raised his brows at me but held his tongue.

I gestured to the librarian. "The map."

She handed the scroll to the captain beside her, who in turn handed it to Chanter. I took it from him.

"This scroll is a map of a cave system beneath the Fold Garrison. According to its directions, this cave system can be accessed through Fold City." I unraveled it on the table, spreading it out for them to see. "My proposition is that you, my captains, march for Fold head on. Draw the attention of the pirates to you. Keep them engaged however possible. In the meantime, I, along with a small party, will slip into the cave system and infiltrate the Fold Garrison from within."

The captains glanced at each other, likely pondering possible setbacks.

"I like it," Minister Chanter said. "Save one thing. You cannot go."

Heat swept up my spine. Here we go again. "And why not?" I demanded. "I know the caves. I've been there. I know the Fold Garrison. I've been there, too. I am the only one who can see this though."

"You are also the only hope Roanfire has should this plan fail."

I scratched my ear roughly, letting out a harsh sigh. "If this plan fails, there will be no more Roanfire." Leaning on the table, I looked over the faces around me. "Why do you think the Dead Forest is that? Dead? Why has it not regrown? And why, for a short time, did it appear to live again?"

They watched me, silent.

"Evil lives there," I began, "a power that has leeched the forest of life for four hundred years. If we fail, this evil will spread. It will destroy everything we know, dry it up just like the Dead Forest."

"How . . . how do you know this?" Captain Alexandra asked, her stern voice shaking.

"I've experienced it firsthand," I said, looking at Chanter's gray eyes. "It's all or nothing this time."

The door to the chamber flew open as a soldier staggered inside and hung on the door, panting. His face was flushed, and his eyes were wide as he met mine. "The Hawk," he breathed.

CHAPTER 31

THE HAWK

"What?" Chanter set his hands on the table and stood. "The Hawk . . ." The soldier swallowed hard. "She's . . . she's here with nearly fifty warriors."

Chanter cursed. "She wasn't supposed to arrive for three more days."

The air in the room ignited with panic as chairs scraped along the floor. Ciri's eyes met mine, wide, terrified. Her face turned a sickly gray. If she was as alarmed by this news as everyone else, I may have underestimated the danger The Hawk posed.

"What's going on?" Ikane asked.

"The ambassador from Toleah is here," I said.

Ikane glanced at Teilo. "And because Prince Leander is missing . . . ?"

I nodded and turned for the door.

"Kea, wait." Ikane gripped my elbow. "How . . . why does this concern you?"

I glanced at Minister Chanter.

"Because King Sander has named her heir to the throne," he said. "Keatep, if she accepts, is the rightful Princess of Roanfire and the only person who can save us now." He stole my arm from Ikane and ushered me from the room.

The whole party followed, trailing us down the corridor, descending the staircase and heading for the Great Hall.

"If only there was time to dress you properly," Chanter muttered as he glanced at my tunic and trousers. "Perhaps we can throw on a regal cape and tiara."

My tunic was fine. It was the one I had donned before leaving. Black to indicate the sorrow our kingdom endured embellished with wine-red flowers and green vines of hope. My hair was pulled back in a low warrior's tail, sleek and clean. "When will you stop worrying about my appearance?"

"Never, because it is everything," he snapped. "Your appearance is a display of power. Gowns and jewels display wealth and prosperity. It shows power, authority, confidence, and self-respect."

"It could also show insecurity," I said. I felt the weight of the new sword against my hip. "Authority, confidence, and self-respect can be delivered in other ways. Besides, is it really wealth and prosperity that we need to convey? What they need to see is strength. That Roanfire is not weak and has the ability to stand her ground. Would you agree?"

Chanter's back straightened as he pondered my words, then he smiled at me. "You've grown," he said, his voice soft and genuine. He looked ahead, marching on with determination. "Do not show any sign of weakness. Stand tall, keep eye contact, and whatever you do, do not touch the hilt of your sword. Rumors of Roanfire's fragility has spread like wildfire. Prince Leander may be understanding, but I can't say the same for The Hawk. If you give her a reason to wage war, she will take it."

We paused by an arched door at the end of a corridor I'd never been down before. Chanter addressed our trailing procession. "Go to the Great Hall. All of you. We will meet you there."

"Wait." I glanced at Ikane, Teilo, Broderick, and Ciri. "These four stay with me."

"Pirates?" Chanter asked.

"The Hawk won't know they are pirates unless we tell her."

"Oh, she knows. Somehow, she knows everything."

"Then why hide them?" I asked.

Chanter smiled, closed his eyes, and scratched at one of his gray eyebrows. "Keatep, two. Chanter, zero," he said with a resigned sigh. "Very well. They can stay. But not a word."

I inhaled a steadying breath as the door opened to the back portion of the dais of the Great Hall. The back of King Sander's and Queen Lonacheska's thrones faced me, empty, cold, and uncertain. Beyond that, an alarming number of Tolean warriors crowded the Great Hall. Regardless of their shrouds and cowls, each one held a physique more impressive than the next, and each one bore vibrant tattoos of skills mastered up muscled arms and shoulders. This was an army. Small and deadly and standing in the heart of Meldron.

My hand slid to my hip as my heartbeat quickened, but I stopped as my fingers brushed the cold metal of my sword. No. I had to fight diplomatically.

A tall, slender Tolean woman, dressed in exotic violet-golden robes, stood on the stairs, flanked by two more impressive-looking Ridarri.

"That is her," Ciri whispered in my ear. "Duqa Alaneek."

The woman's brown skin contrasted beautifully with her bejeweled embellishments and golden paint lining her slanted eyes. But her nose . . . She would have been stunning if it weren't for the large, downturned, hooked feature practically hanging over her red-painted lips. The Hawk. I wondered if she knew her name reflected more than her aggressive personality.

Clearing my throat and squaring my shoulders, I approached. "Welcome, Duqa Alaneek."

The hook-nosed woman cocked her head at me, her golden earrings swaying at her jaw. "Who are you?" she asked in a thick accent. Her voice was much deeper than I would've expected from a woman of her size. "Where is Prince Leander? I wish to speak with him at once."

Right to the point, I thought. Very well. Two could play this game. I could not show weakness. I would not allow her to come into my kingdom unannounced and demand things while threatening us with an entire army. To ashes with Master Chanter's warning. My hand slipped to my sword as I made a noticeable sweep of my eyes across her warriors.

Chanter groaned and looked away.

"An army?" I demanded.

Cold flashed in her dark eyes, but she forced a smile. "There is no law against being prepared," she said.

I narrowed my eyes at her. "Prepared for what?"

She arched an eyebrow. "Shah Milak, the king of Toleah, has dispatched numerous letters requesting Leander's return. Yet the responding letters have been vague and indifferent to his desires, some even evading his demands entirely. You understand we assumed some of the letters were not from our prince."

I swallowed. She was right. Prince Leander had been a prisoner instead of our guest for several weeks. King Sander had forged letters in an attempt to stave off war while he tried to negotiate with the Tolean prince.

How was I going to break the news that Prince Leander was now in the hands of Leviathan pirates?

"He has secured an alliance, has he not?" Alaneek arched a sharp eyebrow.

"I . . . Prince Leander hasn't finalized the arrangements."

"What?" Her dark eyes flashed. "Seven months! More than half a year, and he still has not finalized the engagement? His assignment was to return home once the betrothment was solidified, and yet he lingers, requesting precious resources from Toleah to help Roanfire survive a famine." Closing her eyes, she pressed her fingers against her forehead, shaking her head. "I warned his father about this. He does not have the backbone to fight for what is best for Toleah."

I bristled. How dare she speak of her prince like this?

She dropped her hand. "I suppose with the death of Roanfire's king, things have become more . . . complicated." She eyed me with a dangerous glint, like she knew Roanfire was ripe for the taking. The four dozen Ridarri warriors already inside the castle could overpower and seize control before the day was over.

"Now," she began. "I have stated my business. Who, pray tell, am I addressing?" Her gold-painted eyes scanned me from head to foot, taking in my black tailored tunic, trousers, and boots—just as Master Chanter suspected she would. "Hopefully, I have not exhausted my time clarifying everything to some common errand soldier. I would detest the need to repeat myself."

A flicker of black ignited in my chest. I almost felt as if she were looking for a reason to begin a war here and now. And a part of me wanted to give it to her. I was a soldier, a respected and feared one—at least, that was what everyone kept reminding me. That was the reason Toleah approached Roanfire in the first place, because of my assumed ability to wipe out an entire army with magic. They wanted me because they feared me.

"You have the honor of speaking with Keatep Brendagger," I said. "The soldier to whom you sent your prince to make his bride."

Alaneek's eyes fell to my wrists. "I do not see the betrothment bangle."

"It is not so simple," I began. "With King Sander's passing, negotiations have come to a halt."

Alaneek's lips pulled into a menacing smile beneath her hooked nose. "Then perhaps it is time we showed Roanfire what it takes to make a kingdom flourish."

I took a step forward, my hand now fully gripping my sword. That wasn't an empty threat. "You dare threaten this kingdom after all your prince has done to preserve it?"

"Preserve it?" she asked with a scornful chuckle. "This kingdom is a leech, draining Toleah of resources, taking without giving. And I see why. It has nothing to offer." She scanned me again with such contempt my blood turned hot. "It is leaderless and vulnerable and therefore ripe for the taking."

"Roanfire is not leaderless!" My voice echoed off the stone walls and pillars. Even the chandeliers rang overhead.

Alaneek's eyes narrowed at me, burning deep with challenge. "Isn't it? And who is regent of this pitiful kingdom?"

Master Chanter's eyes burned. I glanced at Ciri, who looked as terrified as I felt. The only face among the crowd not filled with panic was Ikane's. His was filled with a gentle encouragement, like he knew I was meant for this.

"That is what I thought," Alaneek sneered. "By order of Shah Milak, Toleah has the right to occupy Roanfire's capital until all debts are repaid or a new arrangement can be made with its rightful king or queen."

She raised a ring-adorned hand. I knew the signal. Once it dropped, the Ridarri would fall upon us like ants to a morsel of abandoned bread.

The words just slipped. "I am regent!"

Alaneek froze, one of her perfect brows lifting. "You?"

I raised my chin and drew my shoulders back. It was too late to go back now. "Roanfire is under my protection," I declared, "and I will not allow anyone to threaten it or its people."

The hook-nosed woman regarded me for a long moment, then a smile spread across her lips. "Perhaps Roanfire has a backbone after all."

I wanted to smash my fist into her hooked nose. She'd been testing me, seeing just how far she could push before Roanfire buckled.

"You won't object to me verifying what you've just claimed, will you?" she said. "We've had no news of a Princess of Roanfire. My, what a historic moment. I'm sure you understand. I would hate to have my prince deceived in his marriage."

I jumped at this. "You understand that marriage negotiations have changed. Your prince came here to secure betrothment with a war hero, not a princess."

Alaneek frowned. "And where is my prince? Why is he not here?" She peered around my shoulder. "I see his Ridarri, Ciri, and I see Leviathan pirates by your side, but not my prince."

My hands grew damp faster than if I'd plunged them in a washbasin. This was the part of being a ruler I felt very inadequate approaching. This woman had already raised her hand to declare war. What would she do if I told her that her prince had been taken captive by Leviathan pirates under our watch? Feathers, she was going to find out anyway.

"He is not here, is he?" Alaneek asked, danger dripping from her painted lips.

"No, he is not," I said. "Prince Leander was trying to help us with a scouting quest when we were attacked by Leviathan pirates. He has been taken hostage."

"What?" Her voice screeched off the walls like a Deathbiter's cry.

Ciri flinched.

"We just finished devising a rescue when you—"

"Prince Leander Polusmed has been captured by Leviathan pirates, and you stand here with two of them?" Her face grew redder as her hand cut through the air like a sword. "Two Leviathan princes?"

Several Ridarri shifted behind her, their eyes growing hard.

"They are here to help," I said.

Alaneek paced the steps, her violet dress sweeping angrily by her feet.

"We march for the Dead Forest within the next few days," I said. "As soon as our armies are gathered."

She spun on me, pointing one of her ringed fingers at my face. "You . . . you expect me to trust you? Trust them?" Her finger jabbed in the direction of Ikane and Teilo. "I know their kind. I know the feud that has raged between your kingdoms for centuries. We have kept our distance. We have had an unspoken truce with the pirates, and now they have taken our prince." Her eyes flitted about, her hooked nose flaring as she debated the issue within her own mind. Then her gold-painted eyes locked on Ikane.

"Him," she demanded, jabbing her finger at his chest. "We take him."

Four Ridarri moved forward.

"Wait. No."

My protest was ignored as the Ridarri took hold of Ikane, wrenching his arms back, dragging him to her. Why wasn't he fighting?

"You can't do this!"

Broderick lunged forward, pinning my hand to my hip before my sword came free.

"A prince for a prince," Alaneek declared. "Once the pirates release Leander, we will release this one."

Chanter was now by my side, his grip firm on my arm, keeping me from chasing after Ikane as the Ridarri dragged him down the stairs. "You don't understand. I need him! I need . . ." I felt sick thinking about it. I needed Ikane to finish this.

"Take me." Teilo's voice rose above the commotion.

Alaneek raised a hand, halting her Ridarri. "You?"

"Teilo, no," Ikane said.

The young pirate stepped forward, offering his wrists, which were still red, scabbed, and sore from the ropes caused by being held captive by his own brothers. "My value is as much as his," Teilo said. "But without his help, Prince Leander will never come home."

No, no, no. This young man couldn't offer himself. He'd just been freed. All this time, he'd been captive, a tool to control and manipulate Ikane. But . . . I couldn't help Leander without Ikane . . . without . . .

At that moment, a devastating darkness poured into my chest like thick clouds of suffocating ash. Leander was never coming back. He was going to die along with Ikane, Broderick, and Ropert. They were all never coming back. No matter what I did here and now, Toleah was going to wage war on Roanfire.

Alaneek jerked her head. The Ridarri released Ikane and took Teilo by the wrists instead.

"You fool." Ikane wrapped Teilo in a quick embrace before the Ridarri shunted him away.

"One week," Alaneek said. "I give you one week to return Leander to us before this pirate prince dies." She spun on her heel and marched through a sea of Ridarri warriors to the arched castle doors. Her Ridarri dragged Teilo with them, and I could feel Ikane's heart breaking with every step he took further away. Ikane's hands clenched at his sides.

I spun away, burying my face in my hands. This was a disaster. No, more than a disaster. No matter what the outcome, Roanfire was ruined.

"Kea." Warm hands rested on my arms. Ikane's hands.

Didn't he understand the pain he caused? He was going to die. Worse, I was going to kill him.

"Leave me." Shaking him off, I rushed out the secret door behind the thrones. But I didn't make it far. I collapsed against the stone wall as tears exploded in my eyes. My nails dug into stone as I slid down. Streams of water dripped from my chin and onto the black folds of my tunic.

The only way to win—even a little bit—was if I turned myself into something wicked. Destroyed every value I held. Became like her.

And I wasn't certain how I could live with myself if I did.

CHAPTER 32

USEABLE POWER

*S*itting by the uncovered window, I stared down at my open palm in the fading light, shifting my fingers ever so slightly to make the white, blue, and green dust glitter in my skin.

What would happen if I added firedust? Would my hands burst? That pain would have been preferable to the cramping in my chest.

Every color represented one of them. Green—clustered on the skin of my left thumb and index finger—the first dust to sink into the scarred patches on my palms, was Leander. It had been so grounding, like sun-warmed soil in a garden bed.

Silver-white dotted both hands in an even blanket of stars scattered across the night sky. I did not remember feeling anything unusual when it had happened, though the fact that a bounty hunter was trying to blind me kept my attention elsewhere. This was just like Broderick. Slippery and unnoticed yet always there, standing behind me like a protective dragon. Somehow, his encouraging personality enhanced everyone else, just like winddust enhanced the potency of the other dusts.

Finally, thick patches of blue dust clustered around the outside of my palms where I had brushed and scooped up the spilled waterdust from the floor. It had been so soothing, like sliding into a warm bath with my body weightless and floating yet flowing forward with unbridled power. Just like Ikane.

All I was missing was Ropert. Hadn't he said something about the dusts providing him strength when he'd come to the camp uninvited with Prince Leander? He had been so weak and drained when I'd left. If he could harness so much energy from ingesting all four sprite dusts, couldn't I? If only Leander were . . .

I glanced at the door rimmed in the orange glow of Mina's light in my night-darkened room. Perhaps Ciri would know the proper administration.

A black creature slammed into the window beside me, screaming, baring long fangs. Windowpanes rattled as it clawed and screeched. I simply looked up at it. No flinch, no jolt of adrenaline. I placed my fingertips on the cold glass. The creature's teeth hit the window with a *clink* as it tried to bite. Again and again, it struggled, shifting position, changing angle, growing more and more agitated when it did not penetrate the glass.

The poor creature. This wasn't the life it was meant to live. Always angry, always fanatical and desperate. Ending its suffering would have been more merciful than condemning it to this life of torment. I saw myself in this demon bat, striking at Rion but never succeeding, never having the strength to break through her barrier.

"I pity you," I whispered to the creature.

It screeched in return, scraping wildly with its talons against the glass until it bled.

It would have been better for this demon bat to die.

Something tapped against my mind then slipped inside with a painful thrust. Black stars flashed across my vision. Pressing my palms against my eyes, I staggered back. What in the blazes was that? Why did Thrall suddenly feel so . . . so energized? It was a burn, the dark energy of rage scalding my blood, aching and deep, needing a release.

I raised my head from my hands. Where was the noise of the Deathbiter's screaming and clawing? Squinting at the window, Mina's firedust highlighted a heap of something lying on the windowsill outside. A leathery wing waved in the gentle breeze of night.

Dead. The Deathbiter was dead.

What an interesting concept, Rion's voices rushed through my mind. *How does it feel? Was its life energy strong?*

By the burning feathers of the Phoenix, I'd absorbed it. My stomach rolled. Spinning away from the window, I braced myself against the bedpost as my stomach heaved.

Come now. It cannot be that unpleasant. I rather thought you would be elated to discover a source of power that did not involve your loved ones.

I clutched my stomach, digging my nails into my skin. This was not useable power. This was dark and wild, pure rage that only Thrall could use.

Speaking of your precious gems, would you like to see them? She pulled on my mind.

A vision opened up of Ropert hanging on a stone wall, arms dangling from chains overhead, his head drooping. His shirt sat in tattered shreds across his body, revealing the blistered and bleeding stripes of lashes across his torso.

He's strong, Rion said. *He hasn't broken yet. But soon . . .*

She forced me to look upon his face as a thick, crimson streak of blood began to slide from his nose.

Thrall bubbled inside me. *No. You witch! Let him be.*

Oh, I do. Occasionally. There was a sinister smile in her voice. *This fine specimen, on the other hand . . .* Her hold on me swiveled, turning me to come face-to-face with Prince Leander's dark skin. He hung in the center of the cell, bare chested, with arms stretched above his head and dull iron cuffs clamped around his wrists. Innumerable deep purple bruises darkened his skin as if he had been at the center of a beating.

Rion's hand stretched out to him as if it were mine. She cupped his jaw, forcing his head up. Chains rattled as his swollen eyes cracked open.

There they are, she said. *Those golden eyes of sunlight. You wanted to see them, didn't you? Look how they shine, even in this dreadful place.*

Let him go. I was trembling. Trembling and struggling to hold Thrall together. It was going to burst.

Leander's eyes shut as her hand pinched, digging into his cheeks. *You want to see this end?* Her voice was harsh and biting. *Then come to me!*

Red slipped from one of Leander's nostrils.

You witch! I wanted to tear her apart. Thrall did, too, the rage boiling to overflowing.

Careful, Rion warned. Her hand dropped from Leander and rested against the rounding belly belonging to Queen Lonacheska. *You wouldn't want to harm your queen and the future Princess of Roanfire, would you?*

I reeled back into my body, cried out, and released.

Black mist burst from my chest, tearing across my room with a crack of thunder. It ripped through the green canopy of the four-poster bed. It tore into the down blanket. White feathers spun like daggers. The wooden chest splintered and cracked open. The two chairs and table standing by the fireplace turned over, tumbled, and shattered against the far wall.

I hated her. Hated her more than anything. She tortured them just because she could, just to get to me. She knew what it would do to me, and feathers, I wanted to let the rage flow.

But letting it go was wrong.

Digging my fingers into my scalp, I sank to the floor, rocking on my knees.

Using Thrall this way was wrong. It would have no effect on her. The last time I'd tried, she'd simply absorbed it like it was a breath of air.

"Kea?"

I flinched as warm, gentle hands touched my back. It was Ikane. I didn't want him to see me like this. Still, my arms reached for him. Still, I buried my tear-streaked face into his neck. Then I let out a scream against his shoulder, fingers clawing at his tunic, drawing into fists. "I hate her!"

His arms crushed me, rocking with me. "I know." His voice was soft and calm but filled with his own pain. "I know."

"She's torturing them."

"Who?"

"Who else?" I snapped, though I didn't mean to. I pulled away. "Ropert and Leander. They've been beaten and whipped, and Rion . . . oh, Phoenix, Rion is hurting them. Their noses were . . ." My voice faltered as my eyes found Ikane's face. Red. A small crimson drop of blood streaked down his upper lip.

Pain crushed my chest all over again. "No." I cupped his face in my hands. "No. Not you, too."

He wiped the evidence away with the back of his wrist. "I'm alright," he said, his own warm, calloused hand sliding to my neck. He pressed his forehead against mine. "Everything will be alright in the end."

The end. Oh, how I hated the thought. The end that I would bring to all of them, after everything they'd endured. I pulled back, but Ikane held me firm. His eyes closed as he inhaled deeply. "I love you, Little Brendagger. That'll never change."

How could he say that after everything? After what happened to his brother? After he learned what I was going to do to him?

Tears burned down my cheeks, but this time, they no longer stung with rage. Now, they flowed with numbness, an endless disconnected desire to survive and die.

"Kea," Ikane whispered. The familiar scent of mint and steel carried on his breath as his lips drew closer. "Do you remember what I said to you the day we were forced to draw a line between us? The day I returned you to the soldiers of Roanfire?"

I shut my eyes. That pain was nothing compared to what I

felt now.

"You are still a star, Kea. My star. If your light fades . . ." He stopped, then his warm lips pressed against mine, soft and tender, yet mingled with the sense of drowning. I tasted salt. Tasted blood. Tasted pain and sorrow. Tasted goodbye. And still, I leaned into it.

Ikane pulled away. He rested his forehead against mine again, his thumbs brushing the tears from my cheeks. "Please burn strong, Little Brendagger. I need you . . . I need you to guide me home."

What home? Death? Was that the beacon he looked for now? An end? Ever since his body had been restored, I felt as if he was running toward an end . . . like he deserved it. Why couldn't I join him? Life itself seemed to be holding me hostage.

I slumped against his chest, shutting my eyes as more tears flowed. More, more, more. Never enough. Never ending. We were going to march for Fold tomorrow, side by side, face the greatest evil as the allies we had wanted to be for so long. But only one of us was going to survive.

I didn't want it to be me.

CHAPTER 33

CHILLED GLASS

"What happened here?"

My eyes barely cracked open at the voice. They felt swollen and thick, sticky. Sand scratched my lashes as I rubbed them. Finally, they blinked at the sunlight streaming through the crosshatched window, highlighting every piece of broken furniture, shredded fabric, and deadly white feathers embedded in wood and stone.

I had hoped last night had been a nightmare, but Ikane stirred behind me. His warm embrace left my shoulders as I leaned forward, giving him room to stretch and arch his back. He yawned and shook his head. There was something very wolflike in the motion.

Broderick shoved and stepped over the crumpled and broken armchairs piled against the door. He paused at a white feather protruding from the wood of the cracked table. Pinching it with his fingers, he pulled. The soft barbs tore away while the rest of the feather remained fixed. He looked at me. "Did you . . . ?"

"She had a hard night," Ikane said as he stood and straightened his rumpled, tear-stained tunic. He extended a hand to me.

I stared at it. Rough, calloused, suntanned, scarred, human. The hand that had held me, dried my tears, and flowed with the deepest love. But I felt worlds apart from him, so dead inside like everything had turned to dust.

Somehow, I found myself wandering to the window. My fingers fell against the chilled glass. The Deathbiter was still there, its skin torched and blistered by the sun, a lifeless heap on the windowsill. A single, shredded wing hung over the edge, shaking in the breeze.

If only I could use their life energy instead of the lives of those I loved. How many soldiers would we lose to the Deathbiters before we reached Fold? If only . . .

My hand curled into a fist. I could. They were not Rion. They were susceptible to the shredding bursts of Thrall. I could use them and destroy them simultaneously while protecting the main body of soldiers without taking precious energy from Ikane and Broderick.

"Kea?" Ikane asked.

I turned around. "How many soldiers have we assembled?"

"Six thousand and seventy," Broderick answered. "Another two thousand are headed this way from Kaltum. But they won't be here for another five days."

I flinched, looking at the shattered splinters of wood from the chest that had been at the foot of my bed. They wouldn't arrive in time. We had to move with what we had. The pirates would outnumber us, yes, but they were restricted by the walls of the garrison. Only so many could fight.

"Are they ready?" I asked. "Are the captains briefed?"

"They are," he said. "Captain Alexandra's and Sewell's squadrons left at sunrise. Captain Tamian's squadron should be departing as we speak."

"Good," I said. "We leave with the next wave." That was the only way I could ensure I remained in the center to protect them. "Is Ciri ready?"

Broderick rubbed the back of his neck. His lips tightened. "Ciri is in no condition to come with us, I'm afraid."

"What?"

"Duqa Alaneek had her whipped. Fifteen lashes."

Anger pushed the dusty numbness aside. "Why? What for?"

"For failing to protect Prince Leander."

I rubbed my face. How twisted could Tolean justice be? Leander's fate wasn't Ciri's fault. "Is she alright?" I whispered.

"She will be," Broderick said.

"And what of Boma? Any word?"

Broderick glanced at Ikane. They knew something.

"What is it?" I demanded.

"Boma returned last night near death from Deathbiter venom," Broderick said. "Don't worry. He's been healed. But his reason for abandoning his post was . . ."

I jerked my head at him. Why couldn't he just say it? I was tired of asking for explanations.

Broderick sighed. "Boma noticed Sir Ian's strange behavior just before we were attacked by the Leviathan pirates. He—Sir Ian, that is—betrayed us. He was the one who informed the pirates of our presence."

"Feathers, why? Money?"

"So it seems."

I shut my eyes. That explained why I couldn't find him during the attack. Coward. Snake. Wasn't it enough that he boasted about himself being the bodyguard to the future Princess of Roanfire? I was so tired of being betrayed by those I should have been able to trust.

Thrall latched onto this. Fine. I'd let it. Let it wet its lips on something dark until I was ready to use it.

Broderick sensed the darkness. I could see it in his eyes and the way he stiffened. "Kea . . ."

"Is Boma able and prepared to come?" I asked. I needed people I could trust with me when we slipped into the caves under Fold, and that list was growing smaller and smaller. Boma, despite what little I knew about him, was someone I was certain I could trust. His loyalty burned for Leander.

"If Alaneek permits, I believe he can."

"Send for him," I said, "and see that he is equipped with armor from our armory."

Broderick didn't move. "Kea, you . . . breathe, Kea. Take a breath. Let it—"

"Let it go?" I finished. Yes, Thrall was around me, darkening my skin with shadowy vapors. "I will let it go when I am ready. I can use it."

He bit his lip and glanced at the destruction in my chamber. Sadness filled his eyes . . . no, it was disappointment and fear. "You're going down a dangerous path, Kea. I've warned you before. Thrall cannot be—"

"It can," I snapped. "Alder does it. I am doing it right now. Thrall is there. I keep it harnessed like a feral hound and will release it when I see fit."

Ikane inhaled sharply. He glanced away, blinking rapidly, the muscles in his jaw working.

I shut my eyes. I should not have used that analogy. Everything I had said just now made me a mirror image of Alder. The use of Thrall, the darkness, the control, the manipulation.

"Ikane, I . . ."

"It's alright," he said, but I could feel it in his voice. It wasn't. "I should go."

"Ikane, wait."

He paused by the broken furniture at the door, his boot bumping against a cracked leg. "I know you are hurting, Kea, and that I deserve these daggers going through my chest, but I thought you understood." His eyes lifted to mine, green and blue, broken pieces of his soul radiating inside. "Why are you going down the same path Alder did?"

Thrall flashed black, crackling around me. "I'm not. This is what—"

"You are, Kea," Ikane said. "The darkness is around you, rippling through you. I see it, smell it, hear it. It . . . it is dimming your star."

His words were like a punch to my gut, and I took a step back without meaning to. This was just a moment of misunderstanding between us. He didn't know what I had to do to end this. What I had to sacrifice. Neither did Broderick.

"I will be by your side, Kea," Ikane said. "I am yours, heart and soul, always. But I had hoped that, in the end, I would be touching a star and not drowning in waters of bitumen."

Turning away, he stepped over the broken furniture and left.

Everything in my chest clenched. My heart, my lungs, my blood. I felt like a monster had wrung its tentacles around every organ and began to squeeze. Squeeze so hard that even Thrall couldn't make a move.

"I'll have armor brought up for you." Broderick paused before stepping over the furniture. "And I'll send for the servants to take this away."

"You understand why I have to do this, don't you?" I asked. "Look what I did to the Deathbiter." I gestured to the bat crumpled on my windowsill. "Look what I could do with the power it gave me." I glanced around my room. Yes, it was destroyed, but now I knew the extent of damage I could inflict with just one Deathbiter life.

"You used it?" he asked, dismay brimming in his tone.

"Yes." And I wasn't ashamed.

"Life energy, Kea? You took life energy. Stole it and used it. Just like Rion."

"It isn't the same," I snapped. "It was a Deathbiter."

"Do you think she sees us that way? Mere humans? Mortals? Insignificant compared to her godlike powers? It was a living creature, Kea."

"It was a monster!"

"So are we."

My mouth clamped shut.

He rubbed his shoulder—the one with the missing arm—and turned away. "I will see you in the courtyard."

I spun to the window, my hands flexing into fists. Nothing I did satisfied. Wasn't it better for the Deathbiters to die than for us? I was going to destroy the plague and protect our army at the same time. I was doing good.

Thrall turned to me, saliva dripping from its fangs as my anger dangled before it. I wanted to feed it.

But a part of me knew Ikane and Broderick were right. I was going down Alder's path, twisted and dark. But it would only be for a moment. Just long enough to get our army to Fold. I could tame Thrall again, send it to the farthest corners of my mind and ignore it, couldn't I?

The blistered body of the Deathbiter stared at me through the glass.

Couldn't I?

I emerged from my chambers dressed in fragmented pieces of armor. A light breastplate, heavy pauldrons, thick armguards and faulds, leather cuisses, and sculpted greaves that were so polished I doubted they had ever seen battle. This suit of armor was more me than anything I'd ever donned. Royal, but not. A soldier, but not. A wardent, but not. It was a smattering of parts and pieces that created something . . . something strange and unidentifiable.

I paused in the hallway. Ikane was there, dressed in black steel armor, leaning against the wall. His arms were folded across his chest like he'd been waiting for me.

Dismissing the servants, I approached him. "Ikane, I—"

"When was the last time you used your sword?" he asked, not looking at me.

I . . . I had to think about it. I remembered drawing it when he'd abducted me while still in his wolf form, but I did not have the chance to wield it. And I was too injured to handle it when the Leviathans had attacked. I went back further. When Alder had taken Queen Lonacheska? No. When the bounty hunters tried to capture me? No. Even then, I hadn't raised my weapon. The last time I'd raised my sword was when Ropert and I had sparred together after he'd been poisoned by fire from the inside out. That felt like a lifetime ago.

Ikane looked up and scanned me, his green eye shimmering in the dim light of the corridor. Which could only mean one thing: He was irritated. With his eyes locked on me, he pushed off the wall, reached back over his shoulder, and drew one of his swords in a single smooth motion.

I took a step back. "What are you doing?"

"I think you need a chance to remember who you are." He drew the other sword. "Draw your weapon."

What was wrong with him? "Ikane, this isn't—"

One of his swords flashed toward me like black lightning. I staggered back, my hand flying instinctively to the hilt of my sword.

"What's gotten into you?" I snapped.

His green eye sparked as he lunged forward. I had no choice. I drew my sword. His blade rang against mine before it came free of the scabbard. He wasn't holding back. The force of his blow knocked me to the side. Memories of the first time we'd sparred in the training arena flashed through my mind. He was dangerous. He was strong and fast. He was better than I was.

I spun away as his second blade whipped at my leg, my shoulder hitting the corridor wall. My leather cuisses wouldn't have stood a chance against that blow. The tip of his blade sparked against the stone, grinding beside me. "Ikane—" I dropped as another strike raced for my head.

Balling my hand into a fist, I clubbed the inside of his knee. He let out a grunt and staggered back.

Breathing hard, I straightened, feeling my own irritation rise. Thrall licked at it, making me flinch.

"Go on," he growled, green eye flaring, canine teeth sharp and barred. "Use it."

"What?"

"Use Thrall. It's your weapon of choice now, isn't it? Go on."

"I don't want—"

He lunged. I parried both of his weapons, sliding my blade into one smooth arc around them. The tip grazed his shoulder and bit into a strand of his hair as he arched back. Pushing off the wall, I shunted him in the chest. He fell back, hitting the opposite wall of the corridor with a grunt.

"I don't want to fight you!"

His eyes narrowed, the green one burning dangerously. He bared his teeth, showing the permanent sharpness of his canines. "Then let it go," he growled.

"I'm not using it on you!"

His head tipped. "Are you certain about that?"

I glanced at my hands holding my sword. Black mist swirled around the blade, coming from . . . me. Gasping, I dropped my weapon. It rang against the stone floor as I staggered back. How had I not noticed it slinking through my mind, snapping up morsels of pain and anger? It was thick. Thick and fat with dark energy. I had to push it down now.

With a wolflike snarl, Ikane lunged forward.

Dropping to a crouch, I threw up my arms. Thrall lurched at him, ready to burst from my body and level Ikane to the ground. No. I jerked it back like a hound master's leash cutting into an animal's neck. I'd rather Ikane tear me apart than hurt him with this darkness.

Thrall gagged and sputtered. Then it turned its wrath on me.

Breathe, breathe, breathe! I cried to myself.

It didn't work. The darkness was too strong. It latched onto me, sinking into the memory at the front of my mind. The day Ikane and I had sparred. It was rich with fear, easily turned into the anger it so desperately sought.

Call on your lights! Ikane's voice burst into my mind.

I couldn't. I couldn't focus. I couldn't think of anything but the fear of that day when Ikane's swords had crashed against mine, driving me back, his green eye flaring with unnatural light.

This was what he was trying to prove. That Thrall was going to eat at my soul and tear me apart, no matter how much I believed I could tame it. Just like Alder.

A blue streak of light ripped into Thrall, separating the mist as if he'd cut through it with one of his obsidian swords.

Release it, Kea.

I couldn't. If I did, it would rip him apart.

His blue energy touched my mind. Somehow, that was all I needed to soothe the panic inside. I could breathe. I could feel the cool, crisp cleansing of water rush across all the guilt, pain, and anger. Etheric lights sprang forth, like stars awakening in the night sky. Together, we swept over the black mist like a mighty wave on the deck of a ship.

Then it was gone.

"Little Brendagger?" Ikane's voice pulled me back to the dimly lit hallway. He crouched before me, warm hands cupping my cheeks, his swords lying harmlessly beside us. The green smolder in his eye was gone.

Shutting my eyes, I pushed my cheek into his hand. He knew my darkest parts, and still he didn't turn and run. His perfect love took my load, took the blows.

"I'm sorry," I whispered. "I'm so sorry."

"Hush, Kea. You meant well."

"I shouldn't have let it go this far. You were right. You were right all along."

His lips pressed against my forehead. "I am only returning the love you showed me. When darkness possessed all of my being, you still shone. I offered you nothing, and still you called to me. I didn't deserve any of it."

I wrapped my arms around him. "You deserved more," I said. He had been innocent. He had no memory, and under Alder's command, he had no choice. I, on the other hand, had knowingly chosen darkness.

Straightening, I wiped my nose with the back of my wrist and sniffed. I would do better. For Ikane. But how were we going to protect the soldiers from the Deathbiters now? Even with Ikane and Broderick giving me their energy, I barely had the strength to shield a mere handful of us for a few nights. How were we going to shield an army of six thousand?

Unless . . .

I glanced at my gloved hand. Sprite dust. Had the answer been staring me in the face all along? Ropert said we knew so little about them, but he'd arrived at our camp fully energized because he had ingested them. Prince Leander, too, had been miraculously energetically restored after he'd helped me face Rion. What if . . . what if Yotherna and Alder had been using them wrong? Was it really that simple?

It was a blind leap of faith. Doubt was thick, but I had to try.

"I need to speak with Ciri," I said.

Ikane arched an eyebrow. "That . . . was unexpected."

Smiling, I brushed the moisture from my cheeks. "What? Being in my mind hasn't made my thought process easier to follow?"

He shook his head with a smile. "Your mind is rather . . . chaotic."

I chuckled. It felt so good to feel those muscles on my face again. The way my cheeks stretched, the way my eyes lifted. "There's a reason. I promise," I said. Using the wall for support, I stood, bringing him with me. I caught his neck before he stepped away, stretched on my toes, and pressed my lips against his. The kiss was brief but filled with all the passion, love, and light I felt swelling inside. Hope.

He blinked rapidly as I pulled away.

"I love you, Ikane," I said.

At this, he pulled me closer and kissed me again. His hands slid through my hair, pressing us together, melding us into one. I didn't want him to let go. I didn't want to breathe. But a sharp pinch struck my lip, and I yelped, breaking the moment.

"Sorry," he muttered, running his tongue across his sharp canine teeth. "I don't know why these haven't gone away."

"I like them," I said. Even as the taste of blood filled my mouth, I'd endure a thousand more bites to feel him that close to me forever. But that thought was dimmed by what we still had to face: Rion.

I picked up my sword and slid it back into my scabbard. "Thank you, Ikane," I said as he picked up his own.

"What for?"

"For challenging me."

He smiled, flashing those sharp teeth again. "I couldn't bear to lose you like that."

My smile faded. If I didn't find another way, we would still lose each other. "Come on. We need to hurry."

Taking his hand in mine, we headed to the wing where Duqa Alaneek had taken up residence. Where The Hawk now held Ciri under arrest.

CHAPTER 34

ALL FOUR

*H*old a moment, Kea." Ikane pulled me to a stop before we approached the intimidating Ridarri warriors standing outside Alaneek's door. He smoothed my hair and tucked a stray strand behind my ear. His sky-blue and meadow-green eyes scanned me, much like Master Chanter did before I met with nobility.

"And?" I asked.

He smiled. "You look like you."

"You mean, I look a mess."

He chuckled. "You look like someone not to mess *with*."

Oh, how he made me smile. "Wait here," I said. Turning to the door, I gathered a deep breath then approached the Ridarri. Their eyes were hard and slanted as they looked down at me. Feathers, they were giants. And I'd thought Boma was formidable.

"I would like to speak with your prisoner, Prince Leander's bodyguard, Ciri."

One Ridarri tilted his head at me as if he hadn't understood. The other spoke in broken Roanfirien.

"You come no announce. Duqa Alaneek no see you."

I gathered another breath at his tone. "This is not the time to make a formal request for an audience. Your prince is in the hands of Leviathan pirates, and I am doing everything in my power to save him. I don't need to speak with Alaneek. I need to speak with Ciri."

He glanced at his companion, both of them looking . . . unnerved? Worried? Intimidated? Yes, that was it. Neither one of them wanted to approach The Hawk without warning.

Fine. Then I'd do it. Stepping forward, I grasped the lever.

The Ridarri's hand flashed out, taking hold of my wrist. Ikane reached for his sword, but I waved him off and turned back to the Ridarri. "I will take the blame," I told him.

He swallowed, glanced at his companion for reassurance, then released me.

I pushed the door open. "Duqa Alaneek?"

The hook-nosed woman jumped, her dark eyes flashing as she rose from the edge of the bed. I had expected her to have decorated her room in the same comforts of Toleah as Prince Leander had, but she had left the quarters virtually untouched. What caught my eye was Ciri. She was lying on the bed on her stomach with her back of blistered and bleeding lashes exposed to the air. She lifted her head from her folded arms.

"Kea?" she asked.

"What are you doing?" Alaneek snapped. "Get out!"

I blinked. Was that a pot of ointment in her hand? Was she tending to Ciri's wounds? I shook myself. "I need to speak with Ciri."

"You do not come unannounced and demand to see anyone!" Alaneek roared. "Ridarri!"

The men standing guard at the door moved inside.

"No," I said. "Wait. Please. I need Ciri's help. It concerns your prince."

Alaneek paused at this.

"I would have approached this in the proper order of requesting an audience if I had time," I began, "but I don't. I leave within the hour for Fold."

"You . . . are personally going?" she asked in a disbelieving tone. "Placing yourself in danger to save him?"

"He did the same for me," I said. And if my concept proved right, I could actually save him. I could actually bring him home and destroy Rion. None of my friends would have to die. In fact, no further lives needed to be taken.

Alaneek dismissed her Ridarri with a nod, her golden earrings swaying. She set the pot of ointment on the bedside table. "What do you need from Ciri?"

I decided to ask it straight. "Did Prince Leander ingest sprite dust to restore his strength?"

Ciri tilted her head at me then glanced at Alaneek. "I not understand question. In . . . inge—"

"Ingest," Alaneek interrupted. "To eat or swallow." Her tone was sharp and disapproving, like the question bordered on accusing him of using hallucinogenic mushrooms.

Ciri swallowed. "Yes."

"How?" I asked. "I mean, in what order or potency did he do it? Was it a combination of two or three dusts? Which ones?"

Ciri pushed herself from the bed, holding the sheet over her chest as she sat upright. Her dark hair hung over her shoulder like a curtain. She wouldn't make eye contact with Alaneek, who was staring at her with wide eyes.

"All four," Ciri whispered.

Alaneek whirled away, pressing a balled fist against her lips.

"Four?" I blinked. How in the blazes did he do that without bursting the way Broderick's thunder pouches did? Without scarring himself the way Alder had?

"Why do you ask this?" Alaneek demanded, her back still to me.

Should I tell her the truth? Did I have the time and the energy to convince her of the danger Rion posed for all of us? Or would it lead to more questions, more than I could explain? "Because I need the strength the dusts can offer," I said.

Alaneek turned around, her dark eyes scanning me. "You look strong enough."

Feathers, this was what I was worried about.

"Duqa Alaneek," Ciri said softly. Then she spoke in her native tongue, soft and earnest. I discerned Leander's, Yotherna's, and Rion's names, but that was all.

Alaneek turned to me again. I saw something new in her eyes, something I thought was never possible in a face like that. Understanding. She suddenly understood that there was more to the situation than Leviathan pirates holding her prince hostage.

"If I share this with you, you believe you can save him? Truly save him?"

I couldn't promise anything, but this was the closest I'd ever come to hope. "I will do everything in my power to see that Prince Leander returns safely to his homeland of Toleah."

Alaneek straightened. "Equal parts fire, earth, and water dust," she said. "Only pure dust. Anything less, and the balance is disrupted. Once the dusts have reached your blood—it only takes to the count of thirty—then you take winddust. I warn you, it is powerful and strong. It will fill you with a sense of invincibility. But that is not the truth. You are still flesh and bone."

"I understand," I said. I'd felt invincible before, when I'd used Thrall. I knew how mortal I was then.

Alaneek looked at Ciri. "But it is addictive. Once you taste the power, your own strength is never enough." She cursed in her native tongue. "How long has Prince Leander been using?"

Ciri looked down. "Since he was attacked by the dark bats. I try to stop him. He no listen. He say that Lady Brendagger need him strong when . . ."

Another punch to my gut. He did it for me. He did it so that he had more strength to offer when I took his life energy. And he'd given the same concoction to Ropert. My hands balled into fists, leather gloves creaking. Did he slip some to Broderick? Didn't he think that I could have used the strength myself? That he wouldn't have to sacrifice his life—or Ropert's or Ikane's or Broderick's—at all if he had just provided me with this magical remedy?

"Thank you," I said, trying to keep the anger from showing in my face. My jaw ached.

Alaneek retrieved a wooden box from the table, the same box Boma had brought forward when I needed sprite dust to heal Prince Leander. She held it out to me. "This holds full vials of pure wind, water, and earthdust. I do not have pure firedust to give."

I took the box gratefully. "I think I know where I can get some," I said. I cocked my head at her. "Where do you get so much pure dust, anyway?"

Her devious smile returned. "Toleah's secrets are ours to keep."

Very well. I would leave it at that. "Thank you." I bowed to her. "Thank you both. And I apologize for the abrupt manner I approached this. I hope you can forgive me."

"Bring back our prince, and all will be forgotten," she said. "But the terms still stand. One week or the young Leviathan prince dies."

"A fortnight," I bargained. "After all, it takes nearly a week for an army as large as ours to reach Fold. It'll take at least that long to get back."

She nodded once. "A fortnight, then."

I glanced once more at Ciri, who smiled weakly, then left with the box of sprite dust clutched to my armored chest. Now it was time to find Broderick.

Red uniforms filled the courtyard, swimming with armor, supplies, horses, and weapons. I pushed through the crowd to the fountain in the center. Water glistened in the sharp sunlight as it arched from the sculpture of a three-stone phoenix. I searched for a dark cloak, a shadow in a corner, anything to indicate Broderick was here. He should be. He was part of my underground crew.

"Do you see him?" I asked Ikane, straining my neck to look over the crowd.

Ikane shook his head. "I see Boma, though. He's by the fountain."

Soldiers parted for Ikane, eyeing his black armor and deep blue tunic in the sea of red. I climbed the edge of the fountain and peered across the courtyard. So many soldiers. Nearly a thousand clustered together.

I swallowed. This was only a fraction of the soldiers marching on Fold, and I had to find a way to protect all of them when the Deathbiters appeared tonight.

Ikane climbed the fountain edge and stood beside me. "There's Boma." He pointed. The Tolean Ridarri turned to us, his deep-green exotic clothing and copper armor standing out as much as Ikane's blue and black did. His midnight hair was bound in a long braid down his back.

"Boma!" I called, waving a hand.

He shouldered his way through the crowd to us.

But I still couldn't see Broderick.

"There he is," Ikane said.

I followed his gaze, finding the assassin standing beside a group of warhorses, tucking items into the saddlebags. His dark clothing and armor made him nearly invisible in the shadow of the stable.

Jumping from the fountain's edge, I made my way to him. He looked up as we emerged from the crowd.

"There you are," I said. "I've been looking everywhere for you."

"I've readied your horses," he announced. "This one here is for you, Kea. Nightwalker." He patted the neck of the silver stallion beside him. "That one is yours, Ikane. Her name is Gildain. Boma, you can ride Freesia. Are you all ready? Captain Nerian is already at the gate."

He was ignoring me. I didn't blame him. Not after what I'd said earlier.

I caught his shoulder just as he was about to mount his own steed. "Broderick."

He glanced at my shoulder, not at me, his eyes cold and distant. "What?"

"I'm sorry," I sighed. "You were right. I . . . I was wrong to consider using Thrall like that. I should have listened to you when it came to Alder, and I would be a fool to make that mistake twice."

His eyes lifted, his head tilting suspiciously. "What changed your mind?"

"Ikane," I said. "He knocked some sense into me."

A smile tugged on the corner of his lips. "Good."

"And," I continued, "I think I found another way to fuel my energy. But I need pure sprite dust for it. All I am missing is pure firedust."

"You're asking if I have any," he concluded.

I nodded.

"You said pure?"

I nodded again.

He pulled his lips to the side, and I knew what he was going to say before he said it. "I don't have pure firedust. The dust I have I purchased from a Dust Hunter in the market. He doesn't have the cleanest reputation."

"Captive dust?"

"Possibly." He squirmed. "Most likely. I'm not proud of it. But how else do you expect me to make so many thunder pouches affordably? It's a waste otherwise."

I rubbed the back of my neck. I couldn't leave without it. It was what could save him and Ikane, Ropert and Leander. It was what could spare the soldiers pain and horrible deaths from the Deathbiters. If I wasn't going to use Thrall, I needed firedust.

I dropped my hand. "Do you know where I can get pure dust?"

"Maggie *might* have some." He placed heavy emphasis on the word.

I remembered the old healer. She'd tended to Broderick's infected shoulder after Ikane had bitten him. I'd nearly forgotten about her. "Take me."

"We'll fall behind."

"The four of us can ride hard and catch up," I said. "Please. I can't leave without it."

Sighing, he swung up into his saddle. "Alright. Come on."

Maggie Briar, the old healer with shaking hands, had one small vial of pure firedust in her possession, and I gave her seventy-five gold coins for it. I would have given her seventy-five thousand if she'd asked. This was what could save my friends' lives.

But there was a problem. It wasn't enough. Not compared to the thick, heavy vials Alaneek had given me. I didn't know how much I would need to consume to have enough energy to protect the army from the Deathbiters at night. And worse, I didn't know how much I would need to face Rion. This little vial, half the size of my forefinger, no matter how pure, could not be enough.

I pressed Broderick to take me to all the healers within Meldron. The sun passed its highest point and began its descent, and still we had only one small vial of pure dust.

I held it in my fist, pressing it against my chest as we rode to the main gate. I pulled Nightwalker to a halt, gazing out at the trampled earth leading to Fold. The armies had marched quickly, trying to minimize their nights spent in the open—not an easy feat with a militia of this size. I took some hope in knowing that every soldier had armor, whether it be new or old. It would help, but it would not guarantee survival.

"They will be alright, Kea," Broderick said, as if he could read my thoughts. "Roanfire's soldiers are resilient. You and I can heal the wounded."

"Just the two of us? And six thousand soldiers?" The idea alone drained me.

The scar on his lips pulled against his smile. "Thirty-two," he said proudly.

"What?"

"Since the Deathbiters' arrival, I have been searching for wardents to train. I have found thirty-two with the ability to heal Deathbiter injuries."

I wasn't sure whether to laugh or cry at this news. I'd somehow believed we were the only ones with the ability to heal.

"They're not as skilled as you or me. But they will save lives. I have stationed five to every squadron of one thousand men."

"Why didn't you tell me?"

"You didn't give me the chance," he said.

This was good news. Wonderful news. But only five to every thousand? They still needed me. I knew how to use Thrall to save them. It would be effective. But what toll would it take on me? On those around me?

I glanced at the red glow of the vial reflecting on the wrinkles of my leather glove. I had to test this before . . . before it was too late and I found myself in the heat of battle with only the life force of my friends to help me. I had to understand how much I needed, how quickly I burned through it, and most importantly, how much I would need to face Rion's endless power.

But the longer we delayed, the further we fell behind. Perhaps we should wait another night? I shook off the thought. The soldiers were out there now, exposed.

I looked at Ikane. "Will you help me?"

Within moments, I tipped my head back and swallowed a dusty mouthful of equal parts earth, water, and firedust. Only a pinch. I couldn't afford to waste anything if this worked. *One, two, three* . . . Water struck first, sliding down my spine like a cool waterfall. *Twelve, thirteen, fourteen* . . . Heat rushed to every limb, warming my blood and skin as if I were sitting by a campfire. *Sixteen, seventeen, eighteen.* There it was, the grounding stone and roots of earth. *Thirty.* I glanced at the glittering whiteness of winddust waiting for me to consume. It was time.

"Kea . . ." Broderick breathed as I tipped my head back and swallowed.

It soared down my throat, nearly taking my breath away, then rushed through my blood, igniting every sensation of water, fire, and earth into a storm of energy. It was the muscle of the warhorse beneath me. It was the sails of a mighty ship snapping tight in the wind. It was the stone of a fortress wall. This . . . this was incredible. Indescribable.

"Are you alright?" Broderick asked. "You're not going to . . ."

"Burst?" I asked with a grin. "I could fly," I said. "Let's go!"

I kicked Nightwalker's sides and leaned forward in my saddle, feeling the wind rush through my hair and sting my eyes. Still, my horse felt slow. I could have run faster on my own, and perhaps I would.

"Kea! Hold up!" Broderick called after me. "The horse!"

CHAPTER 35

DESCENDANT

*I*t was my fault. The energy had been so strong and so overwhelming that I had completely disregarded the needs of my warhorse. Even for an animal as fit as he was, I should have eased him into the run, let his muscles warm and the blood flow before I pushed. Not ten leagues into our journey, his gait became uneven. I slowed and slid from his back in one smooth motion, leading the horse on foot without pause. We were so close.

Dust—kicked up by the army marching ahead—cast a hazy brownness on the horizon.

Ikane, Broderick, and Boma rode up beside me, all of them panting and brushing sweat from their faces.

"Feathers, Kea," Broderick huffed. "Was that . . . the dust? How did you do—"

"Alaneek told her," Ikane said as he shifted in his saddle. "I still don't see how you can ride like this for hours on end."

"The Toleans know about this?" Broderick asked, glancing over his shoulder at Boma. "Why haven't they used it against us? With their expertise, Ridarri arts, and sprite dust resources, they could have crushed us already."

"Because of Leander. He wouldn't allow—" It struck me, like a rockslide tumbling over my body. I stumbled to my knees. My body shook, and perspiration flared across my skin. A sickening twist curled through my stomach, threatening to expel whatever remained in my gut.

"Kea." Ikane slid from his horse and dropped beside me, taking my shoulders.

Less than a shift in the shadows. That's all the energy a pinch of sprite dust offered. Not even a fifth of a day. I would need to use . . . flaming feathers . . . that meant I would have to use the entire vial of firedust in one night to shield us from the Deathbiters. My fist struck the dirt.

"What's wrong?" Ikane asked.

"It's not enough," I said. "I don't have enough to shield the army from the Deathbiters and . . ."

"And face Rion?" he concluded. "It's alright, Kea. We are here to—"

"No," I snapped. "Don't you see? That's why I did this. If I only had enough firedust, I could use that instead. I wouldn't need to take anyone's life energy. I could face Rion on my own."

Ikane glanced up at Broderick. "Don't worry about that now," he said. "One step at a time. Let us get safely through the night first."

I nodded, allowing his strong arms to raise me up. Broderick slipped down and ran his hands along the slender tendons of my horse's front legs. He cursed. "The right one is hot," he said. "No one can ride him. Hopefully, with some rest tonight, he'll be rideable in the morning."

He didn't say it, but he wanted to. I had been a fool.

"You can ride mine," Ikane insisted. "I need to walk for a few miles, anyway. My rear is killing me."

Climbing into Gildain's saddle reminded me of Alaneek's warning. My own strength wouldn't be enough after using the dust. The temptation to take a small pinch again was overwhelming, but I pushed it down, the same way I did with Thrall. I had to save it. I would use it to protect the soldiers when night painted the sky with violet stars and brought out the nightmares. Not before.

I watched Ikane's broad shoulders and strong strides as he led Nightwalker by the reins. His dark hair hung in a warrior's tail over his swords that crossed at his back. Though he'd known for a while now, he didn't seem the least bit concerned with the fact that Yotherna's plan to end Rion was for me to take his life. Neither did Broderick. Even Leander and Ropert had expressed their willingness . . . no, not just willingness—desire—to help.

Every one of them carried with them an acceptance of their fate, like they knew they were doing this for the sake of Roanfire. For me. It would have been easier for me to lay down my life for them—not the other way around.

I shook my head. I couldn't think about that now. Like Ikane said, we just needed to get through the night, and by the looks of the darkening sky, night was coming fast.

Soldiers took shelter under pines, pressed their backs to the trees, and clustered together with shields as their tents. Positioning myself in the centermost part of the six thousand soldiers, I swallowed the first dose of sprite dust as the opening wave of Deathbiters took flight overhead.

Closing my eyes, I stretched the mingled powers of Etheria and Thrall over the army like a blanket. It was as easy as breathing. The Deathbiters arched away, circling above as if confused by the invisible solid shield.

How did Alder do it? Did he even use a shield like this? Or did he simply command the Deathbiters to refrain from attacking the areas he specified? A sense of pride and hope swelled inside me. I was doing it. I was shielding an entire army of six thousand.

Soon, soldiers dosed off. Even Ikane and Broderick closed their eyes as they leaned against the moss-covered boulder at our backs. Ikane's head dropped to my shoulder. This was good. They needed rest.

I stared overhead, watching the Deathbiters' black bodies soar by, dotting out the stars with their leathery wings. I tilted my head. Their gliding movements were actually soothing— like watching seagulls hover in the wind from the sea—when they weren't attacking or threatening us. Their cries, though shrill, weren't any more earsplitting than seabirds fighting over an abandoned catch from a fisherman's net.

I missed Daram. Missed my home by the sea.

A strange coldness crept across my skin. The smell of dust, body odor, and festering wounds wafted through my mind.

The stars vanished, replaced by meager orange light flickering against dry stone walls. Chains rattled behind iron bars lining the narrow corridor. My hand stretched out, nails polished and painted red, golden rings glittering on my fingers, and an elaborate bracelet decorating my wrist. This wasn't me. This was . . .

The iron gate creaked on dry hinges as she pushed it open. Karreth crouched before the prisoner chained to the wall, the blonde, pretty one with muscles she could have accepted as godlike. Her tongue slid across her lips. She'd tasted his essence before, not far from her own. Heat and power, a strength only emitted by fire.

Karreth, however, was leaning over the young man, black streams of Thrall snaking around his body and gliding over the prisoner's wounds like ghostly vipers.

She stepped inside, ignoring the Tolean Prince who hung just as silent and broken in the center of the cell.

"You still try to reach him?" she asked in Lonacheska's voice. "We have already established that he is immune to your powers."

Karreth's darkness slipped away as he rose, his silver eyes glaring down at the unconscious man hanging on the chains.

"Yes." His deep voice radiated across the prison walls like distant rolling thunder. "But why?"

She stepped beside him, sliding her arm through Karreth's. The young man's body hung there like weakness, beaten, bloody, torn, and broken. Mortal. Yet a strength still burned inside his core, one not so easily fractured.

"Have you reached his mind yet?" she asked. "Have you torn it apart like you did with the pirate?"

Karreth's arm turned to steel in hers as his fist clenched. "No. I can't even find it. It's like . . . like it doesn't exist."

She looked up at him, studying his perfect features and steel-black hair gliding down his shoulders. "You've felt this before, haven't you?"

The muscles in Karreth's jaw flexed. "I have not felt the lack of a mind like his since . . . since Yotherna."

She turned her gaze back to the young warrior. Could it be? The question tore through her mind like the dangerous crack decorating her ruby asylum hanging about her neck. Her rounded belly prevented her from crouching as gracefully as she would have liked, but this was more important than her pride.

She pinched the prisoner's sturdy jaw between her fingers. "Open your eyes," she demanded.

He let out a moan, and his brows furrowed, but his eyes remained shut, swollen. She traced the streak of white hair with her eyes from his temple. So familiar.

Her fingers squeezed until her nails dug into his flesh, forcing his face to meet hers. "Your eyes. Let me see them."

They cracked open. Through bloodshot rims and swelling, his sky-blue irises flickered like a dream—a memory—a curse. She pried her nails from his skin and rose. How had she been so blind to this? She was a goddess—unborn, yes, but a goddess who knew all. Yet somehow Yotherna hid this from her. Curse him. Let him lay in his crippled body and fester in guilt and fire for eternity.

"What is it? What did you see?" Karreth asked.

"Your blood flows in his veins," she said.

"Mine?" Alder's brows furrowed as he gazed down at the young man. "I have not—"

"No, you haven't," Rion said, "but Yotherna has. He bore children of his own, children he hid from you and me. His eyes do not lie. This, my dear Karreth, is Yotherna's offspring. A descendant who holds his immunity to your power."

Karreth's fists drew tight, the dark powers of Thrall rolling from him like smoke. Rion smiled. This was what she adored about her beloved. His fierceness, his loyalty.

"Then I must end him." Karreth's voice rippled with ice.

Rion laced her fingers through his cold hand. "Let me. I have longed to add his life to my reserve since the day I first tasted his power. His essence is like honey. He will add a sweetness to my rebirth that will foster loyalty and love from my subjects."

Karreth took her hand and tenderly placed his lips atop her knuckles. "Anything for you, my darling."

Rion smiled then turned to the young man with the white streak in his hair. This would be more than adding sweetness to her rebirth. This man was adored by her own rebellious descendant. Taking him would establish her dominance over her Phoenix Daughter. It would crush her. It would make her come crawling like an insect, begging her to reunite them.

"No," the Tolean prince croaked from his miserable position. Such a pity Karreth had struck his handsome face. The swelling prevented her from gazing into those golden pools of sunlit eyes.

"You will be next, dear prince," Rion said.

"No." Prince Benroar stormed into the cell. "The Tolean prince is mine. I need him if I am going to take Toleah as well. You've done enough damage to him." The Leviathan prince pulled Leander's eyelids open, checking the life he had left.

Fire sparked inside Rion. What an arrogant fool to think he had any authority over her. She should end him now. Add him to the wretched life of Yotherna's offspring.

Karreth touched her shoulder and shook his head in warning.

Right. Now wasn't the time. She would have them, all of them. In time.

"What brings you here?" Karreth demanded.

"A Roanfirien army has begun its march on Fold," Benroar said. "Six thousand strong."

Rion turned to Karreth. "She comes."

He smiled and gestured to the young blond man chained to the wall. "Then take him. Now is the time."

She approached slowly. This moment was to be savored.

"No." Chains rattled behind her as the Tolean prince found strength to protest.

Ignoring him, she stretched out her hand and slid her fingers through the young man's blond hair that was streaked with white. So soft and luxurious. Shame. Her fist snapped tight and jerked on the lush hair to drag his head back. The young man groaned as she forced him to look up at her.

"Fear not, young warrior. You shall have a place of honor, the first to fuel my rebirth whenever my host is prepared." Her other hand slid across her rounded abdomen, caressing the precious body within. "Whether it be this child or my rebellious chosen one." She leaned forward, brushing her lips against the young man's bloodied ear. "She can't save you this time."

Fire slid through him, shattering the fragile shield around his mind. By the burning feathers of her reincarnation, he was even sweeter than she remembered, strong, vibrant, powerful—

No! The essence of white stars shot at her, pelting her like sand tossed over an eager fire. Rion flinched at the power behind the blow. So intense, so full. Such power was only attained by the sustenance of more souls. But the Phoenix Daughter was alone. How?

Dagger? The young man's mind reached toward the stars, desperate.

Rion let her fire surge. She stole stars, used their essence, fueled her burn. His soul was hers. This was revenge for what Yotherna had done to her beloved Karreth, for what he'd done to keep her from attaining her goal. If she couldn't have him, she would let Karreth resort to the brutality meant for mortal bodies.

By the fire within her, this offspring of Yotherna's would meet his end tonight.

The white stars rushed forward, surrounding the young man's soul like falling stars from the night sky. She hated the gentle hum that accompanied their swarming light. Like horseflies buzzing around dung.

All at once, the stars scattered, like some unknown force disrupted their harmony. Was this a trick? A tactic to surprise her? It seemed the Phoenix Daughter's strength was gone. Not even this young man's supporting power could restore her wretched stars. Smiling, Rion pulled.

Dagger! *The young man cried out as if their hands had been torn apart.*

Ropert! Ropert, no!

Rion smiled. There was so much pain in the girl's voice. Good. Let her understand that she was nothing.

Leaning close, Rion placed her lips on the young man's split and bruised ones. He stiffened like stone as she inhaled all that he was.

Finally, he was hers.

My eyes tore open to raging sounds of Deathbiter cries, bursting thunder pouches, slaughter, and war. I'd lost hold of the magic. I'd lost . . . I'd lost everything.

Ikane stood above me, edged in Mina's orange light, obsidian swords flashing at demon bats whipping by. A dark cut glistened on his brow. Glass cracked in Broderick's hand as he crushed the vial of firedust inside the pouch and tossed it into the air. A burst of blinding light erupted. Thunder cracked against my ears. Deathbiters scattered and screamed. Some fell to the ground, writhing with blistered skin.

My heart clenched. Weak. I was so weak. Drained. The sprite dust had made me invincibly strong for half the night but failed in the most critical instant. When Ropert needed me most.

Searing bile exploded up my throat. No, no, no. This wasn't how it was supposed to happen. I was coming to save him. I was on my way.

Another burst of vomit came up, splattering by my knees. Tears flooded my eyes as I curled over my stomach. He couldn't be gone. This . . . this wasn't happening. This was Eamon all over again. A death I could not prevent because I wasn't there to . . . I wasn't . . .

Black rolled inside my chest like a great mist rising across the black waters of the ocean. No more games. No more playing by rules and morals and virtue.

My mind lashed out, snatching the rotten soul of a Deathbiter from the air. Its body folded and plummeted to the earth as I inhaled it, letting its twisted energy feed the Thrall inside.

The pain wasn't so terrible now. Not with the pain of another creature inside. I released a burst of darkness at a cluster of demon bats diving for Ikane. They disintegrated, ashen parts falling harmlessly across Ikane's body. He raised his arm, shielding his face.

Rising to my feet, I stole another demon soul and another, letting their rage and pain build inside. Thrall took over. This was better. For every Deathbiter I consumed, ten more burst into ash and shredded leather.

"Kea!" Ikane whirled to me. "What are you—" He ducked as a burst of black energy streaked from my hand, shattering a Deathbiter that had been darting for his head. Dropping one of his swords, he gripped my wrist still in his crouched position, nearly pulling my shoulder from its socket. My head jerked.

"Kea, no." The desperate pleading in his voice didn't matter anymore. Nothing did. Only destroying these monsters.

"Hold her," Broderick's voice commanded over the roar in my ears.

Ikane's arms wrapped around my legs. His shoulder slammed into my torso. The world tipped, and my back hit the ground. Straddling his body over me, he grabbed my wrist, pinning my arms to my sides.

"Kea, stop. Come on. Breathe."

I was going to burst. Didn't he realize I could hurt him if he didn't get away? Beside him, a flash of glass glinted as Broderick tore the cork of a vial open with his teeth. I recognized the greenish liquid. It was the same nauseating substance he'd knocked me unconscious with in Glacier Pass the day the Deathbiters took Ikane from me. By the flaming feathers of the Phoenix, I wasn't going to let him do that to me now. I had every right to seek revenge. Every right to fight!

I bucked my hips, rocking Ikane to the side. His shoulder knocked the glass vial from Broderick's hand.

"Kea, stop!" Shifting his balance, Ikane pressed his forearm across my collarbone, flattening himself on top of me. "Come on, Little Brendagger. Breathe."

Deathbiters swarmed behind his head, rolling to the sky like leaves in a whirlwind. Didn't he see that I was protecting him? All of them?

Boma appeared. He took Ikane by the shoulder and lifted him away like he was nothing more than a blanket.

At least someone understood.

Sitting up, I prepared to—

Boma's thick arm slipped around my neck from behind.

What in the blazes? I clawed at him as he lifted my body. I kicked. My throat closed. No. I had to fight. For Ropert . . .

He pressed my head forward with controlled strength, cutting off all my air. Black snapped around my vision, strange in its swiftness. Even Thrall struggled to stay aflame. My muscles strained a moment longer.

Ropert! My mind cried out for him.

Like water hissing over hot coals of a fire, all fight died.

Ropert . . .

CHAPTER 36

FOLD CITY

e can't wait for the army anymore." That was Broderick's voice. "The woods are slowing them down. It'll be five more days before they reach Fold at this speed, and I don't think . . ." His voice dropped. "I don't think they can survive that long."

"What are you suggesting?" This was Ikane's voice, accompanied by the familiar grind of a whetstone across a metal edge.

"We press ahead," Broderick said. "The Leviathans have undoubtedly spotted us. The army is already doing its part in drawing their attention. We take advantage of this, just as Kea planned, cut around, and slip into Fold City from the north. We can be there by nightfall if we push."

The grinding of the whetstone faltered. "And Kea?" Ikane asked. "Something happened to her last night. Something we don't understand. She would not have resorted to that . . . that power otherwise."

A silence stretched through the mild chatter of birds. Last night? Had it really happened? Warm sunlight touched my cheeks, but the sweet sensation was overpowered by an acrid stench of Deathbiter filth and blood. I was terrified of what I would see if I opened my eyes.

"The only other time I've seen her use magic like that was when . . . when the Deathbiters took you," Broderick confessed.

He stopped when my hands curled into fists, clawing at the earth beneath me.

"Kea?"

I rolled onto my side, eyes cracking open to the soil beneath my gloved hands. The vision. Ropert. My eyes slowly lifted, too terrified to see if I was right, too curious to make sure I was wrong. Bodies, both Deathbiter and men, lay scattered through the trees, twisted limbs and wings catching the edge of sunbeams. I shut my eyes again.

A hand rested on my shoulder. Somehow, I knew it belonged to Ikane. Only his touch came with that weight, with that emotion. Oh Phoenix, I didn't want to feel it. Any of it.

"Hey." His voice was soft as his knees lowered to the earth beside me. "Come here, Kea." His strong arms lifted me, pulling me into an embrace. I was shaking. I hadn't noticed until my body pressed against his firm one. And I was weeping. That, too, I didn't notice until a drop fell to the black steel of his pauldron and rolled down his shoulder as if the metal itself was weeping. His hand brushed my hair, dislodging leaves and debris.

"You're safe, Little Brendagger," he whispered into my ear.

Was I? Were any of us truly safe? Rion had . . . she had taken Ropert. That thought twisted in my stomach like a knife, like seven knives, like a hot brand. He couldn't be gone. He was mine. My friend, my brother, my rock. He was always there for me. He was there when Ikane wasn't. He was there when a dream like this revealed Eamon's death. He was there when Rion had taken King Sander . . . always there . . . always.

"What happened last night, Kea?" Broderick asked.

Ikane hushed him. "Not now."

Somehow, those words blanketed my body with numbness. The tears evaporated. The trembling stopped. The clenching daggers in my stomach slid away, leaving an empty hole there. *Not now.* No mourning now. No stopping now.

Slowly, I pried myself from Ikane's arms. His rough hands caught my cheeks as he lifted my head to meet his beautiful eyes. But my eyelids would not lift above his jaw, which was streaked with blood and dirt. I feared if I met his gaze, the pain would return.

"Broderick is right," I said. My voice sounded strange. Hollow. "We need to go. Stop this before it . . . it destroys everything."

Ikane stood, pulling me with him. "To Fold City?" he asked.

I gave him one heavy nod, still not looking up from the crusty brown mud caked to my boots. My greaves no longer shone clean, polished, and battle free. They had made their maiden voyage into battle last night.

"Alright," Ikane said. "We cut north then east, sticking to the tree line. If we hurry, we can slip into Fold City under the cover of night. The Deathbiters won't bother us once we're inside the Dead Forest."

"How can you be sure?" Broderick asked.

"Because of Alder's agreement with the pirates. Wherever they are stationed, the Deathbiters will not go. But we will need to enter the Dead Forest on foot. The dust kicked up by our horses will draw attention."

Having Ikane here was good. He knew the Dead Forest as well as I did, if not better. We'd raided here for months and helped the crippled people thrive—what had happened to them? Torquin? Malese? Had the pirates taken them captive, killed them? Or worse, had Rion added them to her stash of souls? My stomach twisted.

"Come," Ikane said, taking my arm. "The day is half gone already."

Broderick and Boma immediately responded.

"Up," Ikane commanded as we stopped beside Nightwalker. "Don't worry. Broderick says his leg is alright."

I climbed into the saddle and watched as he hurried to his own horse. He leapt up, as if he had ridden horses all his life.

There was nothing he couldn't do. He even knew when to let my sorrow sit. He did the same when the nightmares plagued me, trying to distract me yet always reassuring me that he was there when I was ready.

I followed when he moved. I spurred my horse into a run when he did. I ducked under branches and leapt over fallen logs like him. Trees rushed by as a blur of brown and green. Shadows flashed across our skin as we pushed through the forest and cut around the main force of our army, which was already pressing on.

Broderick was right. They were moving too slow. Too many soldiers against too many trees. The Deathbiters would tear them apart tonight, and a part of me knew Alder would be watching. Another part wondered why Rion did not simply take them the way she had with the pirate army. She had the strength. What was she waiting for?

My shirt clung to my skin as I scanned the landscape through the last of the maturing trees. The Dead Forest, brown and lifeless. I could almost see the Fold Garrison through the haze. Queen Lonacheska was there. Prince Leander and Ropert . . .

"We made good time," Ikane said as he stepped beside me. "Now, we wait for dark."

The pink light of the setting sun filtered through the budding green leaves clinging to the branches overhead. Why couldn't life be this simple? Just run its course like the seasons?

Death was part of living, but Rion had lost that sense of existence. Her mind had become so twisted and heartless over the years as greed took root. And now, she was pulling everyone I loved into it.

Broderick took a stand by my other shoulder, and Boma joined, all gazing out at the remains of dead trees that had been stripped for fuel, leaving a dusty area of open, sloping land slipping to the city below. A hazy, yellow-brown evening light struck the outline of buildings standing at the base of the cliffs, and behind that arose seven thick masts of ships bobbing in the water.

The Fold Garrison towered above the city, standing on the cliffs like a dark citadel with broken towers and scorched stone. According to the map in my pocket, the "safe" entrance to the tunnels beneath the Fold Garrison began where the buildings hugged the base of the cliffs—on the other side of the city.

"Are you alright, Kea?" Broderick asked. "In control?"

I could hear it. He wanted to ask me what had happened last night. I wasn't sure myself, and I didn't want to know. If I ignored it, perhaps it hadn't happened. Perhaps it was a scene conjured by my worst fears.

I shut my eyes. "I am," I said. In truth, nothing was there. No Thrall, no Etheria. I had morphed into nothing. A simple little soldier with only a sword and armor trying to make a difference—and failing miserably.

"What is your plan once we get inside?" Broderick pressed.

I didn't know. All I knew was that I needed to end Rion and that I was going to have to use every speck of sprite dust to do it. But first, I had to get to her. I needed to take the Phoenix Stone from her. And that would mean confronting innumerable hosts of Leviathan pirates and Alder Grayhorn.

Somehow, even with Ikane, Broderick, and Boma at my side, I felt alone. This was something only I could do.

"Here they come," Ikane said as his face turned to the sky.

I hadn't seen anything yet, heard their screeches, or smelled their stench, but I trusted Ikane. He knew. Now was the time to use the strange light of dusk to hide the dust trail we'd kicked up in our descent.

"Alright. Let's move," Broderick said. "Stick to the thickest shadows, and stay low."

I'd forgotten how heavy and stale the air felt here. Even the wind seemed sucked dry by Rion's need for power.

I didn't expect my boots to sink so deep into the parched soil. The muscles in my calves tightened as everything beneath gave way. Without foliage to hold the soil in place, the landscape seemed to move in long ripples down the slope, carrying me with it.

Holding my breath, I sank to my hip, bracing against the dry earth. Dust swirled around me in a giant plume, blurring the shadowy shapes of Broderick and Boma sliding down beside me. Ikane, on the other hand, had slid into the stump of a tree, using it to stop his descent.

Reaching the bottom of the hill, I leapt up and sprinted for the shadow between two buildings on the outskirts of the city. Someone *must* have seen that cloud, even if they hadn't been looking.

Broderick and Boma pinned their back to the wall beside me. Dust and grit crunched between my teeth.

Mina's gift began flickering across my vision, burning most dominant where the shadows were thickest. Ikane's expert movements were fluid as he darted from one tree stump to the other.

Ikane reached us with little more than a flurry of sand at his heels. "Let's move," he whispered.

Pushing off the wall, I slinked forward. This section of the Dead City wasn't familiar to me. My time here was mostly spent traversing between the cliffside dwelling I shared with Ikane, the Dead Forest where we'd ambushed caravans traveling too close to the border, and the main market area where we'd dispersed our loot and trained the crippled people to fight. This section was crumbling away at a faster rate than the buildings sheltered by the cliff. Some were nothing more than a single collapsing wall or the remains of chimney stone stretching to the sky.

I began to recognize a building here and there. The shape of a mended roof, a patched window, an altered doorway. We were getting closer to the market square.

But something felt amiss. It was too silent. I hadn't seen a single soul or the flicker of firelight through a crack in a shuttered window. Invisible hands reached for my chest, squeezing. Had Rion taken them? Had this place turned into a true Dead City?

Ikane's hand gripped my shoulder, pulling me to a stop. His eyes were fixed ahead. If he had still been in his wolf form, his ears would have been twitching.

He pressed a finger to his lips as he motioned for us to follow him down the alley. Soon, muffled voices reached my ears, coming from the market square just ahead. Pushing our backs against the wall, we slinked closer.

"How many times do I need to tell you? The well is dry." The man's voice held an annoyed tone tinged with desperation.

I inched my head around the corner.

Three Leviathan pirates stood by the repaired well in the center of the market, torchlight striking the edges of fur on their shoulders. My breath caught. A fourth man was with them, standing with his back to us. But I recognized his broad shoulders and withered left arm. Torquin.

A sigh of relief raced through my body. If he was alive, there was a good chance the rest of the crippled folk of the Dead City were alive as well.

Torquin raised the burning torch in his good hand, waving it over the well's opening. "It's been dry for nearly a fortnight. We need water."

I frowned. That coincided with the night Alder had freed Rion and she'd taken hold of the landscape again.

A pirate stepped forward and dropped something into the well. Benroar. I leaned back again, watching Ikane. But his determined expression remained unchanged.

A hollow echo rolled up the shaft as the torch fell. "And you want to see the old aqueduct?" Benroar asked. "The one you say sustained you all those years before the rain?"

"Yes." Torquin's voice was firm.

"Will it be enough to sustain my men?"

"Not if they sit idle," Torquin said. Feathers, he was bold. "My people are crippled. We can barely manage as it is."

I leaned out again as Benroar eyed the dry well. "How many?"

"What?" Torquin asked.

"How many men do you need?"

"You . . . you'll let us repair the aqueduct? You'll let us leave the city?"

Benroar scowled at Torquin. "Not without supervision. How many men would it take to bring enough water here?"

"For your eight thousand? At least eight hundred," Torquin said, holding his torch high.

Benroar nodded. "Then I shall assign a faction to you in the morning."

"Me?"

"You know how to survive in this accursed place. I'd be a fool to put anyone else in charge," Benroar said. "Now. Where shall they meet you?"

Torquin turned my direction. I jerked back, slamming my head against the wall in the process. Ikane slinked back with a much more controlled, practiced stealth.

"The aqueduct is up that hill and to the north," Torquin said. "Have your men meet me at the base at first light, and bring every vessel that can carry water. We will set up a watering station here in the market where they can collect their daily rations."

"Good," Benroar said.

"Thank you."

"Hold," Benroar called. "I did not permit you to leave."

A moment of silence fell. I risked another peek around the corner. Torquin had turned away but stood frozen in the street, his back to the pirates.

"You know the punishment for breaking curfew," Benroar continued.

Torquin turned.

"Strip his shirt," Benroar ordered the accompanying pirates.

Ikane's hands balled into fists as Leviathans seized Torquin's arms. The torch fell from his grip as the noise of rending fabric filled the stale night. The flame continued to burn as it lay on the ground, casting terrible shadows on Torquin's skeletal frame.

My stomach churned with ice. He was starving. Somehow, his broad shoulders hid just how fragile his state was. A lump ached in my throat. Malese. If he was this thin, how was his tender wife?

My hand flew to the hilt of my sword as the pirates pushed Torquin to his knees. Boma caught my wrist and shook his head at me. I hated this.

Torquin didn't drop his head or lose his composure as he knelt with arms stretched between his captors.

"Three lashes." Benroar stepped forward, pulling his belt from his waist. "You understand, if I make an exception for you—"

"—then others will think you soft," Torquin finished, a defiant edge to his voice.

Benroar snapped the leather belt in his hands. "Make that four. With the buckle." He took position behind him and raised his arm.

Were we just going to stand here and watch? I glanced at Ikane whose jaw worked like a hammer. Green flared in his eye. His hand, which was braced against the wall, curled and dug into the stone as if it were made of sand. But he made no move. No one did. It would ruin our mission if Benroar were to discover us now.

I flinched as the whip cracked and shut my eyes. No cry came from Torquin. Another crack, and another. The final snap was dulled by a grunt from Torquin's throat.

"Now go," Benroar ordered, "and do not break curfew again."

Ikane glared at the pirates as they dropped Torquin's arms and left the crippled man in the dirt. Torquin braced his one good arm against the earth, his ribs heaving under his bleeding skin. Pirate laughter faded as they went their way. He glanced over his shoulder then pushed against his knee and rose.

"You can come out now," he said.

Ikane's hand dropped from the wall, leaving a perfect imprint in the stone. He rushed forward, catching Torquin before he collapsed again.

The crippled Foldean lifted his pain-filled eyes to Ikane's burning green iris. "You came back."

"I'm sorry," Ikane said. "I wanted to stop him. I—"

"Don't apologize. I knew the risks when I stepped into the night." He sucked air through his teeth, shutting his eyes for a moment. "It was the only way to get their attention. We are dying of thirst."

I hurried forward with Broderick and Boma on my tail, feeling my face burn. Every time I came here, they were dying. Of starvation, of cold, and now of dehydration. This accursed area was no place to live.

"Paige," Torquin smiled at me. "Feathers, look at you. A true warrior princess."

I paused. So they'd heard, too? "Let's get you back to Malese," I said.

His smile faded to something so dark it terrified me. "Malese is gone, Paige. She fought—feathers, she fought. I've never known a stronger woman."

The numb pain in my chest returned. Malese? No, not Malese, too. "When?" I choked out the question.

"Two months. She was too ill, too weak. Nothing we did would have been enough."

I shook my head. He was wrong. I could have done more. I could have petitioned King Sander to help these people long ago. If we had done so, we would have discovered Leviathans sooner. But I had been too absorbed in my own battles.

Now . . . now, I was the Princess of Roanfire. I could make a change. I could . . .

My shoulders dropped. No. After I faced Rion, I couldn't change anything.

"It's not your fault, Paige," Torquin said. "You were Phoenix-sent every time you came to our door. And while we're on the topic, why *are* you here?"

I lifted my eyes to the Fold Garrison's tower rising above the cliffs. "The Phoenix Stone is back."

"That explains the water," he muttered. "Things were returning. We had rain. We had game in the woods and fresh vegetation. Even the fish had returned to this part of the sea. Then the pirates came."

"Do you know what they are planning?"

He shook his head. "Prince Benroar wants to strike hard and fast, take Roanfire by surprise while it is weak and leaderless, but someone else is the driving force."

"Alder," I muttered. "We need to get into the garrison. Perhaps you can help us." Pulling the map from my pocket, I unfolded it and pressed it flat beside the flickering torch still burning on the ground. "Do you remember when I fell from the cliffs and found myself in underground tunnels beneath the garrison?"

"How can I forget? Malese thought you were a ghost."

"This is a map of that place," I said. "There seems to be another entrance here." I pointed to a building sitting near the cliffs. "Do you know which one this is?"

"You're going to sneak into the garrison?" Torquin gazed at us. "Four of you against an army of eight thousand?"

"Roanfire's army is right behind us," I said.

"I always knew you were bold, but this . . ." He shook his head. "May the Phoenix be with you." Ikane lowered him as he leaned down to squint at the map. "That looks like the old smithy," he said, "but I've never seen a door or tunnel there."

I folded the map and tucked it into my pocket. "If there's one, we'll find it."

Torquin clenched his teeth as he straightened. "I'll take you."

"We can't ask that of you," Ikane said. "Not in your state."

Torquin blinked at him as Ikane's Leviathan accent came out clear and strong. "You're a pirate?"

Ikane averted his eyes.

"I see it. You look very much like the pirate prince Benroar."

"I'm sorry for what he did to you," Ikane said. "When this is over, I will make it right."

"We need to move," Broderick said as he looked at the stars glinting weakly through the never-ending thickness of gray-brown haze suspended over the city. I knew what he meant. Black winged creatures circled silently overhead—watching, waiting.

"Come," Torquin said, leaving Ikane's helping arm. "Put your hoods on, keep your heads down, and follow me. A newcomer has taken up residence at the old smithy place. She's no blacksmith, but she knows how to use a sword."

CHAPTER 37

HERBS AND A FORGE

*T*he old smithy stood between rows of other thatch-covered rooftops backing into the wall of sheer cliffs. I glanced up, barely detecting the edge of the tallest tower of the Fold Garrison sitting on the cliffs above . . . where it all began.

Torquin knocked on the warped door. "Hana? Are you here?"

There was no reply.

Torquin pushed the door open and stepped inside. A pungent blend of earthy, herbaceous aromas hit my nose. Moonlight lanced through the thin layer of thatch, falling across a workbench filled with herbs. They hung from the rafters in bundles in varying shades of green. They hung over the windows. They hung from hooks and pegs on the walls meant for weapons and tools. They even hung on the old forge, strung together in an array of brittle blossoms.

Even though Torquin had warned me that this woman wasn't a blacksmith, I'd still expected to smell steel and coal, perhaps even sweat lingering. Whomever this woman was, she was an herbalist and healer.

"I'm not sure when she'll be back. I wish I knew her ways of slipping out of the city. We rely on her more than ever."

Torquin sighed as he leaned on the doorframe. "I could have used her services tonight."

"Go on, Torquin," Ikane said, placing a hand on his shoulder. "Rest. And thank you for bringing us here."

Torquin covered Ikane's hand with his own. "Pirate or not, you have a pure heart. That is how I judge you." His eyes swept over us. "Stop them. We've been suffering for too long. I fear we don't have long before the people of Fold are no more."

He didn't know how right he was.

"That is our goal," Ikane said.

Torquin turned away, moonlight dancing on the bleeding stripes across his back. His walk was slow, but he never swayed or stumbled. He'd lost his son and his beautiful wife to starvation. He was ostracized for nothing but a withered arm and whipped for trying to help the people of Fold survive.

Yet he remained. Alone, crippled, and broken yet pressing on.

Could I ever be that strong?

Broderick removed his glove with his teeth and turned to the far wall of stone where the building backed into the cliff. Leaning over the workbench, he brushed bundles of herbs aside, running his hand along the rough surface. "I don't see anything," he said.

Neither did I. There was nothing to indicate a doorway or passage on the cliffside. There were no crevasses or fissures.

Perhaps it wasn't located in the wall. I glanced at the floor of solid stone. There were no trap doors or cellars, either.

Pulling the map from my pocket, I unfolded it and set it on the workbench. I brushed a dried leaf from the edge as I scrutinized the rows of buildings drawn in faded black ink along the cliffside.

A tunnel was here. It was clearly marked. It stretched into the cliffs, connecting with other passages. Some led to dead ends or simply faded off the page as if unexplored. But one distinct path existed, linking this building to the Fold Garrison.

Ikane leaned over the map. "Anything?"

I shook my head. Strangely, I didn't feel upset or panicked. There was another way. A dangerous way. One I wasn't sure I could duplicate. The manner in which I had stumbled upon these tunnels in the first place had nearly killed me—and Ropert thought it had. His face flashed behind my eyes, glistening and bloodshot, his sky-blue irises wide as I'd appeared. He'd thought I was a ghost come to haunt him. What I wouldn't give to feel him haunt me now.

Boma's head knocked into a bundle of low-hanging herbs. The dried leaves and stems tangled into his braided hair, forcing him to rip it free. Dust rained down and filled the air with sharp, earthy smells. Boma sneezed. It was the only sound I'd heard him make since Prince Leander had been captured.

"Hold a moment," Broderick said. He crouched, inching across the floor toward the cold forge. The unsettled dust from the healer's herbs floated and swirled in the meager light lancing through the thinnest parts of the thatched roof. It curled wildly around Boma's curled toe boots. It would only move that way if air was moving through the room.

I glanced at the air shaft of the cold forge. It was coming from the arched bricks beneath where the ash typically collected.

Broderick stretched his hand inside. "A draft," he said.

Sinking to my knees, I removed a glove and stretched my hand inside. Cold air rushed across my fingers. The entrance was underneath the forge. But why did I feel disappointed? Did I find this path too easy? Was I secretly hoping to fall into the churning waters of the Rethreal Sea a second time and let the waves dash me into the cliffs?

"Good work, Boma," Broderick praised.

The Ridarri only blinked.

"Now," Broderick mused to himself. "How to access it . . ."

The entire forge was set on a stone surface, one that looked like it would move with the right leverage. Ikane set his hands against the stone, planted his feet, and pushed. "It's loose," he said.

Boma joined him. Veins stood out on his neck as he and Ikane dug their heels in. A crack sounded, as if something had jolted free, but the forge remained firm.

Broderick rose. "There must be a lever somewhere." He began moving around the forge, eyeing the corners, sweeping his hand into crevasses.

With Mina's sprite dust illuminating the edges of the forge, I searched for anything out of place. If this was an escape route, it wouldn't be obvious. It would have been kept a secret. Maybe even hinted at in a riddle or depiction on the map. I pulled it from my pocket and unrolled the parchment.

Wait. Something flashed green in the top left corner. The green sprite dust glowing on my palm had illuminated something.

I held my hand over it. Something was there—faint lettering glowing with emerald light. It had only appeared when I'd removed my gloves.

"Hold on," I said and began reading out loud.

> *Glowing coals to heat the steel*
> *Breath to fuel the fire*
> *Blackened ashes hide the wheel*
> *The lever calls the dire*

There was another riddle on the bottom right edge, but I did not read that one aloud. From what I could determine, one revealed the entrance here, and the other exposed the entrance to the garrison. One step at a time.

"What in the blazes does that mean?" Broderick asked.

Glowing coals to heat the steel. I scrutinized the forge, eyes following the stone edges where a blacksmith would burn the coal. *Breath to fuel the fire.* The billows were gone, the leather probably turned brittle. *Blackened ashes hide the wheel.* I leaned down, eyeing the arched vent beneath the forge where ashes would fall. There. Mina's gift highlighted a small, curved lever at the back, tucked in shadow. Anyone who didn't know what they were looking for wouldn't have seen it. I certainly wouldn't have if not for Mina's gift.

"There," I said. Sliding almost to my belly, I stretched my arm inside, gripped the lever, and pulled. A loud click echoed from somewhere deep inside. I scrambled back as the stone platform began to grind and turn. I'd never seen such clever workmanship.

We watched as a wide, gaping hole opened up in the ground, leading into pitch darkness.

"Nicely done," Broderick said, clapping me on the shoulder.

But this didn't feel right. This seemed too easy. After everything I'd endured, could something be this simple?

I peered over the edge. Mina's glow highlighted the stone shaft as it plummeted into the earth. This was it. The hidden entrance to the Fold Garrison. The path that would lead me into Rion's domain.

Rock crumbled against my back as I lowered my body into the darkness. The rope sliding through my gloves let out a gentle hiss. I thought Fold City had been cold, but down here, the temperature plummeted, and the cold scent of iron and water filled my nose. My boots hit the tunnel floor with an echo.

The shaft that stretched before me was rough and deep, burrowing into the cliffs until it was swallowed in pitch-black darkness. Even Mina's gift of sight in the dark couldn't reach that far.

"And?" Broderick's voice echoed down to me. I glanced up, following the line of rope to the entrance nearly fifteen yards above me. Silver light shone behind his head of wild curls as he leaned over the opening.

"It's here," I replied. Pulling my gloves off with my teeth, I allowed my sprite dust-riddled hands to illuminate the map as I unfolded it. Not that I needed the light. Mina's gift outlined everything in an orange-red glow, but the light did help clear the lines drawn onto the map, and a part of me was curious if the dust's glow would reveal anything new.

I'd need to take the first tunnel right then left. It would then split into three, two smaller and one large. I squinted at the markings, following the length of the drawn tunnel. We needed to use the far right one—a narrow passage, from the looks of it. We'd need to pay close attention to every detail, or we would find ourselves lost.

A rock hit my shoulder then another as Boma planted his feet against the rocky side and leaned back with the rope grasped tightly in his hands. Stepping back, I shielded my face from the rocks jarring loose in his descent. Broderick followed, and even with one arm, he had more control than Boma or me.

Ikane dropped into the hole without bothering to brace his feet against the wall. The rope hissed through his hands, and in two breaths, his boots hit the ground with a resonant thud.

If any of us had tried something like that, we would have shattered our knees. But not a Leviathan pirate with bones of steel. And I suspected Ikane's body harbored even more supernatural mutations since his transformation. His teeth, for one. He seemed faster and stronger than before, and his hearing seemed doubly sensitive.

"Show pony," Broderick muttered.

Ikane gave him a crooked smile, flashing one of his sharpened canines. But his smile vanished when his head hit a low-hanging edge. He rubbed the spot, his green eye flaring at the stone like an enemy.

Broderick chuckled. "At least I won't have that problem."

Ikane looked at me. "Let's move. The soldiers are counting on us."

I gathered a deep breath. More than soldiers were counting on us. Leander was. And Queen Lonacheska, and the baby. I pushed back the image of Rion's lips pressing against Ropert's.

Stepping forward, I began our journey through the tunnel. Stone crunched under our boots. Our breathing echoed. The white, blue, and green light from my hands shimmered on the damp edges of surrounding stone, lighting the way.

Reaching the first split in the tunnels, I checked the map again.

"This way."

CHAPTER 38

THE PLACE WHERE SHE TOOK HIM

I stopped by a narrow crevasse. It stretched high and long like a gaping wound. As I peered through, Mina's gift highlighted the smooth linear slabs of manmade stairs beyond. They curved upward and behind a section of rock so I could not see where they led.

This was the right path. This was the way the map showed. But I couldn't get through with my armor. None of us could.

"Did we take a wrong turn?" Broderick asked.

I glanced over my shoulder at the expectant, tired, dirt-smudged faces of my companions. "No," I said and began unbuckling my sword belt. The glow from my hands flashed like strange candlelight across the metal surface of my breastplate and faulds. "There are stairs ahead. We're close. Strip your armor."

My breast and backplate slipped through in two parts, crashing against the stone on the other side. I wedged in after them. Rock scraped against my stomach and chest.

Stumbling out the other side, I gazed up at the tall ceiling decorated with white, crystal-like formations. The light from my hands shimmered against formations that bubbled across the ceiling like a boiling cauldron and others that lanced down like icy spears. Somehow, this place seemed familiar, like from a dream.

I'd seen these stairs before. They'd been white and glowing, smooth like marble as the White Wardent guided me forward. An arched doorway would be at the top. It had to be.

I hurried ahead, stumbling around jagged rock formations, peering around the rock that prevented me from seeing the top. And I saw the door. Arched and faint, hidden. This was how Yotherna had saved me. This was the path that led to the Fold Garrison.

"Kea!" Broderick called. "A little light, please."

I backtracked, bringing the light from my hands to my companions. Broderick slipped through easily. But Boma struggled to twist his large muscles through the narrow passage. He winced as stone cut across his chest and back, tearing his robe-like top. A section broke free and slammed to the ground as he stumbled out.

I scooped up my armor and began replacing it with Broderick's help. "We've reached the end. The entrance to the Fold Garrison is just up those stairs."

"What stairs?" Broderick asked. I forgot he couldn't see. None of them could. They all relied on the light from my hands.

"How long were you down here before?" Ikane's voice was strained as he wriggled his body through the crack.

"I'm not sure," I said, flipping my hair out of the way of the backplate. "It's easy to lose track of time in this place. Torquin said I'd been missing for four days. And Ropert thought I was . . ." My voice faltered, and my arm dropped, forcing Broderick to abandon the buckle on my side.

"Kea?" he asked. "What's wrong?"

I swallowed the growing lump in my throat and blinked. "Nothing. We need to keep moving." I raised my arm again, letting him resume securing my armor back on. Still, my heart clung to the belief that Ropert was alive on the other side of the door. Had Rion truly taken him? Just like she had King Sander? I didn't care if he was one of the keys needed to destroy Rion.

His eyes had been dulled. His smile was gone. I'd never cross blades with him again. I would never hear him tease me or insult someone or beg for pastries.

"Kea?" Ikane's voice drew my attention. He stood before me, palm outstretched. Boma and Broderick were already ahead of me, waiting for my light to guide them up the stairs.

I swallowed, took Ikane's hand, and climbed.

We reached the blended arch and flat wall at the top. Running my fingers along the surface, I found the clean center seam but saw no way to open it. Remembering the second riddle on the map, I unfolded it and read:

Escape through locked stone
The door reveals its jaws
Seek the one that stands alone
The five that look like claws

"Claws . . ." Broderick muttered, his eyes already scanning the surrounding rock. I stepped back, trying to let Mina's orange-red glow highlight anything that would look like claws. But everything here looked like claws or teeth, spears or knives.

Boma touched my shoulder then pointed to the keystone sitting above the door. Two more stones sat on either side, creating the illusion of claws in the rock. The silent man was clever.

"Lift me?" I said.

He laced his fingers together. Placing my boot in them, he hoisted me up. I stretched and pushed on the single stone in the center. It sank into the rock like something had inhaled it. Clicking noises echoed. I dropped back down, listening as the sound of grinding rock reverberated through the tunnel. *Please, don't let the pirates hear this,* I thought.

Broderick, Boma, and Ikane shielded their eyes as hazy light chased Mina's gift from my vision. The smell of something foul raced for my nose. I swallowed. I knew the smell. I'd tasted it in the dream . . . the vision where . . .

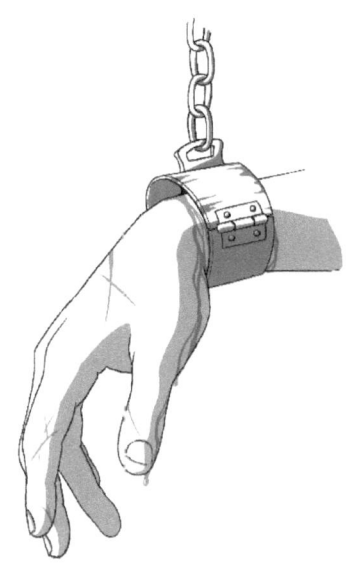

My chest clenched as I stepped into a dank hallway and tightened more at the sight of iron bars lining the wall. The dungeons.

A new coldness swept across my body as I moved forward, eyeing the cells. *Please, don't let it be true. Please.*

Boma suddenly sprinted past me. Gripping the iron bars, he shook. Broderick hurried forward, pulling a tool from under his tunic. In moments, the cell door swung open. Chains rattled as Boma latched onto a figure hanging from iron links in the center.

"Boma?" Leander's voice croaked.

Ikane hurried ahead, but I couldn't. Somehow, my feet had stopped moving. I couldn't lift them. I couldn't breathe for fear of what else we would find inside. Two breaths passed. Then three. I waited.

"Phoenix, no." Broderick's voice came from a corner I could not see.

I shut my eyes.

"Ropert?" This time, Ikane's voice rang out.

My chest snapped tight. I couldn't blink the tears away as I stared at the dark corridor where Rion had walked. My hand flew to my mouth, my breaths morphing into terrible gasps.

Ikane stumbled out of the cell. His eyes shimmered. Pain, so much pain. His lips trembled. He gazed at me. "Kea . . ."

His voice said it all.

My knees gave out and struck the floor as weeping overtook everything. Reality sank into my chest like a knife. It was true. All of it. Rion had stolen my best friend. My brother.

Ikane's boots scuffed the ground as he came to my side, dropped to his knees, and wrapped me in his arms. He buried his face in my neck. "You knew . . ." His voice was as tight as his trembling embrace.

I clawed at his armor. My teeth ground together, trying to keep my wails from drawing the attention of unwanted ears.

"Keatep," Prince Leander said.

I glanced up as he limped closer with Boma carrying his weight under his arm.

His golden eyes shimmered beneath his bruised face. "I am so sorry," he croaked. He looked as beaten as he had in my vision, deep purple-and-red bruising across his bare torso and arms, lip swollen and cut, a gash on his brow. Infected red rings circled his wrists from the iron cuffs. "It was her," he whispered.

I swiped my cheeks hard and stood, desperately trying to keep my lips from trembling. "Get him out of here, Boma," I said. "Go back the way we came."

Boma moved.

"No," Leander protested.

The Ridarri stopped.

Leander's unswollen eye burned into mine. "You need us. All of us."

"I needed four keys," I reminded him. "It's over, Leander. Go, now. All of you."

"What are you going to do?" Ikane asked. He wiped his nose with the back of his wrist, sniffed, and steeled himself.

I placed a hand over my belt pouch, where the vials of pure sprite dust waited to be consumed. "I am going to face her."

"Alone?" Leander asked. "That is madness. You know what will happen if you do."

"Alder is mine." Ikane's green eye flashed as he reached back and drew one of his swords. "You won't deny me that, Kea."

"Feathers, Ikane. He can't be killed. Not until I destroy the Phoenix Stone."

"Then I'll be by your side until you do."

"As will I," Broderick declared.

Leander gathered several gulps of pain-filled breath. "I, too, will not leave your side."

I tore my hands through my hair. "Did you not see what Rion did to Ropert?" I cried. "I will not see that happen to any of you. Go! Go now before I run you through myself." My hand flew to my sword, fingers trembling as they curled tight. A part of me meant it. I would rather see them slaughtered by the sword than stolen and used against me.

"Kea," Ikane's voice was urgent and low. "Hush."

"I'll not be silenced. Get—"

His hand flew over my mouth, driving me back until I hit the wall. "Shh." His eyes fixed on the end of the corridor.

Our breaths stopped as our bodies turned to stone, listening for what Ikane had heard over my roaring voice. There. The sound of footfalls. Murmuring voices.

"Scales," Ikane hissed. "Stay here." He moved his hand from my mouth, reached back, and unsheathed his second sword. The stale air rushed around me as he vanished.

Like a dark blur of silent steel, he reached the end of the corridor just as two figures came around the bend. He silenced the first like a deadly wind. The man didn't even have time to reach for his weapon. The other arched back, dodging the first swipe of his blade. Metal rang as swords connected. Ikane pursued him around the bend and out of my sight.

I tore my sword free and ran.

The noise of steel on steel grew louder until a groan silenced the fight. I skidded to a halt at the base of a flight of stairs and froze. Ikane stood ten paces ahead, his opponent a heap at his feet, facing half a dozen stunned Leviathan pirates above.

"It's Prince Ikane," one of them whispered, his eyes riveted on my pirate.

"My fight isn't with you." Ikane took a cautious step forward. "I want Alder."

The pirate's eyes narrowed. "All hands!" he shouted behind him. "The garrison has been breached!"

Ikane charged like a viper, cutting down the pirates that could not retreat for the others pressing in behind them. I followed, stepping over the body he'd cut down, but there was nothing I could do. Ikane's swords filled the stairwell with black flashes of death, littering the way with pirates.

My palms grew damp as I waited for an opening, anything to help him. At his speed, strength, and endurance, he could probably hold them off indefinitely.

Broderick appeared at the base of the stairs then Leander and Boma.

"What are you . . . ? I told you to go," I snapped at them.

This has gone on long enough.

Rion's heat slammed into my skull like a thousand flaming arrows. I staggered against the wall as if she'd struck me with a fist.

Ikane reeled back, falling to one knee. His swords clattered against the stairs as he clutched his head. Broderick groaned behind me, and Leander collapsed onto the stairs. Even Boma went down, blood dripping from his nose.

I called to Etheria. A shield snapped tight around my mind, bending her flames around it. But my friends. I couldn't reach them. I wasn't strong enough to guard myself and defend them, too.

The pirates surged forward and grabbed Ikane, swallowing him in their midst.

My hands shook as I dug into my belt pouch where prepared vials of sprite dust waited. Snatching the cork free with my teeth, I tipped my head back and swallowed.

"What is she doing?" a pirate yelled. "Stop her!"

Glass shattered as I pitched the vial away and held my sword ready.

One, two, three . . .

I swung at my attackers as the dusts began to take shape, burning through my blood. Just a few more moments.

Sixteen, seventeen, eighteen . . .

My fingers plunged back into the pouch, drawing out another vial. Wrong one. It had to be the white—

A pirate seized my wrist, slamming my hand back against the wall. My fist tightened around the vial. I needed it, all of it, if I was going to—another pirate rushed in, grabbing my sword arm before I could run my attacker through. My bracer rattled against my bones as he smashed his pommel into my forearm, trying to dislodge my weapon. The other pirate shoved my hand back again.

My face went cold as I heard the sound of shattering glass. An eruption of fire, water, and earth tore through my skin. It stung. Feathers, it stung and grew hotter and hotter.

It had happened.

All four dusts had embedded themselves into my skin.

CHAPTER 39

THE TOWER WHERE IT ALL BEGAN

Alder's scarred face flashed behind my eyes. His pink skin, the raised scars, the stretched eyelid, the milky whiteness of his iris. My hand. It was going to happen to my hand—if it didn't dismember me completely.

My sword clattered to the stairs.

"Hold!" a commanding voice shouted.

I barely saw the figure. The heat. Phoenix, my hand.

"Bring them to the tower," the voice said. "All of them. She wants to see them."

I shut my eyes as my arms were drawn back. I had to stop the dusts from bursting like one of Broderick's thunder pouches.

A shield. Yotherna had tried with Etheria. Alder had tried with Thrall. What if I used both like I did when I shielded us from the Deathbiters?

I had no time to think. The burn vibrated down my arm like I held the weight of the entire Gyroh mountain range, the force of the Rethreal Sea in a storm, and the burning glow of the sun in my palm.

Shield, shield . . . contain.

The Etheric lights already surrounding my mind, shielding me from Rion's fire, expanded. I touched Thrall, waking it from the corner, nudging it forward. It reeled back from the light the way the Deathbiters arched away from burning torches or sunlight. I didn't have time to coax it. I turned to the pain I tried to ignore. The heartache of seeing Ikane's face when he'd discovered Ropert. Thrall lunged.

Black and white. Mist around stars. Balance. There had to be balance. Not too much of one or the other. I pushed the blended energy to my hand and wrapped it with the balanced lights, pulling it tight like a bandage. The burn alleviated but continued to pulse with every frantic beat of my heart. Energy trembled with pressure. If I lost focus, it would burst.

I cracked my eyes open, watching my feet blindly move as pirates led me down a corridor. A drop of something red and thick passed under my boots. Then another and another. Blood.

Raising my head, I found Ikane ahead. His arms were twisted back as he was restrained by two pirates, his head hanging low. His feet were unsteady and shuffling—the walk of a man blind with pain.

Rion.

If she wasn't tormenting him, he could have easily fought off his captors.

I reached toward him with Etheria, but the magic keeping the dusts from bursting in my hand began to unwrap like a poorly secured bandage. Thrall was trying to take over. Ashamed, I pulled back, rebalancing the magic. I couldn't help him, any of them, and keep the dusts from exploding.

We began the climb up the spiraling staircase, the one I knew well. The one that led to the tallest tower of the garrison where I'd first discovered the Phoenix Stone surrounded by her den of mummified corpses, the lives she had consumed.

The smell of death and decay no longer filled the air. Instead, it was thick and heavy with dust, something acidic, and dread.

Prince Benroar, who had been leading the procession, paused on the landing. With his hand on his sword, his eyes swept over us, finally resting on Ikane. I blinked, and something shimmered in his eyes that I hadn't expected. Uncertainty? Worry? Fear? His throat moved as he swallowed hard then turned to the arched entrance and stepped inside.

The pirates dragged us forward. I had never expected to find myself in this tower again, seeing the horizon of the sea through the circular pattern of arched windows just as I had in my very first nightmare a lifetime ago. Bitter violet tinged the sky with dawn.

"The intruders," Benroar announced, "as requested."

"Well done."

An unforgettable deep voice radiated against my chest as I was brought forward and forced to kneel on the ground. Alder's tall frame towered in the center of the chamber, his silver eyes burning like a full moon through the haze.

But the image of Queen Lonacheska standing beside him, radiating with the energy of a billion souls, demanded my attention. Her golden hair shimmered like sunlight on wheat fields, her skin glowed, and her dark eyes burned with a ring of red flame. My stomach curdled as her hands absently caressed the roundness of her stomach.

The pirates tossed Ikane at Alder's feet. I winced seeing him so weak, too consumed with Rion's pain to do anything but clutch his head and suck air through his teeth.

Broderick, Prince Leander, and Boma dropped beside him like they were nothing. Every one of them trembled, noses dripping with blood, unable to fight. And all the while, Rion looked on, her lips curled in a knowing smile.

I strained against my captors, aching to retrieve the winddust from my pouch. I could still use it. The power burned through my blood. "Stop it," I snarled at her. "Let them go."

"And why would I do that?" she asked, her voice silky and sweet but oh-so poisonous. Her burning eyes glanced down at the nearest target groaning at her feet, Broderick. "This one is new. I like him. There is a wild power hiding beneath his whispering essence."

My teeth ground together, muscles pulling against the pirates holding me down. My shoulders ached as they forced my kneel into a bow.

Alder's black cloak billowed as he crouched before Ikane. His pale fingers ran through Ikane's dark hair like he was stroking the fur of a favorite pet, then his fist snapped tight, jerking the young pirate's head up by his hair.

Ikane groaned.

"Don't!" I resisted again, despite the stretching ache in my shoulders. Warmth snaked from my hand to my wrist, making it slick and difficult for my captor to keep hold.

"Weakness," Alder spat at Ikane. "Pitiful. Why would you ever choose a body as feeble as this one?" With a jerk, Alder released Ikane and stood. "I gave you power, and you tossed it aside. Ungrateful whelp." He turned away. "Now, you will see exactly what I spared you from."

Benroar flinched. His eyes shot to me, knowing at that moment that everything I'd said about Alder was true. That Alder had transformed his brother into a monster. His hand crept to the hilt of his sword as Ikane let out a low growl through his teeth, but it was filled with more pain than venom.

"It's better this way, my love," Rion said with Lonacheska's voice. "He wasn't worth the effort." She crouched down before Broderick. Her golden hair fell over her shoulder as she cocked her head at him. "He has a sweet face."

"Don't you touch him!" I snarled.

"No?" she asked. "Would you rather I took him first?" Her fingers fluttered toward Ikane.

My heart slammed against my ribs so hard I thought they would bruise. "Don't." I'd intended to sound threatening, but the plea came out desperate and full of fear.

"Or this one?" Rion asked, turning her eyes to Prince Leander who lay on his side, curled in a fetal position. "They are all so lovely. Just like your friend with the white streak in his hair. What was his name again? Ropert Saded?"

Thrall sparked inside, threatening to set my strained magic into a dangerous imbalance. I had to breathe, stay steady, keep the arrow tight and my focus riveted. "Do not speak his name!"

"Then accept my offer!" Rion barked in return.

My hands curled into fists. Remnants of broken glass from the vial dug deeper into my skin. "Free them, and I will consider it."

She tipped her head back and laughed. Alder joined, and a few onlooking pirates chuckled. Benroar's face, however, remained stoic, hand on his sword, watching the scene unfold with wary suspicion. Feathers, I wished he would draw it.

Rion wiped invisible tears from her eyes. "You are in no position to make demands, Phoenix Daughter." She reached toward Broderick, clutching the collar of his shirt in her fist, and drew him to her. I saw the flash of fire in her eyes before she moved.

"Rion, no!"

She leaned forward, and the stone slipped from her collar. The tower burst into a scene of red as her lips planted on Broderick's. His body locked. The tower suddenly felt small, closing in around me. No . . . not Broderick. This . . . this couldn't be happening. This . . .

Broderick's body went limp. She dropped him, wiping his blood from her lips with the back of her sleeve. Her smile burned, but she wasn't fire to me anymore. She was blood. The blood of a billion souls.

Benroar stepped back, eyes growing wide.

I choked on my own breath. The tears burning behind my eyes evaporated, too stunned to surface.

"Now, who is next?" Rion asked, licking her lips as she turned to Ikane and Leander.

"She was right," Benroar breathed. "The Phoenix Stone is here." His blade flashed in the red light from the ruby as he let it fly from the scabbard at his hip. He looked at his men pinning me to the ground. "Release her. Release them all!"

The pirates' grips on my arms loosened.

"Don't be a fool," Alder warned, blackness billowing around him.

Benroar froze.

Rion struggled to her feet, holding her stomach as she turned to Prince Benroar. "Now, now," she began. "Don't be too rash, dear prince. We have yet to build a future together."

"The Leviathans want no future with you," Benroar growled.

This was my moment. My legs coiled beneath me, spurring my body forward as I lunged for Rion. Her eyes flew wide when I crushed the ruby in my bleeding, throbbing hand, and the red light vanished. I jerked the cord from her neck.

Rion clutched her throat and staggered back. "What are you—"

Curling over the jewel, I let go. Let everything go. The magical bandage restraining the pulsing dusts rooted in my skin fell away like a silken ribbon. My teeth slammed together as the raw power of elements flared in my hand, growing hotter and hotter. Tears burned my eyes. This was for Ropert and Broderick. For Eamon and King Sander.

This was for Roanfire.

Pain exploded in my hand, and a blinding flash of lighting burst from my fist. My eyes slammed shut as thunder rippled up my arm and cracked through the tower. The force knocked into my chest, sending me backward. Stone grated against my hip as my body slid across the floor and slammed into the wall.

A terrible ringing sang in my ears, overpowering all other sound. I shook my head. Everything moved so slowly. Even the dust swirling through the tower took a lifetime to reveal a crater of broken stone in the center of the floor where I had stood, resembling the aftermath left by a giant hammer. So much power. Even some of the pillars from the arched windows had been blown out.

Alder, Lona, and Benroar pushed themselves from the ground, stone, debris, and dirt falling from their shoulders. Alder's black form scrambled to Queen Lonacheska's side, and my heart hiccuped as he lifted her from the ground. She shook her head, blinking, trembling as she held her stomach.

Feathers, the baby. I hadn't thought what that could do to the child.

White sparks flashed behind my eyes as I watched Ikane pull his legs beneath him and curl over his ears. My own ears still rang and buzzed. My poor wolf scrunched his face with pain from the noise. But his movements were no longer encumbered by Rion's pain. He was free.

Leander and Boma, too. The Ridarri warrior crawled over Leander, shielding his body from the fragile stones dropping from the vaulted ceiling.

But Broderick remained where he was, motionless, his black leathers dusted with debris.

The stone. Was the stone destroyed?

I glanced at my hand. My stomach heaved at the sight of missing appendages and protruding bone. Worse, an undying crimson glowed amid the blood and burnt flesh of my palm. Averting my gaze, I shut my eyes.

The Phoenix Stone was still intact.

I leaned my head back, looking at the deep black veins spiderwebbing through the cracked stone above. That was what should have happened to the stone. No, the stone should have been shattered, turned to dust.

Yotherna was right. It was indestructible by mortal means. I needed the four keys, the four souls willingly offered to shatter this thing . . . and two were already lost. Two gaping holes ripped through my heart.

The tears came now, blurring the towering midnight figure approaching.

"Foolish, foolish girl."

Even through the ringing in my ears, I could still hear him, feel his voice vibrate against my chest.

"I warned you what would happen if you used sprite dust that way."

Alder reached down and plucked the ruby from my destroyed palm. He turned it in his fingers, gently removing my blood from its surface. "My love—and your new goddess—has amused your insubordination long enough." He spun away. "You should thank her mercy. Were it up to me, she would have . . ." His voice faltered as he held the ruby up to his eyes.

"What is it?" Rion demanded, holding her stomach. "What do you see?"

Alder whirled to me, his steel-black hair whipping around his shoulders. His silver eye was like a dagger ready to burrow into my chest. Even the milky-white one burned. "A crack," he growled.

The word sank into my chest with something I hadn't expected. The feeling when the Deathbiters dispersed in morning light, the hand of a friend reaching out to lift me up, the laugh of a child.

Hope.

Black mist swirled around Alder as he stretched his hand toward me. His suffocating cloud of Thrall jabbed against mine like someone taunting a feral dog with a whip. His cold fingers wrapped around my arm. "It is time, Rion. Take her now. We've—"

A blur slammed into Alder, touched with a small pinprick of vibrant green. Ikane tumbled with Alder to the floor in a ball of savage animal instinct and black rage.

Despite the noise and numb ringing still echoing through my ears, a light *chink* echoed at my feet. I glanced down.

The ruby.

Tucking my crippled hand under my arm, I squinted at its blood-red surface. It was clear. The tiny fracture had opened, brimming with an ember glow as if the sun itself was contained within. Four elemental dusts, a balance of light and darkness, and my blood had done this.

I had two more vials of winddust in my pocket and one more burning with the final three. Would one more explosion be enough to finish it?

"Enough!" Lona's voice cut through the haze.

She had a fistful of Leander's thick dreadlocks caught in her hand. Boma stood nearby, poised but too alarmed to strike. Leander's face was strangely serene as his golden eyes met mine, like he knew his fate and accepted it.

My face grew cold. "No, Rion, don't."

She jerked Leander back. "Then yield to me!"

"It is alright, Kea," Leander soothed. "It is alright."

I shut my eyes, fists tightening, my damaged one feeling strange and numb.

It wasn't alright. I thought I could spare my friends' lives if I refused to use their life energy myself, but my resistance had only given their power to her. My reluctance had been their undoing.

Ikane let out a harrowing cry beside me. I turned just as Alder pushed him off, his face livid and striped with blood, bruising where Ikane had pummeled him. Ikane curled on the ground in a fetal position, clutching his head, teeth slammed together. Fresh blood spilled from his nose.

My eyes flooded with hot tears.

Benroar cried out and staggered back, then every Leviathan in the tower crushed their heads, screaming, groaning, falling to their knees. The roar of pain and agony rippled to the city below . . . and I knew.

"My rebirth is now." Her smile was the bite of a sword, the pierce of an arrow, the sting of poison, destruction. "Become a part of my glorious rebirth, or die with them!" A strange wind rippled around her, warbling like heat on the road in the summer sun.

This was the battle for Meldron all over again. She was going to wipe out another army of Leviathan pirates. And she wasn't stopping there. I could feel her extend further, beyond the borders of the Dead Forest.

I had no more time. I plunged my hand into my belt pouch and withdrew all the vials I had left. Water rippled through my blood, heat warmed my skin, life of the earth solidified in my muscles, and air flowed through my fingertips as I raised them high.

Rion's eyes widened.

My arm jerked to a stop as a cold, white hand snapped around my wrist. "Enough." Alder stood over me, his face streaked with blood, black fumes rolling off his skin. He pried the vials from my fingers one by one.

"No . . ." With every release from my hand, I felt hope slipping away.

As the last one slipped free, Alder pitched the vials out the arched window. Sunlight flashed against the glass as they dropped and disappeared. My heart sank with them, knees giving out. I'd done everything I knew how, and it had been all for nothing. Alder's grip was all that kept me from crumbling to the ground in shame and defeat.

"Bring her here," Rion ordered, shunting Leander's body away. His dreadlocks splayed across the floor as he fell limp beside Broderick and Boma . . . gone. All gone.

Tears blurred my vision as I searched for Ikane. I barely made out his form lying on his side, unmoving, eyes closed, blood trailing down the side of his face from his nose, dripping to the stone floor.

I choked on my own breath.

"Your turn," Alder hissed in my ear, and his cold breath sent an icy ripple down my spine.

CHAPTER 40

LIFETIMES

*A*lder's fingers pinched the back of my neck as he steered me forward. My feet stumbled on the fallen rubble. The sight of surrounding corpses echoed the dark history of this chamber, and she was the center of it all: The woman standing before me in the stolen body of my friend and queen. Her red lips grew into a smile as Alder drove me toward her, steering me between the lifeless bodies of Broderick and Benroar.

I wanted to defy her, glower at her twisted vision of what was life, but I had nothing more to give. Nothing more I could do. I'd lost.

Alder's boot connected with the back of my knee, forcing me to kneel at the hem of her blood-red gown.

Her touch stung as she placed her hand under my jaw and raised my face to meet hers. "Now do you see?" she asked, almost tenderly. "You should have accepted my offer to become my new body when I first presented you with that honor. You could have spared yourself all this heartache, all this loss and pain." She traced my cheek with the tips of her fingers.

Did she truly believe that would have been any more merciful? "You would have taken them anyway," I whispered.

She laughed and dropped my jaw. "True, but you wouldn't have felt it." Her gut-churning smile returned.

How did that make things any better? Wasn't feeling a part of life? Wasn't it experience that sculpted our strengths and weaknesses, made us who we were? How empty would our souls be without it?

My eyes caught the glint of steel lying beside my knee. It was Benroar's weapon, his fingers lax around the hilt. My own fingers twitched. I could snatch it up and plunge it into Rion's chest before she took breath to scream. But it wasn't just Rion standing before me. It was the queen of Roanfire. Lonacheska and her child, the last true heir to Roanfire's throne.

Could I do it? Could I end the Noirfonika line now and ruin any chance Rion had for rebirth in the future? The thought raced through my mind, calculating the benefits and risks of the situation. If I killed Lonacheska, the baby would die, too. Rion would undoubtedly return to the stone . . . or overtake my body before I had the chance to turn the weapon on myself. No. It was too late for any of that. Even if I did succeed in plunging the tip of the sword into my own heart, Rion had the power to restore it. Endless power. She would take my body one way or the other and rise.

I sank to my knees, clutched my shredded hand to my chest, and let my eyes settle on Broderick's body lying on my left. His brown curls, the scar on his lips, the warm blood still glistening under his nose. Leander rested beside him, his face still bruised from the beating he'd taken in the dungeons. Boma sprawled just beyond. Benroar's body had collapsed to my right and a dozen more Leviathan pirates with him.

And Ikane . . . Ikane lay alone somewhere behind me. My neck ached as I turned, looking at my wolf, but all I saw was his back. Not his scarred face or the mismatched eyes I loved so much.

"I'm sorry," I whispered. My eyes closed. "I am so, so sorry."

"It's too late for apologies," Rion snapped. She extended her palm to Alder. Red light flooded her features as he placed the ruby inside.

Alder moved behind me. Grabbing my elbows, he drew them back until my chest ached.

Rion leaned forward and touched the neck of my tunic. "I've waited a dozen lifetimes for this moment." With that, she pressed the burning ruby against my sternum.

Fire tore up my throat, crashing against my skull. It liquified my mind and thrust me aside like something rotten, and Alder's cold grip on my arms vanished.

The stinging faded. The tension in my chest evaporated. The ringing in my ears, the throbbing of my hand, the weight of my armor, the smell of dust and blood . . . all of it floated away like a distant memory.

Once again, I drifted inside the ruby. No matter how many times I found myself here, the emotion was the same, endless clouds of stars rolling around me too vast to comprehend and claustrophobically suffocating. Each star was a life, a creature who had felt and lived. How many were humans, children, infants? How many were animals like my late horse, Gossamer? Was he still here somewhere among the throng? Or had Rion used his life energy a long time ago? And how many of these stars were plant life, trees, grasses, flowers—all the things that could no longer grow in the Dead Forest because she leeched their life away?

Something sharp pelted into me, spinning me off course. The tail of a star streaking by dissolved. Another struck my side, and another. Thousands upon thousands rained forward like flaming arrows in the night, following burning ribbons to the center of the cracked prison.

Fire roared to life in the core, blooming into the form of the beautiful and terrifying woman I'd grown to hate with everything inside me. Her copper skin rippled with flame. Her bone-white hair floated weightless and cold. Her hollow eyes burned. No longer did she warp Lonacheska's beautiful face with her twisted smile. This was her true form. The true nightmare of everything.

"Kea." A rush of blue fell against me, wrapping me in the arms of the man I loved most.

"Ikane. You're here. You're still here." I let myself sink into him as if he could take away all the pain.

His embraced tightened. "Take my energy, Kea. Don't let me become a part of her like this. I'm yours. Only yours."

My light trembled, and I wished I could shed the tears of pain locked so deep. "It won't be enough, Ikane. She's already won."

"I know," he admitted. Somehow, I could feel his fingers slipping through mine, squeezing, giving me strength even without his blue life energy. "But I also know who you are. You are a warrior, a soldier, a protector. You always have been. By the stars in the sky, Kea, I've watched you bleed and give up everything to defend Roanfire. You, my Little Brendagger, have endured too much to give up now."

I held him tight, wishing I could feel the solidness of his arms one last time. Wishing I could smell his scent of mint and wild wolf and run my fingers through his hair. I didn't want to do this. But he'd asked. It was his final wish. Who was I to deny him that?

"I'm sorry, Ikane."

"I am where I need to be, Little Brendagger." His beautiful Leviathan accent rippled through my mind. "And that is with you."

His strength flared through my single star of light. He was the sea and the rain. He was the storms billowing over the ocean and the pale clouds drifting over a meadow. He was a ripple and a tidal wave. A stream and a river. A trickle and a waterfall. And he became my tears.

Laughter filled the rush of swirling stars. "Pathetic. You think one life is enough to stop me? Do you not hear the whispers of thousands in my hands? Do you not see how they burn eternally in me, never to taste of death again?"

I couldn't move.

"But you?" she sneered. "With you, they die."

I wished I could simply shut my eyes and block out the horrible vision of her. Stars screamed at her back, sliding into her like the burning wings of a phoenix, her very essence growing larger and brighter as she consumed them.

"Kea!" A silver-white star crashed into me with such force, it knocked me back. His energy rushed through me with the same intensity of a blasting gale snapping the sails taut on a ship.

"Broderick?"

No thoughts radiated from him as he mingled his energy with ours, pushing all he had to me, giving without hesitation. It was too forceful, knocking the air from my lungs.

"Wait!" I cried. "At least let me say goodbye. Let me—"

"No time." His words raced to me, through me, around me, fading quickly as they became my own.

I cried out, hating every moment.

"Two?" Rion mocked, a million voices laughing with her. "You think you can defeat me with two souls?"

I knew I couldn't, and that was what hurt the most.

"She has three." A green star flickered beside me, defiant and sturdy.

It was Leander.

Rion's glowing white eyes narrowed. "Foolish young prince. I should have taken you when I took your cellmate." She lashed out with a whip of fire.

He whirled to me, vines of emerald energy wrapping around my core.

A cry overpowered the screaming of the stars, one so close I thought it could have been Leander. But I hadn't absorbed him. I hadn't used his power.

He turned, finding that a different star had moved into the path of Rion's strike. Its leafy glow was not quite as pure as Leander's but still strong, vibrant, and determined.

"Boma!" Leander's voice was in a panic. "Boma, no!"

Boma's energy warbled with pain, and he was ripped away like the roots of a mighty oak torn from the earth. Leander cried out as Boma's energy fell into the endless cloud of stars moving together in one mighty swell, rotating around Rion's growing inferno. She was taking them all, burning through their energy like dry tinder in a bonfire.

"Do what you can, Lady Brendagger," Leander whispered. "You have not failed in our eyes."

Whether I wanted him to or not, Leander pulled me to him and wrapped his light around my silver-blue tinged star like the shelter of the pines that had protected us from the Deathbiters at night.

The power they gifted me was unlike anything I'd ever experienced. All the force behind a cavalry of a thousand warhorses could not compare. All the rage of the sea burying a ship under giant waves became like a model ship in a bottle. Was all this power truly not enough to defeat her? My three stars, my three friends, lives willingly sacrificed for a kingdom that wasn't even theirs? Even without Ropert, I had to try. For them.

"Go on." Rion smiled. "Three souls are no threat to me. You needed the fourth, and he is mine. You will all be mine!"

The power surging inside me melted together to form the weapon I knew best. "You are a warrior," Ikane had said. "A soldier, a protector." The blade grew long and sharp, glowing with an edge of blue-green light, reminding me so much of Ikane's eyes. The hilt balanced the weight of the blade with perfect precision, and the cross guard unfurled with the wings of the true Phoenix. Not the one Rion was trying to become. But the bird that returned life to everything.

The corners of Rion's blood-red lips curled up with a taunting edge. She shook her head as if I was nothing but a child holding out a brittle stick in the face of a wolf.

Perhaps I was. Against all her power and roaring energy, I was nothing.

And yet, the sacrifice of my friends was everything.

With a battle cry, I surged forward, streaking toward her like an arrow from Broderick's bow, and aimed the sword at her chest.

She laughed, and with a wave of her hand, a wall of trapped and trembling stars moved between us. For a moment, I was blinded as I crashed through them. Stars scattered like shards of glass.

I didn't see her move. I didn't see her hand as it caught my throat, stopping me like a low-hanging branch in the path of a galloping horse. The paralyzing flame rolling through me cut off the last remaining ember I had. Her hollow eyes enveloped me in white nothingness as she drew me to her.

"Now, you all belong to me," she hissed.

"Hey! Scary fire lady!"

That voice! I knew that voice!

CHAPTER 41

REBIRTH

*L*et them go," he demanded.

Rion's brows furrowed as her eyes lifted to a star behind me. "You... How did...?" She flinched when she found a single thread fluttering aimlessly beside her, untethered to a star, a life.

Her moment of panic was all I needed. I sliced upward, severing her hold on me, cutting into her arm and through a handful of threads holding stars. Rion clutched her arm to her chest as they scattered like birds released from a cage.

I spun backward, aching to be near that familiar voice and brother-in-arms.

"Ropert."

His star radiated beside me, red and strong, and somehow, I could sense his crystal-blue eyes watching me. Laughing, brimming with his usual mischievousness.

"Hi, Dagger. I was wondering when you'd show up," he said.

I wanted to laugh and cry, pummel him and embrace him.

"We don't have much time," he said. "But I brought some recruits."

Clouds of stars swarmed behind him, churning like a hurricane storm over the sea. The energy was so thick that bolts of blue, green, red, and white lightning tore through it.

"They're here for you," Ropert said. "We all are."

This was . . . this was incredible. Unbelievable. This was what I needed to destroy her. This was . . . wrong. I couldn't take lives and use them the way she did.

A star flickered forward, tiny compared to the others. "I give my life to you." The voice was young. A child's.

Another star followed, this one larger and more vibrant. "We have spent centuries imprisoned here, waiting to become the life-blood of a goddess who cares nothing for our souls," she said. "End this, Princess of Roanfire. Our lives will mean something to the future if we can do our part to save it. Save your friends. Restore those whose hearts still beat with our lives."

Without warning, she touched her energy to mine. I gasped as she filled my core, swelling with light like the rising moon over water, and leaned into Ikane's waning energy.

The child also tipped toward me, her essence like the breath of wind, rushing to Broderick. Another became a green valley and flooded to Leander. The sword in my hand dissolved into three lights, blinking at me like friends awakening from slumber. Ikane was back! Broderick and Leander. The stars had brought them back!

They didn't stop pressing in around me, suffocating me with the energy of the rising sun, a mountain, rain, budding leaves, a candle flame, an earthquake. With every life willingly given, my lights doubled, tripled, expanded too quickly to contain. I was going to burst.

"No!" Rion screeched, but I barely heard her. "They are mine! Those stars are mine!" The stars behind her pulled against her in unison, turning into chains at her back.

More life energy seeped into me, and the cloud never seemed to grow any smaller. I could have wept for all the life she had taken. "No more," I whimpered. "I can't . . ."

Ropert flashed with command, halting the onslaught of stars.

"They only mean to help," he said.

I knew that. But Phoenix, the power was too much. Yotherna had warned me that one life willingly given was worth more than a thousand stolen lives. And all the stars here seemed suddenly willing and eager to give me all they had.

I already had more than enough to destroy her twice over.

"Take their energy, Dagger. You can restore Ikane and Leander and Thundercrack."

"Hey," Broderick warned.

Ropert's light flashed with a grin. "You can save them the way you saved me."

"And you?" I could feel the pain welling up inside me.

He flickered sadly. "I'll always be with you, Dagger. You can't get rid of me."

"Oh, Ropert." I wanted to embrace him but feared that if I did, I would absorb him, too. "I wasn't there for you. If I had only come sooner, Rion wouldn't have . . ." I choked.

"Hey." I could almost feel his finger tap under my chin. "Stay strong, Dagger. You've got this."

It was the exact thing he'd said to me the day I'd lost my temper on the training field years ago in Daram, when everything was simpler.

"May I make one request?"

"Anything," I sobbed.

"Remember me?"

I let out a sob. I would never forget him, even after my own life returned to the phoenix. "Every year, on this day, we will have a celebration in your honor," I vowed. "Just like the Harvest Festivals we used to have in Daram. A feast, music, dancing."

His mischievous smile radiated through his red light. "Only pastries allowed."

My laugh was filled with weeping. "Alright. Only pastries," I promised. "And a new one filled with apple."

He turned to Broderick. "You'll take care of her, Thundercrack."

"I will," Broderick replied. "And . . . I don't mind being called that anymore."

Ropert smiled.

"Ikane." Ropert flickered beside the blue light of the Leviathan pirate. "We never did get to spar," he said.

"I would've let you win," Ikane answered. "Like I did with the horse race."

Ropert laughed, then his red light burned with seriousness. "Love her, Ikane. I've never seen her fight for anyone the way she fights for you."

"I will," Ikane promised.

"One more thing." Ropert paused, Rion's distant screaming rolling behind the surrounding stars. "Take my body home, to Daram. And tell Ciri I . . . I wish we'd had more time together. I never thought I'd say this, but I think . . . I think I was falling in love."

That last part broke my heart. After all these years, he'd finally found someone who could impress him, some beautiful woman he didn't feel like he would break. "I will," I said. I would do everything he asked and more.

His light opened to me like his arms opening for an embrace. I fell into him, and he filled me with more than energy. He filled me with love.

Stars surged together, eager to be a part of their own liberation, eager to lend me even a fraction of their stolen life. Humming vibrations swallowed all sound. White filled the cavernous red, overpowering Rion's burning brilliance like a clean sheet wiping away blood.

I didn't even hear her cry out.

CHAPTER 42

VERDANT

 My eyes opened. Somehow the air smelled of summer rain despite chucks of stone continuing to fracture and drop from the vaulted ceiling, leaving streams of dust to glitter in the sunlight streaming through the open windows. There was life here. I could sense it, feel it beneath my body, touch it in the air.

I rolled to my side, coming face-to-face with Queen Lonacheska. Her dark lashes remained closed against her cheeks in the perfect image of sleep . . . or something else. I swallowed as I reached toward her and brushed her golden hair behind her shoulder to let my fingers rest against her throat. I felt a heartbeat. Strong, steady. She was alive, and she was free.

A chunk of stone cracked from the ceiling above her. Springing to my knees, I rolled over her body, hearing the clang of rock hitting the metal backplate armor I wore. I'd never moved so fast. Nor had moving like that ever been so effortless, even with my hand—

My hand.

I lifted it from the ground beside Lona's golden locks. My stomach flipped at the sight of blood and protruding bone where my fingers had been. I tucked it against my chest as trembling overtook my body. Shouldn't I have felt more pain? I was missing over half my hand. Perhaps it was the lingering energy of thousands of lives that continued to flow and ripple through my muscles that numbed it.

Broderick stirred beside me, then Benroar. The entire tower rippled with pirates waking, groaning, and pushing themselves from the ground. They wiped blood from their noses, glancing at each other, the unconscious queen, and me.

Across the way, my wolf lifted himself up, his mismatched eyes immediately bright as they found mine. Feathers, he was beautiful, so full of life and energy, like he was flooded with a hundred stars. I had thought he was gone. I had said goodbye, thinking that I would never feel him close to me again.

Springing to his feet, he hurried to my side, stripping his tunic as he went. Crouching beside me, he wrapped my destroyed hand inside the warm fabric and used the leather lacing to bind it tight.

Tenderly, he tucked my hair behind my ear and pressed his forehead against mine. "You did it, Kea." He inhaled, almost like it was the first time he could do so since we'd met. "She's gone."

I closed my eyes, inhaling his scent of mint, steel, blood, and lingering wildness. "No," I whispered. "It was Ropert. Ropert and the stars."

I felt him nod. "Ropert," he agreed.

Ikane pulled away, brushing my cheek with his thumb as a smile spread across his lips. I hoped it would never fade from his face again. His eyes flickered to my lips as he leaned forward.

A kiss. My heart fluttered at the thought. A pure kiss without Rion infesting any part of us. Something real and untainted.

I closed the gap, pressing my lips against his, melting against them, running my fingers through his hair. A tear slid from my closed lashes. I had given up hope of ever having this moment.

I pulled away as a chunk of stone dropped from the ceiling, struck Ikane's shoulder, and tumbled away. But he drew me back, his lips hungry and searching. His sharp canine tooth pinched my lip, making me flinch.

Only then did he pull back and rest his forehead against mine again. "I'm sorry," he whispered.

I wasn't, but another chunk of stone crashed beside us, the size of an iron helm. The tower groaned. A rumble sounded as a deep crack etched its way across the domed surface, sending a shower of sand across us.

"We need to move," Broderick said as he hovered over Lonacheska's body, shielding her with his cloak.

Ikane scooped the queen from the ground like she was lighter than feathers. "Help Kea," he said to Broderick.

I barely noticed Broderick come to my side as my eyes fell on Prince Leander. He curled over Boma's unmoving body, dreadlocks hanging over his bowed face as he pulled the Tolean warrior's head to his chest. His shoulders shook, and tears glistened in his eyes as he rocked, though I did not hear him weep.

My heart ached with his. I knew exactly the pain he felt. Boma had given his life to save Leander. He had been one of the first victims of Rion's attempted rebirth, and I could not bring him back. Not with all the power of billions of stars.

Even unflexed and limp, Boma's muscles remained the envy of any warrior. I'd seen what those muscles could do. They'd moved with the grace of the wind, struck with the speed of a viper, and hit with the force of a mountain. My moments with this man were few, but Leander . . .

I saw a mutual love and respect between them, much like . . . like what Ropert and I had shared. A bond that transcended blood. Brotherhood. Leander's silent, faithful, ever-present warrior, friend, and brother was gone.

As was mine.

I set my jaw as my hand began to sting and throb. We would not leave Boma here.

One of the pillars standing between the circular row of arched windows shifted. Rock and debris struck the ground.

Broderick stepped to Leander and placed a hand on the prince's shoulder. "Leander? We need to go."

Leander glanced up. Pain shone in his golden eyes, but his face remained calm, almost numb as he nodded and pulled Boma's arm over his shoulders. Leander's legs barely shook as he shrugged Boma's body onto his back and rose. He carried his bodyguard from the tower.

Benroar stepped beside me and slid his sword back into the sheath at his hip. "I . . . misjudged you," he said, not looking at me. I could tell this was not something he did often. He glanced over his shoulder. "It was them."

He followed Leander from the tower, leaving me to glance back at what he had indicated: Alder, the only body remaining in the chamber. His black cloak rippled as falling stone dusted it in gray sand. His long hair sprawled around him like streams of liquid steel. And his eyes . . . they stood wide and frozen, aimed at the glittering red fragments of the Phoenix Stone lying in his open hand.

A shadow tore through me, mixed with hatred and compassion. What had this man endured to become so twisted? What sort of a life had he led that made him so loyal to Rion? Everything about him was a shadow to Yotherna, like the difference of the moon to the sun . . . just like Thrall and Etheria.

Strangely, I didn't feel the powers churn so vibrantly inside me. They felt almost like a ripple versus a tidal wave or a flickering candle instead of a roaring blaze. They were a ghost of their former selves. Just as Yotherna had designed, once the curse was destroyed, the princesses of Roanfire no longer needed to hold this magic. Lonacheska's daughter would be born pure and free. Roanfire would be reborn in a way Rion could have never imagined.

But this also meant that Yotherna was gone. Was he lying on the bed of pillows with his milky-white hair cascading down his shoulders like the silken petals of lilies? Were his eyes closed or open like his brother's?

Regardless, the brothers of light and dark were no more.

And neither was Rion.

"Come on, Kea," Broderick tugged on my sleeve.

I turned away then paused. Something green flashed near the windows. Squinting, I stepped closer. It was a glossy ivy leaf—green, full, shaking in the gentle breeze. Was it . . . possible? Despite the urgency to escape the unstable tower, I cast my gaze out the nearest window.

Verdant life stole my breath. The hillside had turned into a blanket of dappled green treetops with leaves unfurled and glittering as the rising sun cast its glow across the landscape. It breathed and moved, as if maturing before my eyes. Open patches that had once been fields of death and dust swayed with blades of grass, and bursts of yellow, white, and blue wildflowers unfurled like scattered stars. Dead stumps turned into beds of green. Vines curled up the side of the tower. Shrubs and thick leafy plants dotted the cliffside.

This was all happening through the power of the stars. All the life Rion had stolen was returning to the earth. Ropert was here. In the trees. In the grass and flowers, in the smell, in the air brushing against my skin. He was a part of everything.

"Kea, now," Broderick urged.

Closing my eyes, I inhaled, smiled, and turned away.

Thank you, Ropert. You will be missed.

I followed Broderick from the tower. Even with urgency pumping through my blood and the throbbing rising in my hand, a lightness infused my step. I hadn't realized how Rion's influence had slowly ground me into the dirt like the weight of armor dragging against the muscles of a tired soldier. For the first time since leaving Daram all those years ago, I could breathe.

The roar of the collapsing tower raced after us. The earth shook beneath my boots. I braced myself against the wall as dust and debris rolled down the spiraling stairwell like a giant gale, striking my back with a blast of sand.

As we stumbled into the corridor below, we were greeted by several dozen Leviathan pirates. Those coming from the tower hurried to their comrades, and whisperings began. Eyes flashed to me and my bandaged hand as the stories started. I noted several glances toward Queen Lonacheska in Ikane's arms—or was it Ikane they were looking at? Their wayward prince?

Leander lowered Boma's body to the ground, propping him up against the wall as Benroar pushed a side door open.

"Bring the queen here," he urged Ikane.

Ikane slipped inside where a cot stood ready, draped with furs and woolen blankets. The room smelled of Lona. I assumed this had been her prison before Rion had taken over. He gently laid the queen down and tucked her legs onto the bed.

"We need to return her to Meldron," Ikane said, keeping his eyes averted from his brother.

"Aye, that we do," Benroar agreed.

Ikane glanced at me as I stood in the doorway beside Broderick. I leaned against the frame, my body suddenly feeling strange. Almost like the lightness I felt inside was getting carried away.

Benroar followed Ikane's gaze. "There is much we need to make amends for."

Ikane's eyes rose in surprise as he dared look at his brother.

"Ah, don't look so astonished. Your girl there has proven wise and formidable and persuasive. She's not half bad to look at, either. I wouldn't mind seeing more of her as we begin negotiating peace agreements."

Ikane choked. "P-peace? You mean it?"

"You've got me convinced," Benroar announced. "The problem will be convincing Accalon."

Ikane leapt forward and pulled his brother against his chest, arms trembling in the embrace.

"Scales, Ikane," Benroar croaked.

Ikane released him quickly. "Sorry," he muttered.

Benroar arched his back, and several pops resounded. "Just . . . don't do that again. I can't handle all this touchy-feely stuff you're doing today."

Ikane smiled. He'd longed for his brothers to accept him. Any of them. Teilo had been the only one, and now he had two he could count on. Two who could help him persuade the Leviathan pirates to make peace. I found myself smiling at the beauty of the reconnecting brotherhood flowing between them.

"Kea," Broderick cried. His arm shot out, catching me before I collided with the floor. It was strange how much the room narrowed in. When had the Fold Garrison become so hot? There was no fire here.

"Her heart beats too slow." Ikane was by my side in an instant, crouching over me as he gently lowered me to the ground. He brushed my hair back. Despite worry filling his handsome features, I would have been content if his face was the last thing I ever saw.

"It's shock," Broderick said. "Her hand. The pain . . ."

CHAPTER 43

REMEMBER THEM

*M*y hand felt like it clung to Rion's fire. It pulsed with a raging heartbeat, stung, and sent sparks of pain through my arm. A groan escaped my throat.

The touch of a gentle hand against my brow was an afterthought. "Keatep?"

The voice was feminine, warm. My eyes cracked open, blinking at the hazy image of Queen Lonacheska leaning over me.

"She's awake," Lona called over her shoulder, "and she's in much pain."

Broderick appeared. "Drink this," he said, holding a tin mug to my lips. I raised my head, desperate to drink anything he offered, anything to make the burning stop. The liquid was tinged with bitter herbs but flowing with the soothing, pain-numbing rush of windsprite dust. I dropped my head against the pillow and shut my eyes, aware of the dust's power spreading through my abdomen and expanding to my limbs. Every muscle sighed as it reached my hand, settling like a cold blanket.

My face relaxed, and I inhaled.

"It's only—"

"Temporary, I know," I finished for him and sat upright, taking in the chamber. We were in the same room in the Fold Garrison with the single cot where Ikane had set Lona on this very bed. Only I was in it now, and Lonacheska was sitting beside me.

"My queen," I bowed my head to her and brought my fist up to my chest in a soldier's salute then let out a yelp. I had used my wrecked hand.

"Oh, no need for that," Lona said quickly. She gently coaxed my bloodstained, bandaged arm back to my lap. Her smile was natural and sweet, with pink color touching her cheeks and lips. She'd shed the red gown for a simple cotton dress and a shrug of spotted gray-and-white seal fur provided by the pirates. Her golden hair hung in a loose braid over her shoulder. She looked wonderful and real. Reaching up, she brushed my hair behind my shoulder and stroked it, her dark eyes studying my face.

"We are in your debt," she said.

I stared at her. Our relationship had been strained when she'd discovered that I was King Sander's bastard daughter, but it had slowly grown into a mutual understanding when she realized her unborn child would face the same fate as I did—or worse—if I didn't stop Rion. She'd sought my counsel on more than one occasion and did everything in her power to help me, even defying King Sander's orders. But her touch now was motherly, tender, and loving like I was her own flesh and blood.

"Can you ride?" she asked. "Your hand is badly damaged, and we do not have the tools nor the skill to tend to it here. Healer Bandock may be able to prevent it from being amputated."

I swallowed and nodded. As long as Broderick kept me supplied with his pain-numbing herbs and windsprite dust, I could ride.

She stood and turned to Broderick. "Let the others know she is awake. We ride within the hour."

Broderick bowed and slipped out of the room.

"What about you?" I asked, glancing at her stomach. She had grown. "Should you be riding in your condition?"

"I just survived being kidnapped, trekking halfway across Roanfire with a madman, and endured the mind-warping assault from an ancient witch-queen. I think I can manage a short ride back to Meldron."

I almost regretted asking.

"Yes, Lady Brendagger. I can ride."

I swung my legs over the edge of the bed. "Where are the others? Is Prince Leander . . . alright?"

Lona's eyes fell. "He has taken the loss of his bodyguard very hard. He has not spoken a word, but perhaps he will speak with you."

I felt a renewed stab as I remembered where my own bodyguard, Ropert, had been murdered. I stood, feeling a strange pressure build in my hand as I held it to my chest. "I will speak with him," I said. "Has . . . has Ropert's body been recovered?"

Lonacheska nodded. "Recovered and reverently wrapped and adorned with thyme, peppermint, and cedar for our return to Meldron. I am truly sorry for your loss, Keatep. I knew he was more to you than a bodyguard."

I swallowed the pain building in my throat. It was fresh and raw, unlike the pain of losing Eamon. Still, it would always hurt. It would always be a wound, but over time, I knew it would be easier to bear.

"He will be honored," Lona assured me. "Both Ropert and Master Eamon will live on in legacy and legend."

"Thank you, dear queen." I bowed.

"Please," she said. "No. You do not need to bow to me. You are King Sander's daughter, a rightful princess of Roanfire." She raised her hand before I could speak. "I know you don't want the title, but I do hope that you will consider a position close to me, as an advisor."

"I . . . I would be honored, Your Majesty."

She pursed her lips and gave me a sideways glance.

"I mean . . . Lonacheska."

"That's better," she smiled. "Come, I will take you to Prince Leander."

Freely walking along the corridors lined with staring pirates felt strange. I paused. A man in a crimson uniform sat nearby, and another, and another, mingling with the pirates. I turned to Lona.

She smiled. "Prince Benroar has been most agreeable. I believe we are entering the first stages of peace between our people."

My heart fluttered. "Does Ikane know? Where is he?"

"He is working closely with his brother. I have not seen him for some time. Shall I send for him?"

"No. If things are going well, I don't want to interfere."

Lona stopped at a curtained door. "Leander is in here."

I pulled the tattered curtain aside, and my eyes flared immediately with Mina's firedust at the gloom. Leander sat on the floor, back against the wall, hands propped on his knees with Boma's covered body lying beside him.

"Leander?" I stepped inside and let the curtain fall.

His head rose quickly, his golden eyes falling on my bandaged hand as I sank to the wall beside him. "Lady Brendagger. What . . . ? Why are you here? You should be resting."

"Everyone is worried about you," I said.

Leander's face grew numb as he glanced at Boma. "It should have been me."

His words struck me harder than I thought. How many times had I yearned for the same thing? Wishing with all my heart that I could die and spare the lives of everyone I cared for. But I had to accept their sacrifice. I had to understand that if the roles were reversed, Ropert would be the one standing over my body, wishing the same. In the end, no one truly came away the victor.

"I was raised to be a key for you, Kea. It was my task. Mine . . ."

"Leander."

He swiped at his cheeks though I didn't see any tears glittering down his face.

"You are lamenting his sacrifice, what he gave to save your life—our lives. Would you have felt better knowing that he stood in your place, looking down on your body the way you look at him now?" I paused, letting my own words sink in for Ropert. "Let us honor them, Leander. Open a place in your heart, and let Boma's love for you live on like I will do for Ropert. We will relish them. Accept them. Honor them."

Leander shut his dark lashes, and shimmering droplets of tears trailed down his cheeks. He pressed his lips tighter. "I accept," he whispered. Then he looked at me. "But what will become of me now? I was meant to die. What do I do with the life Boma has given me?"

I didn't have an answer. "I suppose we will figure that out together."

"What about your Leviathan prince?"

"What?"

He didn't look at me. "You love him. That much is clear."

I felt heat rise to my cheeks. How insensitive could I be? Leander had lost his closest friend, and I had let my passion for Ikane take over, openly kissing him in front of the man who'd come to ask for my hand in marriage. His words echoed through my memory. *I am not doing this for Roanfire.* His eyes had burned so vibrantly when he'd confessed this.

"I did not allow myself to dream of a life with you," he said. "I knew it could never be." His gaze turned back to me. "Dare I hope for something more?"

My heart hiccuped. "Leander, I . . ."

"I understand." He looked away. "Your heart has always belonged to Ikane. It is better that way."

I touched his arm, but he flinched away.

"Do not make this more difficult by showing me pity. It will only spur me, and I do not wish to destroy your happiness."

I retracted my hand, a strange sensation of guilt festering inside me. I opened my mouth, but nothing came. What could I say? I did love Ikane. More than anything, my wolf was the center of my world.

I pushed against the wall and stood. "We are leaving for Meldron shortly," I said. "Shall I send for help with Boma—?"

"No," Leander said quickly. "I will care for him."

I bit my lip, hesitated, then turned away. What had I done?

What was to become of Leander now? What was to become of our kingdoms and the treaty? What was to become of the marriage arrangement?

CHAPTER 44

ROANFIRE REBORN

*S*unlight rested on my shoulders as I followed a light strumming melody through the path of endless orange poppies and blue cornflowers of Meldron's garden. The castle grounds had never looked so lovely, so rich with color, so full of life pushing through the soil. Even the hedges bore thick crowns of green far sooner than our normal season permitted.

Willowy arms decorated with the jewels of spinning green leaves swayed in the warm breeze. Birdsong darted from tree to tree, twisting to the cloudless summer sky—a sound that was only just returning after the disappearance of the Deathbiters two weeks ago.

I lifted my freshly bandaged hand and gently held it in the other for support. My fingers—or lack thereof—still ached. Healer Bandock was able to save most of my hand, but the gruff old sage had warned me that I would probably feel pain the rest of my days. I had yet to regain full movement of the remaining two fingers.

The strumming melody grew louder as I neared a hedge filled with sweet-smelling white blossoms. It was beautiful and fresh, like the music Broderick used to play on his lute. The music stopped abruptly.

"Ugh. My hand is cramping again."

I paused. That was Ikane's voice.

"You're getting better."

Was that Broderick?

Placing my feet more carefully on the gravel, I leaned around the hedge to find Ikane sitting on a bench with a stunning six-stringed lute in his arms. He was shaking out and flexing his fingers. "Do you think I'll be ready by—"

Broderick stood abruptly, his eyes snapping in my direction. "Kea." His tone was chiding.

Ikane jumped up, sweeping the lute behind his back as I stepped out.

"Sorry," I muttered. No matter where Ikane was, I always seemed to end up spying on him. "I heard the music. It's beautiful, Ikane. I didn't know you could play."

A rosiness filled his cheeks as he bit his lip. "I can't. I mean, I couldn't until two weeks ago . . . give or take."

"Why didn't you tell me you were learning?"

Ikane glanced at Broderick. "Because . . . well . . . it was supposed—"

"It was supposed to be a surprise," Broderick interrupted. "He was going to play at the festival tonight, at the unveiling of Master Eamon's and Ropert's memorials."

"You were?"

"I'm not sure I'm ready," Ikane admitted.

"You are," Broderick said, clapping him on the shoulder. "I'll leave you two alone a moment." He paused beside me. "You will make an excellent advisor to our queen, by the way. I look forward to the announcement tonight."

I swallowed. "As long as you remain *my* advisor."

"It would be my pleasure and honor." He gave me a hasty bow.

"And member of the Lost Limb Brigade?" I added, holding up my bandaged hand.

He smiled, touching his stump to mine. "When did you come up with that?"

"Just now."

He chuckled. "That was about as good as Ropert would have done."

I gave him a weak smile. How I missed Ropert.

"I'll see you tonight." Broderick waved his good hand absently as he left.

Ikane cleared his throat.

I turned to him as he sat back down on the bench and patted the empty space beside him. He lifted the lute by its neck and draped it across his lap.

Gathering the fullness of my shimmering copper skirt around my legs, I sat. It was the only clothing I could comfortably slip into without the use of both hands. Once I learned how to use my two fingers, I was certain I could buckle a tunic and a sword belt again. But I wondered if that person was who I was anymore.

Ikane strummed a weak tune then placed his hand over the string to silence the instrument. "This is harder than it looks."

"What made you decide to play?"

Ikane shrugged. "Because . . . well, because Broderick can't anymore. Because of me."

My smile faded. "You don't need to prove anything."

"I do," he said. "For myself."

If that's what he needed, then I would support him.

"How's your hand?" he asked as he set the lute aside.

I glanced at the bandages. "It hurts. Bandock says it'll probably ache the rest of my life."

Ikane gently took my bandaged hand and placed a tender kiss on the back of it. "That was a brave thing you did."

I had to wonder if it was more reckless than brave. If I had simply done as Yotherna had instructed, my hand would probably still be intact. I glanced at my other palm, where blue-and-white sprite dust continued to glitter. No, if I had done as Yotherna had said, Ikane would not be beside me right now. Broderick and Leander would be gone, too, and none of the stars would have found true peace in standing up to Rion.

"I heard that they've begun to restore the Fold Garrison," I said. "Now that the waters are clear, it will be a main port for trade with your people."

"I never dreamed I'd hear those words." He grinned openly, showing his forever sharp canine teeth. Although they were a constant reminder of what he'd been through, they displayed who he was. My wolf.

"Torquin is heading the repairs," I said. "He's been able to clear out all the—"

"Kea?" Ikane cleared his throat. "I . . . I'd like to ask you something, but I'm not quite sure how. I don't even know if it is appropriate."

"What is it?"

He stood and began pacing the ground before me, rubbing the back of his neck. It reminded me so much of the time he'd come to my chambers all those years ago, torn with the decision to kill Roanfire's new king or not.

"I'm not the same man I used to be."

"Neither of us are."

He glanced down at my bandaged hand. "I want to be with you, Kea. More than anything," he finally whispered. "But after what I've done . . ."

"It wasn't you," I said quickly. I wished I could help him see that I did not blame him. "I love you, Ikane. I never stopped."

"Have you . . . spoken with Prince Leander recently?" His question was hesitant.

I shook my head. Leander had not even looked in my direction during our journey back to Meldron. It was like he'd shut out everything in the world, including friendship, after Boma died. But Duqa Alaneek continued to hound me and Queen Lonacheska about a union.

"You . . . well, he . . . he's a good man, Kea. A kind man. A prince who can protect you. And he's never hurt you the way I have."

I tilted my head at him. "What are you trying to say?"

"Well . . ." Ikane pulled his bottom lip through his teeth. "He asked for your hand in marriage first."

My heart swelled and throbbed. He was asking. He was asking me to marry him! I jumped from the bench. "Yes, Ikane. Yes." I gripped his hand tightly in my good one, my sword-fighting hand, the one I would continue to fight with. "I choose you faster than your swords can fly."

But . . . this wasn't my choice. When my royal heritage had been revealed, any marriage agreements had become up to Queen Lonacheska, and thus far, negotiations were well underway with Toleah.

"Nothing is settled yet," I assured him as much as myself. "A union with the Leviathan pirates is a priority to Queen Lonacheska. There is hope."

"Are you sure you want me?" he asked.

I curled against his solid chest, and his arms surrounded me. "Yes," I said. "I do."

"Lady Brendagger!" A maidservant's voice interrupted the moment. I pulled away as she jogged toward us, huffing. "It's Queen Lonacheska."

Alarm flared inside me. "Is she alright?"

"The baby," the maidservant panted. "It's time."

I glanced at Ikane.

"Go," he said, smiling. "This is a new age for Roanfire."

I arrived just as a handful of servants exited Queen Lonacheska's chamber carrying soiled towels and blankets, pitchers of water, and other items. The grumpy old healer, Bandock, stepped out wearing a smile. I paused. I had never seen him smile before. But the smile fell flat as soon as his gray eyes fell on me.

"You're late," he snapped.

"I came as soon as I—" I stopped myself. I didn't need to explain myself to this man. "Can I see her?"

"Enter at your own risk." He shrugged.

I wasn't certain what he meant by that, but I slipped inside, anyway. "Lona? I whispered. The curtains were drawn, and a hazy light filtered inside. The firedust in my eyes flickered in and out, highlighting the edge of the four-poster bed where Queen Lonacheska sat. A sweet, indescribable smell filled the room.

"She came fast," Lona said. The smoldering light from the fireplace flickered against her drained features and the small bundle wrapped in a white knitted blanket against her chest.

I sat on the edge of her bed as Lona lowered the corner of the blanket to reveal the baby's wrinkled face and dark hair. Her tiny lips hung open in the shape of an O. And in that moment, I fell. Fell in love with everything about her. Everything I had endured had been worth it. All the loss and pain and heartache had saved this little human being. Tears blurred my vision.

"She's beautiful," I breathed.

"Do you want to hold her?" Lona asked.

Feathers, did I. I glanced at my broken hand, uncertain. What if I dropped her?

"Don't worry," Lona said. "She's small enough." The queen lifted the infant princess and placed her into my good arm. She was so small, so light and fragile, so pure.

"What is her name?" I whispered, unable to take my eyes from her dark lashes and plump cheeks.

"Eliana," Lona said. "Princess Eliana of Roanfire. It means 'rising sun.'"

"Eliana," I whispered, swaying with the child against my chest. I saw King Sander in her. My sister. "She is perfect."

Lona leaned back against her cluster of white pillows, smiling. "I hate to speak of diplomatic things in moments like this, but the new ambassador to the Leviathan people must be announced this evening at the festival."

"You want me to announce it?"

"No," she said. "Minister Chanter will have that honor. But I was hoping that you would accept the position."

"Me?"

"They respect you."

I licked my lips. This . . . this was perfect. "Would it be possible to take things a step farther?"

She tilted her head at me.

"Ikane has expressed a desire for marriage," I said. "A prince who is just as formidable as—"

Lona held up her hand. "You love him?"

"I do."

She smiled softly. "And what about Prince Leander?"

My smile faded a little, and I bit my lip as I looked back at the tiny princess in my arms. "I . . . could learn to. If it is in Roanfire's best interest."

"Ah, my dear Kea," Lona sighed. "You don't need to keep sacrificing everything for the kingdom. I don't know what is in Roanfire's best interest. Nothing is certain. All I know is that life is short, and it is nothing without happiness."

Did that mean . . . ?

"You and Prince Ikane Ormand of the Leviathan people have my blessing," she said.

I could not keep my smile contained.

"But we will need to sort things with Toleah. We are indebted to them."

I nodded quickly. "Thank you, my queen."

"One more thing," she said. "I need someone to head the duchy of Fold. It will serve as a port of trade with the Leviathans, and it will be an ideal location for my ambassador."

I bit my lip. Why couldn't I stop looking at Eliana? "I . . . wonder if that task is better suited to the people already there," I said. "Torquin would be an excellent leader. Don't let his withered arm fool you. He's the most honest, loyal, and hardworking man I've ever known. And he already has connections with the Leviathans." Not the best ones, but I saw no need to delve into those issues now.

Lona nodded thoughtfully. "I agree."

We sat in silence a few moments longer, watching the baby sleep.

"I suppose," Lona broke the silence, "there is another ideal location for the ambassador to the Leviathan people to reside. One with a prominent port for trade. It will need a lot of hard work and patience to rebuild."

I barely heard her. Eliana's lips were moving ever so slightly, pink and perfect. Why did Queen Lonacheska want to send me away from her? I never wanted to leave my sister's side—even if she was my half sister. I wanted to be by her, protect her, watch her grow.

"You wouldn't be interested in rebuilding Daram, would you?" Lona asked.

My head jerked up. What did she just say? "Daram?"

Lona's nod came with a knowing smile.

"Feathers, yes!" I couldn't keep my voice lowered, nor could I keep from nearly leaping from the bed. Eliana flinched at my sudden movement, but she settled back into sleep quickly, even against the excited beating of my heart. Daram! My home. I could hardly imagine it. I hadn't been back since I'd been given the assignment that changed my life.

I would rebuild it to what it was, and with Ikane by my side, it would be better than ever before. We would build a stronger Roanfire as we worked with the Leviathans and the Toleans instead of remaining at odds with them, abolishing Rion's legacy once and for all.

With the ancient evil queen gone for good, our future was bright. And it was even brighter with Eliana in it.

The rising sun of Roanfire.

NOTE FROM THE AUTHOR

I have a confession to make. I have never actually *ended* a book before. I mean, I've written books that have endings, but nothing as final as Kea' story coming to a close. She has been with me for so long it is strange to think about my life without her. It's almost like saying goodbye to a dear friend who is moving away. It's hard, and it hurts somehow. I feel a little empty.

But the void will be filled. New characters will take her place and new stories will develop.

There were some plot points in this story that I was unable to resolve in the time I was given, so stay tuned for more Roanfire adventures told through the eyes of fresh characters and new kingdoms.

ACKNOWLEDGEMENTS

My writing life would not be possible without my provider and rock, my pillow and my heart; my husband, Matthew Miller. He held my hand, watched me cry, and listened to me rant as I worked through story issues and debilitating personal doubts. There would be no Roanfire without him. Thank you, Matt. I love you most.

A special thank you to my crew of Roanfire Alpha Readers. I felt like Kea when she gathered her team of reconnaissance soldiers. Steph Johnson, Laurel Bingham, Amber Kizer, Jennifer Gilmore, Trina Tolman, Author Jennifer Ann Schlagg, Maria Olson, and Author Jae Cooper. Each one of you came with a special talent and varying viewpoints, and when brought together, it was well rounded and thorough.

Thank you to my editor, Melissa Frey, for her meticulous work to make sure everything was cohesive, flowed, followed a good timeline, and is polished. Seriously, she's incredible.

And I must give a huge thank you to the Rogue Writers, a tight knit community of fantasy authors and artists who always have my back.

Thank you again to my dear friend, Brandon Ho, Creative Director of Goldenworks Entertainment, for pushing me to do more and checking in to make sure I'm still writing. If you need a feel-good hallmark movie to watch, check out "The Bookworm and the Beast."

Not to forget another important person who has helped me tremendously, especially with writing the back blurb of my books, Justin Fike, author of the Farshore Chronicles. He has skills!

What kind of a mother would I be if I didn't thank my boys for giving me inspiration for Dust bombs! They were the ones who came up with the "Sprite Dust Explosives" that Broderick creates.

As I was wrapping up this novel, my computer baby had a heart attack and died. Everything I had been working on was stuck in a black hole. But leave it to my wonderful brothers, Ruben and Jon Kackstaetter to come resuscitate my life and this book.

And thank you to Studio Madness! I would not have held it together without my group of sisters holding my hand as my computer baby went through surgery. Rachel, Trina, and Ruth—every one of them talented in their own way with art and entertainment. What can I say? I come from a family of artists.

ABOUT THE AUTHOR

C.K. Miller lives near the Colorado Rocky Mountains with her husband and three handsome boys. Along with copious amounts of hot chocolate and writing, she can be found drawing, working in the garden, practicing martial arts, or studying natural medicine.

www.ckmillerbooks.com